SEEDS OF OUR
FUTURE

LEONARD J. DISANZA

Cover design by: Derek Murphy
Layout design by: Jake Muelle

ISBN: 978-0-578-48236-1 (Paperback)

First Edition: June 2019

Printed in the United States of American

Published By
LennyDoesRants

For my wife Sally Patricia DiSanza, who has wholeheartedly
supported and encouraged me through this long process.

I'd like to take this opportunity to acknowledge my debt to my first beta readers Janis, Catherine, and Bill, for the excellent feedback they provided on an early draft and to my final beta readers, Lawrence, Laura, William, and Carolyn, for their valuable insights on a later draft.

I would also like to thank my writing coach and editor, Karen Aroian (www.aroianeditorial.com), who guided me on both the development and editing of this story. A wellspring of ideas and insights, she is a master at bringing a novel's literary elements to life. She believed in me, took me on a journey far beyond my first and second draft, and always balanced truth to kindness as she justified rewrites I honestly didn't want to do — again. Thank you, Karen!

TABLE OF CONTENTS

CHAPTER 1

2033: THE BEGINNING OF THE END

*A*s I begin to write in this notebook, I must confess that it wasn't as if we didn't know what was happening to our climate. We did. We turned a blind eye.

Like everyone else, I was distracted by the normal trappings of life. But the increasing series of disasters were serious, and they were happening all around me.

I was 39 years old in 2033, when solid ground first shifted under me. As an internationally known chemist, I should have . . . I don't know what I should have done. The acceleration in climate changes seemed unstoppable.

We had known for years that glaciers at the poles were melting, but the current rate was alarming. Tides began rising. Hurricanes and tornadoes grew stronger and more frequent. Droughts lasted longer. Earthquakes hit unexpected places, floods worsened, and now the volcanic eruptions.

At that time, I had an extensive battery of scientific publications. I spoke at conferences around the world, and my research was funded by the University of California, Berkley. Yes, my colleagues and I knew what was happening to the climate. We even knew the reasons: more gases polluting the atmosphere from fossil fuels, fewer trees in the rain forests, more methane gas from factory farming of cattle, chicken, and pigs and an exponential increase in the human population.

The earth was warming. I should have taken things more seriously.

My wife Martha was an obstetrician, practicing at a local hospital. Between long hours at work, we were busy carting our boys, Paul, 6, and Mark, 9, to their sporting events. Busy. Too busy to pay attention. The climate changed each day, but we simply went about our lives like nothing was wrong, lulled into acceptance and submission.

Except for the fact that our little coastal California community of El Cerrito was experiencing rain for the umpteenth day in a row, things were mostly ordinary on that warm day in April.

It must have been a Thursday afternoon. That's the only day Martha and I could get home early to prep dinner together. From the sound of furniture banging upstairs, we knew the boys were horsing around, and as long as we heard more giggling than crying, we wouldn't intervene.

"You on call tonight?" I asked, always finding her schedule hard to keep track of.

"No, I'm home. How 'bout you? Guess you'll be going back up to the college after dinner?"

"Nah, I think I'll just work on my article from here." Talk about procrastination. She knew me so well. My article on simultaneous ionic and covalent bonding in high temperature superconductive metal oxides was due to a scientific journal in less than two weeks. "Hell," I said to cover my tracks, "You know with everything that's going on these days, does this article matter? I mean a year from now, when the world is coming to an end, is anybody going to give a damn about this stuff?"

"Not sure I understand all that, but I liked the part about bonding at high temperatures. Works for me." A smirk beamed across her face. I knew that look, as well as every other look she had in her arsenal. I had studied that pretty face not just for the eleven years of our marriage but for all the years I had chased after this woman as an undergrad at UCLA.

Martha made quite a first impression walking in front of me on the quad toward our freshman English class. Thick blonde hair glowing in the California sunshine, bouncing up and down with each step. Hard, muscular thighs of a runner, a slight curvature rounding out her backside. Oh, those legs.

When I heard her respond in class, I realized that she was probably the smartest person in the room. She continued dating jocks until late in our junior year. I had dated my fill of empty heads in high school and waited to make a move. A torrential downpour, a slippery sidewalk, and an umbrella were all it took.

Yes, her smirk telegraphed that no one who was waiting for the end of the world would care about ionic and covalent bonding occurring simultaneously in a metal oxide superconductor.

"Seriously, honey," she said to me, "All of us at the hospital, we're asking ourselves the same question. What matters these days? Nobody has an answer. We go on pretending everything's normal. . . and clearly every doctor knows it's not."

"Yup, that's what I mean." I continued pounding out perfectly shaped burgers while she sliced onions and other veggies for grilling.

Martha stopped chopping and turned to me with a serious look, "Sim? Listen. . . do you hear that? What are the boys doing up there?"

My shoulders involuntarily began to shrug upward, and a creepy feeling shook its way down my back. "That's not the boys."

"Then what the hell was that?"

I went to the window. The grumbling noise grew. "Oh my God, look up on the hill. Damn, the ground is moving. Get the boys right now. We need to get out of here. Boys get down here," I yelled.

"Paul, Mark, hurry! I mean it. Get down here, now!" Martha shouted as she ran to the stairs like a bear intent on snatching her cubs from danger.

"Momma, what is that? Do you feel it?"

"I feel it, baby. We need to leave. Come on, hurry."

"Mark, hold on to your mother's hand. Paul grab mine. We have to go right now."

"But Dad, what's happening? What's that rumble?"

"It's a mudslide coming down the hill." I told him, "The ground must be too wet from all the rain. We need to run, OK?"

"Sim, the cars?" she asked me in a shaky voice.

"No, forget them. It's too late, they're not usable," I said as we ran from the house. "Go! Run sideways!"

"Which way?"

The memory of a guy I had seen interviewed on TV after a mudslide popped into my head. He told the reporter that he had followed a group of dogs to safety. The idea seemed reasonable. "Follow those dogs. They sense the vibrations. They'll go . . . where it's safe." But I was just pretending that I knew what I was talking about.

"Daddy, the mud is going over those houses," my son Paul told me while pulling on my arm, obviously wanting me to stop to turn back to look. I refused. Instead I pulled him closer. "Don't look back. Squeeze my hand. Run with me."

"Run, boys. Oh my God, Sim, our neighbors. Do you think they got out?"

"I hope so," I said unconvincingly. "They had the same warning we did." But I didn't believe what I was saying. If they hadn't gotten out when we did, they probably couldn't survive.

Eventually we stopped running. We came to an elevated area with large well-anchored boulders outside the mudslide near the entrance to the hiking trail my family and I had visited many times. From here we had a clear view of our house. I tried to catch my breath, but then our home shuddered, as if it were a piece of cloth, more like a flag blowing in the wind than a sturdy structure. The walls rippled. The house tore loose from the foundation. It's hard to describe how sick I felt watching our house and cars and possessions methodically twist and turn down the hill.

"Sim, that's our house! Boys, boys, stay right here with me. Don't you move an inch," she commanded.

"But Momma, look, our house is leaving. It's running away!" Paul cried.

"I know, baby, I know. Just stay still."

Each of us watched in horror, as our home of eight years squirmed down the hill and collapsed as easily as a toy, breaking into pieces of wood and metal and glass, which were swallowed by mud.

My mouth and lips went dry in the seconds I had to think about neighbors who might be trapped inside this monster sludge. It was a mess of furniture and cars and pieces of housing. Then the mudslide shifted and flung itself in our direction. We ran farther up the rocky boulders. A foul odor invaded the air, a thick palpable smell with ozone from the electrical flashes mixed in with the dust and crud of the shattered sheetrock, wood, and glass. It choked me to my knees.

The four of us reached a temporary haven in an elevated cluster of rocks as mud from below sprayed up at our feet. We remained hunched with our hands on our knees, alternatively viewing the carnage and protecting our faces inside our soiled shirts. The smell and the dirt grabbed at my throat.

Martha broke the silence. "Is it just me? I don't hear the rumble noise anymore. Sim, it's gone, isn't it? Sim...?" Her eyes looked glassy. Mud trailed down her face and neck. "Think it stopped?"

Paul and Mark were oddly quiet, intently watching us for confirmation that the danger was over. Martha tapped my arm, as if for an answer.

"Maybe," I whispered, wrapping my arm around her shoulder and straining to listen. The groan of muddy debris seemed at least temporarily to have stopped. Now there was nothing but an eerie quiet. "All I hear is the rain."

"I don't see the ground moving anymore," her voice cracked.

I wanted to stop shaking and coughing, but my body couldn't. I wasn't sure what we should do next. Part of me knew it was time to step up, get a hold of myself, and offer the certainty they expected. I pulled my wife and boys firmly against me. Enwrapping them, I did the only thing I could think of, I prayed. "Let's pray for our neighbors . . . and give thanks that we're safe. Dear God . . . ."

* * *

Four years later, in 2037, after the world had completely gone to hell from volcanic activity, drought, heat, flooding and lack of food, two government agents knocked on our apartment door.

People everywhere were sick and dying. Mark, our eldest, was desperately ill. The agents did not ask me to join other scientists at a secret subterranean research facility. They demanded. I gave a million reasons why they should pick someone else, find a smarter chemist. I insisted there was no way I was going to leave my family and a son who was sick. Unless they came with me, I wouldn't go. But they told me *no, my family couldn't come with me. They said where I was going was a dangerous top-secret facility with limited space and limited resources and was no place for children.*

Seeing how frustrated I was, Martha turned and gave me that look. The look that telegraphed, 'You know you're the one, you know how to make things better' -- a hopeful look that told me that she could take care of herself and our boys. At that point, my resistance stopped. Martha, Paul and I huddled together around Mark. We prayed, and we cried.

I guessed that I might never see them again, at least not in this world. I think Martha knew it, too. I grabbed a photo album and my bible and said a final goodbye without knowing where I was going.

CHAPTER 2

2121: THE JOEY VISIT

Standing in front of her filmy apartment mirror, Mary dragged the brush through her long red hair. Again. As if that's going to help, she thought. This morning before work she had places to go. Try harder, she reminded herself as she battled through knots. Another obstacle to remind her that she was stuck. The promise she had made to herself and to her friends, despite the difficulty of this daily struggle, was that she would recover a happier, more positive outlook on life.

She did a final check. She had no idea if her blue sweater and gray slacks looked nicer than usual. Maybe not. She envied her best friend, Ena. Restrictions from the Program didn't seem to bother her. She marveled at how Ena always managed to find a way to go along with restrictions. So odd, but Ena was happy, something Mary desperately wanted in her own life.

As she pulled a tangle of silky copper strands from her hairbrush, she caught the reflection in the mirror of the large paper calendar hanging behind her. She had taken this calendar from her workplace in an act of defiance. She no longer cared how closely her managers monitored the office supplies. The large red X over the square for Wednesday, April 16th, 2121, marked her younger brother Joey's nineteenth birthday. Will next week's happy occasion be his last, she wondered.

His dementia was now in the advanced stages. An Outcast, he was the last living member of her family. He had been admitted into the Care Place about 18 months after the death of their parents, Sim, Margreet, and younger sister, Amasa, in a fire. The accident still weighed on Mary's mind. She tilted her head back and shrugged her shoulders as the guilt from not being with them on that fateful day engulfed her.

Why, she wondered, had the Program allowed Joey, given his status as an Outcast, admission into the Care Place? It was strange, but she was grateful he was now close enough to visit, especially this morning before her own doctor's appointment before work. She hoped today would be one of his better days.

In the last few years, she had come to accept that Joey's mind and cognitive skills were diminishing. On most visits, she would find him off in his own altered reality, one taped together with pieces of memories mixed with bits of wild fantasies. Sometimes he would tell her stories of hunting for secret papers or trying to escape. When she found him like that, floating off the grid, she listened agreeably. Challenging him would be pointless.

As she walked out of her apartment door, she reminded herself to keep expectations low and the visit short. She could not be late for her monthly clinic appointment. Last month, Dr. Brisko, who was more surrogate father than doctor, blew up. "I've done so much for you, your brother, your father. Please don't disrespect me like this." His tone was more desperate than angry. She wasn't sure why that stuck with her, but she vowed not to be late again.

Mary tightened her coat collar and braced for the weather outside. "Another depressing Buffalo day," she muttered as she stepped out of her tiny apartment. She hated the incessant dismal weather in this barren overcrowded place. Then, in what seemed to Mary to almost be repudiation for her thoughts, the wind instantly picked up and a gust slapped against her face. "And, there goes my hair."

The cold gray April skies forced her to shake her arms vigorously, as if that might remove the depressing thoughts. Not another day of sadness, she told herself. Think about how happy Joey will be to see you.

As Mary walked toward the Care Place, she marveled how Joey, despite the severity of his illness, had managed to survive another year. She looked forward to reminding him that he would be a year older next Wednesday and the plan she had to celebrate his birthday with him.

Why hadn't she been able to get him to talk about the years that he had been gone? What must it have been like for him to live as an Outcast on the other side of the wall? Mary was curious, but Joey refused to discuss what had happened to him back then. Now, as his dementia advanced, those details were probably gone.

When she arrived at the facility, she headed straight to Joey's room. He called it a prison but transferring him to a room with a window seemed nearly impossible. Positioning herself on the edge of his bed near his head, she watched him sleep. She thought about how pleased she had always been with the care her brother received, the way the staff treated him, especially his nurse, Lucinda, who kept a devoted watch.

She noticed how small and hollow Joey's cheeks appeared with little fat remaining to hold them up. Most of his thick reddish hair was now gone. The small amount that remained was graying. She took his hand, which was cold and looked almost transparent. As she pulled up his covers, she saw additional sores tearing at his arms and shoulders. On her last visit, she noticed a cluster of small tumors developing on his leg. She asked Lucinda about them but never got a clear answer. She guessed that Joey had other tumors that were wreaking havoc on his brain and organs. What could Lucinda – or anyone else – do at this point?

She stood for a moment to admire the framed picture on the otherwise empty dresser across from his bed. A young athlete with long lean muscles stared back. She mused how earlier in his youth he had been so mischievous while at the same time exuding such charm and confidence that everyone around him was taken in by it, except for her. He was too handsome, too jovial for his own good. He had been a rebel, always resisting, but in the end, it destroyed him, mind, body, and soul.

Still, she missed that version of her brother and wanted to scream with rage for what the Program had done to him, casting him out at such a young age. Leaning closer to him, she ran her fingers across his forehead. That movement opened his sleepy eyes. Groggy, he stared at her for a moment, seeming to enjoy her touch. Slowly he pushed back the covers and placed his hand on her arm, "Mary? Where've you been? I've been waiting for such a long time. We need to get out of here."

"I'm here now, Joey," she said, leaning over her brother. "You know I work, and I come to see you as often as I can. How are you feeling today, sweetie?"

Joey grasped at her coat lapel and struggled to pull himself to her face. His eyes scanned the room. "We need to leave, jog into the hills, get Jude, then find Emad's collection. We'll be safe when we get out of here. But Mary don't tell them. They'll try to stop us. They always do. Daddy told me they would want to stop me from escaping. He said they intentionally cause bad things, that's why they built the care site, to save themselves."

Again, the same story with the mountain, Jude, and Emad's collection. Crazy talk. "Yes, Daddy was right, they did build the Care Place, and you're here in it now. But, little brother, today would be a bad day for a jog. It's ugly and cold outside. Believe me, you don't want to go out there. Let's wait for a better day, then we'll jog in the hills together, I promise. And I'll keep your secret, I won't tell them about our trip."

Joey slumped back on his bed and turned his head toward the wall, "You're not listening. It's not safe here." His demeanor now turning to sadness.

"It'll be all right, Joey," she said, hoping to distract him, "I'll take you for a little walk down the hall, but first let's visit. I want to know what you've been doing."

Her questions and conversations with Joey were quite ordinary. They had to be. She asked him what he had eaten that day for breakfast and if they had given him a shower that morning. With his dementia, he was no longer capable of discussing much beyond the mundane. Knowing how bright he used to be saddened her.

Joey starred at her. "Sometimes I don't eat the poison they feed me. I'm too smart for that."

"What are you talking about? They don't give you poison. They take great care of you, especially Lucinda."

Without warning Lucinda brushed past Mary, startling her. "Good morning! Yes, I do take good care of Joey," Lucinda said, "but now it's time for morning medications."

How long had Lucinda been standing there? For the most part, she had been pleased with Lucinda's constant care of her brother, but her hovering seemed a bit excessive. Did Lucinda give this much attention to her other patients?

As Lucinda approached Joey's bed, Mary stood and gave her the Program's obligatory hug. After their brief greeting, Lucinda bent over close to Joey but, as she came near him, he abruptly turned his head away.

Sensing his displeasure with his caretaker, Mary spoke up causing Joey to turn and face her, "It's OK, Lucinda. I'll give him his meds."

Lucinda paused with a look that sent a chill through Mary. "Fine. I'll leave his cup over here where he can reach it. Sometimes we try not to swallow the pills," she said as she swung around the bed to take readings and mark Joey's chart. "We spit them out when we think no one is looking. Isn't that right, Joey? Make sure - he takes - them all," she punctuated.

Her curtness made Mary wonder if Lucinda was having a bad day. "I will . . . and I'd like to take him for a walk down the hallway . . . with his walker, of course, if that would that be all right?"

"We like our walks . . . don't we, Joey?"

At the sound of Lucinda's voice, Joey's head once again turned away from his nurse.

"Make sure he takes all those pills and drinks that water," she repeated and left the room.

"Here, turn around," she said, handing Joey his pills. "I'm not sure what that was all about, but you heard Lucinda. Finish taking these pills, and then we'll go for our walk."

Joey squeezed his face, almost snarling while holding his hand to block his sister from making him take the pills. Then he quickly acquiesced, maybe knowing this was a fight he would lose. He swallowed the pills as his big sister carefully watched to make sure he didn't spit any out.

What were these pills, she wondered, that made him so set against taking them? She would ask Lucinda later. Then she helped Joey struggle to his walker. "That's good, we're almost there. A few more steps. You can do it." She placed the cup, which was still partially filled with water, in the holder on the side of his walker. They traveled through the hallway at a snail's pace, but she didn't care. She was pleased that Joey was still walking, this might be the only exercise he would get all day.

Lucinda was standing at her cart preparing medications for patients. When they were directly alongside of her, Joey reached down, grasped his cup and raised it toward his lips, as if to toast her and take a drink. Lucinda briefly nodded in approval. Then, in quick motion, Joey flung the remaining water in her face. She lurched backward, banging into her cart, which also caused Mary to jump. Witnessing the chain reaction, Joey burst out in laughter.

"What's the matter with you?" Mary scolded Joey like a mother, a role she had unwillingly assumed throughout their youth. "Why did you do that? Tell her you're sorry." She glared at her younger brother, then at Lucinda. "I'm sorry. Are you OK? I don't know why he did that."

Joey squinted his eyes, stiffened his upper body, and yelled, "Don't! She's the bad one. They built the care site, and we need to get out. She wants to stop me from leaving! They're poisoning me!"

She had never witnessed an outburst like this from her brother. Her instinct was to mother and calm him. "It's all right. I told you, this is the Care Place. They care for you here. It's safe. You shouldn't take out your frustrations on Lucinda. She's trying to help you."

"No!" he shouted. "Dad found out these are the people who cause everything bad to happen, especially her. They want to control us. It's not safe here. They listen to our conversations."

Lucinda grabbed a towel from her cart and slowly wiped the water away from her face. Then she bent over, placing her face directly into Joey's and, in a firm tone Mary had never heard from Lucinda before, yelled, "Now stop."

Joey tilted downward and covered his head, as if his nurse was about to strike him.

At this point Mary did not know what to think. Why did he flinch? Surely Lucinda would never hit him. Was it possible for nurses to be able to hit patients?

The commotion in the hallway caused others to come out of their rooms. A toothless woman, wheezing in her wheel chair, had watched the whole thing. "Good for you, Joey, good for you. She's a bitch, ain't she?"

Mary continued stumbling over herself, repeating apologies. Her pale face turned a deep red, almost matching her hair.

"It's just water," Lucinda said, brushing the incident off.

Once again, a chill trickled down Mary's back. Would this incident make Joey's life harder? She grabbed his walker and wheeled him back to his room. "I'm so disappointed by what you did. You have no idea how lucky you are to be here."

Joey turned his head around to look at her. "Lucky, sis? Are you sure?"

She wasn't sure of anything. Lucinda was upset. She could sense there might be consequences. When they reached his room, she helped him get out of his walker.

For a moment, he stopped and smiled coyly at her. Then he made a fake spitting motion toward the floor. Giggling, Joey shouted, "Here, sis, look what I found! Lucinda wants you to take this. Swallow!" He bent from the waist and pretended to pick something up but, as he did, he teetered to the point of falling.

"Hey, steady there, funny guy, you keep that pill," she said as she grabbed him by the back of his waistband. "Where you going? Don't you dare fall. You'll drag me with you. What's so funny? Come on, let me help you get into bed." Just like that, the dementia had almost instantly changed his mood from upset to happy.

Her visit had lasted longer than she planned, but she decided not to leave until she was certain her brother was asleep. She listened to him giggle until something changed, and he began sobbing.

"Come on. Don't cry. Why are you crying? Next week when I come, I'll bring you a birthday cake. We'll celebrate."

Joey reached for her, though he could barely hold his eyes open. "Can we have a party?"

"I think so . . . if you promise you'll behave."

He searched her face, confused. He looked as if he had more to say, but something more powerful at work in his system shut him down.

She knew he'd already forgotten about the water incident. She bent over and kissed him. On her way out, she nearly collided into Lucinda. Standing outside of her brother's room again? This was getting ridiculous. "Lucinda, we just bump into each other, don't we?" She made a lame attempt to lighten the moment but kept moving.

Lucinda seemed equally surprised to see Mary still on the floor and turned to walk with her. "It's my job to check on my patients. You made sure he swallowed all his pills?"

"He took them all, and now he's asleep. Again, let me apologize for his behavior, I don't know why he did that," she said, more annoyed than sorry.

"It's fine. We're used to that kind of behavior. They make up stories and act out like children."

"He thought it was funny, as if he were a child again. He gets mixed up. Usually I listen and agree with whatever he says. I try not to make him upset. Today wasn't a good day for him. Do you happen to know why?"

"No idea. Next time tell me more about what he says. Maybe we can figure more things out."

Ridiculous, she thought, how could anyone figure out what was going on in Joey's head? What more was there to know, and why would it matter anyhow? How strange the day was turning out. And now Lucinda was walking her down the hallway? Seriously? A few feet from the exit, Mary stopped. "Lucinda?"

"Yes?"

"Joey takes a lot of meds. Maybe if he didn't take so many, he'd make more sense. Are they all necessary? I've asked for a list of what he's taking. Aren't those meds why he gets as weirded out as he does? The drugs make him groggy so, I mean, could they be . . ."

"They're for pain," Lucinda snapped. "You don't want your brother to suffer, do you? The meds work together to keep him calm. He needs every one of those pills. Here's how it works: doctors order medicines, and nurses monitor patients. We don't mess with doctors' orders. Get it?"

Lucinda's tone caught her off guard. She wanted to let it slide because the visit had already made her late for her own appointment, but she couldn't. "Fine, and since we're clearing things up, please get me that list of his medications," she whipped back. "I want to know what he's on."

"I've got others to check on. See you next time."

"Yes, with a list of my brother's meds in hand." What was with her? Lucinda's supervisor was watching from down the hallway. When Lucinda approached her supervisor, she leaned in and mumbled something to her ear. Mary couldn't hear what was said. Are they just going to stand there and watch me leave? Now emboldened by their gaze, she waved goodbye.

With every step further from the clinic, she felt relief. She wanted to chalk it up to Joey's bad day, but the place bothered her. Why did Joey react as if Lucinda was going to hit him? Had that happened before? Should she check in on him more often? When would she have time to do that? She felt guilty that she hadn't asked about his increasing sores or, given how he flinched, checked the rest of his body for bruises. She felt like a failure. Had she been wrong about his treatment all these years? What about the other patient's comments? The Care Place staff had always been kind to Joey. She wanted to believe that.

CHAPTER 3

TREK TO THE CLINIC

At 23, Mary was attractive, intelligent, and a loner. She was tall, and her distinctive complexion gave rise to gawking, which she found tiresome. Almost no one had red hair. Her fair and freckled skin was rare among the Program community. She was aware that her looks were outstanding, but feeling as if she stood out for things like hair color and freckles only made her cheeks more red.

She had a good job, her own apartment, so why, she wondered, wasn't she happy? For one thing, even as a child she had been the type of person who desperately wanted friends but was rarely successful at making them. So, she was lonely sometimes.

Growing up, she enjoyed being around her younger brother and sister though, in her mother's absence, was often forced to act more like their mom than their sibling. Joey reminded her so much of her father. They were the gregarious sort of males who could make you smile when you were sad. Everyone wanted to be around them. Though she loved her father and her brother, she was jealous of the attention they garnered.

Joey also had another side to his personality. He could be mischievous to the point of mean, and his rebellious streak frequently got him into trouble. His actions often presented a problem for her parents in their dealings with the Program. She imagined her father probably behaved similarly when he was a boy. She rationalized that it was their similarity that made Joey her dad's obvious favorite.

She was much more like her mother, reserved, maybe a bit standoffish. The few traits she inherited from her father weren't much to brag about. Like him, she was stubborn, argumentative, and emotional.

She loved her mom but, as a teenager, realized that the woman had issues. Sometimes she would come home to find her mother in bed crying. Other times her mother was nowhere to be found. Mary resented being a substitute parent, but she always performed as expected.

Despite her mother's absence and her father's overt favoritism of her brother, things in her childhood were not all sad. She had fond memories of the times her family spent with Doctor Brisko, her father's best friend. Doc was always there for family celebrations and on every other happy occasion. He was like an uncle or a stepfather, and she felt close to him. He was worldly and intelligent, and he always made himself available, patiently listening to her many questions, especially her concerns with the Program. He was kind, but sometimes, like a father, he could be stern if he felt her questions and insights became too negative.

She hoped Doc would not be too upset with her this morning. Her visit with Joey had gone longer than she planned and, for the second month in a row, she would be late for her clinic appointment with him.

The wind bit through her as she raced toward the clinic. She shrugged her shoulders, desperate to pull her head into her coat, like a turtle into its shell. Her hope was to keep the cold air from rushing in and freezing the back of her neck, but the plan wasn't working.

She despised this harsh climate. Shivering, she reminded herself how lucky she was that the Program didn't make her live and work farther away, near the factories or fields. That long walk to the clinic for her monthly shots would have been much worse. Why, she thought, did commoners like her have to walk everywhere anyway? Committee members had drivers. Why couldn't workers like herself have vehicles?

She increased her pace to a trot. Ahead she could see two guards and a third person. The guards looked as if they were attempting to apprehend someone, which was rare to witness. The man pulled free, and Mary realized he was running straight at her with the guards following close behind.

For an instant, she froze on the narrow sidewalk, not sure which way to move. As the man ran by, he reached out and pushed her aside, causing her to temporarily lose her balance. Tripping past her, one of the guards reached out and grabbed him by the collar of his tattered coat. Mary caught herself but felt an uncomfortable twist in her left ankle.

As the guard attempted to pull the man backward, the culprit swung around in a twirling motion and used his right hand to punch the guard in the face. She had never seen anything like that before. The second guard then caught up with them and tackled the man to the ground. The guard who had been punched kicked the man twice in the midsection. Writhing in pain on the ground, he yelled out and then curled up in submission.

Mary stood with a gathering crowd and gawked in horror. This exhibition was so unusual. No one fought with each other in the Program and certainly not with a guard. Because of their monthly injections, common workers couldn't fight without extreme physical consequences. Yet they had just witnessed a man and two guards in an altercation, and neither the man nor the guards had gone into convulsions.

He had to be an Outcast, Mary guessed. The likely reason he was on their side of the wall was that he was either a spy or trying to get medical attention. Only an Outcast, she thought, could have behaved so aggressively without having a violent convulsive attack. As for the guards, she had heard a rumor that they undergo some form of secret intensive training that allows them to temper their body's response to intense situations such as these. These guards, she thought, must have had special personalities in the first place to be so rigid.

As the guards dragged the man away, Mary heard her own thoughts in other bystanders' voices. "What will happen to him?"

"What will they do to him?" In seconds, the guards and the crowd were gone.

Though her ankle complained, she managed to keep her pace. Breathing hard, she arrived at the entrance to the clinic. She grabbed the door handle and watched her warm breath drift in the cold air. She paused long enough to wonder what she hated more each year: these monthly injections or the cold.

Mary checked in at the front desk. Immediately, three other patients in the waiting room jumped up to greet her, offering a hand or hug, the traditional Program greeting. Without thinking, Mary smiled warmly and stretched out both of her hands to the greeters, a move that prevented others from hugging her. She despised fakeness but accepted that she lived in a cramped community, where almost everyone knew everyone and, it seemed, everyone was somehow related to everyone else. In memory of her family, she mastered the minimum that was expected by the Program and made shaking hands look good enough.

CHAPTER 4

DOC'S EXAM ROOM

Doc's nurse Delilah was still up to her old tricks. She called Mary to the front desk in a curt tone she made sure everyone could hear and lit into her for being late. Again, the sour-faced ritual. Mary had been getting her shots regularly at Doc's clinic for years. She had no choice but to accept that Delilah enjoyed her position of power. Lording over certain people was her thing. Whether Mary was late for her appointment or not, public shaming was a certainty here. Why fight? She imagined Delilah was jealous of her relationship with Doc. Oddly, though, Delilah didn't appear to even like Doc.

Mary accepted the lecture with her head hung, as was expected by Delilah's captive audience. Then the nurse whisked her to an examination room. Doc was already there, pacing, and slammed the door.

For a moment, he said nothing. His face was puffy with sweat as he glared at her. Mary took off her coat and smiled sheepishly. She wondered how she had known this man her entire life while so much about him remained a mystery.

Her father had told her that, before she was born, Doc had been paired. He had a son, but something bad must have happened to the boy and his mother because Doc never made any mention of them. Some day she would ask, but today wasn't that day.

Doc flipped through her chart. "No doubt Delilah informed you of your tardiness?"

She nodded. Though she thought of him as a second father, it dawned on her how odd Doc sometimes looked. He could be very animated, moving his arms in large gestures and contorting his face into strong expressions. Physically, he was a short, balding, pudgy black man. She guessed Doc must be in his late fifties since he had been a childhood friend of her father. He had been in poor health for as long as she could remember. Her father had told her that Doc had developed a heart condition that affected his lungs. He could easily get out of breath if he became too excited, which often happened when she butted heads with him. Despite his gruffness, he reassured her, and she was usually glad to be in his presence.

Doc put down her chart and stopped pacing. He looked at the fiery red-haired young woman he had helped raise. He couldn't have loved her more if she were his own daughter. He had high hopes for Mary – and one of those was for her to lead a happy life. He had delivered her as a baby. She represented his surrogate family. He had no other. Naturally, he worried about her. She was still mourning the loss of her parents and sister. Her brother Joey seemed to be the only sparkle in her life, and now even that light was dimming. He was concerned that when Joey died, things would be worse for her.

Trying his best to be fatherly, he let his face display his irritation. "Last month you promised me that this was not going to happen again." Because he felt responsible for Mary, he held back certain truths about her dad, himself, and the Program. Conveying that information might be detrimental to her disposition. Eventually, he would have to come clean. Given Joey's decline, that time was approaching.

She shrugged her shoulders. "I know, Doc, but while I was walking here, a fight suddenly broke out between this man and two guards and . . . "

He cut her off. "No doubt one of those damn Outcasts again, stealing something or someone. Anyway, that's no excuse. Leave a little earlier next month. Get here on time for once. You're not my only patient."

She guessed that Doc was more likely disappointed than upset. "Doc, I know you really don't think that way about those poor Outcasts. Now, come on, how about a hug?"

"We're preparing new injections based on your most recent blood test results," he said, patting her back. "They should be ready shortly, but first let's talk about something I see on your chart. You've had another violent episode? With convulsions?"

She pulled away, embarrassed that she had lost control of her emotions and gotten into a shouting match over paperwork with a guy from work at the Distribution Center. He had accused her of incompetence, something that might apply to others but would certainly never apply to her. Unfortunately, the situation escalated. She wasn't proud of losing control, something that she had been taught never to do.

Doc misinterpreted her embarrassment for lack of interest. "This is serious, young lady," he scolded. "The effects of these convulsive attacks on the human body are cumulative. You know that. You must control your emotions. You're young and healthy but, with as few as four or five of these attacks, you can die. It's a bad way to go. Now describe to me in detail what happened during the attack."

Mary bent over, illustrating how she buckled in pain during the attack. "I was really angry after this guy intentionally bumped into me, so I slapped him. Left finger prints on his pretty face, I think," she said, giggling. "Of course, that's when all hell broke loose with severe full body cramps."

"Yup, a big part of the symptoms. Go on."

"My head was splitting, like it was going to explode. I couldn't see. I couldn't focus. This loud ringing in my ears made my heart race in my chest."

Doc shook his head. "Everything you've described is typical with these attacks. The headaches and blindness were from the high blood pressure, deadly high! If you don't learn to control yourself, the anger is going to kill you. What's your brother Joey going to do if you're not around? Is that what you want?"

"No. No, of course not, but it is sort of my personality, who I am. You of all people know that about me."

He reached out and took her hand. "Listen to me carefully. Your father would want me to counsel you, so please don't give me this personality shit. You know, how about we put something extra in the injections to calm you? You know we use a little Chlorpromazine."

"Absolutely not!"

"It's the same medicine that we give to the youngsters to calm them. The drug centers them, calms them. Believe me it's safe. They all take it. You took it as a kid. Let me help you with this. Why not give it a try?"

"I said no. And your little drug didn't work so well on my brother when he was a kid did it?"

"Joey was always a special case, his physiology is somehow different."

"Hmm, and I know why they really give children those drugs. They do it to dull and control them!"

"Mary you're overstating, it's simply to calm them. Anyway enough, you're being stubborn as usual. But young lady you keep in mind about what I've been warning you about." For a moment Doc closed his eyes then opened them and stared at her in silence before continuing, "Now tell me about Joey. I haven't seen him in a while. How's he doing?"

"Frail. He looks bad. The sores on his arms and legs aren't healing. He can't hear or see well. Some days are OK. Most days, he's lost in dementia. He still recognizes me, though, so that's good."

"We've talked about his progression."

"I know, but it's sad. He looks so old. This year he's gone down quickly." She paused and perked up. "Next week I'm bringing him a birthday cake to celebrate his nineteenth. I think he'll like that."

"I'm sure he will. You know, there's nothing more any doctor can do for him. You need to understand he's going to decline rapidly now. But he's lucky he's lived this long and has you, such a caring sister. And we're lucky that we got him into that facility, aren't we?"

"I guess. . ."

"What do you mean, 'I guess'?"

"I mean, I know. I appreciate what you did for us."

"We worked hard to get him in there. I owed that to your family. I don't know of any other Outcast who has been admitted to that place. You do realize that? We're lucky."

"I'm not sure about the lucky part. Things aren't too lucky for him, and it doesn't feel lucky that Mom, Dad, and Amasa are gone."

"You know that wasn't what I meant by lucky. We all do what we can for Joey, but we can't fix this. The others have been gone almost four years now; we can't change that. I think your family would want you to try to move on with your life, get out of your funk and, you know, be happy."

Before Mary could respond there was a knock at the door. Delilah entered, carrying a tray of needles. Neither nurse nor doctor said a word. Once Delilah turned to walk away, Doc twisted and contorted his face and stuck his tongue out, showing his dislike for his nurse.

After the door closed again, Mary said, "Nice. And you teach anger management?"

"A perfectly legitimate management strategy," Doc mumbled. "Now, up," he said pointing to the exam table.

Mary hopped up onto the exam table, laid face up, and pulled up her shirt. Doc administered the monthly injections into her stomach. "Damn, will these shots ever stop hurting?" She sat up slowly and took a moment to gather herself.

"There's something else, something important that I need to give you. I think I've put this off long enough — maybe too long," he said.

"There's more? Can it wait until my next visit?" she asked, reaching for her coat. "I already feel sick and need to get to work. I've taken off too much time today."

"No, this can't wait," he said, carefully locking the door in a way that produced the least amount of noise. Then he pressed his index finger to his lips, signaling her to be quiet. He continued speaking now in a low whisper voice. "You know your dad and I grew up together and how close we were. He gave me something to give to you if something happened to him and your mom. You're the oldest, and I've been waiting for years to give you this. I think the time is right."

Doc slid his roller chair over to the built-in medical supply counter behind him and removed one of the small lower drawers. He turned the drawer over, dumping the contents onto the top of the counter, and then removed a thick envelope that had been taped to the bottom. Holding it in his right hand he rolled back toward Mary and extended his arm, offering it to her. As she reached out to take it, he gently pushed her hand down. "You can't open this here. I need you to hide it. Don't let anyone see that you have it."

"What is this?" She watched him fidget with the envelope. Sweat began beading on his brow. She had never seen him so nervous.

"I don't know for sure . . . but, if it is what I think it is, then you need to be extremely careful with it. The information in this could be dangerous."

From the serious expression on his face, she knew she needed to pay attention to what he was saying. She took the envelope, carefully flattened it, and pushed it into her bag.

Doc wiped his brow and seemed calmer. "I have patients waiting. Maybe we'll talk about all of this another time." He stood up.

Mary followed his lead, not daring to ask, "All of what?"

He unlocked the door, again putting his finger to his lips. "See you next time, Mary. Say hello to Joey for me," he called out into the hallway before disappearing into the next examination room.

CHAPTER 5

IMPATIENTLY WAITING AT WORK

Mary sat at her desk, trying to be inconspicuous, which only made her more paranoid. Who had seen her come in late? Would she be questioned? She absent-mindedly rubbed the back of her neck. Calm down, she told herself, no one knows what is in your bag. She lowered the bag softly to the floor and then, using her feet, guided it under the desk and out of sight.

For all her education, Mary's position at the Distribution Center was that of a glorified accounting clerk who audited resources. She had been stuck in the same mindless job for three years. Minutes passed like hours. What was in that damn envelope, and why was it dangerous? She was dying to rip it open.

From the left side of her desk, she reached for the top folder from her incoming tray and pulled out the thick stack of papers. Each paper represented a separate invoice denoting material, supplies, or finished goods that had arrived at the dock from one of the numerous factories and farms that existed inside the walls of their compound.

She noted each invoice in her receiving ledger: number, date of arrival, place of origin, temporary warehouse storage bays and sub bins. Each day her Outgoing tray on the right side of her desk mounted as she made new folders containing shipping invoices. Her bosses appreciated her productivity.

From the entries in her shipping ledger, she produced invoices that noted where materials were to be sent by truck, date of disposition, and bays and sub bins where material or goods were housed. Mary then placed each shipping invoice in its own folder with the name of the destination and date of demarcation marked on the outside.

Sometimes the monotony of accounting made her want to scream. Still, she prided herself on doing accurate work. She reminded herself that she was valuable to her bosses. They gave her special latitude, which meant she could go to the Care Place to see Joey. Her heart rate calmed as the pile of shipping folders in her Outgoing tray grew.

Though she dreamed of being promoted to a better job, she had no trouble convincing herself that many were worse. Working in the fields, food processing plants, factories, or especially the pharmacies would be dangerous for an outspoken woman. From childhood, she knew the Program expected her to work hard without drama or emotion. She learned to display a smile of gratitude to managers and hid how much she hated the drudgery.

Besides, this job was temporary. The Program would soon pair her. She was healthy, of breeding age, maybe even past her prime. She loathed the idea of these forced pairings and population control contracts, but she knew that eventually her name would be added to the pairing list. That was the way it worked.

Traditionally, girls were paired as early as the age of sixteen, but for some unknown reason, that wasn't happening anymore. As she gazed around the room at the workers sitting at their desks, she wondered why the Program was waiting so long to pair these singles. She had heard that newly paired couples were also being forced to sign contracts to have fewer babies.

Attractiveness between the paired individuals wasn't a priority for the Program. The Program dictated who your partner would be and how many children you would have. Your mission in pairing and breeding, as in everything, was to be happy about the opportunity to serve the greater good of the community. If you weren't happy with the Program decisions . . .

"Mary. . . ? Mary! Are you daydreaming again? Get up, come on. What are you waiting for? They want us down at the dock immediately," her coworker and best friend Ena chided.

In a daze, Mary gave her friend a baffled look.

Like Mary, Ena was overqualified for her job in the Distribution Center. To relieve the mundane, their daily highlight was gossiping as they walked through the halls of the center. They looked out for each other and enjoyed each other's silliness. They cherished the time they had together, talking, arguing, gossiping, and laughing, which solidified their sisterhood. Ena was a striking woman of medium height, dark eyes, dark complexion, and short black hair. Mary called her perfect, though the two women had differing opinions about life in the Program and their personalities, appearances, and backgrounds were as opposite as could be.

It irked Mary how Ena fit in and stood out for all the right reasons. Her relaxed attitude permeated almost every aspect of her life, including her ability to accept Program rules. What made her most attractive was that she did not take herself or her circumstances too seriously. She didn't care how she dressed or what people thought of her.

When it came to the pairing of couples, Ena thought the Program had an acceptable process. She looked forward to being added to the list, to being paired, and to having children. She felt it would be wonderful to have three children, live in a bigger apartment, and have a better job, all of which were perks that came along with pairing. Mary, on the other hand, abhorred everything about the system.

Ena had been shy and somewhat fearful as a young child, a mama's girl. She was smart and pretty and, because of that, many children from the nearby apartment complexes were eager to play with her. While she enjoyed playing with them, she was a cautious child, never straying too far from home. Unlike the other children, she was not adventurous, and she rarely got into trouble.

She had learned an attitude of restraint, growing up in a family of strict rule-followers. Her father had taken many opportunities to remind her that if she did what was asked by the Program and followed all the rules, she could be happy and safe throughout her life. She took this advice to heart. As an adult, she lived by it faithfully.

Ena, unlike Mary, had grown up under a strict religious structure. Her family was private about their faith, but at the end of each day they always prayed together. This daily prayer routine continued until the day Ena reached puberty and was officially confirmed into the Program. Shortly after, her father left her and her mother to start a new family.

"Mary, come on!" Ena said, this time shaking her mildly. With that, Mary snapped out of her daze and slowly walked around to the front of her desk. Though Mary and Ena had been molded by entirely different family circumstances and had differing opinions about life, they loved each other dearly.

"Sorry, I didn't hear a thing. Wow, where is everyone going? Is this a drill or something?"

Ena grabbed her arm, attempting to pull her along. "Maybe, but Reyanne told me the rumor mill has it that this might be a fake drill. Word is the Program management is using it to search desks for stolen office supplies." Ena's giggle echoed above the sound of their shoes tapping down the stairwell. "And, as always, there was Reyanne, on her usual soap box: 'Those bastards give us less and less while they get more and more, blah, blah, blah, and here they are worried about office supplies? What a bunch of shit.' Can you believe she said that out loud?"

Reyanne was a friend to both women. She was tiny and feisty, a survivor. Everyone knew her as the go-to gossip. While people admired her for surviving an abusive childhood, they either followed or avoided the troublemaker. On occasion Mary found her irritating, but she also knew Reyanne was generally on target with rumors. "Hey, Ena, did I just hear you curse? I've never heard you do that before."

"Well, I was just repeating what Reyanne said," Ena muttered, embarrassed by the comment.

"Ena, who wouldn't agree with Reyanne about all that? So what if a few desperate employees feel that they need to take a few office supplies to trade on the black market for basic necessities? As always, the Program makes things worse, don't they?"

Now Ena was beginning to regret that she had opened this subject.

"Wait, wait," Mary said, the potential seriousness of the situation now sinking in. "I need to get something."

"What?"

"I need to grab my bag."

"No one's going to steal your bag. If we're not on the dock in two minutes, we're going to get in trouble."

"Just go on ahead. I'll catch up."

"All right, but you better hurry. I'll wait here."

"No, go on. Go. I'll meet you there."

Ena shook her head as she watched her friend run back up the stairs. Really, she thought, risking trouble for a stupid bag? How stubborn, like her opinions about the Program. Why did she have to be such a pain? Mary was a loyal friend, and Ena adored her intelligence and spunk, but in moments like this, she worried that someday Mary's stubbornness would get her into trouble.

Mary's mind raced as she considered what was the safest thing to do. What if Reyanne was right? What if this wasn't a drill? What if they really were checking desks for stolen supplies? Wouldn't they also check women's bags?

At her desk, she bent down and reached under for her bag. She looked around before yanking out the envelope and quickly burying it between thick folders of receiving invoices on her Incoming tray. She glanced around again. Clutching the bag, she ran through the hall.

Ena was still waiting at the bottom of the stairs. "Finally. Would you please pull yourself together? First, you're late, then you don't hear me standing right in front of you, and now you're acting weird over your purse. What's with you? Let's go!"

The women stood on the dock as the last employees arrived. When everyone was present, management scolded the workers for taking so long to assemble.

Ena didn't dare look over at her friend but whispered, "Guess this was just a drill."

"Maybe."

"Hey, at your desk . . . you seemed lost in another world. What were you thinking about?"

"Nothing in particular, just daydreaming, I guess."

"Well, aren't you lucky to have time to be bored. I'm really behind in my work."

Mary wondered if Ena ever daydreamed about anything other than being compliant, being paired, and being a mom. "Yeah. Me, too."

Back upstairs, the girls said goodbye. As Mary turned in the direction of her desk, she noticed a manager alongside a guard, who was dragging away a sobbing coworker. She and everyone one else watched as the woman tried to cover her face in fear and embarrassment. What had she stolen, and what kind of punishment was in store for her?

She felt terrible for the woman and an uneasy feeling in her own stomach. Farther down the hall, her boss Able was standing at her desk. She panicked. Her heart rate quickened. A guard was with him. She knew not to run, but she strained to see what was in her boss's hand. Had they found her envelope? What was in it that was dangerous, and what terrible punishment might she be in for?

As she approached, she caught her manager's eye. He looked nervous. She knew he had been pleased with her work. Would he stand up for her now? Gathering herself, she walked while keeping eye contact. Maintain your poise, she thought, always appear confident. Her throat was burning.

"Boss?"

"Mary."

"May I help you with something?"

"We found this new unopened box of folders in your desk drawer," he said, waving a box of manila folders back and forth, as if he had discovered a stolen bar of gold. "This is a full box, Mary. You know how precious paper is."

Mary was aware that paper products were precious. She had been taught their value repeatedly throughout her childhood.

She remembered one particular day as a young girl. Her mother had not been feeling well. To give her mom time alone to rest, her father had taken her and Joey on a walk. He told them he was taking them to a secret place but that they should never go there without him. After walking for what seemed like a very long time, they came upon an area by the side of an old abandoned building not far from the wall. The Program had been using the area to store dead trees and reclaimed wood and paper.

Mary remembered looking up at the huge pile of logs and wood and thinking that it was higher than the tallest building she had ever seen. While they stood in front of the massive mound of logs, her father told them that all new buildings and paper things, including new books, were made from this giant pile. He told them that everything in the pile had value and that they should always try to reuse things.

"Supplies have been disappearing, Mary," Able said in a stern and louder voice, signaling that she wasn't paying sufficient attention. "And management refuses to put up with theft. Why do you have an entire box? You're not thinking of taking this home, are you?"

Mary had never seen him act so gruffly. She slowly and deliberately corrected her posture as she processed the ridiculousness of his question and the fact that they had not found something possibly much more incriminating. At the same time, she knew she should be careful not to embarrass her boss in front of the guard or her colleagues.

"Of course not. I have that because," she paused to clear her throat and point at the stack of outgoing shipping folders in her Outbox.

Able stared at the pile.

Mary registered the subtle shift in his grimace as the stupidity of his question dawned on him. "As you know, boss, I reuse whatever folders I can as many times as possible, but still I go through almost a full box of new ones every week for outgoing invoices."

Attempting to save face, he continued his questioning. "But do you need your own full box packed away in your desk?"

"Well, sometimes I go through a pack a day. I mean, I could make individual trips to the supply cabinet for each folder . . . back and forth . . . if that is what you want me to do, but that doesn't seem efficient, given the goals and standards you set at the beginning of the year."

Able had no choice but to address the guard. "Actually, Mary is one of our best employees in the entire distribution center. Let's move on."

The guard looked blankly at him and said nothing.

Mary breathed a sigh of relief once they and the crowd that had congregated behind them were out of sight. She had dodged a bullet, but she needed to get that envelope out of the office. She cautiously slid the envelope out from between her incoming invoices and back into her bag.

After a stressful day that made her stomach injections hurt even more, she finally arrived home and took a moment to gaze at her tiny apartment. She felt no connection to the musty room, painted a dreary brown that had faded years ago. Her kitchen area was regulation-fitted with a table, two chairs, one lamp, a bed, and her only prized possession, her bookcase. She had one window that no longer opened. It overlooked three abandoned neighborhood buildings. She closed the rickety blinds, sat on her bed, pulled her bag close, and let out a long breath. "Deal with this," she muttered, and with one hand quickly tore open the top of the envelope and pulled out the contents. Inside she found a letter from her father and a very old tattered notebook.

CHAPTER 6

DAD'S GIFT

Mary trembled as she held the four-year-old letter from her dad. As she held the paper, her father's voice came rushing back.

April 15, 2117

My dear children:

Some of the things you are about to read, your mother and I decided not to disclose previously. We felt this knowledge could be dangerous. Understand that although you may feel we concealed things or misled you by their omission, we felt this was something we did to protect you. In my heart, I know your mother and I withheld this information for correct reasons. Knowing our intent, please do not judge us harshly.

Since you are reading this letter, you know by now your mother and I are deceased. Our hope is that each of you are well and happy. Before disclosing any further details, I would like to caution that for your safety, you should probably not let anyone else read this letter or see the contents of the envelope.

Along with this introductory letter is a second letter and a notebook that belonged to your great grandfather, my grandfather Simian. At the time he was writing in the notebook, he was one of the original members of a group of scientists trying to save humanity. Later, along with others, he was instrumental in the development of the Program. He died before you met him, but I can tell you he was an intelligent and wonderful man.

Scientists like your great grandfather were given a heavy burden to bear, and they worked diligently under great duress. Their task, their burden, was to try to save humanity from extinction, and they succeeded. In the past, your mother and I have mentioned that he was a hero, and I will do my best to add more to his story. Reading the notebook and these letters will help you understand that history.

Your great grandfather kept this notebook, a post-diary of sorts, to detail what went on leading up to and during the development of the Program. All of them involved in the operation at that time were under strict orders not to document anything. The official record was only to be made by management, supposedly to ensure that confidential information was not accidentally disclosed. During the days of that operation, those in charge had little tolerance for disobedience.

Scientists who did not keep policy were cast out of the Program to the Earth's surface to die. Your great grandfather, however, felt that a first-person documentation of history was important. I believe he was also suspicious of those in charge. He wasn't sure they would truthfully record this important history. He felt the world deserved an observer's record in case the history was distorted in the future by those in power. Please keep the value of this notebook and all contents of this envelope in mind when you care for it.

Parts of what you will read will not be new information since the Program and your mother and I have taught you the open history. Other contents contain sensitive information that you have not been told. After you finish reading the notebook, please read my second letter. In it, I share additional information that your mother and I hid from you. As will become clear, this information is dangerous, and those in power will not want it made public.

I leave this documentation and what should be done with it in your hands. My personal view is that history should be preserved. I trust you will carefully consider the consequences of whatever actions you take.

May the God that I have taught you is Creator of the Universe watch over and protect you. Goodbye, my family. Know that we greatly loved each of you and always wished you the very best. Our hope is that all is well in the world and you are happy.

Dad

Mary stared at her father's handwriting. Before placing his letter on her bed, she smelled the paper in search of his scent. Then she reached into the envelope for the second letter but could not find it. Tired, and with her hands mildly shaking, she stroked the cover of the notebook. This notebook is a big deal, she thought. In the past she had collected a few old books from before the climate change, but this 100-year-old notebook was much more valuable. She opened to the first page.

CHAPTER 7

THE NOTEBOOK, 2033 THE BEGINNING OF THE END

As I begin to write this notebook, I must confess that it wasn't as if we didn't know what was happening to our climate. We did. We turned a blind eye.

Like everyone else, I was distracted by the normal trappings of life. But the increasing series of disasters were serious, and they were happening all around me.

I was thirty-nine years old in 2033, when solid ground first shifted under me. As an internationally known chemist, I should have . . . I don't know what I should have done. The acceleration in climate changes seemed unstoppable . . . .

* * *

. . . I'm determined to write more in this diary concerning the history during the climate change and my time in this secret facility. The catch is, and I should have noted this earlier, that site management has forbidden us from recording things for security reasons. I have my doubts. Anyway, I will write when I can, especially if I think something is historically significant, and I will try not to get caught.

Here is the history as I remember it.

In hindsight, the public, or at least those of us from the scientific community, should have been more alarmed when the tremors first began. They were small, and they were happening in places that had never experienced earthquakes. Even that oddity didn't trigger our attention. We missed the significance of the tiny quakes, those neon signs in the night flashing danger ahead. As I think back, I still remember conversations my wife and I had when we learned of these events.

"Hey, Martha, did you catch this?" I had asked her after seeing a clip on the news.

"Catch what? What are you talking about?"

"On the news, they said there were small earthquakes in Dover, Delaware. That's odd, don't you think? I never heard of earthquakes in that part of the country, have you?"

"No, but I'm not so surprised. Haven't there been all sorts of weird places having tremors this year? Where was that last one? Oh yeah, Wichita, Kansas. Come on, Kansas earthquakes? That was about two months ago. Remember?"

Well, it turned out those Dover mini-quakes did little damage, but I was curious, so I approached Ron Bartlett, a colleague of mine at the university. He taught civil engineering, and his doctoral research had focused on the strength of concrete buildings during quakes.

"Hey, Ron, what do you think about those Dover tremors the other day?" Turns out Ron was way ahead of me. He had already been asking other colleagues the same question.

"That was strange, so strange that I contacted a seismologist friend at UCLA. He has been spending a lot of time lately researching all the tremors around the country in the places that don't normally have quakes. Let me tell you, he's concerned. I mean big time."

I decided it was better not to share what Ron told me with Martha. She had enough on her plate with all the attrition on her staff at the hospital.

Unfortunately, Ron's UCLA friend was right. Those tremors turned out to be very significant – precursors of the floods, sink holes, earthquakes, tsunamis, volcanic eruptions, fires, and landslides that followed. They were early indicators of strange things going on above and below Earth's surface.

The second link I and other scientists missed was the worldwide increase in volcanic activity. Ron wondered if there might be a connection, but his seismologist buddy told him he found no reason to link the tremors occurring in odd places to all the new volcanic activity.

"Hell," he told me one afternoon over coffee in the cafeteria, "My buddy told me historically fifty to sixty worldwide eruptions occur each year. He thinks it's simply a statistical coincidence that so many eruptions are occurring simultaneously these days. He doesn't believe they're linked."

I believed him and dismissed the anomalies. Soon, however, it was difficult for anyone to dismiss the volume of weird things going on, especially all the volcanos.

Political leaders were proclaiming in the papers and on the news that the volcanic activity was nothing to be concerned about. This was simply a literal case of Mother Nature blowing off steam. Only a few months later, things got serious.

One day, Ron and I were in the faculty lounge, watching a TV interview with two climatologists. They were debating whether the volcanic eruptions were a cause or an effect of the climate change. After watching that interview, we both grew more nervous.

Debates on more fundamental issues were also taking place between scientists and politicians. The majority of scientists and others who believed in anthropogenic global warming used events to further their agenda for more regulation and restrictions on sources of dirty pollutants. Government officials, a handful of scientists, and climate deniers who did not accept the manmade impact argument used the same circumstance to argue that nature and not man had more of an impact. This camp argued that any manmade causes of climate change were minor compared to Mother Nature.

It turned out neither group had grasped the magnitude of the looming apocalypse. Climate change was happening, maybe in fits and spurts at first, like two steps forward, one step back, but it could no longer be denied. And scientists were now alarmed by the magnitude of the changes.

Two things happened that eventually caused scientists the world over to question their knowledge of the geology and climatology of our planet.

First, a strange regenerative effect emerged between the accelerating climate change and the increase in volcanic activity. More volcanic eruptions forced more climate change, which in turn seemed to force more eruptions. This regenerative effect was completely unexpected, and it sent almost all members of the scientific community into panic.

The second observation was the increasing explosive nature of the volcanic eruptions. Many Plinian eruptions occurred simultaneously, producing large plumes of gasses and particles. Nothing like these eruptions had ever been seen.

While all this weird stuff was happening, the main concerns for scientists were the problems directly associated with the climate change itself: flooding, temperature extremes, extended droughts, increasingly violent storms.

Life was certainly getting harder, but what could we do? We went to work, lived our lives the best we could, and listened to the news.

I can hear Martha as if it were yesterday. "Sim, we're seeing so many cases of melanoma at the hospital. But why? Anyway, I want to look you and the boys over very carefully and make sure I don't see any lesions. Then you'll check me."

"Sounds good." That evening we checked everyone. We didn't find anything.

At this point, scientists were not sure what to do, so they settled on arguing theory: were manmade pollutants or volcanic gasses to blame for the atmospheric changes? All the while, the invisible volcanic gases and particles they were talking about were slowly destroying the ozone layer, which turned out to be the cause of all the new melanoma cases.

I, like others, was aware that in previous decades, scientists, politicians, and governments had worked together to eliminate or reduce manmade aerosol pollutants which were known to be detrimental to the ozone layer. These chemicals included chlorofluorocarbons (CFC's), hydrofluorocarbons (HFC's), methyl bromide, methyl chloride, as well as other gases and elements such as halons, chlorine, and bromine. Through rare collaboration among nations, humanity had managed to abate disaster and the ozone layer had self-healed.

That bit of history concerning the ozone layer gave some members of the scientific community a reason for hope, but others found little solace in that event. The situation this time of course, was different. It was nature itself that was the nemesis to the layer in the form of gases spewing from volcanic eruptions not manmade aerosols.

I had read that scientists believed chlorine and bromine gases blasting from volcanoes into the atmosphere would have minimal or at worst temporary negative effects on the planet. They were aware that chlorine and bromine were detrimental to the layer, but conventional wisdom stated that the amounts of these chemicals emitted during a volcanic eruption would be exceedingly small.

Something else they believed was encouraging. Normal moisture in the form of rain and ice in the atmosphere would remove or wash these gases clean before they could cause damage.

What was not expected, though, was the exceptionally large concentrations of these gases in the simultaneous Plinian eruptions. The measured concentration of these gases were tens (if not hundreds) of thousands of times greater than what would have been predicted. These Plinian eruptions had violent explosions. Deadly gases and particles blew deep into the stratosphere, reaching the ozone layer. This unsettling knowledge changed everything for scientists around the world.

Wide holes formed in ozone regions above the volcanos. The layer, behaving like a skin stretched tightly over a drum, was about to tear. Ultraviolet A (UV-A), ultraviolet B (UV-B), and ultraviolet C (UV-C) poured onto unshielded and unprotected planet Earth. The ozone layer thinned. With each day, danger increased.

"Damn," I remember Martha saying, "this is scary. You won't believe how many still born babies I'm delivering. My ophthalmology buddies? They're overrun with cataract and blind patients — and melanoma cases are through the roof."

"So, what do you suggest?"

"I'm not sure, but I'm worried about the boys playing outside, getting too much sun. How about we limit their exposure? Just keep them occupied indoors."

"Oh?" I challenged. "Sure, that's going to go over big."

Mankind, through its use or misuse of the planet, had unleashed the sun, the god of warmth and life. Sol Invictus had turned into a demon, Earth's mortal enemy. With the ozone layer diminished, our sun's daily *invisible death rays were silently punishing every living thing on Earth outside of cockroaches and wasps.*

First to die were Phytoplankton. Deformed in early development, entire species of sea creatures rapidly became extinct. Horrific mutations appeared in animals. Mammals produced extra partial limbs or malformed organs.

Martha saw what was happening to humans firsthand. Patients came into her hospital blinded by cataracts, dying from melanoma, and suffering from strange diseases related to zombie bacteria. Weakened immune systems had no way to deal with these new strains of bacteria, leading to the rise in disease. The death rays were changing proteins in the DNA of plants and animals. People were dying, and unfortunately the world was unprepared and unable to cope.

To prevent outright panic, world governments tried to downplay the seriousness of the situation, but the public wasn't stupid. They knew they were being misled. They lost faith in their governments, politicians, news media, and us, their science and medical communities.

An angry, frightened public was looking for definitive answers. Some people were convinced the initial eruptions were caused by man, due to underground nuclear testing. Others believed the depletion of water and petroleum in the ground that had been cooling and lubricating the continental plates was the problem. Still others believed the eruptions were linked to oil exploration and recovery, such as fracking techniques or other manmade events. Finally, the conspiracy theorist assumed that intentional experiments by nefarious governments — Russia, China, and North Korea — were to blame.

Religious fundamentalists proclaimed God was reigning his fire down on a world of heathens for their immoral activity and that the rapture was at hand. Doomsday cults formed over the world. People prayed for forgiveness and at the same time hoarded water, food, guns, and supplies. Governments were unable to repress the panic. It was rampant.

Unfortunately, as the planetary disaster continued, strange diseases appeared in humans. Most frightening, humans were aging prematurely at an accelerating rate. Everywhere you looked, people were developing progeria, Werner syndrome. They were shrinking in stature. As their bones and organs weakened, their failing immune systems opened them to disease.

Soon Martha was drafted out of obstetrics to help in other areas of medicine. She saw young people whose body organs performed as if they were already old. She also noticed how those who hadn't gone through puberty seemed to be spared the strange aging progeria-like malady.

We witnessed desperation closer to home, too. Decaying human and animal carcasses scattered everywhere because cities and towns didn't have enough healthy workers to safely collect and dispose of the dead. This meant water and food supplies were contaminated, further spreading disease and death.

"We're struggling at the hospital, Sim. We're seeing severely decreased fertility. The birth rate is approaching zero. I seriously believe humanity could go extinct. I mean, what the hell have we done? What kind of world are we leaving our boys?"

"Not a good one, that's for sure," I replied, wishing I could have said something comforting, but it would have been a lie. Like everyone else, I was frightened to the marrow.

The world decayed in front of us. Without healthy manpower, wars halted. Armies disintegrated. Soldiers with aging disease succumbed or simply dropped their weapons and ran away to die with their families.

News outlets and communication networks collapsed as they were abandoned. People were too weak to work. Food shortages became a major problem, crops were poor, farmers and truckers were sick and dying, the railroads weren't operating, and grocery store shelves were empty. Infrastructure around the globe slowly collapsed.

∗　∗　∗

Mary's head swooned from fatigue. She dropped the notebook on her bed and rubbed her eyes. She could read no more. As a child she had been taught about the climate disaster, but those facts had always seemed so distant, just history, not real. Reading her great grandfather's account however, brought that history to life.

CHAPTER 8

THE SECOND LETTER

Mary knew that a group of mostly scientists had lived through the climate disaster and saved humanity and created the Program. She also knew her great-grandfather had been one of those scientists.

As a young girl, she loved hearing her father talk about what an intelligent and brave man her great-grandfather was. Her great-grandfather was a hero.

She was intrigued by what she might find next in the notebook, but she needed sleep. Arms outstretched, she yawned and sank into her pillow. Despite her exhaustion, she tossed and turned through the night. In the early morning, she lay starring at the cracking gray painted ceiling. Certain she would not be able to go back to sleep, she got up.

In the bathroom grooming, she heard someone pounding on her door. Startled, she threw on a cherished robe that had been her mother's and made her way to the door. Who, she thought, would be at her door this early?

Paranoid, she turned back toward the bed to verify that the envelope was hidden. Nervously, she held her breath and partially opened the door, sticking her head through just enough so she could talk. There, on the other side, was her neighbor, Adrienne.

"Oh, so you are home? I'm sort of surprised to see you. I mean, you didn't come out last night. Everyone else did, not you. . . you know, during all the commotion?"

Mary looked at her inquisitively. "Good morning? Uh, what commotion?"

"Really? The commotion outside your door! A guy was snooping around. I saw him, he was right here, leaning down by your door. I yelled at him, and he ran off. Then I contacted the guards."

"By my door? Huh. Guess I slept right through it."

"Doubt that would have been possible," Adrienne flung back, suggesting Mary was lying. "The guards passed right in front of your door, looking for him. All the other neighbors came out. So . . . they didn't knock on your door?"

"No, I'm sure I would have heard that. Did they catch the guy?"

"Nope. I don't know. I don't think so. The guards commanded us to go back inside, but he probably was some filthy Outcast, casing our building, looking to rip us off. Anyway, I was checking up on you. You're all right?"

"Yeah, fine thanks," Mary replied, "just . . . I need to get ready for work. Thanks for checking on me. So very, very . . . thoughtful of you. See you later?" Mary thought to herself that this woman had probably never met an Outcast, yet here she was, comfortable with disparaging them. She wished she had what it took to confront Adrienne about Outcasts, that her brother was one, but it was too early in the morning to chastise her for her ignorant prejudice.

"Yeah . . . sure," Adrienne said, walking away.

"Oh, and Adrienne, let me know if you hear anything else."

Adrienne twisted her head back, obviously surprised by the comment, and gave Mary a cold stare before walking into her apartment.

Mary knew this neighbor didn't like her. The feeling was mutual. Many of her neighbors, she suspected, were snitches. Program snitches got special perks, which made her cautious of people like Adrienne. "Thank you!" Mary made sure she shouted before locking her door.

She washed her face, wondering how she had been able to sleep through all the commotion. "Guess I must have gotten more sleep than I thought," she said, mumbling aloud. But why would a person be skulking near my door? Who was he? Would he be back? Am I in danger?

As she finished buttoning her blouse for work, she thought back once again to the envelope's missing letter. She needed another appointment with Doc. Maybe he would know what happened to it.

CHAPTER 9

THE NOTEBOOK: HOPE FOR SURVIVAL

While walking to her apartment that evening, she noticed the dim orange glow around her building. Security lights. The sight was surprising since the lights on the old building rarely worked. Mary liked seeing them shine on the narrow walkway near her door. Between that and the crisp evening air, she almost felt a spring in her step.

Reaching her apartment, she unlocked her door, stepped inside, and was immediately greeted by an unusually strong musty odor.

"How horrible," she muttered to herself, twisting her lips in disgust. Knowing it would be nicer outside, she dared herself to read the notebook on her walkway in the fresh air. Surely, she could read it safely on the walkway since her neighbors basically never left their apartments in the evening. If they did come out and spot her, she'd just conceal the notebook by sitting on it.

Of course, she might encounter the person who had been snooping around her door, but she assumed that with the security lights on, he was unlikely to reappear.

Resolved that this evening she would live dangerously, she tightened the top most buttons on her coat, wrapped her only scarf around her neck, and grabbed the notebook. Using her free hand, she dragged through the doorway the only kitchen chair that didn't wobble and placed it in the walkway snuggly against the wall.

* * *

A full two years after the disaster started, I learned that the United States and other governments had been planning a way to save humanity. With the consultation of scientists, the U.S. had directed public and private resources to build an immense underground laboratory facility, unprecedented in size and scope. I did not know at the time that the site went by its acronym, CAIHR, located near Buffalo, New York. When I found this out, I realized the location for the facility was ideal.

Buffalo had been a city that was naturally shielded from the sun's rays due to its low number of direct sunshine hours per year. The region also offered low exposure to other natural disasters such as earthquakes, volcanos, hurricanes, and tornadoes. Of course, cold weather was Buffalo's downside, but mountains of snow would give it half a chance at a continual water supply.

Anyway, I soon learned that various governments had cooperated by donating scientists to work at the site. Included in this group were the best and brightest geologists, engineers, biologists, immunologists, virologists, geneticists, physicians, pharmacists, and research scientists from other disciplines. When I think about it now, I realize this group of individuals probably represented the greatest assembly of diverse scientific brain power in the world. Brilliant minds, working in a fantastic research facility, presented the best chance of survival for humanity.

But I get ahead of myself.

Military chaperones grabbed me from my family and flew me to Buffalo, New York, where I boarded a military helicopter.

"Welcome aboard Little Bird, Dr. Walker. Strap in. Put your headset on," the pilot commanded.

Knowing little about military aircraft and somewhat nervous about being in a helicopter, I asked, "Little Bird?"

"Little Bird, MH-6s, the model of this chopper. Great lineage, great bones."

"Good to know. So, where are we headed?"

"Old ski resort in Coldon, New York, now the CAIHR site."

"Care?" I said.

"No, C A I H R," he replied spelling it out letter by letter.

"Got it, CAIHR site. An acronym obviously?"

He nodded, "Been ferrying people like you there for months. Heard you scientists are supposed to save the world. Now buckle up and put your headset on. We lift off after the others get here."

"Others?"

"Three more."

"Be there soon enough," he clipped, as if telegraphing, "You ask too many questions. We're done."

The first person to arrive was an older Asian woman. She said nothing to me or the pilot and quickly sat and buckled in. She had obviously flown in a helicopter before. When she looked settled, I offered her my hand. "I'm Sim. Dr. Sim Walker, chemist."

"Dr. Haruko Ishizaka, immunology. Glad to meet you," she said in broken English. Little did I know at that time what a good friend and hero Dr. Ishizaka would become. Next came Dr. Sang Wook, a world renown physicist, whose journal papers I had followed for years. The last person to board was Konrad Daimler, a German electrical engineer. Konrad, like Haruko, would also become one of my heroes, though for a very different reason.

Once we were buckled in, the chopper lifted off. After about 15 minutes, it circled before making its final approach. Our destination came into view below us. I had never been to Coldon, New York before, but the small mountain jutting from the surface was certainly no longer a ski resort. A forest area of many acres had been cleared around the base of the mountain. From the air, we could see the tops of giant wide fortified structures that seemed to barely protrude above the ground. These buildings didn't appear to have any surface level access. We later learned they were silos, giant storage buildings, used to hold precious building resources, food, equipment, and medical supplies. Obviously, this place had been designed to be self-sufficient for a long period of time.

Numerous other structures became visible. Using his long skinny finger, Konrad, the engineer, pointed and shouted gleefully into his headset as if he was trying to get above the noise of the chopper, "Look on your left, what a huge farm of windmills and solar panels."

"*Clearly, for site power generation, maybe also for pumping water for drinking and cooling,*" *I responded.* "*You know, to capture the sun and breezes from Lake Erie.*"

Konrad cranked his head around as the chopper circled, and he looked off into the distance. "*Yes, I believe you're right, Dr. Walker. And did all of you notice that large array of terrestrial and satellite antennas?*" *Haruko and I both nodded, though we obviously weren't as excited about seeing them as our new friend Konrad.*

As soon as we landed, three armed soldiers ran from the surrounding wooded area and approached the helicopter. One of the men appeared to be a United States general. The men quickly ushered us out of the way of the blades of the helicopter, making a short jog across the yard through a thick metal doorway. Once inside, we faced a group of armed soldiers.

"*I apologize for the rush. We needed to get you in ASAP so that chopper can refuel and get the hell back out there. Let me introduce myself. I'm General Walter Tishman. I'm in charge of this site. Welcome to CAIHR.*"

Each of us introduced our names and specialties as the general shook our hands. "*We'll take a quick tour of the facility, show you to your quarters, then you can rest. Let me remind you that you are now in a secret and totally secure facility.*"

I remember hearing the general say those words and thinking that this might be his attempt at humor. Obviously, all of us were quite aware it was a secret facility, but I was wrong to think this man was joking. He was quite serious. I didn't know him yet, but later I came to realize he wasn't the type of man who would ever joke about anything.

Our site tour got underway, led by the general, who stopped briefly at certain junctures.

"*We built this campus almost entirely underground. In the belly of this short Buffalo mountain, we are very secure. The entire site is in concentric circles with the largest being the outside hallway, where we are now walking.*" *He was clearly proud of his site. I wondered if he had been involved in the design.*

As our tour guide pointed out different things, I could see that Konrad was impressed with the general and with the facility. He leaned over and whispered, "*Much planning, many resources needed to construct such a place. Fantastic, no? I think work on this enormous place began many years ago. You agree?"*

I nodded out of politeness, but in my mind, I thought the site may have been originally designed for a different purpose, like an emergency operations center or wartime command post. Irony was that we were at war but, for the first time in human history, we were battling the climate, not people.

As we walked further along the curved yellow tiled hallway, I asked the general about the meaning of the cryptic site name, CAIHR.

"The name is not important."

I felt disrespected. Not knowing the unspoken rules of the new world order began to sting.

Without missing a beat, he continued. "On your right is the infirmary. Hopefully none of you ever have to use it." Only later did we understand the significance of that statement.

"On the right you can see the door to the communications rooms. Let me enter the code, and we'll peek inside." When he opened the door, we entered a large conference room that housed a giant oak conference table. Admiring the impressive table, I mentally counted twenty-five matching chairs surrounding it, each in front of a computer station.

"Behind this door are two additional conference rooms, nothing special. Moving on . . ."

I don't think he realized when he dismissed the rooms as "nothing special," he tipped his hand. Like hell nothing special. Later I learned those rooms were only accessed by people with higher security clearances than us lowly scientists. Who they were, I never knew.

We walked back into the outermost circular hallway. Our next stop was the main computer room. After another series of door codes, we saw a cavernous room with many bays of computers and other electronic machines. The soldiers sitting in front of the computers turned to look at us. The uniformed men and women in brown and beige fatigues seemed surprised to see us. They quickly stood and saluted.

"At ease," he told the desk soldiers, who turned out to be the guards he had stationed inside his IT command center. We later learned he had stationed guards everywhere. "I have an important announcement." He signaled the four of us to fully enter the room. "Meet four of our newest

scientists: Dr. Walker, Dr. Ishizaka, Dr. Han, and Mr. Daimler. All experts in their fields. They will help us get out of this mess."

I felt a little embarrassed to be referenced in that way, and their blank stares didn't help either. I hoped his faith wasn't misplaced.

With his parting "Carry on," we marched back into the hallway. At this point the tour took a strange turn. When we approached the next two rooms, the general simply pointed, implying they were either unimportant or secret. Either way, we kept walking. Were these places he never expected us to go?

"Here are the kitchens. Note the water and waste treatment bay." We moved on. "Now a place you'll like. Make a point of spending time here. We have a large workout area, including an indoor track. Work out to stay healthy. In your spare time, of course."

"Wow," I whispered to Dr. Ishizaka, "it almost feels like a college tour."

"I'm glad you like the facilities, Dr. Walker, but this place will lose the feel of a college visit once you get to work." When I looked over, the general was frowning.

"No, sir. I'm certain of that. I didn't mean to minimize the seriousness of our situation. I'm sure you are right." If nothing else, I thought to myself, he had good hearing.

Our tour continued at a faster pace.

"Down this hallway, note the four laboratory bays on your right. You will be spending most of your time in them." He turned looking directly at Konrad and Sang, who had been whispering between themselves, "I realize you are anxious to get in them, but first you need to be versed in the rules. You'll get a closer look at these tomorrow and every day from now on. These labs are among the best-equipped in the world."

Doctor Han spoke excitedly, "I can't wait to get in there."

"I sense that, Doctor. I assure you that will happen soon. Moving on . . . to your right, the fabrication centers, equipment maintenance bays, and manufacturing areas." By now the general's voice was becoming curt, almost authoritarian. Clearly, he was tired of playing tour guide.

"On the right, male and female sleeping quarters. Appropriate quarters only. Find your locker and bunk numbers. Freshen up, change

into your scrubs, rest. No talking. People are sleeping. At 18:00, guards will escort you to a rules and expectations meeting. After the meeting, my staff will assign you access codes and introduce you to a few of your peers. Wait for your escort. Absolutely no wandering. Questions?"

Before I could ask, "When do we eat," soldiers swarmed around the general, talking urgently. Then he was gone.

Haruko, displaying a smile, spoke first. I still recall her broken English. "Are we in the military now?" Everyone chuckled politely, as professionals do, but we were all thinking the same thing.

CHAPTER 10

REYANNE'S DEAL

"Hey, Mary. Have a minute? Walk with me. I've got to deliver this stuff down the hall."

"Sure, let me grab some folders of my own, and I'll drop them off on the way. So, you're back at work then, feeling better?"

"Yea, I'm fine. Walk." Once away from the clutter of the other desks, Reyanne came clean. "Actually, I wasn't sick that day you covered for me, but thanks."

"You weren't? Then, where were you?"

"Shh, damn, not so loud. A small group of us were . . . having a clandestine meeting at my apartment."

"At your apartment? During work hours? That's kind of risky, don't you think?"

"Not really. We figured the safest time for us to meet was during the day when all my nosey snitch neighbors would be at work."

"Go on, you've hooked me."

"A bunch of us are frustrated by the shit treatment we get from those assholes on the leadership committee. We want to organize a work stoppage, like in the ones in the old books. A walkout."

Mary chuckled under her breath, "A walkout. For real? You must be crazy. What would that accomplish?"

"A lot, and don't think I don't know how you feel about the Program, or I wouldn't be talking to you. I've heard you're a dissident at heart. Aren't there a million reasons for us to resist those bastards? For instance, we protest what they do to us when we get sick. Like, if you're so sick, they send you to the Care Place."

"Sick? I guess I'm not following. We go to the clinic for the monthly shots. If we're sick, doctors take care of us – run tests, give us medicine, that sort of stuff. Then if we're seriously ill, they send us to the Care Place. What am I missing?"

"Obviously, you haven't been paying attention lately. The Care Place has changed. The word is people are going in and never coming out. Except maybe for managers and committee members, nobody leaves the Care Place alive."

Mary chuckled, "Where did you hear that? That's the dumbest conspiracy theory anyone has ever come up with."

"It's not theory. Remember that guy, Jeffrey, who used to work in my group? When he got sick, he went in there and never came back."

"That's ridiculous. He probably works in a different facility now, or maybe he's home recuperating. I go there all the time to visit my brother Joey. That place is mostly full of old people."

"Mary, I'm telling you, old people aren't the only ones dying. Something bad is going on there."

"Well, I haven't seen it." But as she spoke, Mary thought about how Lucinda might be treating her brother. She had seen Joey flinch, and she wondered if Lucinda had ever hit him. She couldn't imagine it and dismissed the thought. "I think you might be reading things that aren't there."

"OK, that issue aside, the leadership committee is dangerous in other ways. You agree with that, right?"

"I certainly do."

"So, shouldn't we make sure every worker understands that? And shouldn't we find a way to resist those bastards? Mary, there's power in numbers. Only seven were able to get to my meeting, but I already have over two dozen names on a list that's growing. If enough of us were involved in a work stoppage, we could cripple the Program, bring them to their knees. Their comfy little lives would be affected. They'd be forced to deal with us."

"And what about their response? You think they'd just take it? There'd be severe punishment for everyone. You're talking about people's lives here. That sounds reckless to me."

"Then reckless might be just be what we need. I say screw the bastards."

"I can appreciate that you're frustrated. I am, too. You certainly don't need to convince me about how horrible that committee is, but I don't agree with your method. People could get hurt."

"Fine, you don't like my methods, but don't expect us to just sit back and continue to put up with their shit. Me, I'm going to keep working to organize this walkout. So, I take it from what you're saying that I can't I count on you to be involved?"

"It's not just me I'm worried about. My brother is in the Care Place, and I don't want him mistreated because of something stupid I do, like participating in your walkout."

"I get it, but at least take a little time to think things over. Maybe you'll change your mind when you see how many people want in on this. We need all the good people we can get."

"Reyanne, as long as my brother is in there, I'm not going to change my mind."

CHAPTER 11

THE NOTEBOOK: RULES AND EXPECTATIONS

"Mary, are you sick this morning? You look green." Able sat on the edge of her desk, flipping through her outbox.

"Yeah, I think something I ate disagreed with me, boss," she mumbled, turning her face away from him and holding her head in her hands. But as she said that, her gut wrenched, and she quickly stood up. Her cheeks puffed outward involuntarily, and she pressed her right hand firmly against her lips to prevent a disaster. Able quickly jumped backward, stumbling to avoid being spewed upon.

"Oh hell no," he exclaimed in a disgusted tone of voice. "Go home before you make a mess and get everyone sick." Mary wanted to apologize, but Able was already speed walking, with his hand over his own mouth. Feeling her stomach and chest contract once again, she ran down the hall, making it to the bathroom just in time.

She felt somewhat better after she cleaned herself up and wondered about the food the Program had been doling out lately. Lately the food smelled bad. She guessed the committee members ate fresher food. Common workers such as herself ate what remained. Whatever food had upset her stomach, she decided her boss was right, she needed to go home. She strode back to her desk and grabbed her yellow bag, thrilled to have permission to leave work early.

After a walk in the cold air, her stomach felt better. She smiled to herself, thinking what a treat it was to be home without any chores or need to be anyplace. Gleefully, she grabbed the notebook, sat in a chair at her kitchen table, and opened to the green strip of cloth she used as a marker.

* * *

Other newcomers like us attended the meeting, but Sang, Konrad, Haruko, and I all sat together. And, new officials told us the objective for the facility was to find a way to save humanity from the effects of the climate change but, of course, we already knew that. The expectation was for people to work daily ten-hour shifts in their primary roles and then, if required, help with site maintenance. The concept, officials said, was to house the least number of scientists and support personnel to conserve the resources for the longest time possible.

A few minutes into the presentation, Sang turned to us. "I am anxious to get to work. My poor family. Dying. So many others, dying in my sweet Korea, and here I sit in a stupid meeting. Time to solve this thing. Quickly." His voice was shaking.

"Hey, I'm with you. My oldest son was so sick when I left him, and my wife is a doctor, but I'm not sure she or anyone else can save him. I'm all for getting in those labs and starting work right now, tonight, but . . ."

As I spoke, a fresh wave of anxiety hit me. With so many new things to process that day, I had managed to stop worrying about my family. Once again, the guilt returned. I had left my loved ones. They were counting on me to save them. God only knew what shape they were in. I tried my best to calm down and think positively. I kept reminding myself that we were in a fantastic research facility with a world class collection of scientists. I remember believing, like Sang, we could solve this thing together. I needed to be hopeful, and I needed to believe this to the depts of my soul or I would go crazy.

That night after the meeting, Sang, Konrad, Haruko, and I were taken to another room to meet other scientists. The diversity in this assembly of experts was amazing – hundreds of men and women of all races, ethnicities, religions, and nationalities. People from all over the world, from many backgrounds, religions, and cultures – atheists, agnostics, Jews, Moslems, Catholics, Buddhists, Hindus, and Protestants – met and talked. Though we didn't yet know each other, we seemed to be connected by a common fear and common goal. All of us were humbled by the power of nature that was destroying our world and by our powerlessness to aid our loved ones.

Over the next few days we settled into teams. Haruko and I became members of the life sciences team. Sang and Konrad were added to one of the numerous physical and engineering teams. Though we did not all work directly together, the four of us remained good friends and talked as often as we could.

We continued to meet other scientists, technical support people, and managers who reported to the lesser generals. Over time, we also met guards and managers who, like us, were men and women of many nationalities. Surprisingly, a few of them were as young as seventeen or eighteen.

The guards, who were always present, ensured site security from outside intervention and maintained strict internal order. Most reported directly General Tishman. Also reporting to him were two other generals and tens of professionals, who functioned as project managers. These managers tried to keep the many research teams focused while containing the big scientific egos.

It was inspiring to see that these teams never faced any discrimination in leadership roles or assignments, regardless of their sex, race, sexual preference, religion, or ethnic background. Everyone felt compelled to work hard toward the common goal.

With all the pressure on us to perform, Sang and I decided to use the exercise rooms in what little spare time we had. We met almost every evening at the track. It was a great comfort to have him to talk to as we jogged.

But even in our leisure time, the general restricted much of what we did. Endless rules and regulations. "I hate how they treat us, like we're soldiers instead of scientists," Sang confided.

"Yeah, but I tell myself we have to suck it up and live with that as long as we are making progress." My response placated him, at least temporarily.

With socialization, as with everything else, management had zero tolerance for rule violations. Punishment was both quick and harsh. Fraternization among men and women, heterosexual or homosexual, was neither encouraged or discouraged, but we had tight restrictions. No matter the type of relationship, pregnancies were forbidden as well as any verbal or physical fighting.

With the exception of surgical sterilization, many forms of birth control were available to us. As a result, the punishment for pregnancy was essentially a death sentence, since both parties were immediately banished to the surface. These outcasts had no chance of survival.

Such extreme punishments acted as an incentive for people to be careful in their relationships and to get along regardless of their differences. The expectation was for everyone to make an important contribution and nothing, including personal relationships, was to get in the way of work.

Another strict rule that Haruko and I often discussed during our work in the lab concerned how the Program dealt with illness among workers. This was a hot button issue for her, not so much for me. To combat the spread of disease in close quarters, the rules dictated that the sick person would be immediately quarantined. Haruko, an immunologist, had no problem with that, but if physicians were unable to quickly diagnose, cure, and send the patient back to work, the patient was left with two terrible options. Either they could be euthanized and cremated or banished to the surface. Either option, a death sentence.

"How can you agree with this rule?" she would rant, whether you agreed or disagreed. "People can't control if they get sick. And isn't every scientist or support person needed? I thought everyone here was an expert, valuable. Otherwise, why would they be here? This rule is inhumane."

On points of social justice, I tried not to challenge Haruko. It took less time to nod and continue doing my work. Besides, I accepted the harshness of the rule. When I had time and felt brave enough, I did argue with her. "We have limited time and resources to find a way to save our loved ones. We don't have the luxury of spending resources on people who can't be quickly cured."

"That's a cruel excuse. I don't accept."

Truth be told, I wasn't sure that I totally did either, considering the medical advancements on what conditions could be cured. But we had the greater good to consider. That's what mattered. No individual was indispensable or could be allowed to crater the entire effort.

All of us, and maybe Sang more than any of us, talked about families we had left languishing on the surface. The problem was we were not allowed any direct communication with them, another ridiculous restriction dictated by site security.

The general and his reports had a massive array of radio and internet-enabled computers, storage, and backup systems, which were used to gather and archive information. The fact that they had direct access to news at the surface while we didn't was a point of great contention.

We understood the primary usage of these internet-connected computer systems was to search for specific information requested by our research teams. That was good. If we wanted a search, we had to submit a request through our team leaders. Upon completion of the search, the data was then appended to the massive archival database and made available to us on an intranet computer system. Bottom line, we got the search data we requested but had no access to what was happening on the surface or knowledge of our loved ones.

"What do you think they are trying to hide from us?" Konrad once asked me.

"I don't know. Maybe there really is a valid security concern. I mean, imagine what would happen if desperate people at the surface discovered us. They might storm the site to get our stash of food and medicine. Then humanity would be screwed."

"But I often wonder how bad it must be for them."

"I feel guilty that I'm safe in this hole in the ground while my family is suffering. I think all we can do is work hard to quickly find a solution. But that's not going to happen unless we all come to a consensus on what the priorities are and soon."

Scientists agreed that when the volcanic eruptions ceased, and the ozone-destroying chemicals dissipated, the ozone layer would begin to self-repair and the climate would moderate — speculation based on the history of the ozone layer. Decades earlier, international cooperation to reduce CFC's and HCFC's had resulted in improvements to the layer. Now we wondered how much time an ozone layer that had been extensively damaged would need to sufficiently repair for humans to live on the surface?

Sang had his own thoughts on this subject. "I think the ozone layer could repair fairly quickly, maybe less than a year." I felt he was being optimistic because others I spoke to thought it could take decades. Who really knew, so why share their pessimism with him?

Anyway, the primary question we needed to ask was when would the volcanic eruptions stop? No scientific data existed to speculate, so we chose to believe that eventually Earth's underground lithostatic pressure would subside, and the eruptions would end. If we were wrong, or if the eruptions outlasted our resources, then our work wouldn't matter anyway. Humanity would end. We chose to believe the eruptions would end before our resources were depleted.

Like Martha, Haruko and most everyone else on our life sciences team believed that most of the adult sickness, cancers, and deaths could be attributed to the impairment of the immune system, which was directly caused by exposure to the UV rays and which left humans susceptible to disease, including accelerated aging syndrome, which destroyed the bones and organs and limited reproduction. If we wanted to reduce the incidence of disease, what we needed was a way to protect humans from the rays and the bacteria. Even my Martha knew this.

I remember the day Haruko told our team, "Bolster the immune system so we slow the death rate while increasing the fertility and birth rates on the surface." Nothing to argue there. She was convinced that with the population rate stabilized, we would then be able to focus our time and remaining resources on resolving many other issues presented by climate change. The majority of scientists in and outside of our group agreed that we should tackle the issue of stemming disease before all others.

With that, each research team was tasked with finding a way to beat the exposure problem that had resulted in so much death. The most obvious solution involved a form of mechanical shielding to protect against the rays and disease. Konrad and Sang's engineering team proposed a solution. They wanted to totally encase humans in a *protective space suit designed for planet Earth. The suit would offer protection from both UV and biohazards.*

One evening while we were working out in the exercise facility, Sang gleefully told me how far his team had progressed. "We're almost there," he said with a big smile on his face. That was probably the first time I had ever seen him so upbeat. "In just a few days," he continued, "we'll have the first suits ready for surface tests. I'm so hopeful about this."

I was a little skeptical about their solution, but maybe I was biased since my team was also working on an alternative. Nevertheless, I found his enthusiasm contagious. After we finished working out, he told me to follow him.

"I've got something important to show you in our lab." He used his code and opened the lab bay doors to a huge room full of people and electronic equipment. Toward the back, I saw what looked like metal or woodworking machinery. Everyone was busy working, except for one fellow, standing in the middle of the room with a gigantic smile on his face. It was Konrad.

"Welcome to our hell, I mean, our lab," he said.

"Pretty impressive facility you guys have here," I commented.

"I asked Sang to bring you by tonight. We have something to show you."

"Now what could it possibly be?" I said, pretending not to notice the large robotic-looking space suit that was hanging nearby.

Konrad turned me around, "Look here. This one is the first model that we fabricated. In the back room, we store five better versions that I can't show you. And guess what?"

"Let me guess, this thing walks on its own?"

"No, but we could do that if we wanted. No, Sang and I are in the group of five people who are going to test the suits out in a few days."

"Well, congratulations, I guess. And you believe this contraption can protect you from the rays and all that disease out there?"

"That's the idea, my friend. I'm totally confident these suits are the answer we've been looking for."

A few days later Sang and Konrad and the others conducted their test on the surface. The victory was that everyone came back safely. The problem was that the suits predictably proved too bulky, making it hard to move. While every team applauded the engineering group's effort, the conclusion was that the suits would make it too difficult to farm or do manual labor. The suits could be useful in the short run, but a better and more practical scheme was going to be required for the masses.

While the results were unfortunate, the effort had at least offered a glimmer of hope. My life science team now had a chance to propose the solution that we had been working on. Our research had started by looking for clues in plants that were known to be radiation tolerant. We discovered the plants accomplished this feat by utilizing UV absorbing secondary metabolites and UV sensing protein molecules. Our team also investigated spore Bacillus species that could survive strong radiation.

In addition, we studied research that had been conducted on mammals that were living in the extreme radiation levels around the Russian Chernobyl nuclear disaster site. Once we were armed with an understanding of nature's way of dealing with radiation of all types, we compared the similarities between the UV-induced aging malady and the accelerated aging disease, progeria. Haruko, who was the most experienced scientist on our team, was our research lead.

"What we need," she told us, "is a combination of drugs to boost the immune system, not just for the rays but to protect against all those odd strains of bacteria out there."

"That's obvious," I replied, "but what drugs and in what combination?"

Fortunately, Haruko already had the answer. "The drug cocktail we need is probably composed of heavy doses of human growth hormone, melanin, vitamin C, carotene, Thiol-based antioxidants, and UV absorbing metabolites." Then she added, "For total protection, we still need UV-blocking eye glasses and body creams."

The team agreed her approach was correct. This scheme had merit. We knew that the things that boosted the immune system and protected us from the rays also had the advantage of making people less susceptible to other pathogens and carcinogens. If we could make people's immune systems stronger, the overall population would have less incidence of disease and death. Nothing could be more logical.

For months we researched and did experiments to determine the correct drug cocktail. Now we had a plan. The next step would be human trials in a test group.

The general insisted that for the first trial we use people from the entire site and not just our team. The response to asking for volunteers for this trial was simply amazing. Everyone wanted to be involved. I marveled at how many scientists and support personnel showed the courage to volunteer for this dangerous assignment. The only people who were not allowed to volunteer were General Tishman, the managers, and the guards. In fact, so many scientists and support personnel volunteered that a lottery was required to determine who would participate in the study. Haruko and Konrad were among the final group selected by the lottery.

The General, who often had conflicts with the strong-willed Haruko, thought she was too valuable to participate in the test group. Standing her ground, she insisted that she be a member of the test group in the study. After all, she argued, she had been selected by the lottery along with everyone else. Fortunately, her stubbornness turned out to be a good thing.

All the participants in the trial were considered heroes. The tests began, and this group of brave souls was injected with the drugs and then exposed to the surface under controlled and concealed conditions.

The initial results were terrifying.

The drugs proved toxic to all but one of the participants, Haruko. Our dear friend Konrad, one of the test subjects, had an allergic reaction and died quickly along with many others. Haruko, Sang, and I were terribly shaken by this horrible test result, especially by the loss of Konrad. Everyone on the site was devastated. At first, we discussed whether we should continue on this path or terminate and move on to a different solution. It was Haruko herself that answered things for us.

"I don't yet know why I was spared," she began. You could have heard a pin drop. "But I survived without any signs of the aging syndrome or any other surface diseases. As a scientist, I know we have good information in that outcome. We can't abandon this," she declared. "Otherwise they died for nothing. They wouldn't want that. Let's understand what worked for me. The answer is in there somewhere."

As usual she was right. We were eager to examine how Haruko had not only survived but thrived. After reviewing the experiment and analyzing her biology, we concluded for this to work safely each person *would require a specific ratio of the drugs tailored to their particular physiology. We also concluded that we should administer considerably lower doses. In the double-blind trial, Haruko had been given one of the smallest doses. We discovered that the proper tailoring of the drugs could be determined by analyzing the blood of each potential participant.*

Now we found ourselves in need of a second trial. But who would be willing to volunteer knowing what happened the last time? Braver souls.

Haruko was the first in line for the second trial. Sang and I stepped up, too. We wanted to be in the trial out of respect for our friend Konrad. To their dismay, Sang and Haruko were not accepted. Haruko hugged me tightly and whispered, "You are my hero, Sim. Best wishes."

Fortunately, we all survived the second trial. The results, however, revealed we would need reoccurring monthly injections for continued protection. This requirement seemed to be a small price to pay for surface trips.

Everyone was ecstatic about this news. If things at the surface improved, we might be able collect sufficient resources to make the supply of the drugs available to all. For now, we would rotate surface trips, inoculating one or two people from a small group. The trip duties would include bringing back specific resources, conducting experiments, and performing routine maintenance on surface items, such as the solar panels and wind turbines. We now had hope.

CHAPTER 12

THE KABAK

Mary entered the creaky doors of the Kabak. Doc looked up from his drink surprised to see her. He leaned over to his associate, taking his arm as if to lift him from their rusty table. They both stood to greet her.

Mary tried to adjust her eyes to the dark room. She was well-acquainted with this place. The Kabak was the only place where the working community felt comfortable and safe to relax. Many people, including members of her own family, had frequented the bar over the years.

This was a shabby establishment. Always had been. The common workers who built it never worked from a design. No one ever worried about it being an actual building or being safe. Instead, the Kabak grew organically, as men and women cobbled it together over time, people long in the past who initiated construction with just a crude overhead hanging. They made the roof by collecting large discarded pieces of sheet metal bolted together. A few clever folks managed to awkwardly but securely stringing the roof up with cables between the outside of two old buildings. Over the ensuing years, the roof held so they added other panels until the Kabak eventually became a fully enclosed, if not rickety, structure.

Odd furnishings garnished the floor and walls, a mishmash of discarded items. Community donations gave this spot its ambiance.

Its attraction lasted out of pride and loyalty. By and for the common workers.

The only light that graced the place was what managed to pass through the partially covered set of glass front doors that workers had removed from a nearby abandoned building. They intentionally constructed the Kabak with only one way in and one way out, ensuring that anyone who entered was clearly visible to every patron. Visibility was an important feature because guards and managers were not welcome and could be quickly spotted. On the rare occasions they did enter the room, all conversations instantly turned silent, and patrons would stand and leave.

"Well, how nice running into you here. Mary, this my coworker and very good friend, Doctor Chivas." Turning toward Chivas, Doc continued, "Mary is a patient of mine and family friend. You've often heard me talk about her."

Mary leaned in and hugged Doc and then reached her hand out to his coworker, "Hello, Doctor Chivas. Glad to meet you."

She scanned the face of the stranger in front of her, wrinkled and adorning sparse whispers of gray hair. He had the kind face of someone's grandfather, but he also exuded a regal confidence. She liked the calm about him and felt he must be older than Doc.

"Please sit with us, Mary."

"Thank you, I will, but I can only stay a few minutes." The place smelled like stale kvass, and Mary immediately recalled how much she disliked the place. On too many afternoons, she had accompanied her father here. Usually she would be told to wait outside while her father went in, reappearing shortly after, holding up a harrowing version of her mother with droopy eyes, slurred voice, and unsteady gate. Her father would wrap one arm around her mother's waist, and the three of them would stumble home. She looked around the room self-consciously, thankful not to recognize anyone other than Doc.

"We were having a kvass. Would you like one?" Doctor Chivas offered.

"No," she said, forcing a smile, "I don't know how you drink the stuff. It's so sour." More than the nasty taste, Mary considered drinking a bad idea, given she had witnessed firsthand how alcohol had negatively impacted her mother. Then she reminded herself she had not come to judge. She was searching for answers.

"You get used to it. I love it. We both do," Doc replied. "Then what can I get for you?"

"Nothing, thank you. Sorry to barge in on your. . ."

"Nonsense. You're not barging in," Dr. Chivas interrupted, thumping his hands rhythmically on the metal table. "Glad to meet you. Doc B. talks about you all the time."

"Really? Uh-oh, good things, I hope?" she attempted to joke, knowing how regularly she irritated Doc.

Everyone laughed. She felt both delighted to meet such a friendly face and also a little awkward. Who was this Dr. Chivas? Obviously, Doc's sounding board, but why hadn't she met him before? They seemed so close. She wanted to like him but was somewhat uncomfortable not knowing how much he knew about her.

"Of course. Doc has nothing but good things to say about you," Chivas replied, recognizing a hint of insecurity. He rose from his chair with an air of benevolent royalty.

Mary had never met anyone as peaceful as this man. The contrast between the two friends was startling.

"Thank you, good to know. I . . . I wish you didn't have to leave so soon." Mary cringed as the half-truth slipped. She would have enjoyed more time with him, just not now. She needed Doc alone.

"No, it's time. We've been bending each other's ear for an hour, and I need to get back to the clinic. You two visit. Again, nice meeting you. B., I'll be talking to you."

"I feel bad running him off."

"Don't. Chivas and I meet here all the time. Maybe too much. He's a special friend and a very influential man in certain circles." Once again Mary wondered how it was possible that the man that she had just met was such a friend and yet she had never heard mention of his name?

"We enjoy each other's company, and this about the only safe place to talk about things we shouldn't," he laughed. "So, what's up with you, young lady?"

"Honestly Doc, I'm not here by accident. I need to talk to you. I went by your office, and Delilah told me you were here. I thought I'd take a chance and look for you."

"God damn it! That woman, son of a bitch. You know, I've told her a million times not to tell patients where I am when I'm not in the office. She doesn't listen to me, we just can't stand each other, and she's the nurse they assigned. I've been stuck with her for 16 years."

Doc threw back what looked like his third kvass, slamming the glass to the table. "But, in your case, I don't care that she told you where I am. I make an exception. I'm always glad to see you. Now, what can I do for you? Have you reconsidered those anger management drugs? Changed your mind, I hope?"

Mary squinted, hoping he might already know what she wanted to talk about. "No, that's not it."

"Then what?" he said, waving his hand for a server to bring another drink. The serious expression on her face prompted him to lean forward. "Oh wait . . . does this have something to do with . . . ? Damn it, Mary! I should have known."

Hearing Doc speak too loudly, she covered her face in embarrassment. Other patrons were staring at them. "Doc," she whispered, "maybe a little quieter?"

He took a deep breath, held it, and exhaled loudly. "I warned your father that some things were better left unsaid. Damn it, I warned him."

Mary smelled Doc's breath and wondered what he was saying. Did he already know what she came to ask him? Had he read the notebook? "You warned him about what? What was better left unsaid?"

"Not here," he mumbled. "Let me settle up. We'll walk back to the clinic together. Meet me outside."

Exiting the Kabak, the two walked through a small parcel of land known to everyone as The Park. Of course, it wasn't a real park, not like the ones she had read about anyway. The committee would never have allowed such a wasteful use of space. No, she knew each inch of land was considered far too precious for anything like that. Instead, this abandoned barren parcel was embellished with nothing more than a few improvised benches that workers had made and placed here and there.

As a child, her father had warned her not to play too long in this place. He had heard rumors that many years prior the Program had buried large amounts of toxic waste on the parcel. Mary wasn't sure if that rumor was true, but she knew that management and the guards must believe it because they always walk around the area and not through it, making it a safe place to talk openly with Doc.

Doc stopped by one of the homemade benches and sat down. He banged his feet together kicking away the dirt from his shoes and looked at her sternly. "I warned your father about the sniffing around he was doing. Bad things happen to people when they question and begin to investigate things. I warned him that passing on information to others could be dangerous for everyone. I wish he had never given me that envelope."

Exasperated, Mary leaned over and whispered, "What are you talking about? Can you be more specific. Please."

"I can't be more specific. He never gave me details, only that he was investigating something within the Program. I only know that he was messing around in things that he shouldn't have been messing around in. Take my arm. I need to get up and keep walking."

Frustrated by his answer but realizing he either couldn't or wouldn't give her any additional information, she decided to bring up the missing letter. "Was the envelope you gave me the original? I mean, is there any chance the envelope tore or did anything happen that caused you to put the original contents of the envelope into a new envelope?"

"The envelope tore? What are you asking?" Confused by her question, he shook his head. "No, the envelope I gave you was the one your father gave me, the original. I didn't know what was in that notebook – and didn't want to know. I hid it under that drawer. When he gave it to me, I taped it to the bottom of the drawer, and that's where it remained until I gave it to you."

"But you do know that it contained a notebook?"

"I guessed that his grandfather's notebook must have been in that envelope. Your father told me about it years ago, but he never let me read it. From the stiffness, I assumed the notebook must have been in there.

"OK, so, in one letter, my father references a second letter, but it's not there."

"I don't know anything about any letters."

She tried once again to read his facial expression. "Well, my dad said in the first letter that after I read the notebook, I should read the second letter, but there isn't a second letter."

Doc stopped cold. "Implying what? That you think I removed it? Why on Earth would I do that? You think I stole the . . ."

"No, of course not," She interrupted as she noticed the change in Doc's tone.

"Listen to me. I never looked inside that envelope. To be honest, I was afraid to know what was in there. I didn't take any letter or anything else." Then he raised his voice and carefully enunciated each word, "Your father was messing around in things that he knew could be dangerous," he paused, glaring at her. "Hiding that envelope has been a big burden and sacrifice. You have no idea the anxiety it's caused me."

Mary stepped back. She had never seen Doc become so defensive about anything.

He could see she was dumbfounded. "All right, maybe it's time for you to hear something else." He signaled to her to come closer. "I'm going to tell you this as someone who cares deeply about you. Please, let this be a warning: you cannot ask questions about the content of that notebook. In the Program, people get killed for asking questions."

The sound of those words rang in Mary's ears as she gave him her full attention.

"I think – but I don't have any proof – that your family's fire might not have been an accident. It might have had something to do with whatever was in that envelope."

She pressed her hands over her mouth, trying to hold back a scream, but a tiny shriek squeezed out anyway. "What?"

Her squeal caused a woman walking toward the Kabak to glance over at them. Doc waved and smiled. When she was out of sight, he squinted at Mary in disapproval. They kept moving. "I think it may have been because your father discovered things the Program didn't want anyone to know. Listen, these people don't mess around; you don't get second chances. Whatever you read or learned from that notebook, leave it in the past. Leave things alone. I'm warning . . . no, I'm begging . . . for both our sakes."

Frustrated, Mary picked up a pebble from the barren ground and threw it as far as she could across the park. She needed a moment to compose herself and picked up another and fiddled with it. "Why would you think that wasn't an accident? What else are you not telling me?"

"Nothing. Nothing else, I'm just suspicious. I've always wondered what your family was doing in that old building and the timing of that accident.

About a week prior to the fire, your father came to my office. He was extremely nervous. I'd never seen him look so spooked. He didn't say much, but he slid that envelope across my desk with instructions to hide it and said that he might have more items for me later. He scared me to death. I freaked out. I mean, by giving me that envelope, he was involving me in danger. What could I do? I loved him like a brother so, against my better judgement, I did what he asked. I hid the damned thing. The timing of the fire afterward and where they were when it happened was suspicious — too soon after that handoff."

Mary stopped for a moment. "But you don't have any evidence, right? It still could have been an accident. And if it wasn't an accident, why would they bother killing my mother and Amasa?"

"Maybe the Program thought your dad confided in your mom. Or maybe your mom and sister were simply collateral damage. What I'm trying to say is that you need to be careful. Whatever information you now have is dangerous. Possessing it puts us both in danger."

She tried to digest what she was hearing. "Doc, when I finish with the notebook, I want you to read it, then we can talk about it." She could tell that he was surprised by her comment, but he said nothing. He leaned over, kissed her on the forehead, and walked off in the direction of the clinic.

CHAPTER 13

THE NOTEBOOK: SIDE EFFECTS

Mary could hardly wait to get home from work and read the next section of her great grandfather's diary. Her routine bordered on obsessive. Her clothes had not been washed in a week, and she had nearly run out of food. She dumped her things, grabbed a small bowl of rice, settled into bed, reached underneath for the envelop, pulled out the notebook, and read.

* * *

It soon became clear to everyone on the life science team that the drug cocktail had strange and frightening side effects. After a few injections, the drugs became highly addictive. Stranger still, they could cause the recipient to have violent attacks. I witnessed this happen to Aharon, a guy who worked in the fabrication shop. One day he got angry at a coworker and hit him. A guard called me in to witness the effects of his attack. It was terrible. We watched in horror as he as he winced from full-body cramps, grabbing his head and shaking while vomiting. Then he yelled that he couldn't see or hear as we stood by powerless to help him. The episode stopped when he slumped to the floor. We had trouble finding a heartbeat. The attack nearly killed him.

Attacks triggered by anger were obviously quite serious, and most doctors felt that multiple attacks might be deadly. They examined people who had similar attacks and discovered elevated levels of adrenaline and cortisol in their blood. It was as if they were experiencing a massive heart attack: high blood pressure, high heart rate, shortness of breath.

Haruko, who had been so fundamental in the development of the drug cocktail, addressed these concerns at our team meeting.

"Everyone should be aware that the addictive side effect of this drug has proven powerful. Withdrawal from the injections can lead to depression, sickness, and possibly death. That being said, we should put our concerns in context. It should be remembered, that to maintain protection from the rays and disease, anyone in the rotation plan for surface trips must have monthly injections for the rest of their lives. And, unfortunately, we will have to learn to deal with other side effects."

Many of us found this information sobering. I wondered if using these drugs might be a mistake. Jogging on the track with Sang later that evening, I brought up the subject.

"Listen," Sang rebuffed me, "if the injections enable us to survive at the surface, that gives us a chance to save our families, right? So, in my mind, nothing else matters. I don't care what the side effects are. These injections are worth it. The addiction doesn't matter if we have to take them for life to survive."

I wasn't convinced, but Haruko and most of the other scientists felt the same way as Sang, so I went along.

We still had a chance to minimize other side effect, the possibility of the violent attacks, especially since we were working under high stress in a cramped environment. But after numerous meetings without a resolution, a frustrated General Tishman laid down the gauntlet. "No one leaves this meeting until we have a plan on how to combat this issue."

At the time I was impressed that this stern man appeared to have such great concern for all of us. Later, I came to believe he was more worried about his guard team and their ability to control us.

We all had a vested interest in solving this issue, but the only thing we could come up with was that everyone had to commit to develop a calm, nonaggressive posture toward each other. Confronted with the possibility of death for all parties involved in any altercation, we had no other choice but to learn to control our emotions, especially anger.

Interestingly, this conciliatory stance toward others eventually became the root culture of our little society.

Now that we had a drug cocktail that presented a potential solution to survive at the surface and a way to deal with the bad side effects, we had an opportunity to consider other questions.

Since Haruko and I worked together every day, we had numerous opportunities for serious discussions about some of the many lingering questions. The biggest question concerned the goal of saving mankind outside of the site. As usual Haruko had a way of getting right to the heart of things.

"I doubt our plan to save humanity on the surface was ever realistic. I mean I don't see any way to reach that goal. At best, maybe we collect enough material to manufacture sufficient drugs for everyone here. But we'll never have enough to inoculate people at the surface."

I had been thinking the same thing, but I had found it too painful to speak out loud. "I've been denying it. I just didn't want to dash anyone's optimism, mine and especially Sang's."

We were not alone in reaching that conclusion. Slowly and painfully everyone on site began to accept the notion that it was unlikely we would ever see our families and friends again. The goal of developing a solution to save humanity had been accomplished, but it existed only for ourselves. This was devastating news.

"Everyone at the surface is going to die, aren't they?" Sang asked. "And there's nothing we can do to help them. I guess I've been kidding myself." We grieved together for our loved ones.

With this realization came another looming question. Had those in charge ever really intended for us to save humanity on the surface? I wanted to ask the general, but I knew even if he had the answer, he would never share it with me.

As scientists, maybe we had been the foolish ones, simply living in denial, lost in our work and in the arrogant belief that we could save our families. No matter, it was now obvious the original plan most likely never included survival for the people at the surface.

This understanding led us to examine other fundamental questions, including the original cause of the climate upheaval.

One day, Haruko bluntly asked me, "What do think caused the climate change . . . mankind?"

"Hell if I know, but I think mankind certainly must have done something to accelerate things."

She shrugged her shoulders as if it didn't matter. We had no answers. She did make me question, though: if mankind were at fault, then was the climate change accidentally or intentionally instigated? Then again, did the cause of the climate change matter at this point? Whatever had instigated the devastating change, we were the only remaining humans on Earth likely to live through it.

Only one indisputable truth existed: if humanity was to survive, then we were it. Of all the limited resources we had carefully conserved on this site, the one that proved to be most precious, in the end, was ourselves. Each of us now had greater value than at any time previously in our lives. Each of us was a precious genetic resource. We alone represented the future of humanity. The initial euphoria we had in finding a solution for survival on the surface dissipated. One day, so depressed, I attempted to lighten the mood. It backfired.

"Haruko, what do you think? Isn't it sort of funny that our little group here wasn't selected to include the most artistic, athletic, or attractive people, only the most intelligent and educated? I mean, is that how you would have picked us, or would you have chosen a more diverse set of qualifications?"

But as I should have expected, her face gave away how little she appreciated my logic. I didn't wait for her to reply, "What that means is, the people on this site will be the only ones responsible for . . ."

She held up her hand to stop me.

". . . the continuation of the legacy of humanity," I trailed off like a lost little boy. She clearly had heard enough, and I wasn't at all sure what I had done to offend her.

"Attractive?" she dryly replied as she shook her head. "Some things do not change with intelligence. Men." I was so ashamed, I couldn't bring myself to apologize for days after that, which only deepened my sadness. The brilliant immunologist, Haruko Ishizaka, was a woman. How did I miss that?

Through the grief we continued our experiments, working was our way of coping. Fortunately, before we depleted our resources, the volcanic eruptions ceased, allowing the climate to slowly become more hospitable. Without volcanic eruptions, researchers on Sang's team could begin to measure and study the conditions on the surface, especially that of the ozone layer.

"Our results," he said, his bottom lip habitually pooched and downturned when he shared research results, "show that the ozone layer is repairing, but at a much slower rate than we hoped. I'm afraid that we're witnessing healing at a glacial rate, more on the order of decades rather than years."

When he said that to me, I decided I was not going to let that information dampen my outlook any further. "No doubt that is disappointing news, but we can survive up there and, to quote you, 'that's all that matters.'"

Yes, Earth was certainly not in its best shape, but it was inhabitable – or, more accurately, would be again. With the proper monthly injections, humans could one day survive on the surface, at least for short periods of time.

CHAPTER 14

ENA

Other than Doc, Ena was Mary's most trusted friend. Whenever possible these women hung around together, especially during work. They both worked at the Distribution Center, had similar jobs, were both in their twenties – healthy, educated, and single. Over the past few years now they had been expecting that they would be added to the pairing list. They were perfect candidates for breeding, but pairing seemed to be happening later and later and only for the few.

During their walks on break, conversations usually revolved around life in the Program. But the women were smart. Everyone in the community knew that the leadership committee used perks to incentivize the identification of dissenters, and this produced a general climate of distrust among workers. So, the friends kept their discussions discreet, though their competitive streaks also kept conversations fiery.

From the start of their walk this afternoon, Mary sensed Ena had something she was dying to share. "Ena, just spit it out."

Before she could get the words out, a tall, attractive young man slowed his pace long enough to acknowledge Mary with a disarming glance and nod. After he moved on, Mary turned to her friend, who had already guessed what she would ask. "That's Edward," Ena said, smirking. "He works here in distribution, I think. Did you see? He winked at you."

"I doubt it," Mary replied, "but he sure is cute, isn't he? You know him?"

"Nope, not really, just who he is." Ena grabbed her friend's arm to resume their walk. "I've seen him around."

Realizing she had been caught staring at this man as he walked away, Mary accepted she had no comeback. "Don't you wonder what lucky girl will be paired with that guy? Wait, I'm sorry, what did you say? You know him?"

"Need more time to gawk, or are we walking? Walk."

"Silly, I am walking," Mary said, a little embarrassed that she had been caught gawking. "Now what did you want to tell me?"

"Did you catch Emily's coat this morning? Everybody was talking about it. It was beautiful, not plain like ours."

"Sure did, and that Emily is such a pretty girl, isn't she? Don't you wonder how she got that coat?" Mary replied, displaying an obvious smirk.

"Oh, quit that. You know something. Tell me."

"Come on, Ena, you must have heard the rumors about her, all the stuff about her and our big boss – and that she has a girlfriend – and that she's pregnant."

Ena gasped, "Pregnant? Nooo…!" She caught herself and lowered her voice. "I didn't realize she'd been paired. Lucky girl, I guess? Who is she paired with?"

"I'm telling you, she's paired with our big boss."

"Ew! What? Oh, Mary, no. Shoot, her poor girlfriend. That mean old guy is so fat and ugly, and he already has children. His daughter Kisha works here. That freaks me out!"

For a moment Ena's mind wandered. The mention of Kisha's situation reminded her of what had happened in her own family when her father left them to start a new one. She and her mother never really recovered from that loss.

"Poor Emily," Mary continued unaware that Ena had drifted off for a few seconds. "Can't imagine her girlfriend is exactly happy, either. Surely, those girls realized that eventually they would be paired . . . and not with each other. Probably never thought it would happen with that old dude."

"Officially paired and pregnant. So curious. Why do you think the Program paired her with that old slob? I thought it was usually young with young."

"Evidently the rules get bent for the powerful. He wanted her, so he got her."

"Wow, paired."

"Typical of the Program," Mary continued. "They make all the decisions, don't they? Where to work, where to live, what clothes we have, what food we eat, and who to have babies with!"

Ena's body stiffened, bracing for the oncoming typhoon. "OK Mary, yes, they make major decisions for us, but they also do a lot of good things . . . and you know that."

"Ha! Like, what?"

"Well, if we didn't have the Program, how would we get the protection shots? We'd die from the UV rays without them. They give us an apartment, food, clothing, education, all that sort of stuff. And there aren't any wars or prisons like the old days. People don't fight or kill each other like they used to before the climate change. That's good, isn't it?"

"Ena, tell me," Mary exclaimed as she watched her friend squirm, "who are the 'they' you're talking about who give us everything?"

"We [illegible] but we know their names."

"Tha[illegible] who 'they' are. Those cretins are just [illegible] do they live? Certainly not in our shitty ancient apartments. So, answer this then, why don't ordinary people like us ever get to be members of the leadership committee anymore?"

"I didn't realize we ever did get to be on that committee. I guess we're not trained leaders. They must have special training, leader education, or something. I don't know. . . the Program does lots of good things."

"No, it doesn't. They just look out for themselves, and things are not supposed to be like this. Ena, don't you ever wonder why they keep us locked behind this wall? What's out there that they're hiding from us?"

"Maybe they just want us to be safe. Protect us from the dangerous Outcasts."

"Well, I think it's something else.'

"Here it comes. Wait for it."

"They're keeping us as slaves. And damn it, they've been changing all the rules so they can stay in power and lord over us forever. We're addicted to drugs they've weaponized that we can only get from them. They've got side effects that make us completely nonaggressive. I mean, it's perfect. A perfect setup, they drug the children to control them and drug the adults to keep them addicted and dependent. Anyway, Ena, who do you think you're kidding here? I know you don't believe the Program is all that great."

"I never said it was great. I said it works, which is different." Ena paused, thinking about her friend. Why couldn't Mary understand that if you just accepted things, it was possible to be happy.

"Yeah, well how many times have I heard you say that you hate how fake everyone acts? All the fake smiles and hugs, everybody pretending to be happy, and how they act like they care about you when they don't. Come on, everyone pretends they're fine with things, but we know they're not. They're afraid to question anything. It's safer to be quiet and fake it."

"Enough. I've heard all this from you before. Can we change the subject now, please?"

Mary shook her head in disbelief. "No, for once we need to talk this out. Listen to me, they lie, control us, play God with us."

"Fine, we'll talk it out, but God? Coming from you, Mary? You don't believe in God . . . and they don't kill people. That's simply not true. You can't say things like that here at work."

"For your information, I might believe in God, just not the way you do. And they *do* play god. They pair us, so they can carefully 'tune' the genetics of our offspring. Please. And they toss out teenagers and adults like garbage when they think they cause too much trouble. Make them Outcasts, like they did with my brother. And what about the fact that they kill off the babies and children that aren't perfect! The ones they call defective, that don't measure up to their precious standards. Are you also going to pretend you don't know about that?"

"Quit being so dramatic. They don't *kill* defective newborns. They let them pass. Babies shouldn't live that way, deformed, suffering in pain. What kind of life would they have? This way is better. And yes, they pair us. So what? Isn't intentional genetic planning smarter than simply relying on chance? As for the troublemakers, they get what they deserve."

Hearing a reference that might apply to her brother Mary's face puckered. "What's happened to you, Ena? Remember my brother is one of those Outcasts – one of those troublemakers. And, listen to you, "intentional genetic planning?" What have you been drinking? And why would you think letting babies die is somehow better for them? It isn't."

"Once again you're overreacting. Calm down, OK? No more killing talk, or I'm leaving." Ena said, her voice now audibly cracking.

Ena's head instantly wrenched backward as a hand reached from behind them and rested on her shoulder. Mary, equally startled, spun around to see who the hand belonged to. If someone from management had heard them disparaging the Program, the consequences could be devastating.

"Girls," Reyanne said, giggling at their stiffened bodies. "For shame, I thought you two never disagreed on anything and now I find you twins are arguing."

"Damn you, Reyanne! You shouldn't go sneaking up on people like that."

"Oh please, I was just messing with you two. Anyway, why were you yelling?"

"We weren't yelling," Ena replied, now noticeably calmer realizing it was their coworker and not someone from management. "We're discussing, that's all," she continued nervously trying to cover for the actual conversation.

"Discussing what?"

"Nothing really, all the gossip about Emily. Mary disagrees with the pairing,"

"Shit, Ena, everyone disagrees with that pairing! It's just weird! But we know why that happened, don't we?" she teased.

"We do?"

"Really, Ena? That manager was connected, perks for him. Boom, he gets the young girl, they get paired, and shit, she's pregnant. Simple."

"How come everybody knows about this but me?"

"Maybe you shouldn't be so naïve? Anyway, it's likely our unfortunate friend won't be working much longer. She won't be living around here either. At this point, I don't know whether to feel sad or jealous."

"Then where will she live? His daughter Kisha works with us, and she and her mom still live around here."

"You don't get it, Ena. That boss is a big shot now. He's moved on from Kisha's family. No, Emily will live with him in the other section, where they're supposed to be building that new place. All the big shots will live there."

"And how would you know about any of that?" Mary asked sarcastically, still irritated that Reyanne had surprised them and interrupted their conversation.

"Because my guy, my partner Ajay, he's an engineer, working on the design of those buildings. He says the apartments in that complex will be incredible. Huge. Four and five rooms with all these beautiful furnishings. Nothing like our shit. He's always complaining how much he hates working for those assholes, but it's his job. Drives him crazy, knowing they get more perks every day, all at our expense."

"But you say Emily will get to live in a brand new five-room apartment?"

Reyanne's face twisted. "Ena, are you for real? Do you think Emily gives a shit about any of that? You think she wants to be pregnant with that bastard's baby . . . for a new luxury unit? She's a lesbian, for God sakes! She wants to live with her girlfriend, not that fat son of a bitch."

Ena's face reddened as she sheepishly replied, "I know, I know. That wasn't what I meant. You said yourself you don't know if you should feel sorry for her or be jealous. But if she has to be with that guy anyway . . ."

Reyanne had heard enough and turned to Mary, looking for support. Hearing none, she said, "Sorry ladies, I need to run. I have work to do. See you later, and oh, girls, feel free to go back to arguing."

"Yeah, sure, thanks for permission. We'll do that," Mary replied, pleased that she was finally leaving.

Mary moved close to Ena and whispered in her ear, "To answer your question, before Reyanne rudely interrupted us, I think the Program may have murdered my family."

Ena lunged backward but not before pushing her friend away. "Shh! We're still at work! You can't say stuff like that here. Your family died in a fire – an unfortunate accident – everyone knows that. You know that."

"Well, I used to think it was an accident. Now I'm not so sure. I think the Program had them killed."

"Mary, people are watching! I'm sorry, but I need to get back to my desk. I have a lot of to do."

"My mistake, Ena. I thought I could talk to you about anything. Never mind then."

Ena reached out for Mary's hand. Mary refused it, pulling away.

"Come on, don't be like that. You can talk to me about anything, but somewhere safe, not here. Please. Can we just get back to our desks?"

Mary huffed as she turned down the hallway, leaving Ena behind.

CHAPTER 15

THE NOTEBOOK: RECYCLING GAME

The day dragged on longer than usual. Mary was relieved when it finally came to an end. Back in her apartment, she threw her coat and bag on the table and plopped face down on her bed. She had no appetite. She was disgusted with herself.

When would she learn? Her best and only real friend Ena was entitled to her own opinion, no matter how different it was from hers. Why did she feel compelled to bait and argue with her? They were never going to see eye to eye about the Program, why not just accept that? And the possibility that her family was murdered was just too dangerous to share with Ena or anyone else.

She resolved to behave better. That might also appease Doc and keep her head and stomach aches to a minimum. Frustrated, she reached under her bed and pulled out the notebook.

* * *

In time the climate improved, the air became safer to breath, and the temperature returned to a more normal range. Rain and snow fell in somewhat more appropriate amounts for the region around Buffalo, though certainly not what it had been before the change.

With the moderation, we put together four pairs of scientific teams to explore and collect resources on the surface. I was assigned a slightly younger person than myself, an Italian scientist named Francesca, a semiconductor physicist and member of Sang's engineering team. Our goal on each trip was to venture as far as we felt comfortable from the safety of the underground site.

At first, we were cautious, and we moved like zombies, mesmerized and horrified by a world desolate and devoid of life. The earth's surface we encountered was nothing like what we had known. Despite the fresh snowfall, this was a gray world. The atmospheric soot, a thick layer of sludge, composed of dirt, ash, and debris, had rained down on nearly everything.

I was already acquainted with sludge since I had been a member of the early surface rotation team. One of our early goals on those missions was to clean the gunk from the solar panels and windmills. The buildup invariably caused them to run inefficiently. Now, we have to deal with much larger quantities of it.

On warm days, when the fresh snow partially melted, gruesome things revealed themselves. Remnants of a former culture pushed up and peeked through the dirty snow. Partial skeletons, unrecognizable pieces of anatomy that winds and floods had scattered. Horrific reminders of what happened while we were safe in our subterranean world.

One time, Francesca lifted the edge of a large thin rock, exposing a mangled ball of decaying matter and, along with it, a suffocating odor. She squinted as she let the rock fall and turned away, nearly losing her balance.

"Oh, Sim," she said, "I think I might faint. Hold on to me."

I couldn't help but make light of it as I reached out to brace her, "Steady. I've got you. Whew, that's the smell of rotted material carried by methane gas. Nature at its worst."

She nodded, taking a moment to regain her breath. "That was bad."

"Could you tell what that thing was?"

"I don't want to think about what that was. Come on, let's get away from here." Francesca's face had belied her, and I did not say any more.

My attitude sobered as we walked. Was the decaying matter someone's child or pet? And that made me think, how had my family died? Where were their remains? I did my best to push those thoughts away.

The further we walked, the more the trip depressed us. In every step over fallen trees, we saw the destruction to plants, animals, and structures. The dead wood would be valuable for paper production and building repair, but nothing seemed to be growing. We marked the spot of these trees on our makeshift map, so workers could come collect it later.

Through a clearing a half mile west of us, Francesca and I noticed piles of brick, stone, glass, and rusted metal that resembled buildings, probably the remnants of houses. They had been ravaged almost beyond recognition by the extreme weather. As we walked around these piles, we noticed a few buildings appeared to have survived. We were excited until we looked inside. Their interiors had been gutted by wind and water. All that remained were more mounds of sludge.

In this new world, everything that had been made by man and God had been destroyed. One clear stretch revealed a number of cars and trucks and other large items in odd positions and places, plenty partially buried in mud. Most vehicles looked as if they had been ruined by the same high winds and acid-filled caustic rain that had eaten away at them. From the volume of vehicles, we could tell we were on what was formerly a road or highway, and these vehicles probably ran until the last precious drop of gas depleted, leaving their owners stranded and consumed by the monster elements.

Each of the thousands of scattered items we found from town to town — the buildings, the cars — were logged and inventoried. Slowly the curiosity of these discoveries wore off, and our mindset concerning them changed.

After we submitted our reports, the Program assigned teams of scavengers to test for toxicity, retrieve, and clean the things that could be used or repurposed. This system kept workers busy with reuse and reinventions. We all became part of the ultimate recycling team in this new world.

Occasionally we would find paper products that had not been totally ruined, like books and office supplies. To Francesca and me, finding salvageable books was like finding gold. But mechanical parts, especially if requested, became the most prized gifts that we could bestow upon the technicians back at the site. Men and women, like my friend Aharon, gleefully worked on rebuilding or cannibalizing things — guns, vehicles, generators, and pumps. In turn, these same men and women became our heroes, the rebuilders of metal and machinery, and we celebrated them. Each time we could cobble something back together, or repurpose an unusable item, we felt a deep sense of satisfaction. So much so, Francesca and I found ourselves constantly in competition. Collecting things became our game. We were the king and queen of recycling in a world full of trash.

Carpenters and architects emerged from our team of scientists. Groups got together and built new structures out of the wood we salvaged from dilapidated buildings and the dead trees. With the aid of electricity from our solar panels, Sang and his team of chemical engineers actually distilled methanol from the otherwise unusable pieces of wood. They also were able to make paper which turned out to be important since we documented everything.

Once we had a few functional vehicles, methanol became an important energy source. By collecting decaying organic matter, we could produce methane, ethanol, and biodiesel fuels, which enabled us to run generators, vehicles, and many types of machinery.

Of course, collecting this material was valuable, but it also produced an uncomfortable moral issue: were the collected remains animal or human? It was disconcerting to think we might be disturbing the dead to make fuel.

With time, we began moving easily from the underground facility to the surface world and back and spent more time above deck. We accepted that the injections offered us safety from the rays, but psychologically we remained frightened of the sun. We were cautious about being outside too long in the daylight. The sun provided electrical power through our solar cells, but it was no longer our friendly life source. It was a killer.

"Maybe we should go back now. We've collected a lot and been exposed all day," I told Francesca. "The sun seems stronger today, it might be dangerous for us to stay out here any longer."

"Oh, you're such a baby," she replied. "You just want to get back because today you've collected better stuff than me. You're so damn competitive."

"No, really. We should limit our exposure. Let's not push it."

"OK, we'll go back, but you're a liar."

I was not the only one worried about too much sun exposure. Other teams had been tasked by the general with constructing tall surface shelters in close proximity of the safety of our mothership, the site, for that very reason. These buildings could be used as escape havens in case the sun flared and poured rays on us that the drugs might not adequately deal with.

Over time a dense village was constructed where everyone could quickly walk to work, and live, and play. Now with safe places on the surface and the original CAIHR resources dwindling, we turned our attention to food production.

Not surprisingly, few plants suitable for food could grow from our reserves of seed stock. The crops that did grow yielded poorly. Plants such as rice, soy beans, and sorghum could not tolerate the UV rays. A few mutant strains of wheat and other vegetation grew through experimentation, at least to a meager extent. With this discovery, the life sciences team under the direction of Haruko worked to genetically engineer radiation-hardened plants and seed stock. Using these newly modified seeds, the food production improved. We were still hungry most of the time, but we did not starve.

CHAPTER 16

DEATH

Mary remembered the first day her brother stopped recognizing her. She began noticing when Joey had been unable or unwilling to speak and guessed from the contortion of his face that he might be in pain. Then came the shift in Lucinda. She refused to discuss Joey's condition, only lingering long enough to curtly tell Mary that he was already receiving the maximum dose of pain killers allowed by his doctors. At this point, Mary had no way to impact Joey's care. She could no longer reach him.

A few days after Mary's visit, her little brother died. Consumed with guilt, she wondered if she should have challenged Lucinda more aggressively about his drugs and treatment. She was too late. Joey was gone, and now none of that mattered. His suffering was over, her only consolation.

Shortly after his death, the Care Place notified her, as sole next of kin, that she would be able to participate in combined funeral service for Joey and a few others. She felt lucky that Joey would be included. She wondered if he would become the only Outcast ever allowed in such a ceremony.

Mary sprinkled Joey's ashes over a small unmarked designated square of land where, she had no doubt, countless other ashes had been sprinkled over the years. She tried not to be bitter. Doc held her hand. His hand remained in hers at the burial site through the duration of the secular service. It was an emotional day, and she greatly appreciated Doc's presence, comfort, and support. It was not lost on her that Doc, while not related by blood, was now her closest family member.

"You know, in a way, Joey was my hero," she said as they walked slowly on a worn path away from the patch where she had sprinkled his remains. "I'm certain many times he was in pain, but he never complained. That's sort of heroic, don't you think? I miss him. I miss him so much. Now, I'm it, the last living member of the family."

Doc took hold of her arm and placed it under his own, "You still have me, and he was more of a hero than you may know."

"Yeah, you think?"

"Did your parents ever tell you the entire story about the situation with Joey, the Program, and your sister? Surely you're aware of all of it by now."

"Maybe, but I figured out most of what I know by myself." She responded tilting her head, somewhat perplexed by his question and wondering if there was more that she didn't know. "The day the Program guards came to take him away, you know, declaring him an Outcast, everyone was so upset. Nobody wanted to talk about things. After Joey was gone, my mom took a turn for the worse. She had been a wreck for years, so I couldn't talk to her about what happened, and Dad never seemed to be around. And when Mom and Dad were at home, the subject of Joey was too sensitive, so I had to figure a lot out for myself. I remember seeing you often, but you never spoke about it, either. It was just taboo."

"Well, it wasn't my place to talk to you about those things. You were smart. I always suspected you knew what really happened and why."

"Not at first. Originally, I thought the Program sent Joey away because he was trouble, always misbehaving, running away, constantly doing bad things that caused my parents issues with the Program. It wasn't until later that I realized that being a problem child had nothing to do with his becoming an Outcast."

"When your brother was about nine years old, your mother's blood tests showed that she was pregnant with your sister, and that, of course, was reported to the Program Committee."

"Yes, of course I knew my mom was pregnant with Amasa."

"Well, then I guess you knew the pregnancy violated your parents' pairing agreement. Under their contract, they were only allowed to have two children. I suggested they terminate the pregnancy. Your parents wouldn't consider it. Did you know that?"

"Not at the time, but I figured that out."

"So, you knew Program rules meant your parents had to either abort the pregnancy or later decide who would be officially confirmed in the Program, Joey or your sister."

"That was so horrible. And I hate the damn Program for doing that to my family. I hate them."

Doc nodded. "To think they had to choose between them. Terrible."

"Wait, why wasn't I in the mix?"

"After puberty you were officially confirmed as a Program member. You had signed your contract. You were already getting the adult injections. No, you couldn't be in the mix, only your younger brother and sister."

"I do remember that now. Doc, that whole situation killed my parents . . . especially my mom."

"It did kill them. It was a bad time. Three years later, when Joey reached puberty, the Program decided they needed more girls than boys, and Joey was out. Just like that. He was declared an Outcast. Your sister would have been in the Program when she reached puberty, but with the fire . . . "

". . . that never happened."

"No."

"Poor Joey . . . All my mom's crying, outbursts, drinking. It's understandable, isn't it? Her sadness affected all of us."

"Your mom was a good woman, and what happened would have ripped apart any parent. In a way, I think it was a blessing that at least they didn't have to make the ultimate decision. The Program made it for them. I don't know how any mom and dad could make that choice."

"Doc, why do you think my parents didn't tell me everything? Didn't they trust me?"

"You were seventeen when Joey was sent away. Old enough to be paired and have your own babies. I'm sure they thought you were smart enough to figure out what was going on."

"Do you think Joey understood all along the tough choice they were going to have to make? If he did, that must have been so hard on him. Maybe he was trying to make things easier for my parents by always getting in trouble. You know, so they would choose to keep Amasa instead of him?"

"I never thought about it like that, but he was certainly a smart and insightful young man."

She pressed against Doc, drying her tears on the shoulder of his coat, "I'd like to think Joey lived the way he wanted to. He always was a rebel."

"He would have hated being in the Program, especially if he knew it meant your sister would have been cast out. So please cut your parents a little slack, especially your mom. They had heavy things on their minds back then. Don't be too angry at them or me for not spelling things out. I really believe they thought you knew everything."

"Thanks for being honest with me. It certainly wasn't your place to have to tell me anything, back then or now."

"Well, anyway . . ." Doc fumbled, "how about we put the sad stuff away for the rest of the day? I do have good news, if you'd like to hear it."

"Please, I could use some."

"I just got this a few days ago," he said, pulling out a folded paper form from his coat pocket. "Once I sign this document, you're officially on the pairing list."

Mary's stepped back. "What did you say?"

"All I need to do is sign that you are healthy enough, and you'll be on the list. The Program will pair you, and soon you can be raising your own children."

"Are you kidding me? That's terrible news."

"What? Why?"

"I don't want to be on that damn list! I don't want to be paired with anyone. I don't want raise children in this horrible place," she said, pushing the paper away from her face.

"Why are you raising your voice? I thought this would be good news."

"Well, it isn't."

"You . . . you don't want to be paired? Don't want to have children of your own? Mary, this is the way it's done; this is the way it works. It worked that way for your parents, the way it's worked for decades."

"Not the way it works for me. Absolutely not. I don't want to be on that damn list. Don't you dare sign that. You keep me off that list!"

"Calm down a minute, will you?" Doc shot back, raising his hand. He had foolishly hoped that when Mary had the distraction of a family, her disposition would improve and she could find a way to happiness. "Then you're saying you want me to do something about it? Is that it?"

"Could you?"

"OK, let's think this through. I guess I could change your health report. Why don't we say that you have emotional problems? Maybe in need of anger management? That might stop any prospects of pairing, especially with your mom's background. And with you, young lady, emotional instability and anger management wouldn't be a stretch."

Mary blew off his poor attempt at humor. "All I want to know is if that's possible, because that's what I want. Can you do that for me – without the sarcasm?"

"If that's what you want, but . . ."

"No buts. Please keep me off that list."

"And, promise an old friend that you will leave all that stuff about the fire and what you've read in that notebook alone. Take charge, and help yourself lead a normal, happy life. You can't change the past. Move forward."

"Getting me off that list would make me normal and happy."

"If that's what you want."

"It is."

Doc took Mary's arm again as they walked. "We've said our final goodbyes to Joey. Could we leave now? I'm feeling drained."

Before turning off the path, they saw an oddly dressed young man running toward them. He was a teenager, Mary guessed, maybe 14 or 15 years old. Instinctively Doc placed himself in front of Mary in a feeble attempt to protect her. The boy was too quick and, despite the block, managed to get around him. He grabbed Mary's hand and moved close to her. She found his brashness stunning, and she froze in place.

"You're Mary, Joey's sister, aren't you?"

"Hey! Get away from her," Doc yelled. "What do you think you're doing?"

"Stay back, old man," the boy whispered, raising his hand. "Just a couple of questions. I'm not here to hurt anyone."

"Yes, Joey is . . ." she stumbled, catching herself and turning her head toward his sprinkled ashes, "I mean, was my brother. That was his funeral. You knew him?" Mary looked intently at the boy in odd, ragged clothing. "You were at Joey's service," she said, as if working out a puzzle. "Why?" She remembered thinking he looked out of place, but the detail seemed unimportant at the time.

"He was my mentor and friend. So is Jude," the young man replied. His blue eyes peered deeply into hers. His stare made her uncomfortable as if he was scanning her soul, checking to see if she was trustworthy. Where had she heard the name Jude before? It sounded familiar. Then it dawned on her . . . Joey. He had mentioned someone named Jude numerous times.

After a minute or two, they heard a small group of people from one of the other funeral parties walking toward them. Doc shouted, "That's enough. Now, get out of here – leave us alone."

Upon seeing the group, the boy immediately dropped Mary's hand and ran off without another word.

"Did you know him," Doc asked?

"No. I've never seen him before, well, other than possibly earlier today at the funeral. What about you? Have you ever seen him?"

"No, never. He said he knew Joey, and he obviously knew you were his sister. That can't be good."

"How does he know me, but I don't know him? And he mentioned someone named Jude. Maybe that's an Outcast friend of

Joey's? Now that I think of it, on a couple of occasions in the Care Place, Joey mentioned someone with that name. I thought he made him up. You know, part of his fantasies, but Jude must have been a friend."

"The boy obviously wanted to . . . share his condolences. Be careful. My gut tells me you'll be seeing him again but, with those ratty clothes, he's probably an Outcast. They're dangerous."

* * *

Back in his apartment, Doc thought about how brave Joey had been and how depressed that fact made him feel. Mary wasn't the only one grieving. He, too, had lost his best friends, and today marked the loss of yet another member of that family, the only family he had spent appreciable time with his whole life.

He found funerals exhausting, and this one caused him to remember how much he missed his own son and maybe even his crazy partner. Those losses stung, and he recognized he would never get over grieving them.

His responsibility now was to Mary. She still had a chance to be happy, and he wasn't about to let her self-destruct – or bring him down with her. The young man who approached her after the funeral would be his next worry. Trouble was coming.

CHAPTER 17

THE NOTEBOOK: THE PROGRAM

The day after the funeral, Mary wrapped herself in a blanket and paced her apartment, knowing she had to calm down. While she was grateful that the Program had allowed her to participate in the community funeral service, she also knew that every worker in the Program who had ever died had their ashes sprinkled over that same small plot of land. How disrespectful of the dead, she thought. Maybe she shouldn't have gone to that service. Maybe she should have just kept Joey's ashes and spread them somewhere else. Maybe that would have been more appropriate since he was, after all, her rebel. And, what about his friend, the boy who approached her at the funeral? Who was he, what else did he want to tell her?

She walked to the rusty porcelain sink in her tiny kitchen, filled a cup of water, and boiled it. It smelled odd, maybe worse than normal, but she drank it. She needed a distraction from all the sadness. She thought that maybe more of the notebook might be just the ticket.

WHY DIDN'T SHE READ *** the whole thing AT ONCE?

To survive in our new world, we required some form of order or government, a structure of leaders and workers to manage our precious resources.

It was important, we felt, for all adult members to have a turn rotating through positions of power and working citizen. The governing body we decided upon would be a leadership committee with members selected from the people. With this concept in mind, we used a lottery system, to select the first leaders. The committee consisted of 30 people from the community and one from the general corps, each with one vote, each serving a 4-year term, and with half the committee changing out every two years. A simple majority of the 31 sitting leadership members was required to change or institute any rules. We named this governing structure, our new society, the Program.

"This Program committee is a good thing, isn't it, Sim?" Francesca asked me one day, making more of a confirming statement than asking a question.

"Yes, it seems fair, and I'm proud that our little community came up with it."

Everyone in the community had a job to do and a responsibility to everyone else. The goal was to reward each person with monthly inoculations, a job, food, shelter, education, and medical care. With our governing structure now set, life on the surface could once again begin in earnest.

The most immediate problem was combating hunger. With the meager food production from our farms, we needed to manage all resources, including our population.

To accomplish this, the Program carefully selected the healthiest individuals for breeding, paired them, and dictated the number of offspring allowed under contract. Women of prime child-bearing age could be paired with more than one male, and men could be paired with more than one woman when this was dictated by exceptional genetics.

Each healthy child planned by the committee was initiated under contract into the Program at the age of puberty. Upon becoming an official Program member, adult inoculations were initiated, and the community agreed to support that person throughout his or her life. By carefully planning and population control, work, food production, housing, and other items, the limited resources could be managed for the benefit of all.

Like others, I did my part. I was nearly forty-nine years old when the Program decided to pair me with a younger woman, Pricilla. Together we produced two wonderful children, our daughter Phoebe and son John. I will try and write more about them later. If you are reading this diary, perhaps you already know about them?

You should also know that I will never stop missing Martha and my boys. I think about them every day. I hate knowing I was powerless to save them. They are my heroes, and I will love them forever. I am happy to say I have contributed to the continuation of humanity through Phoebe and John. Raising them convinces me that our Program will work for the benefit of humanity.

I, like the rest of the community, was convinced one of the most important functions of the Program leadership committee was to ensure proper matching of the population to the available resources. This included selectively breeding humans for the best possible future. The committee had its fair share of problems to face. We quickly learned that breeding and population control was a tricky business.

Couples began violating their pairing agreement by having too many children. To deter this, the Program enacted a rule that in the event of an unapproved pregnancy, an abortion was mandatory. This rule elicited great push back from the community and, for years, it was a matter of continuing debate at committee meetings.

This problem was compounded by the fact that surgical sterilization was never allowed since nothing was to interfere with the Program's flexibility, based purely on genetics, for additional children outside of the original pairing contracts. This flexibility was considered a necessary part of the selective breeding process, which aided in producing the best genetics for the future society.

I served my term as a member of the leadership committee during that turbulent period, and we chose to review the population control policies and the harsh rules associated with them.

New to my term my old friend and confidant, Haruko, quickly cautioned me about the dealing with this hot button issue. "Be careful here, Sim," she warned. "This issue is explosive. What you and the committee decide will greatly affect the legacy of this community."

I did my best to heed Haruko's warning. After much deliberation, we, the committee, enacted a new rule in place of mandatory abortions for pregnancies outside the limits of the contracts. With this new rule, any child born outside of the contract would be allowed to live in the society until he or she reached puberty and then would be cast out. Being cast out meant the young adult would be banished from the community, denied access to its resources, and sent to live in the wilderness without inoculations. This compromise was based on the belief that prepubescent children consumed few resources and that at puberty they would be mature enough for survival on their own in the wilderness.

This new rule was accepted as less harsh than the previous rule and was considered more humane. Under the new rule when a young adult was cast out, he or she was given a small amount of food and one booster inoculation for protection from the rays. The booster shot would be the first and last protection drug that the person would receive. Families were discouraged from having contact with the young adults casted out. Severe penalties existed for those families or anyone else that violated the committee ruling by attempting to share food, resources, or give shelter to the cast out. The new rule was controversial but proved to be an effective deterrent to overpopulation and was begrudgingly accepted as necessary.

This class of young adults became known as Outcasts. They were subject to many cancerous diseases and eventually the Early Aging Syndrome. Most died quickly. There were cases, however, where young and surprisingly healthy Outcasts caused problems for the community. With only the booster shot, they did not suffer the side effects of the protection drugs, and they could be aggressive. To protect our vulnerable Program community from hostile Outcasts, General Tishman decided to use armed guards to police the perimeter of the compound.

Unlike the Outcasts, a young adult reaching puberty within the Program received monthly inoculations. Those younger than puberty did not need protection from early aging but were still subject to many cancers and other UV related immune system disorders. The adult protection drugs were too harsh for a child's developing immune system, which posed a dilemma for us.

Once again, the community turned to the life sciences team to find a suitable solution for the younger members. As in the past, Haruko led the way, developing a milder daily oral cocktail for the children.

This cocktail, which also had a calming effect on the children, was not as effective as the adult drugs and needed to be augmented with UV resistant glasses and body creams. To ensure further protection, children did not go outside during the peak sunshine hours of the day.

With these problems solved, our new community thrived. One lingering issue was the objectionable side effects of the adult injections, especially the violent attacks.

To address this problem, Tishman put together a new team to investigate ways to mitigate this. For the first time, Haruko was not involved in the effort. She had some sort of falling out with the general.

Work progressed without her help, and doctors eventually conducted human trials. Unfortunately, despite a rumor that they had made significant progress, an acceptable solution was never found. Then the team abandoned the effort. This was odd, and I wondered if this would have happened under Haruko's leadership.

Without a solution to mitigate the drug's side effects, we accepted the addiction as necessary and minimized the possibility of violent attacks by controlling our emotions.

This still posed a dilemma for the General and his security forces. Now that his team was working back on the surface where they needed to take the protection drugs, how would they be able to act aggressively if required?

A partial solution to their problem turned out to be a long and extensive training regime of mind and body. They determined that through extensive training, the security forces could at least minimize the extent of any violent attacks while performing their protection duties.

The community soon learned that the guards had found a limited solution to the aggression issue. Sang asked me the question that was on everyone's mind. "So, why don't we all get this training?" His question sounded good to me. I'd certainly take the training, if they let us.

Ironically, Tishman himself soon addressed the community with his answer. "This course of training is far too intense and dangerous to administer to anyone except to those that absolutely need it. People can die, so I have told the committee that only the guards should take it."

With that he quickly squashed our hopes, and we moved on.

* * *

It was done, she had read his entire diary.

Mary closed the notebook, gently lifting it to her face. Breathing in, she hoped to capture any remaining scent of her great grandfather.

She felt strangely connected to the sacrifices made by all the people of the notebook almost a 100 years ago. These were not figures in history, these were her people, her brave ancestors. Ripped from their homes, they left everything and everyone behind in a desperate attempt to save humanity before time ran out.

She thought about how hard it must have been to live and work in that cramped underground tomb, without having any connection to their families on the surface.

They did eventually find success, she was proof of that, but not without great personal cost. Emerging from that hole they found the world they once knew gone along with the lives of their loved ones. This was a harsh new world full of obstacles to survival yet, once again, they soldiered on. With slowly acquired gains, their group aspired to create a new society, one in which each person held great value, with everyone having a chance to govern. What wonderful goals they had, she mused.

A century later, she wondered what those ancestors would think of the current Program, a society now ruled by a locked-in privileged few, with most of the spoils going to them.

She knew the answer. They would hate it.

CHAPTER 18

A MEETING OF MINDS

Meeting socially with a coworker was highly unusual. Apartments were small. Thin walls had big ears, and a general unease and distrust hovered over everyone. People understood how to behave: be happy, perform your job, never complain, smile when expected, offer the obligatory greeting, return directly home after work. About the only times people gathered socially were parings, funerals, and official holidays that honored Program heroes.

By now Mary and Ena had gotten past their little spat and while they knew it was unusual for people to visit, work had been busy, leaving little time for girl talk, so the two friends arranged to meet at Mary's apartment after dark. They picked a low-traffic time to meet to avoid being seen.

During her life, Ena had never seen any other apartment apart from the one she grew up in and the one she now lived in. She was curious about Mary's and imagined it to be better than her own. To her disappointment, it was not. One thing did catch her by surprise – so many books on Mary's make-shift shelves, neat lines of old spines and pages, tattered from climate change. Where did she get them all?

Mary watched her friend admire her collection. Everyone knew old books were a cherished commodity, most had been recycled long ago to reclaim the paper. She invited Ena to borrow any that caught her eye. Ena's hand slid gently across the shelf, as if the knowledge within each book could somehow pass to her.

After her drab apartment tour, Mary detected a hint of disappointment on her friend's face. She watched as Ena peered out the window, looking at the abandoned buildings across the street. She guessed that she had been hoping to see a nicer studio in a nicer area instead of another standard issue unit in an unremarkable setting. With that she tossed Ena's coat on the bed, and the two friends sat in hardback chairs, facing each other across a teetering card table, which she stabilized with a touch of pressure from her left knee.

Ena was the first to break the ice. "I'm sorry about Joey. I feel bad. I know you must miss him very much."

"I do. I miss him every day. In the end, he didn't recognize me. He was in bad shape, and I'm certain he was in pain. Knowing that, I think, hurts the most.

Ena rose from her chair and moved behind Mary gently rubbing her friend's shoulders. "I'm sorry I couldn't be with you at the funeral. I wanted to come, but work . . . I asked . . . they wouldn't let me off."

"I know you wanted to be there. It was a combination funeral . . . not that many people, so don't worry about it. The strangest thing hap. . ." Mary cut herself off. "Hey, here's a thought. I know it's a cold night, but how about we go out for a short walk? The air is so stale in here. I'd open that damn window, but it's been stuck for a year. I could use some fresh air. What do you say?" Mary began nodding pointing to the walls and her ears in an exaggerated fashion, hoping to encourage agreement. Ena caught the code; the walls might be listening.

"That would be nice. Grab my coat, and we'll go."

Outside, the initial warmth from their coats quickly dissipated, and the women picked up their pace in a futile effort to keep warm.

"I have something exciting to tell you," Ena burst.

Mary braced herself, guessing what might be coming.

"I'm on the pairing list," Ena exclaimed.

Mary knew Ena had waited her whole life for this moment. As an only child, Ena had repeated in nearly every conversation they shared how she wished that she had other siblings to play with. She resented that her biological father had left her and her mother when she reached puberty. He and the Program agreed to pair him a second time, robbing her of the chance to love a sibling. Worse than leaving, he never had the decency to contact her after he left, let alone include her in his new family.

She envied people like Mary who grew up in a complete family. How wonderful it must have been to have had a brother, a sister, and both a mom and dad. Now that she had been added to the pairing list, she would have a chance to build a big family of her own.

"That's what you've always wanted. I'm . . . I'm . . ."

"Stop. Please. You're not a good liar or good at faking it, Mary."

"That's not true," Mary snapped back, knowing full well that Ena had caught her. "I want you to be happy. Being paired is just . . . not something I want, that's all . . . but I'm happy for you, really. Maybe I'm a little sad because I won't see you as much?"

"Getting paired doesn't necessarily mean I'll leave for another job." Without effort, she was beaming again. "I wonder if my guy will be handsome . . . or ugly. Oh, that would be bad!"

Mary took the opportunity to get back on board with her friend's happiness. "Handsome, of course."

Her tone reassured Ena that she had her best friend's approval and blessing. "Exactly. They wouldn't dare pair me with an ugly guy!"

The two friends hooked each other's arms and walked faster.

Ena loved being around children. She had dreamed of becoming a teacher. The Program had decided not to fulfill that dream, but she now embraced the pairing system because it meant she could raise her own. She knew this wasn't the life Mary wanted, but she was glad to see that her best friend could at least share in her joy.

"Your turn," Ena pivoted the conversation. "What did you want to tell me that you couldn't say at work or back in the apartment?"

Mary's mood changed as she began to relate the details of what Doc had told her about her parent's impossible decision to choose between Joey and Amasa.

"That's horrible, you never told me that. And your poor parents, they picked Joey to become the Outcast?"

"They didn't get to choose. The Program made the decision for them. Joey was forced out. The Program needed more girls. Losing Joey just about killed them, those years of not knowing what had become of him broke my mother . . . and contributed to her drinking."

Mary had never shared the cloud her family had been under, and it struck Ena for the first time that Mary's idyllic childhood had, in reality, been terrible, maybe even more devastating than her own.

When Ena was a child she had worshipped the idea of growing up in a big family with siblings, but the Program, the very system that was supposed to protect Mary's family, had betrayed all of them. "I can't imagine what your family went through, and what you're going through now, but I am here for you. You can lean on me."

The two continued to walk in the cold night air before Mary regained her voice. "You're a good friend."

Pained, Ena thought about Joey's final hours. "Hearing all this makes me wonder how your brother got to the Care Place in the first place."

"Doc Brisko somehow made it happen. Maybe once my sister died, they were more receptive. Who knows?"

"Why don't you ask him? Aren't you curious?"

"Funny, I spent so much time being grateful that Joey was in there, I never thought about why, not that it matters anymore." Mary drifted for a moment then turned, "I do have something else to tell you. Something weird happened at the funeral."

"I can handle weird," Ena brightened, eager to shift Mary's sorrow.

"When Doc and I were leaving the ceremony, a young man ran up to us and grabbed my arm. He said he knew Joey and a friend Joey talked about named Jude. Before he could say much, he ran off."

"You didn't recognize him?"

"No, I didn't recognize him and neither did Doc."

"If you and Doc don't know him, do you think he was . . . an Outcast, begging for help or something?"

"Nah, he looked healthy. I mean, his clothes were tattered, but don't all teenage boys look that way?"

"How strange . . ."

"Yeah, it was. Hey, if you're ready, let's go back inside. I can no longer feel my toes."

"Glad you said that. Let's run!"

As Mary unlocked and entered her apartment, she stepped on a torn piece of paper. She examined the scrap for a few seconds before picking it up.

"Keep moving. It's freezing out here," Ena whispered, playfully tapping Mary's back.

But Mary didn't move. She did not recognize the handwriting and was certain that the paper had not been there before. Then she looked at the large gap at the bottom of her door and realized that someone must have slipped the note under while she and Ena were out. An odd sensation rose from her stomach to her throat. She turned, looked down the hall, and yanked Ena inside before locking the door. She then dragged her kitchen chair over and barred the door.

"Hey! What are you . . . . ?"

Mary covered Ena's mouth. "Stay away from the door. Close the blinds – now."

"What's going on?"

Mary held up the note and thought back to her strange conversation with Adrienne. Someone had been snooping around her apartment and wanted her attention. "Come into my bathroom when you're done."

The two of them squeezed into the small bathroom together. They looked at the badly scrawled writing and pieced the words out loud. "I think it says, '*Jude, blue building, 10:00PM tomorrow, don't be followed,*' Mary whispered. "Here, you read it."

Ena brought the note closer to the light. "I think you're right . . . but you absolutely can't go. It could be a trap. That Outcast. He wants to kidnap you."

"Those silly rumors. Outcasts don't kidnap people. And, to be fair, why do you assume whoever wrote this is an Outcast? It could be from someone in the Program. A spy from this building."

"Ahh, an informant . . . that's even more interesting," she said with an unexpected upturn in her voice. "Maybe that's the real reason the guard made your boss stop at your desk last week. They've been watching you."

Mary wrinkled her brow. "The blue building . . . where could that be?" She said, not actually expecting an answer.

"Wait, I think I know." Ena ran out of the bathroom to the window. She lifted the blinds. "We walked right by it tonight. Look."

Mary followed, surprised that her friend was capable of solving the mystery. She approached the window and pressed against the cool glass, searching the moonlit foreground. A block over, on the side of the abandoned building, she could see blue graffiti in the shape of a large arc.

"You think that's it? I've lived here for years, and I've never seen anyone near those buildings. Ever."

"I'm telling you. That's the blue building. We'll go together for safety. Don't argue with me on this," Ena said, buttoning her coat back up.

"Wait, a moment ago, you were telling me not to go and now, suddenly, you're so brave? I don't believe what I'm hearing."

"I want to go with you. I mean, I'm afraid. You know me; stuff like this frightens me to death, but it's . . . Mary, I want to experience something exciting before I'm paired!"

"And, if this is a Program informant trap, what then? We could both get in trouble. That could mess up your pairing. And, if it is an Outcast, then who knows what they might do to us. Didn't you just said they kidnap people?"

"Yes, and didn't you just say that was a silly rumor?"

"Maybe, but I need to go. You don't."

"No one needs to go, but if you're going then I'm going with you." Then Ena grabbed and squeezed her. "Take me with you. Please. This is . . . fantastic!"

Mary resigned herself. Her best friend would not be denied.

CHAPTER 19

THE BLUE BUILDING

"Ena, please! Not here at work," Mary said the next morning, racing up the back stairwell to her office hallway with Ena on her heels. "I haven't even had a chance to get to my desk yet."

"But . . ."

"Your desk is that way. Go. I'll see you tonight."

Mary spent the day regretting her decision to let Ena accompany her. Why couldn't she bring herself to say no? The more she thought about it, the more she wondered if taking Ena to the blue building would be a mistake. The note said not to be followed, but Ena's enthusiasm caught her off guard and was hard to squash.

Besides, she knew it would be safer to have someone with her. Now, the question was, who would be around to tell the authorities if they were kidnapped?

She guessed that since the note referred to Jude, it must have been written by the boy who spoke to her at the funeral. If he was a friend of Joey's, she wanted to talk to him. He said he didn't want to hurt anyone, she reminded herself. Pushing her worst fears aside, she got back to work.

Mary and Ena agreed to wear black and work late that day so, once it turned dark, they could hurry through the neighborhood streets toward the building with the blue graffiti. On the way, Ena pulled out a rusty flashlight and pointed it in the direction of the building.

"Are you crazy?" Mary said, grabbing the flashlight. "What if the neighbors see us? Hurry, duck in over here," she said, pushing Ena into an alcove of an abandoned building. "Don't turn that damn thing on again. Where did you get that anyway?"

"I found it in the basement of my building. I took two batteries from work."

"You stole from work? You, Miss Rule Follower? What were you thinking? You're always lecturing me on how closely they monitor supplies. Put these batteries back tomorrow exactly where you found them. Remember the fake fire drill?"

"Well, I took them, and it was fun. I've never stolen anything before in my life," she said, flashing the light again.

"Put that away. Why did I agree to let you come with me?"

"Come on, relax, this will be handy inside that building."

Mary knew Ena was too naïve for the trip. What Ena didn't realize was that because this trip was about Joey, it could be dangerous. Exasperated on the one hand, Mary was secretly proud to be watching her friend unleash herself, like a kid who nabs a piece of candy and eats it before anyone with power can take it away.

The women entered the abandoned building through the entrance closest to the blue graffiti scrawled on the outside wall. It was dark inside, but Mary quickly displayed a facial expression that cautioned Ena not to dare turn on the flashlight.

Wide-eyed in the dim light, the two silently explored inside the dingy building. Mary wondered if they even had the right blue building. Ena kept walking. Mary couldn't believe her confidence.

They were careful to step over old rusted junk piles strewn everywhere. A dripping sound emanated from a dark corner of the hallway, just beyond the room they were passing. They approached the sound and found themselves standing in a puddle of water. A bad smell came from the puddle. The floor was slippery, so they held on to each other's forearms for support. Shocked, Mary felt rough, calloused hands from behind cover tightly across her mouth.

Someone was doing the same to Ena. Both women squealed as they were pulled harshly to a seated position on the cold wet floor.

"We're uncovering your mouths on the count of three. If either of you scream or try to fight, I'll kill you both, plain and simple," the shorter of the two shadowy figures said, swinging a pipe back and forth for them to see. His anger apparent as he and his partner came out from behind them.

Mary fixated on the shadowy figures. In the dim light, she realized their assailants, again, were teenage boys. She had never in her life seen anyone other than the police act so aggressively. She didn't think people could behave this way and survive, and yet here they were.

She continued to bring the boys into focus. The taller assailant resembled the boy who approached her at the funeral. "I said not to be followed," he growled. "Who the hell is this? Why is she here?"

She was right – he was the boy from the funeral, obviously the same person who had slipped the note under her door. Having figured out who he was made her feel like she had a bit of leverage to speak up. "It was too dangerous to come alone. This is my best friend, Ena. She's like a sister to me," she said, hoping to appease them.

The young man stopped swinging his pipe and looked at his accomplice. They appeared to be confused about what to do next. Mary and Ena exchanged glances. Whatever these boys had planned, they hadn't expected Mary to bring a friend.

After a few minutes of whispering, the taller boy from the funeral spoke. "I'm Axel, and like I told you, Joey was our friend. That's why we're here. That's why we wanted you here. Joey was a good guy. He taught us lots of things and told us that you were his sister, that you could be trusted. Now I'm not so sure."

"He was right. You can trust me. You can trust both of us. Since you boys knew Joey, I guess you must be Outcasts?"

"No, we're not Outcasts, we were born on the other side of the wall but like others, we are children of Outcasts. Joey and his partner were Outcasts," the boy with the pipe said speaking up.

Mary gasped, "His partner? You're saying my brother had a partner?" The women looked at each other in disbelief.

"She died. We've been taking care of their boy, Jude."

"Jude? Holy shit," Mary yelled as she jumped to her knees, "Joey has a son? I don't believe it, Ena. He never told me he had a partner or a son."

"Sit down," Axel's accomplice said, pressing his pipe into her shoulder. "We promised him we'd let you know about Jude if something happened to him, and that's what we're doing. First, we needed to be sure about you . . . but we don't know that one."

"I told you. She's my friend. You can trust her."

Ena, now feeling braver, spoke for herself, "I won't say a thing to anyone."

"Be quiet, lady. We risked our lives to be here, and if we hear you say anything about us, your friend Mary here will never meet Jude . . .", Axel threatened.

". . . because we will sneak into her apartment when she's sleeping and kill her. Get it? We know where you live, don't we, Mary?" the boy with the pipe finished.

Mary flinched. Ena slid a little farther back from the boys.

"We came here for Joey, not for you," Axel added, "We have no loyalty to you."

Ena, now trembling from the cold water she was sitting in, kept her wits about her. "I was at Mary's apartment when she got the note, and I made her bring me for safety."

"Axel," Mary interrupted, "My brother told you to trust me, right? Well, you can. He wouldn't have said that if it weren't true."

Appearing to be somewhat more comfortable, he replied, "We'll see if that turns out to be true."

"You guys look strong and healthy. Why aren't you sick from the rays like the other Outcasts? Won't you get sick, like Joey?" Mary asked, moving the conversation along.

"Not us kids. We don't get the sickness. Only some of the parents who were Outcasts," the boy with the pipe explained.

Ena's curiosity took hold of her. "You said you risked your lives to meet here? But the Program doesn't hurt people. They might make you go back to your side of the wall, but they would never hurt you."

"Lady, are you naïve or just plain stupid?" Axel snarled. "If they can catch us, they sure as hell kill us. They might cut off our heads and throw them over the wall for our families to find."

Ena leaned a little closer. "The Program would never do that. They don't hurt people, not even Outcasts. I've never seen them hurt anyone."

The shorter boy became incensed and started banging his pipe on the surfaces surrounding them. "You're idiots! You live sheltered little lives on your side of the wall. They're lying to you. The Program has killed so many good people. Let's get out of here, Axel. This was a waste."

"Don't leave," Mary pleaded. "We've lived in the vicinity of that wall all our life, but we don't know anything about what happens on the other side. You boys took a risk we can't begin to understand. I want to thank you for that. You came tonight to tell me about Jude because Joey told you to, and if my poor brother were alive, I know he'd thank you."

Hearing Mary's voice crack, Axel calmed down. "Fine, but you better believe what my friend is saying. The Program kills Outcasts to terrorize our community, to keep us on our side, away from all of you. Joey told us a lot of bad things about the Program, but he also made us promise that when he died, we would come find you. And that's the only reason we're here."

Suddenly rustling noises from outside the building echoed through the broken glass windows. The four of them froze silently in place until the noise stopped.

Axel whispered, "We need to get out of here, Raj."

"But I want to meet Jude," Mary blurted out.

"Next time, if there is a next time," Axel cautioned. "Any one of us could be dead by then, especially if you open your big mouth again. Now get out of here. Either of you says anything, we'll know, and you'll never see Jude. Expect the worst if you screw up."

"Wait. That noise is gone. Can't you stay and talk? I want to ask you so many things. Stay a little longer," Mary pleaded.

Trained and disciplined, the boys turned the closest hallway corner and were gone.

Later that night, after hand-washing the mud out of her outfit, Mary wedged a chair against the door and left several glasses scattered on the floor. If anyone came in, she was convinced the noise would wake her up. She thought that precaution might help her sleep, but she tossed – hot one minute, cold the next – thinking about what those boys had told them.

Should she believe that they were children of Outcasts? That her brother Joey had a partner? That she had a nephew, Jude, and that he was being treated well by these aggressive boys? That they didn't get sick? The questions overwhelmed her. She wanted to believe the boys because, if their story was true, then she had family. No way would she do anything to risk the chance to meet her nephew. She vowed not to discuss this with anyone other than Ena . . . and, well, maybe Doc.

CHAPTER 20

DOC'S EXPLANATION

"You have to understand," Doc told her, "The aftermath of that fire was a bad time for everyone. You were a wreck. Joey was dying somewhere on the other side of the wall. I was grieving the loss of my best friends and doing the best I could for their kids. Out of the blue, Program officials urged me to admit Joey to the Care Place."

"But Doc, why would the Program want an Outcast in that facility? It is strange, isn't it, caring for a dying Outcast? It doesn't make sense."

"Oh, but it does. First, appearances. Admitting Joey into the Care Place made the Program look good to the community. A family dies in a horrible accident – and they agree to care for the wayward son? It made the Program look pretty magnanimous, don't you think?"

"But . . ."

"More importantly, diversionary tactic. It squelched any conspiracy theories about the accident. No one was going to believe they would kill your family and then take in your Outcast brother, right?"

"That sounds . . . ."

"Finally, safety. By then Joey was senile, so it was safe to let him in. He didn't present a threat to the Program. They knew you would visit him, and they could listen in on your conversations. If he ever divulged what he and your father were doing, their strategy would work better than planting a snitch in his room."

No sooner had the words come out of Doc's mouth than Mary blew up. "That damned Lucinda, always lurking nearby while Joey and I were talking!"

"If they thought he had told you anything, you probably wouldn't be alive today."

"All Joey and I ever talked about was what he had eaten or if he had a shower. That old witch Lucinda must have been bored to death, listening in on those conversations."

"Who knows, but you can bet she was listening and reporting on you both."

"What do you think Joey and Dad were working on? Mom and I suspected Dad was secretly meeting with Joey and possibly other Outcasts, but Dad never talked about it. Mom was worried that he would get in big trouble."

"I knew he was meeting with your brother. I warned him, but he never listened to me."

"So that's where I get it from," Mary said, trying to lighten the mood.

"Ha, got that right!" he said, "you're certainly a lot like him, maybe more than you think. Anyway . . . on the day of the fire your dad was supposed come by my office. That never happened. Now I wonder if he would have given me that missing letter you were looking for."

"Damn it, I can't stand not knowing what he was up to, and I hate everything about the Program. I can't wait for a chance to expose their so-called leaders as the liars and murderers that they are."

"You need to stop. If they think one of us is sniffing around asking questions, or if they discover that notebook, things will get bad. Very bad. I appreciate where you're coming from, but your father's work is over, done, in the past. You need to leave well enough alone."

"I'm not sure I can, no matter how nice they were to let Joey die in that place."

"Mary, listen, they have no tolerance for snooping. If you start, you could get us both killed."

"I want to know what my father was doing. Now that Joey's gone, it's up to me to protect . . . Damn, I want revenge."

"Protect what? I can't lose you. You're the last survivor of your family – and mine."

"I may not be."

"What? What are you talking about?"

"Promise me you won't freak out and that you won't tell anyone, or it could really mess things up."

"I'm not in the mood to promise anything to anyone, including you. Talk."

She proceeded to tell Doc about Ena and her clandestine meeting with the boys in the blue building.

"What were you two thinking? You could have been . . . ."

"They aren't Outcasts," Mary blurted, "not really."

"Well then, what the hell are they, and what do they want with you?

"You're not going to believe this, but Joey has a son. That's why these guys wanted to meet. Did you hear me? These guys were Joey's friends. I have a nephew named Jude."

Doc looked at Mary, shaking his head in disbelief. "That's impossible. Ridiculous. You've been duped. Joey couldn't have a son. He wasn't healthy enough to make something like that happen. What if those guys were Program informants? Did you think of that?"

"I did, but they weren't. They said they had witnessed how the Program kills people. Doc, you've got to believe me. They are children of Outcasts, not Outcasts themselves. The whole time they were worried about being caught on our side of the wall. They were two strong and healthy young men. They said none of the children of Outcasts get sick. You met one of them, the boy at the funeral. His name is Axel. He looked healthy, wouldn't you say?"

"Those guys are lying to you. That Axel has to be a skilled informant for the Program. I'm a doctor, damn it. If they are living as Outcasts, they can't be healthy."

"You're wrong."

"This is so dangerous. Don't you dare meet with them again."

"I can't promise that, Doc. I want to meet them again. If Jude is my brother's son . . . ."

"Stop being so naïve. You've now endangered me and your friend Ena, seriously endangered."

"Do you hear yourself? You became involved the minute my dad handed you the envelope. And yes, Axel obviously knows who you are, or he wouldn't have felt safe coming up to us at the funeral. He knows who we both are. Joey must have told him."

"You have no idea how bad this could get. Let me think . . . let me think. When do you meet them again?"

"They control the timeline. Last time, one of them slipped a note under my door after Ena and I went for a walk. When we came back to my apartment, we found the note saying where to meet."

"Why was Ena at your apartment?"

"Doc!"

"Never mind. You both may already be in trouble. We all could be. I want to be there next time you get together with these guys."

"I'll ask, but I won't mess up my chance to meet Jude."

Doc was flabbergasted. "You don't know that Joey has a son. If the boy wasn't at that meeting, he probably doesn't exist. Those guys are after something else. We need to figure out what, and you let me come along next time."

"What possible reason would they have for meeting me other than to let me know about my nephew?"

"Outcasts hold people for ransom, food, medicine, information, whatever they want. They are desperate kidnappers, and you're too trusting. You do realize that place on the other side of the wall is a penal colony, right? Do I need to spell it out? What happens there to naïve young women like you? Believe me, I'm more familiar with their criminal mindset than you know. I've had run-ins with them."

"I knew you'd freak out."

"Damn you, Mary. Why wouldn't I?"

CHAPTER 21

QUESTIONS

Ena was now the only person she could talk to since her discussion with Doc had ended so poorly. She left with a nagging feeling that maybe Doc wasn't telling everything about why Joey was admitted to the Care Place. His explanation seemed implausible, but his concerns about the boys seemed logical and added to her unease.

She was conflicted about the meeting in the blue building. If those boys were Outcasts, they should have been sick. Were they really children of Outcasts? Doc said it was impossible for them to be healthy, but they were. Maybe they were really informants from the Program, but then shouldn't she or Doc have recognized them?

She guessed Axel and Raj, if those were their real names, could have lied about everything. But if the meeting wasn't about Jude, why meet? Was it wishful thinking to hope for a nephew? Or maybe they were playing into her fantasy, using the story about Jude to lure her to the building. Would they have told her more if Ena hadn't accompanied her or if they hadn't heard the rustling outside the building?

"Are you kidding, Mary? I loved the excitement that night. I was scared to death, weren't you? I'll never forget Raj, swinging that pipe. That boy is mean. Things could have gone so badly, but you kept your cool. Do you believe Joey could have fathered a child?"

"Maybe. When the Program ripped him from us, he was still healthy, so I guess he could have fathered a son. We didn't see each other for years. By the time he moved into the clinic, he was in bad shape."

"And, if your nephew does exist, guess you'd want to raise him here?"

"Oh yeah, like the Program would really let me raise an Outcast? That would never happen. Think about it, if offspring of Outcasts don't get sick or need injections, would the Program want that information to get out? They'd kill us both before they'd let that get out."

"Kill you? A bit melodramatic, don't you think?"

"No, you heard those boys. They are witnesses. Not only did the Program force my brother to become an Outcast, we now have confirmation that they kill people."

"Well, no, I wouldn't say that. I get that the Program forced your brother to become an Outcast. That was tragic, but your parents broke the rules; they violated their pairing agreement, right? Eventually the Program let your brother into the Care Place. That was a good thing. You told me they took good care of him, proof the Program isn't bad. How much evidence is enough?"

"What about killing my family? What category would you put that in?"

"You keep going back to that and, I'm telling you, everybody but you accepts that as an accident. You don't have any proof to suggest your family was murdered. Isn't it just as likely that you'd be suspicious about anything that involves the Program?"

"I'm not the only one. Those two boys said the Program kills Outcasts."

"I heard them, but that doesn't mean I believe them. We don't know who those guys are. Why should we believe anything they said?"

"Then why would they lie about that? Why would they risk their lives to talk to us if that wasn't true?"

"We don't know that they risked anything. I was right there with you, hearing and seeing the same things you did. The difference is, I don't necessarily believe them. They could have made that stuff up. The whole point of the meeting was about Jude, so why didn't they bring him?"

"Doc asked the same thing. Maybe they did bring him, but they were holding him back to see if they trusted us."

"They wanted you to meet Jude, but they hid him? That doesn't make sense. If he existed, they would have brought him along. Why hide the boy?"

"Maybe because I didn't come alone. "

"Oh, so it's my fault they kept Jude in hiding?"

"They told me to come alone, and I didn't. I let you come along. I messed up."

"Look, I didn't twist . . . well, maybe I did twist your arm, but I think something bad might have happened to you if I hadn't come along. Maybe rape or a kidnapping or worse. Anyway, forget about Jude for a moment. What did they say that makes you believe they knew your brother Joey? At the funeral, did that boy offer you any proof?"

"He didn't, but . . . "

"All right then, the bottom line is, only after you meet Jude and can prove he's really Joey's son will we know if this isn't just a story. The meeting was exciting, but there's no reason to believe them."

"Huh. Well, I disagree. And I will prove that Jude exists."

"Great. I hope that you do, but until that happens there isn't much else to say about this, is there?"

"No, there isn't."

"Good, then for once we actually agree on something."

CHAPTER 22

HERO'S PARADE

N o one worked on Hero's Day. Today was a time for celebration and for all members of the community to visit.

As Mary scanned the crowds from her window, she noticed the guards. She expected their presence, but their numbers this year seemed to have doubled. Anxiety rose inside of her. She expected snitches would be scattered among the crowds, but no way would the Program ever tolerate dissident behavior, so what were they expecting?

Ena arrived early to Mary's apartment so they could walk together to the parade. Mary pointed out the number of guards. Ena said nothing. Mary asked her how her week had gone. Ena said nothing. She was clearly somewhere else with something more important on her mind. "All right, you're way too quiet."

"Really?"

"Out with it."

"I have . . . great news."

"Who is he?"

"Oh, Mary, his name is Jorge, and we met for the first time a few weeks ago, and we've been together a few more times since then, and you're my best friend, and I couldn't wait to tell you, and you know that I love you, and I've been anxious to share this with you, but I just didn't want to jinx it by saying anything until the pairing was certain." Ena put her hands to her face and giggled with embarrassment.

"Wow, that happened fast," Mary said, watching Ena hyperventilate. "So, tell me, what is he like?"

"He's good looking, maybe not handsome but very nice. I like him a lot. You've probably seen him working on the dock. He's a supervisor but more hands-on."

"That is big news." Mary gave her friend a hug. "What happens now? When do you officially get paired? How does all this work?"

"In a few weeks, we'll sign the pairing agreement. And that brings me to what I've been wanting to ask you. I would love for you to be my witness at the ceremony and celebration, I mean, if you want to."

"Want to? Why wouldn't I want to be your witness?" Mary had no idea what that meant, but she didn't want to spoil Ena's fun.

"They told us we might be allowed to have two children in the future, but for now we can have one. You'll see when you witness the agreement. We want a family, you know, soon after the ceremony. I can't think of anything else. They said when we get pregnant, or possibly before, that we'll get a new apartment. A nice big one."

"Your dream has come true. I'm happy for you Ena. And I've never been a witness to a pairing before. A new experience will be good for me. You'll continue working?"

"Yes, but after a baby comes, I might get reassigned. Don't worry, though, that won't be for a long time. Isn't this great?"

"When do I get to meet this guy?"

"We might see him today at the parade. He said he would be around. You're going to like him. You'll see."

"I'm sure . . ."

"He's about four years older than me, almost twenty-seven. He's a few inches taller, broad shouldered, very muscular, sort of stout. He lifts a lot at work, so he's very strong. He has a dark olive skin tone like mine, and he has the cutest cheek dimples you've ever seen and another one in his chin. Sort of a rough-cut face, but he's not tough at all. He's kind and calm and thinks we're going to have beautiful children!"

"He sounds wonderful. I hope we see him today. Ena. . . you're not going to tell him about our private discussions or about the meeting in the blue building, are you?"

"Oh no, no, no. Our secrets are our secrets. I'm not going to tell him about any of that, but it's important that you're happy for me. Are you happy for me? Please, it's important."

"Of course, I am. I want a partner, too, but I want to be the one to pick him. I might get sort of jealous of this guy, though, if we don't get to spend time together, you know?"

"Don't be silly. I'm sure we'll be gossiping and spending time together same as always."

"I hope so. Now, let's get to the parade. We need to be seen."

CHAPTER 23

THE PAIRING EVENT

Mary had never been to a pairing celebration. She had read about weddings in many old books, but she knew this celebration wouldn't be anything like those big affairs. Program pairings were not religious ceremonies. People didn't congregate and, when they did, they didn't talk about faith. In fact, the only religious person she had ever met that talked about beliefs was her father.

As a child, except for witnessing her father pray, she had little exposure to religion. Once, when she interrupted him while he was praying, he brought her to his lap and told her about a creator God that made everything in the universe. At the time, she was happy to have her father's attention. Regardless, today's pairing was simply a party to honor Ena and Jorge.

Mary also knew the couple was not required or expected to stay together for life. The reason for pairing was strictly biological. The Program enforced the production and raising of the proper number of children. Paired couples were only required to stay together until the youngest child reached puberty and could be officially confirmed into the Program. Once they signed their own contracts, their parents could choose to stay together or go their separate ways. One parent, however, was always required to continue raising the children until adulthood. In some cases, the Program would pair each parent with a second partner to produce additional offspring, as Ena's father had done.

Mary soon learned that Edward, Jorge's handsome friend she had seen around work, would witness for him. As witnesses, she and Edward had been sequestered to read the contract before the signing. After entering the room, they sat near each other at a small table. The document immediately distracted Edward, so she took the opportunity to carefully observe him. He had deep brown eyes and bushy eyebrows and was a head taller than her. She envied his wavy black hair.

Together, they navigated through the legalese and were able to confirm that Jorge and Ena were currently authorized to have one child with a Program option to have a second within five years. If for any reason they could not produce the first child within the allotted time frame, the Program could void their contract and pair them with other selections.

Unlike Mary, Edward often dealt with contracts at work, and he took the time to explain the basics. He revealed that most contracts contained three to four essential terms: the names of the parties, an offer, an acceptance, and a form of consideration. Mary could tell he took the role of witnessing for his friends seriously.

After reviewing the contract, and seeing the restrictions on childbearing, she found it hard to believe that Ena didn't seem to mind these details. The contract only served to reinforce what a ridiculous system couples had to bear, but she decided to hold her tongue and roll along with things.

Mary, being predisposed to disliking the entire pairing concept, was surprised that being a witness had not been totally distasteful. Her fellow witness had a pleasant demeanor, turned out to be intelligent, and had opinions about pairing that were not unlike her own. On the contrary, witnessing had been an agreeable exercise.

Nevertheless, her head pounded as she added her signature, agreeing that this contract represented what her friend wanted.

Edward sighed a little too deeply as she slid the signing document to him, and his pen hesitated long enough to notice. Mary was relieved to see that he was not a fan of the forced pairing. That's when she knew he would not voice his concern to Jorge or Ena. This was their day. Theirs were the only opinions that mattered. She could tell he felt the same way.

After the signing, the guards collected the document and swiftly removed them from the room. Mary squinted as her eyes adjusted to the late afternoon light. A blur of happy faces greeted them, and she reminded herself to switch; this was Ena's day.

The thought of spending time with Edward made Mary brighten. This evening she would try and get to know him. Maybe they could become friends.

For someone who disliked crowded gatherings, she liked being a person of importance at Ena's pairing. She assumed her role as witness and best friend with style, greeting guests, visiting with acquaintances from work, and checking up on Doc, who had accompanied her to the celebration. How nice to be distracted from her cares. She reminded herself to thank Ena.

Watching nearby, Doc picked up on Mary's interest in Edward. His strong facial expressions made her head tilt up, and he was pleased to see her smiling for once.

As the celebration wore on, the noise began to grate on Mary. Thirsty, she grabbed a cool drink and moved to a less crowded area, away from the lights and chatter. She found an empty table and leaned her back against it. She enjoyed the quiet, gazing into the mass of guests. Ena and Jorge had invited so many people. She figured most of them must work with Jorge because Ena had little family and only a handful of coworking friends.

Off in the distance she noticed Edward visiting with two women who were having a good laugh about something. She wasn't surprised. Maybe she would get to spend more time with him, too, at Ena and Jorge's. She was imagining what a dinner party at Ena's big apartment would be like when something tugged on her dress hem, frightening her back to reality. She looked down below the table. Mostly out of sight was Axel. Again.

"Damn, you're everywhere. Stop scaring me like that. Why do you do that?" she scolded, catching her breath.

At first, he just smiled without responding. Her boldness reminded him of Joey. They were definitely related.

"What are you doing here, anyway? Program managers are everywhere at this ceremony, and all these people are from work. You shouldn't be here. We could both get in trouble. This is dangerous for you – and for me," she said looking down, darting her eyes to make sure no one noticed her lips moving.

"I'm taking a risk. I'm glad this time you understand that. I've been following you around all evening, waiting to make my move. If you want to meet Jude, come with me right now," he whispered.

"What? I can't just leave. This is a party for Ena. Remember her? It's her pairing celebration. I was her witness. People will wonder what happened to me."

"Everybody's drunk and visiting. You'll be back before you're missed."

Mary began to panic. Why now? Why the rush? But she couldn't risk challenging him.

"Listen," he warned, "do whatever you want. I'm leaving in three seconds with or without you. If you don't come with me now, though, that's it. You'll never meet Jude."

"I haven't heard from you in months, and now you show up here, of all places, with demands? I'll come, but I want to bring someone with me."

"Impossible." Axel grabbed her hand. Mary gasped, and they sprinted off behind the folded table that shielded them from the party into the dark. Safely out of sight, Axel slowed to accommodate. Soon, they came upon the wall that, for her entire lifetime, had appeared to extend forever in both directions. Looking at this giant structure, Mary again wondered, had this wall been built to keep outsiders out or keep insiders in?

"We live on the other side," Axel whispered with a definite sense of pride.

Mary looked upward at the structure against the night sky. "I've never in my entire life been this close to the wall. We were taught that the guards didn't like us to get near it. But this close, it looks even higher. I just don't think I can climb over, especially in a dress."

"Don't be stupid," Axel replied. "We don't climb it." At that moment, he saw a guard patrolling slowly along the top of the wall. Axel yanked her down and froze, hoping the guard had not seen or heard them. After the guard had passed, he gave Mary instructions. "If you try to scale the wall, the guards will shoot to kill. Stay low. Follow me. And, keep quiet if you don't want to die."

They hugged the wall, walking another 5 minutes before Axel stopped and bent down. Using his hands, he brushed away debris that covered a heavy wooden plate. As he lifted it, a young boy popped up from inside and held the cover open. No words exchanged. Axel flashed a light into the tunnel, cupping it with his hands to make sure the guard wouldn't notice any reflection. He took Mary's hand and guided her down the ladder inside. The other boy, who looked like a younger version of Raj, stayed behind.

"What about him?"

"Don't worry about him. He'll stay hidden until we come back."

"Isn't that dangerous?"

"He knows his way around the wall."

Except for the close proximity of Axel's light, Mary walked blindly through the tunnel. Axel's rough hand held her wrist tightly as he led her through the cold, wet interior. He warned her where to step and not to step. "Keep moving. We don't have much time to get you back before anyone notices that you're missing."

They exited the tunnel on the Outcast side of the wall minutes later. Mary looked back toward the wall that was now about a hundred yards behind them, trying to orient herself. As they walked, the ground in front of them was covered with small tuffs of grass, just as she had seen in photos in Doc's old books. She had never seen grass before, and she couldn't stop herself from touching it. At one point, Axel admonished her. "Stop that. What are you doing? Move faster. We don't have much time." Mary complied until they came upon Raj, who was holding the hand of an angelic red-haired toddler.

Axel released Mary's arm, and she fell to her knees, "A little Joey," she blurted and reached out for him, but the boy hid behind Raj, clinging to his pant leg. She guessed her tears frightened him, but she couldn't stop. "He's . . . darling. Hi, Jude! You look just like your daddy, you know that?"

Raj moved up and said defensively, "As we told you, Joey's son, Jude. He's three years, very shy."

Mary noticed a difference in Raj tonight. He wasn't at all harsh or scary as he had been in the blue building, swinging that pipe and threatening them. "What a wonderful little boy you are, Jude. If you want to come closer, I'd love to hug you."

Axel went behind Raj and took the little boy's hand, guiding him forward, "Don't worry, we're here," he coaxed. "Jude, this is your Aunt Mary. We told you she would come to see you. It's OK, you can hug her."

Slowly the toddler moved closer to Mary. Again, she reached out. He touched her hand and giggled, pulling away before slowly moving back toward her.

"What's your name?"

"Jude." His voice fell off, almost too quiet for Mary to hear.

"I'm your Aunt Mary. I'm your daddy's sister."

"I don't think he remembers much about his father. And he never met his mom, she died having him. We don't have doctors here," Raj explained.

"Jude, would it be all right if I hugged you? Only a little hug, not a big hug," she teased.

The boy slowly moved closer to her, and she enveloped him. Then he let out a happy high-pitched squeal and squirmed away.

"Jude, would you like to sing a song together? I can teach you one." But once again he backed away and buried himself behind Raj's leg.

Raj turned to her. "He'll come around. He doesn't know you yet, but he will."

Mary was ecstatic. How wonderful, she thought, to meet her brother's son. All this time she had wondered if the boy was real, and here he was, in front of her. She couldn't soak him in fast enough. While the three of them played peek-a-boo with Jude, she gathered more information about her brother. "Tell me how you came to know Joey."

"He was like a big brother to us and a good friend," Raj jumped in.

"He taught us a lot of things," Axel added, now speaking in a noticeably softer tone. "He was our mentor. We were with him nearly every day until we brought him back to the other side."

"Your mentor? Tell me. what did he do?"

"Every evening after chores, if it was still light enough outside before we ate, he would play the book game with us. He really enjoyed that game, and so did we."

"What's the book game?"

Raj was quickest. "One of us would grab a book from the old building, any book at all, and we'd open to any page we wanted, then Joey would read it. If we liked the book, he would read it to us from cover to cover. We liked a few of the books so much that we had him read them to us again. He sometimes got sick of that." Both boys snickered.

"Every day after he read to us, he would teach us something about reading and writing," Axel added.

Mary felt her face redden. She was proud to know how admirably her baby brother had acted. What a mature father figure Joey had been, she thought. A very different man had grown from the mischievous child she had raised. "And what were your favorite books?"

"Oh, for sure, making pottery," Raj replied.

"Really?"

"He's right. We read that book many times. Raj, remember how we made a lot of clay pots and cups and tools? Joey was the best at making the pottery."

"Joey made pottery? I'd love to see it."

Axel stopped talking for a moment. He made eye contact with and older man off in the distance. Whatever the man had signaled caused Axel's demeanor to abruptly change, "That's enough fun and games for today. You've met Jude. Now, do you want to see him again?"

"Absolutely."

"Are you willing to help us with a few things we want in exchange?"

"If I can . . . I guess . . . why not?" The words came out without knowing what she was getting into. "What kind of help?"

"We'll tell you when the time comes. And if you cooperate with us, you can see Jude again. We might need information about the Program."

"But I won't do anything bad – don't ask me to do that."

"We're not going to ask you to do anything bad. See over there, that crumbling building? It's full of old books, from a school library, we're guessing. That's where we got all the books Joey read to us. The building is in bad shape, but a lot of the books are still good, and we been removing and collecting them."

Hearing that, Mary's eyes lit up. She loved the old books, everyone in the Program did, and here they had an entire library full of them. "So, how can I help?"

"Only a few of us can write or read . . . and not very well. Maybe you could teach us, like your brother Joey was doing? We might also ask you to maybe bring us supplies or get us answers to questions, things like that.

"And if I can do that, then I'd get to see Jude?"

"Right. Now say goodbye. It's time to go." His voice now clearly changing to a rougher tone.

"Can I ask some questions first?"

"Make them quick."

"Are there more people like you, I mean, children of Outcasts?"

"Yes," he said with a sigh, obviously tiring of her questions. "There's a small group of us," Axel replied, "There'll be more. See that group of people over there? They're like Raj and me, first or second-generation children of Outcasts."

"They don't get sick? No injections?"

"No, no injections or doctors or anything. Most of us don't get sick. Now let's stop wasting time. We need to go. Next time we meet I'll show you things that will help you understand more about us, if there is a next time, so you can figure stuff out for yourself. You've met Jude now, so we're good?"

"Completely. You kept your word. I love that little boy. Jude's mom was an Outcast, too, right? If she hadn't died during childbirth, would she have gotten sick?"

"You're making me angry now. She was already sick. If you want to see Jude again, stop talking about being sick." Then he grabbed Mary's arm and pulled her from the ground in a way that made it clear his patience had run out. "Up. We have to get you back to the party."

Jude, hiding once again behind Raj's leg, peeked his head and arm out, and Mary placed her hands in his. "Bye for now, Jude. I love you, my beautiful boy. Your daddy would be so proud of you . . . and I'm proud of you, too," she said as Axel pulled her toward the tunnel. It killed her to let Jude's fingers slip loose.

She was convinced that Axel could retrace their steps back through the tunnel blindfolded, though she had no idea how long it must have taken the Outcasts to build such a system. As they approached the same portal near the party, Axel signaled for her to climb the ladder and leave. Mary leaned in and whispered, "Thank you. I'm so happy that I finally met Jude. Please let me see him again. I'll do the best I can to help you with whatever you need."

"There is something I want you to do for me."

"Anything."

"That doctor you were with at the funeral, Brisko? Ask him what's in the final injection they give the Outcasts before they throw them out of the Program."

"I can answer that, the last injection is a booster shot to help protect them from the rays of the sun, at least for a while."

"Maybe, but you ask old Doc what he thinks. He might have a different answer. Watch it, though, if he's not a good friend, things might get ugly. You better consider that before you ask him."

"Believe me, the purpose of the shot is common knowledge, so I'm not worried." It occurred to Mary that life on Axel's side of the wall forced children to grow up quickly. That might also explain why Joey had a partner and a son he never told her about.

"We'll see about that. Just remember, if you tell anyone about this tunnel or this meeting, you'll never see any of us again, including

Jude, understand? Now, get back to your celebration." Before Mary could argue, Axel melted back into the darkness. Mary had no idea where she was. She panicked for a moment, getting acclimated. Then in the distance, she saw the party lights and walked slowly toward them.

CHAPTER 24

DIRT

Mary pushed her way through a crush of party guests, feeling as though she was the happiest person on Earth. As she searched the crowd for Ena, she became keenly aware that people were staring at her. At first, she thought she might be imagining the attention. She loved the dress Ena made for her and looking down at it noticed that at the bottom it was covered with thick streaks of dirt. She forgot about sliding along the edges of the tunnel.

A short distance away, Edward saw her and called out. "Mary! There you are. I've been looking for you. Where've you been? And what happened to your dress?"

"Yeah, I tripped in the dark. Look at this dirt on my dress."

Edward cocked his head slightly.

Mary brushed away as much dirt as possible. Despite her laughter, she could tell that he wasn't buying her story. "It's silly, really. You don't know this about me, Edward, but I'm very clumsy."

"I've been looking for you, that's all. Where'd you go?" he persisted. "I was hoping we could spend time together. You know, visit, get to know each other."

Mary was impressed that a man she hardly knew might be able to catch her in a lie. "Oh, I needed a little time, that's all," she brushed him off. "I had a headache and needed a break from all the noise. I'm not into crowds. Then I tripped. Anyway, let's visit now."

As they walked and talked, Ena and Jorge approached them. "We've been looking around for you, Mary. Wow . . . your dress," Ena said, turning to Edward with a questioning look on her face. "Edward, what happened to her?"

"Don't look at me. She claims she tripped and, regrettably, I wasn't with her to catch her fall," Edward reported defensively.

"Hey guys, I'm standing right here – and I'm fine. End of story. How are you two enjoying your celebration? This has been a spectacular day!"

"Why don't the two of you come back to the tables with Jorge and me? There's still food left, and we can get you cleaned up."

As they walked Ena gently pulled Mary aside and whispered in her ear, "Are you all right? He didn't try anything, did he?"

"Of course not. He's very nice."

"Good, because I think he's smitten with you. He told Jorge that he thought you were smart and beautiful."

"Really?" Mary said, hugging Ena as they walked. "I can't thank you enough for a picture-perfect day, well, outside of a muddy hemline."

CHAPTER 25

CELEBRATION TALK

"So, you and Edward, huh?" Ena meddled as the girls walked through the work hallway. "Jorge told me you two have seen each other quite a few times since the party. But you didn't think to mention that? Edward keeps telling Jorge how great you are."

"Ena, are we kids again? I've seen him a few times. Don't go making anything big out of it. And obviously we know one more thing about Edward. He can't keep a secret."

"Now who's in a huff? I'm not making a big deal out of anything. But the very fact that you didn't mention it and that you're continuing to see him means you're . . . interested, right?"

"I like him. Are you happy now?"

Ena added a self-congratulatory bounce to her step.

"How are things going with you and Jorge, now that you're officially paired and all?"

"I enjoy being with him. I really do."

Mary couldn't help thinking how odd the pairing of Ena and Jorge seemed. They had only met a short time ago and now they were committed by contract to have a child. This and the fact that they seemed to enjoy the arrangement were almost too hard to accept. How could Ena be glowing? Her acceptance of this arrangement with a stranger, as good a guy as Jorge seemed to be, was difficult to comprehend.

"Mary, I want you to be happy, but you realize that Edward is on the pairing list, don't you? For your own sake, maybe you shouldn't get too attached. Maybe just keep it light."

"Practicing your parenting skills already?"

"It's none of my business, just that I care about you. Alright, no more talk about Edward. What'd you think of our pairing ceremony?"

"I had so much fun. Thank you for asking me. It was a true highlight of my life."

"It was perfect, wasn't it? Thank you for agreeing to be my witness. I wouldn't want anyone else by my side. You're my best friend, you know. A little uptight, but I can live with that," she said smiling.

"Thanks, I think."

"You looked gorgeous in that dress, too, even if it did get suspiciously dirty by the end of the evening."

"Clumsy. I had a headache, so I thought I'd rest away from the crowd for a few minutes, but it was dark and when I got up, my shoe must have caught on a small hole or something. Before I knew it, I tripped and fell. I went down."

"If you say so. Seeing Edward again?"

"As a matter of fact, I am. And you can wipe that grin off your face. I told you, don't make more of it than it is. I'd appreciate it if you don't say any more about it to Jorge. Our talk is between us."

"I know that, but Jorge is Edward's close friend. They can talk about whatever they want, including the fact that he likes you *and* he's on the list."

"Damn it, Ena, stop pushing, will you?"

"Fine, fine, lets change the subject. Have the boys from the building contacted you again?"

Mary was caught a little off guard about the direct questioning about the boys. She and Ena had not discussed this subject since their last little confrontation. She did her best to keep her composure sufficiently to lie and not be caught. "Not yet," she replied. "But they obviously know how to contact me if they want to. Whatever. If the stuff about having a nephew is true then I hope they do," Mary said a little too defiantly, feeling her cheeks flush once again. "You haven't discussed anything about that meeting with Jorge, have you?"

"I told you before, what happened that night is between us. Strange that they haven't contacted you again. They wanted something from you." Ena starred at her curiously.

Mary felt her cheeks flush and worried that Ena might be able to read her expression. "Whatever. I should get back to my desk," Mary said, leaning in for a hug before her face gave her away. "You two threw a great party. I'll never forget it."

"Yeah, me neither."

CHAPTER 26

ENLIGHTENMENT

"Mary, back so soon?" Doc asked. "It's not yet time for your shots, is it?"

"I need to talk to you about something else," she confided, "something important." Mary thought back to Axel's question: did she trust Doc? She did, but he opened a sliver of doubt in her mind. Things she couldn't reconcile gnawed at her, like Doc's unsatisfactory answer about how he was able to get Joey admitted into the Care Place. On the other hand, she knew this was probably just silliness. Of course, she trusted him. He was her father's best friend, her guardian. Surely, she could ask him anything.

"Wait a minute. Did that kid from the funeral contact you again?"

"That's not why I'm here." Mary was getting better at avoiding the truth. "I need to ask you something that's been on my mind. Are you one of the doctors who makes someone an Outcast? I mean, do you administer the final booster shot?"

"I'm the man who delivers beautiful babies, who grow to become accomplished surrogate daughters who barge into my office to give me a hard time. You know this about me already. Why do you ask?"

"Well, I want to know . . . what's in the final shot?"

"Are you asking about the chemical makeup?"

"I mean, is it different from the shots you give me every month?"

"It's a booster shot, you know that. Why are you asking?"

"You're evading the question," she said, surprised by his response. "Is it different or not?" Doc's pause was deafening. "Oh, so you're not going to tell me?"

"I will, but you're not going to like the answer. Sometimes unpleasant things are necessary. They're in place to protect us, to protect you."

"Be straight with me. I'm not a child anymore."

"Sit," he ordered. "Generations ago, yes, they gave a booster shot. It bought the new Outcast additional time and helped to stave off disease for a while from complications from the rays to their immune systems."

"What's different now?"

Doc slumped in his chair and rubbed his face. "No, it's not like your monthly shots, not like what it used to be. It's a shot that guarantees things will be over quickly. It ensures the person will get sick sooner."

"What? Wait. That sounds like the opposite of what it used to be. Are you saying it's a lethal injection? That's. . . that's murder. Why would the Program do that? Did they do that to Joey? Did you know about this? You didn't tell me or . . . or stop it?"

"Listen to me. The new Outcast would eventually die anyway. This shot simply weakens their immune system, makes them more susceptible to diseases, like cancer. Bottom line, they die quicker. I assure you it's more humane, better than the alternative for everyone."

"What alternative? Everyone who? Hell, why doesn't the Program just poison or shoot them if that's what all of you believe?"

"Because, Mary, that would be murder. And anyway, we both know how important appearances are to the Program. They would never execute them. Think of the community outcry. "

"Oh . . . my . . . God! Who are you? I need to leave."

"Stop, Mary. The shot doesn't make them sick. It simply makes them more susceptible to disease."

"That's just semantics!"

"You're wrong. There's a big difference. And you don't have a right to look at me or talk to me that way. I told you, I don't give final injections. I had nothing to do with whatever shot Joey received. I loved that boy. If I could have done something to stop him from becoming an Outcast, I would have. It was out of my hands."

"How I hate deceit, all these lies. I hate this Program and everything about it."

"Per usual, you refuse to see the bigger picture. It's not only because it's more humane. They administer that shot because Outcasts have caused trouble. They've stolen from us, they've kidnaped our children. We can't stand by and let that happen."

"I don't believe that excuse to justify murder. The Program administers that injection knowing they'll become sick and die. What a horrible thing to do to another human being. And if they were going to get sick and die anyway, why bother?"

"I told you why. You don't want to believe that Outcasts have done bad things or that the Program has to take distasteful steps for the good of everyone, but it's the truth. You say you're not a kid anymore? Then stop being so naïve. Do you think people like us could stand up to an aggressive Outcast who has never had protection drugs? Of course not. When new healthy Outcasts steal or kidnap, we're defenseless. They're leaches on our resources, on our society. Yes, they give them the shot so they probably get sick sooner, less time for them to cause trouble and, with any luck, they die on their side of the wall."

"How unbelievably callous of you. It makes me sick, hearing you, a doctor, buy into this thinking. I hate what the Program has done to good people like you."

"Listen, you barged in here, demanding to know the truth, and I told you. I don't make the rules. You've been protected in ways you're not even aware of and handed everything. Maybe try being appreciative, happy."

"Be happy? Are you serious? My mother, father, and sister are dead, possibly murdered. Joey is dead from a shot that the Program gave him. How can I be happy? Who are these monsters making our rules? No, I'm not happy, and you shouldn't be happy, either."

"Don't tell me what I should be, young lady. And, for your information, Joey likely didn't die from the final injection. He lived much longer than its supposed effectiveness. Your father didn't do you any favors by saving that notebook. Things have changed. Back when that was written, Outcasts weren't stealing, threatening, or kidnaping people. Not everyone has the stomach to make rules that protect our way of life. The Program figured that little fact out long after your great grandfather finished his notebook. Do you think you could do it, be a Program leader? Easy to complain when you don't feel threatened, when you're always safe and protected by others."

"I could be a leader, and I wouldn't behave the way they do. I understand the difference between right and wrong. What they do is wrong, and shame on you for trying to justify their actions to me."

"You're convinced the Program is so bad, but who is starving, freezing, living on the streets? Who doesn't have a job or get life-saving medications? No one. Everyone is taken care of. We're a peaceful community. We share everything – the population, the resources, the food, the medicine. It's all carefully balanced, and the Program leaders manage that. Otherwise we would live in chaos."

"I can't believe what I'm hearing. You told me you thought the Program killed my family."

"Yes, I told you that, and I also maintain the Program does many good things. You forget. Your father broke the rules. He knew his decision would get him into trouble. But he did whatever he wanted to, even to the point of endangering his family and friends. I recognize my honesty in divulging that history has put both of us in jeopardy. So, it's your turn now. You tell me honestly, why are you asking about that booster shot? Who made you ask?"

How did he know? Mary's mind raced as she tried to think of a believable excuse. She realized she couldn't tell Doc that Axel had asked her to find out about the final injection, that could possibly jeopardize future visits with Jude.

"Joey got sick so quickly. He . . . he died too soon. That's not how life is supposed to be!"

"What are you talking about? He lived for years longer than any Outcast I know, and I did what I could for him. I helped get him into the Care Place, and you told me on many occasions that you thought they took good care of him until his last days. What else do you want from me?"

"I no longer think they took good care of him, and I can't believe you don't have any human compassion for the Outcasts."

"Compassion for Outcasts? You're talking to the wrong person. I won't support criminals and kidnappers. Now do you have anything else for me, or are we done here?"

Mary could feel her face warming and her heart rate climb. She needed to go, she thought, if she didn't want to experience another violent episode. She knew Doc wasn't the enemy. He was brainwashed by bad experiences. "If you're going to lump all Outcasts in the same basket, we're quite done," she said calmly. "You can't believe they murdered my family and at the same time think the Program is good. That's not rational."

"Your doctor and closest friend, not rational? OK. I can live with that. But let me remind you, both our lives are now in your hands. Say something outside this room about the final injection and see what happens – to both of us. I probably should have lied, but I didn't. I respect your right to know. I don't make the rules but, unlike others, I do not to break them and put people at risk."

Mary felt the sting of that statement, and it hurt to hear Doc's intentional cruelty. "Got it, Doc. Your secrets are safe with me." Mary said, no longer attempting to conceal her disdain. She had the answer Axel wanted but, in the process, probably lost a good friend.

"And you've told me a lot about yourself by not answering my question, young lady." With that, Doc left the examination room.

CHAPTER 27

TEST RESULTS

A few weeks passed before Axel surprised Mary, this time on her walk home from work. He pulled her into the recessed front entryway of an abandoned factory near the blue building. "Ready to see Jude again?"

"I wish you would quit sneaking up on me."

"No time for manners."

Axel quickly led Mary to a tunnel in the back alley of the factory. "We wanted to see if we could trust you to not tell anyone about the other tunnel. You didn't disappoint us. We're sealing this tunnel soon. It's too exposed, but it'll be all right for us to use tonight."

"I didn't tell anyone about the tunnel or our meeting."

"That was smart," he smiled. "But, of course, we knew that. I asked you to do something for me. Did you get it done?"

"How can you be sure I didn't tell anyone? Do you follow me around and listen to my conversations?" Mary asked, surprised that he knew she hadn't told anyone.

Axel waited for her answer. He knew she wanted to see Jude more than he needed confirmation about the contents of the final injection.

Mary broke the tense standoff. "I spoke to Doc. He's not involved with the final injections, but he knew about them." She paused, thinking how hard she been hard on Doc and that now, in a way, by answering Axel's question she was betraying him. She felt guilty.

"So, what did he say?"

Without Doc's efforts, Mary would never have been able to visit her brother. He didn't give Joey that final shot, and he didn't make the rules. Doc loved her brother and would have done anything for him. Yet here she was, dishonoring one of her best friends.

"Well?" He said displaying his impatience.

"The Program gives Outcasts something that impairs their immune systems and makes them get sick sooner and die quickly."

"And what now? Do you still trust him?"

"I do. He's a victim of the system, but he has no sympathy for Outcasts." Mary bowed her head sadly as she thought to herself that her brother had been one of those unfortunate people that had been given that final injection. She was confused by his lack of concern. "Axel did you hear what I said? The Program intentionally infects them. That's murder – and all you ask me is if I trust him?"

"I heard you."

"You're not surprised by this information?"

"Not surprised. Our spies move back and forth through the tunnels every day to collect intelligence. All you did was confirm what we already suspected."

"Then what was the point? That confrontation may have cost me a good friend." Now she really felt guilty for betraying Doc's trust. "Who told you about the booster shot?"

Axel's face reddened, and he gritted his teeth and growled. "For the last time, I said to drop it. Now do you want to visit with Jude or not?"

Hearing his tone of voice Mary, backed down. "Of course, I want to, but I don't appreciate being manipulated. That's going to stop if trust is the goal here."

"You help us, we help you. It's that simple," he said, now calmer, making sure he had the final word. "He's waiting. Later I have something I want you to see."

"Oh wait, damn it! Damn it. I forgot someone's coming by my apartment later."

Exasperated, he yelled, "You either want to see Jude or not."

"I do, I want to see Jude . . . but you expect me to drop everything on a moment's notice, as if I have no other plans? Maybe next time, you can . . ."

"Do you honestly think I operate at your convenience?"

"Never mind. I'll make up something. Fine, let's go."

As they came out of the tunnel Mary saw a small group of people who appeared to be performing a ritual, bowing up and down and waving their arms high in the air. When they saw Mary, they stopped. Mary pulled back.

"They're gawking mostly because you look like Joey and Jude and your dad and partly because you're a pale white woman with red hair," he said, laughing. "They are praying to the Lokapalas to give thanks for our land and food and for protection from our enemy."

"Lokapalas?"

"Yes, our god."

"But who do they want protection from?"

"You. The people on the other side of the wall."

"And you said my dad came here? So those people know who I am, that I'm Joey's sister?"

"They do. Otherwise, it wouldn't be safe to bring you. Wait here, I'll get you in a minute."

Mary found the wait excruciating. In the distance, Raj and another person from the group walked over to Axel with Jude. Raj acknowledged Mary with a tilt of his head. Finally, Axel walked back toward her holding the little boy's hand. Mary gingerly approached, hoping not to startle him. Jude did not back away.

As Mary played with the boy, an overwhelming feeling of happiness came over her. She loved storytelling and playing hand games with her nephew.

After ten minutes Axel declared, "OK, you two, it's getting late. Jude needs to go. The group is waiting for him. Anyway, I need to show you something outside the dead zone before dark."

An older man from the group came and took Jude's hand from her, and they marched away. Mary lingered, waving goodbye kisses to Jude who, as he waddled off, kept turning his head back and stumbling over himself to see her.

Axel tugged on Mary's right arm, "Come on. You had your visit. We need to move now."

Reluctantly she turned toward him and started walking. "What did you say about a dead zone? Like for people's ashes after they die?"

"No, we don't burn our dead. Look down at your feet."

Despite his encouragement to keep moving Mary stopped and bent over with her hands on her hips staring at the ground. "Uh-huh, I see little plants, but . . ."

"The elders tell us that before the Program invaders moved the wall farther onto our land, they sent their guards here to destroy anything in their path. They killed many resisters.

They tore down the old buildings and cut down all the trees and plants and hauled everything away. When the land was cleared, they sprayed plant poison everywhere. Then they built the new wall.

"The elders prayed for help from the invaders and the Lokapalas answered their prayers. She punished the guards for the bad things they had done. Within days of spraying that poison, some of the guards died. Now come on, let's get out of here. Hardly anything grows here anymore. Let's hurry. I want to show you a better place."

For a slight moment, Mary was distracted by what he had said. She wondered if the Outcasts prayed to their god for protection from the Program, then who was more powerful, the Lokapalas, Ena's god, or her father's god? Whose god was best? But her father had taught her there was only one god, the Creator of the universe. Then whose side was the Creator on?

She followed Axel down a dark, rocky slope until they came upon a large field that was surrounded on three sides by trees. Looking upward in amazement Mary gawked at the rows and rows of trees.

"Wow! So many tall trees, and they are covered in leaves. It fantastic, just like the pictures in the old books."

Realizing that she was fixated on the grove of trees, he pointed downward with his finger.

"Trees, yes, but I want you to see something different. Take a good look at this field. See how full and healthy-looking these plants are. This is where we grow our food. What do you think?"

"Ah, I don't know. I've never seen a field like this. So many tall plants. Actually, I've never seen a field before."

"I guessed you hadn't," he said, chuckling. "I'll tell you something else that will surprise you. Your dad saw this."

"My dad? I wish he had told me about this place when he was alive."

"When you get back, I want you to check out the plants growing in the Program fields. That's your next assignment. Check out your fields."

"OK, but how. . . ?"

"No more questions. Just do it. Time to leave."

*   *   *

On the Program side of the tunnel, Mary felt a chill in the night air as she walked back to her apartment. What an incredible evening, she thought. She had played with her nephew, seen a grove of tall trees, a field full of plants, and learned about a new god. The world she had grown up in now seemed small.

When she arrived home, a note was on posted the door. Her heart sank. She guessed it was from Edward. She knew he would be annoyed, especially since she had been the one to invite him over. She was torn between seeing Jude on the fly and planning her evenings with Edward. At this point all she could do was hope he would understand. She loved how their commitment to each other was growing. The last thing she wanted was to disappoint another important man in her life.

CHAPTER 28

EDWARD

Mary woke up from her nap to a banging on her door. It was Edward, both miffed that she hadn't been home and anxious to see her. "I came by last night at your request, but you weren't here. You did ask me over, didn't you?" Once he saw her face, his frustration melted away. "What's going on? I thought we had agreed to meet?"

"I'm sorry. My boss gave me something to work on at the last minute, I couldn't leave," she lied. "Please come in," she said, peering down the hall.

"Look," Edward softly scolded, once Mary locked the door, "Let's set basic boundaries. If you're not going to be here, don't ask me over."

"I know. I couldn't get away . . . I wish I had a way of letting you know."

"On top of that, when I came by your nosy neighbor caught me hanging out in front of your door. She started quizzing me – who was I, what I was doing, how did I know you."

"Damn. That was probably Adrienne. What did you tell her?"

"I made up something about a work project that I needed to talk to you about, but I'm sure she didn't believe me. I had to tell her my name and where we worked, or she would have gotten more suspicious. That woman is crazy."

"Yeah, I've had run-ins with her, too. She's not to be trusted."

"Then this afternoon, this guy Peter I sometimes work with tells me that a manager came by his office along with a guard, asking questions about me."

"They were asking questions about you? Why?"

"Got me. They wanted to know how often Peter and I work together, how I interact with others. The manager wanted to know if he thought I was I good at my job. Did he have any issues with me, was I a problem, stuff like that. Then he asked if he thought I was a loyal worker and loyal to the Program."

"Loyal to the Program? Uh-oh, now that's not good. Wonder why the inquisition?"

"It could have been a routine Program loyalty check, but it also could have been instigated by that damn neighbor of yours. Anyway, Peter is a good guy. He told them he only works with me sporadically, but when we have worked together things have gone smoothly. He said I was a very good worker and completely loyal to the Program. I couldn't thank him enough."

"That does make me wonder who else they might have talked to about you? Anyone else say anything? What about your boss?"

"No one other than Peter mentioned anything. Of course, that doesn't mean no one else was interviewed. People get scared and go silent after they're approached by the Program."

"No doubt."

"But I don't think this was coincidence. I think that woman neighbor of yours snitched on me."

"Maybe. We'll never know. Come here. You've had a rough 24 hours. Let's put it aside, OK?"

"Listen, Mary, all this sneaking around we're doing is weirding me out. And, if I get paired, we certainly won't be able to—"

Mary cut him off. She didn't want to hear Edward's lecture on Program rules. "I hear you. It weirds me out, too, but I promise, when I ask you over next time, I'll be here. You won't have to hang outside my door ever again."

"Well, if I weren't on that damn pairing list, we wouldn't have to sneak around. We could be together, live together." As the words tumbled out, Edward pulled back, worrying that it was too soon to talk fantasy.

"Are you saying you want to live together? You would get off the list . . . for me? Once you're off the list, you'll never be able to have children. You probably wouldn't be allowed back on the list, either. Think of all the things you'd be losing – no kids, no pairing ceremony, no nice apartment."

Edward pulled Mary close. "I want to spend every moment with you, not a stranger on a stupid list. I'd love to get off. You know I would."

"Well, here's a crazy thought. If we could convince them there's something mentally or physically wrong with you, we might be able keep you off the list."

"Is that possible?"

"I told you that's how Doc kept me off that list."

"That's you. I guarantee no doctor is going to do that for me."

"Why's that?"

"Because there's nothing wrong with me."

"So hard to be you, Mr. Perfect," she said, patting his back.

"Yeah, it kind of is," he said, lifting his face as he came in for a kiss.

"I'll talk to Doc – who, by the way, is not very happy with me right now. He's had enough time to cool off, I think, but I should probably ask nicely."

"What did you do to upset him?"

"Why do you assume *I'm* the guilty party? We had a father-daughter spat, is all. Anyway, if Doc gets you off that list, you might never be able to get back on."

"I told you, I don't care. Let him get me off so we can be together, which is what we both want. Right?"

"Yes."

In the past, Mary had always been able to wrap Doc around her little finger, but would things be different now? Would he take such a big risk for someone he didn't know? She imagined she'd have to bend on one knee and apologize before she could ask for his help. "Now," she said, grabbing Edward's collar with a coy smile, "Why don't you stay and let me make it up to you for leaving you hanging the other night."

"Sounds like an invitation I can't refuse."

CHAPTER 29

MURDER

Mary was dying to see Ena and Jorge's new apartment, so when Ena extended the invitation for her to visit after work, she grabbed her coat and started off.

No sooner than she had moved away from her desk and stepped outside, Reyanne approached her out of nowhere. "Mary, wait up. I need to talk to you."

"You always seem to be surprising people, Reyanne. Any chance whatever juicy gossip you have can wait until tomorrow? I'm running late."

"This isn't gossip. I'm extremely upset, and this can't wait. I'll walk with you."

"OK, walk. Why do you sound so angry?"

Reyanne looked in both directions, making sure no one was listening, then leaned in and whispered, "Mary, this is serious, and you're one of the few friends I can talk to about this. People are disappearing! This friend of ours who works with my Ajay, Gus Weisman, he's an architect. The guy and his pregnant partner have completely disappeared. Ajay said Gus was vocal at work about the extravagance of that place they're designing for those committee bastards. Now this couple is gone. We're so upset and really worried about them. Ajay's convinced that, for some reason, the Program is desperate and is doing terrible things. Mary, they might be systematically eliminating people – murdering them! Shit, you have to think this is frightening, right?"

Reyanne was unaware that, to Mary, murder was a particularly personal subject, but it wasn't something she was about to share with the company gossip. "Murder? Don't you think maybe you two are jumping to conclusions? Being a little paranoid? What do you actually know about what happened to this couple?"

"I'm pissed. Don't you dare accuse me of being paranoid. The couple has disappeared. Damn it, listen to me. They're gone! We went by their apartment and a new couple has moved in. And that couple didn't know anything about Gus or his partner. I'm telling you, they may have been murdered."

"OK, OK, I see you're upset, calm down." No sooner than Mary had spoken those words than she began wondering if she was now sounding more like Doc than herself. "Gone, but that doesn't mean they were murdered. If Ajay said the guy was a complainer, then isn't it just as likely the Program reassigned him somewhere else as punishment? Maybe he's working somewhere in a shitty factory or out in the fields? If that's what happened, they've probably been moved to an apartment closer to their new work assignments."

"Ajay's convinced that's not what happened. They evaporated, I'm telling you. He thinks those bastards did something bad, really bad to them."

"Reyanne, there's no reason to jump to extreme conclusions yet, especially murder. I hear everything you're saying. I'm taking you seriously, but what do you want me to say?"

"Well, you can start by saying you believe me. Hell, you can also say we need to do something about this. That's why I'm talking to you. And I don't think you're taking this seriously."

"Reyanne, please stop," she said, taking Reyanne's hand, "I am. You're right, it certainly is possible something bad happened to them."

"So, what should we do?'

"Give me a moment to think," she said, mimicking Doc's go-to when he didn't know what to say. Then she realized the solution was right in front of her. "I know someone who might be able to get some answers, see if they've been reassigned to the factories or fields. In fact, I'll be seeing this friend tonight."

"Good, and your friend can find that out?"

"Yes . . . well, maybe. He's a manager and interacts with lots of different people in his job, not like us, so he has connections. I'll try to see what I can find out from him but, in the meantime, you have to promise you'll stay calm. No more freaking out, or all this anger will get you in trouble. So, I said I'd try to help, and now I have to go. Go home, Reyanne. Stay calm and go home." Mary waved her hand, turned herself around, and walked off toward Ena and Jorge's new apartment.

"I'm counting on you, and I'm not freaking out." she called out as Mary walked away, cringing at the thought of people being murdered.

The short conversation impacted Mary more than she wanted to let on. If people were dis[illegible]gram was capable of murder, which m[illegible]n family had been murdered and th[illegible]. Once again, the bad feelings she had temporarily suppressed about the fire resurfaced, and her thoughts turned to revenge. More than ever, she was resolved to understand what her father had been up to and why her family had been targeted. Reyanne had no idea the rage she had just unleashed.

CHAPTER 30

ENA'S NEW DIGS

Ena loved many things about her new life. Her wonderful partner, the big furnished apartment, and a larger food budget represented the beginning of a dream she had embraced since she was a young girl: to be paired and have a big family. She was giddy about the potential of her new life, even if her childhood had forced her to be a realist.

Sometimes coworkers, even friends, mistook Ena to be naïve or in denial, but those characterizations were mistaken. Ena was neither. She was fully aware of how the Program made life difficult for common workers like herself. The Program was always present, always in control, even when it came to her personal life. It was their purview, not hers or Jorge's, as to whether she would be allowed to have a big family. They dictated her life down to the work she did at her boring job, where she felt her talents and intellect were definitely underutilized. They controlled the availability or scarcity of food, clothes, furnishings – everything. When it came to getting the upgraded apartment, which she appreciated, she knew the Program controlled where it would be located, which unit it would be, and what used furniture would be included. She understood that many times choice was not available to workers.

It wasn't that Ena was unaware of the restrictions in her life or that she blindly followed the rules, rather it was that she accepted her situation and still found a way to be happy. She wished her friends could understand that about her, that she literally willed herself to be happy. Now, how nice it would be, she thought, if Mary could at least get on board and rejoice in her happiness. Tonight would tell, because her best friend was coming over for dinner to see her new apartment. Ena was hopeful that the conversation would be pleasant, and everyone would enjoy themselves.

*   *   *

Before knocking, Mary told herself not to spoil Ena's fun by mentioning the upsetting conversation that just transpired with Reyanne or by pointing out how unfairly the Program treated people. Mary realized Ena's apartment would be much nicer than those assigned to single people. While that pissed her off, she vowed to show the face of a good guest for her friend's sake. She'd ask Jorge to check about Ajay's friend when she could speak to him privately, but tonight she would be gracious.

The grand tour commenced immediately after she arrived. Ena made big gestures as she pointed to the walk-in kitchen, which was only slightly larger than the one for singles. Her point of pride, however, was that the kitchen didn't have a bed in it.

As they walked around the apartment, Mary got a whiff of a faint chemical odor she recognized but couldn't identify.

"It's paint," Ena squealed. "I didn't even care that the only color they had was the same old gray. Our walls have been freshly painted. Can you believe it?"

The odor reminded Mary of her childhood and how much attention the grimy walls in her own apartment needed. She knew that wasn't likely to happen, given recent scarcity issues.

Ena continued the guided tour into the main room, which contained twice as much furniture as Mary had ever seen — a slightly worn couch, large cushiony chair, and dining table with four chairs near the kitchen wall. A bookcase leaned in the corner of the room, flanked by a floor lamp adjacent to the table and chairs. Walking on, Ena took her friend's hand and gestured to the couple's bedroom.

This room included a small closet, nightstand, and dresser. The large bed was one of the few perks that average paired workers could get.

"What can I say, Ena? You have . . . room!" Mary realized she had to do better. "And, how nice – a real bedroom."

Ena beamed. "We love it! It's wonderful to have a real bedroom, you know? No bed in the kitchen!"

"It is wonderful."

Before Ena could judge whether Mary's tone was sincere, Jorge answered a knock on the door. "Edward! You came. Good to see you, man!"

Mary, walked around the corner, surprised to see him. "They didn't tell me you were coming," she said, looking at her friends.

"Jorge let me know you were going to be here and invited me to tag along. He didn't think you'd mind sharing the tour."

"Not at all," she said, giving him a hug. "This is so nice, the four of us together. And, Jorge, I was just telling Ena, I love your new place. Thank you both for the invitation."

Jorge looked at Ena. He had been trying to reassure her that Edward brought out the best in Mary, and now she could see it, too. "Well, the two of you were witnesses at our pairing. You're our friends."

Jorge grabbed Edward and gave him a manly squeeze, "Best friends! Ena has been dying to have you over to show this place off. Sit down. Let's visit. Ladies, did you know that Edward and I grew up together? We were best friends long before we worked at the center. He worked there first and became shipping coordination manager. I joined later. Of course, my job is better than his. It's much more physically demanding to work as the supervisor on the loading docks."

"I've been told by reliable sources," Edward added, "that my buddy Jorge here can load and unload faster than any of the dock workers who report to him. And I've also been told that his crew is in awe of his strength and stamina."

"In awe?" Jorge replied, somewhat embarrassed by the compliment. "That may be stretching a little, but my guys respect me," Jorge said. "I still don't understand how you work at a desk all day. Doesn't that make you crazy?"

Edward stood and motioned to Jorge to follow his lead, then jokingly he pushed against his smaller, more physically stout friend who was unmovable and pushed back. "Make me crazy? No, not at all, buddy. I love my work, who needs weather?" he said, laughing. "Not everyone thinks it's a dream job to work where it's freezing cold or burning hot."

The two men continued pushing against each other as the girls looked on amused by the testosterone fest. "You know, Eddie boy, you're doing pretty well standing your ground for a kid who was always so sick and scrawny," Jorge remarked to his taller adversary. The two of them pushed as hard as they could. Neither wanted to be the first to yield. Then Edward tickled Jorge, and they both busted out laughing.

"No fair, man," Jorge whined.

"Sorry, but not my problem," Edward raised his hands and backed away, laughing.

"You were always the sorry one, brother," Jorge said, shaking his head as he sat and wrapped his arm around Ena.

Hearing that Edward had health problems surprised Mary and piqued her curiosity. "Wait, you're saying Edward was scrawny as a kid?"

"Tell her, Eddie boy, tell her how I used to have to stick up for you all the time when we were kids."

"Ladies I'm afraid that what Little Man forces me to confess is correct," Edward responded as he sat down. "I was sickly. In fact, my mom and dad were worried that the Program would declare me defective, make me an Outcast when I reached puberty. But that didn't happen because at around eleven I became healthier and bigger and . . . I filled out."

Even as he kept up the façade, his friend Jorge's words stopped him cold. A flood of memories reminded him how often his mom took him to the doctor and how often he got sick to his stomach and could not eat. His chronic illness reminded him of how inferior he felt to the other children, especially other boys. None of them – not even Jorge – realized how much scar tissue that illness left. None of them knew that he still had to remind himself daily that he was all right, as strong and worthy as anyone else.

"From where I'm sitting, you certainly filled out nicely," Ena teased. Mary and Ena cheered as Edward rolled his sleeves up and flexed his biceps.

Jorge played along. "Hey, you don't need to go looking at my buddy that way. You've got me now."

"Don't worry, honey, you're the only one for me." Ena leaned over and kissed Jorge, and he hugged her back.

Edward sat next to Mary and hooted. Jorge playfully kicked at Edward's shin and kept missing. They all laughed.

Mary was pleased to see these childhood friends horsing around. She liked seeing Ena and Jorge so comfortable and affectionate. She enjoyed being this familiar with friends, and she was crazy about Edward. Her fantasy, though she knew it never could happen, was to be paired with this man she loved and bear his children. This must be what *happy* feels like, she thought, as if her memory had been wiped clean.

More than anything, Ena wanted Mary to be happy, but what would happen to her once Edward was paired? Would her loyalty be caught between Edward's new partner and Mary? The inevitability gnawed at her.

After visiting a while longer, Ena brought out a pasta dish she had prepared in her new kitchen. She had more food coupons now that she was paired, and she invited guests to enjoy her bounty. The four friends ate and drank as they continued to laugh and tell stories.

Another hour passed before Edward stood and announced that he needed his beauty rest. While Jorge and Ena laughed, Edward winked at Mary. He grabbed his glass and made a final toast to the new couple, wishing them well in their new digs. Everyone stood as he thanked them for the invitation. Then he dramatically dipped Mary in his arms and kissed her. Edward took her by surprise, and she blushed. He had never dared to do anything like that in front of others. It was dangerous and embarrassing, but she liked that about him.

"Slow down, big guy! How much have you had to drink?" Jorge questioned, walking Edward out of the apartment and down the walkway.

"Whoa, after that grand exit, I think it's time for me to leave, too," Mary said.

"Well, before you go," Ena said, walking into her bedroom, "come back here for a minute, will you?"

Mary instantly recognized the shift in Ena's demeanor. She could feel a lecture coming.

Before Mary stepped fully into the bedroom, Ena pounced. "You do realize he'll be paired soon, right? It's none of my business but are you sure you know what you're doing?"

"Come on, Ena. We had such a good time tonight. Can't you quit worrying for once? We enjoy each other's company. Plain and simple."

"Mary, I love you, but we both know it's not that simple. It's obvious that guy is crazy about you. He couldn't take his eyes off you. I'm just worried about the both of you once he's paired. Hon, you're playing with fire here."

"You're my friend, and I appreciate the concern, but it's under control . . . and, Ena, respectfully, like you said, this really is none of your business."

"OK." Why couldn't Mary see the inevitable, Ena thought, that this was going to be a disaster, resulting in heartache all around?

"It's late. You've done a beautiful job hosting us, and your new place is great. I'm very happy for you," Mary said, reaching out and to give her friend a hug.

Ena reciprocated, though uncomfortably. "Well, I'm glad you came. Do you want Jorge to walk you home?"

"Nah, I'm fine," Mary replied, gathering her coat and purse. "See you at work? Good night, Jorge. Thanks again for the invitation." Mary breezed along the apartment walkway and into the night air as Ena and Jorge waved arm in arm from their doorway.

Around the corner, Mary saw Edward waiting. She slipped her hand into his, and the two kept walking.

* * *

"Ah, now I'm tired," Jorge yawned. "I think our first dinner party in the new digs went well, don't you? Everyone seemed to have a good time."

"Sure, it went fine, it's just . . ." Ena paused, gazing at the table where the four of them had sat to visit.

"Just what? I thought everything went great."

"So, you not at all worried about the two of them? Because I am. I'm really concerned about Mary. She's had such a tough life. When he gets paired, which he surely will, she's going to be devastated. She pretends like she has things under control, but she doesn't. And I can't talk any sense into her. She's too stubborn."

"Ena, darling, they're our friends, but that's none of our business. We need to stay out of all that. They're both adults. They know what they are doing. And if you ask me, I think those two should be together. If the Program doesn't let that happen, then that's a damn shame."

"Well, when Edward's paired, we'll have to pick up the broken pieces for both of them."

"Then that's what we'll do, that's what friends are for. We'll be here for them."

Ena was resigned, for the moment, that there was nothing she could do to fix the situation. "That's not the only thing bothering me. I didn't mention it earlier because I didn't want to spoil our party."

"OK . . ."

"I heard a rumor today at work. The Program is cutting back on food for singles and paired couples who don't have children. That's us, Jorge."

"I haven't heard that one, but I wouldn't be surprised. We've been scheduling fewer pickups from the farms, so there might be truth to the rumor. I heard some interesting gossip myself this afternoon. Want to hear it?"

"You know I do."

"So, the guards dragged away this guy named Batista, who works at one of the processing plants, and an Outcast today. Caused quite a commotion. Evidently, this Batista was caught diverting finished goods to the Outcast. Pretty brazen, huh? Guards caught them both in the act. I'm betting tonight things are not too good for either one of them."

"Gosh, will anything bad happen to them?"

"I don't know, Ena, that's pretty serious stuff. What they did won't be taken lightly. But, for sure, they'll make an example of the Outcast."

"How so?"

"Parade him around for a while. Imply that Outcasts are the problem, the reason for all the scarcity."

Ena thought back to the escapade at the blue building and what Axel and Raj had said. It made her think that maybe those boys had been telling the truth, and they really had been Outcasts. That gave her a slight chill. She would break her promise with Mary and tell Jorge about that trip, just not tonight.

"But that can't be true."

"No, of course it's not true, but that won't matter to the Program."

"Hmm, disturbing. Hey, hon? We really did put on a good dinner party tonight, didn't we?"

Jorge wrapped his arms around her from behind and squeezed gently. "We certainly did. Now shouldn't we go and try to protect our food allowance?"

"What? Oh, you mean my rumor?" she asked, smiling. "Yeah, let's go work on that. Beat you to bed."

CHAPTER 31

THE FIRST TO BLINK

Mary continued her monthly clinic appointments with Doc, but their stubborn resolve meant they were cordial, not much more. She wanted to thaw their relationship, not just because she needed a favor, but because she missed him. For détente to take place, she would have to make the first move.

As Doc approached, Mary pulled him close and hugged him for an extra moment longer than usual. "I love you, Doc."

"Young lady, I thought we weren't talking?" He couldn't hide how glad he was to hug her. "OK, let go, we're talking." With that, the ice between them broke.

"Of course we're talking. We just strongly disagree about things, that's all." Mary worked hard not to sound smug.

"We do argue well. Now tell me, what can I do for you?"

"Doc, really, I am sorry that we fought. And what makes you think I need something? Can't I just miss you? I know you didn't do anything bad to Joey. You're the reason he was admitted into the Care Place, so thank you for that. I'm upset because the Program gave him that final injection."

"That's completely understandable."

"But I am grateful that you helped him. You've always been a good friend to me and my family, especially my dad."

"I loved them, and I love you like my own. I am not mad at you. I am worried about where you will end up with your intense frustration toward the Program. I've been . . . overprotective of you."

"Doc, you may not always be able to protect me."

"Tell me why you're here. I know you must want something, otherwise you'd be far too stubborn to be the first to apologize."

She brightened. "You do know me well, I'll give you that. But let me clarify, I didn't actually apologize, did I?"

"Coy as ever, which means I'm right. You need something. Tell me."

"As a matter of fact, I do need your help, but it's sort of for someone else."

"Well, now, there's a twist."

"There's this guy . . ."

"From the pairing celebration . . ."

"Yes, Edward. Was I that obvious?" Mary looked up, but she couldn't read Doc's face. "Anyway, he's on the list or soon will be. We're both afraid he could be paired soon."

"Let's see, so you want me to find a way to get him off the list? Before he's paired? Like I did for you?"

"Yes, that's it! Could you? Would you? I mean, is that possible?"

"Without seeing him and examining his medical history, I can't say for sure, but if there is, it might not be without risk to him or me. Surely you realize, even if this works out, that you two will never be a sanctioned pair. Neither one of you will be deemed suitable to have children. This is very serious. Are you both sure this what you want? No children, ever? And if you became pregnant, the Program would force you to have an abortion. At that point, life could get worse for both of you and maybe for me."

"I've told you I never want to raise children in the Program anyway, so that won't happen. I just want to know if you'd look into things for us?"

"Possibly. First, I need to decide if Edward is good enough for you. Second, I would need to accurately assess if this guy truly realizes how stubborn and self-righteous you can be. Third, if he is ready for a life of pain," he said, displaying an ear-to-ear grin across his chubby face. "I hope this means you're distracted enough by this guy that you've stopped thinking about Program revenge," Doc continued. "That's a dead end, a place with no future. Remember you can destroy what you two have if you get caught messing with the Program. Make the choice to forget about justice and focus on leading a happy life."

Mary shook both his arms like jump ropes. "So, you'll see him? You'd do this for me?"

"I'll need to see if I can transfer him, so he becomes my patient. Then we'll find a believable reason why he's not fit to have children. If all that happens, then they'd likely remove him from the list. But Mary, he'd have to agree to go along with whatever I dream up. Is he the type of guy who can work with me?"

"Whatever you say. Here's an idea, what about Anger Management?"

"Oh no, that one belongs to you. Leave Edward to me. He needs to understand the dangers of faking a diagnosis. Send him soon, but I make no promises."

"He'll be there, don't you worry. He does whatever I tell him."

"No doubt.. Now tell me more about the man."

CHAPTER 32

FULL DISCLOSURE

As Mary opened the door to her apartment, Edward grabbed her and twirled her around. "I think we've got this," he exclaimed. "I saw Doc, and the plan is that I've got an inherited genetic disease, Tay-Sachs, and with that I should never be allowed to have children. He'll say it was missed in the previous genetic testing."

"And, the Program will take his word for it?" After he put her down, Mary pulled him closer and kissed him, "That's fantastic news!"

"I feel really good about this. I know it's going to work. And Doc told me stories about you. Like, how he had delivered you as a baby and how your dad was his best friend. He was surprised by how little you told me about your family. He also said you were just like your father and your brother, stubborn, but I told him I already knew that."

"Why would either of you jump to *stubborn*? If I'm stubborn, I am in good company."

Edward tilted his head and then thought wiser. "Once we are together, will we live at your place or mine?"

"Hey, slow down, sweetheart. Doc's right. You deserve to know much more about me and my family before this goes any further, and you might not be so eager to get off that list after you hear this."

Edward sat down. "All right, you've got my attention. Let's have it."

"Well, there are things I probably should have told you earlier. I am involved in stuff you may not like."

"Are you talking about that night at the party, when you ran off with that other guy?"

"He's part of it, but . . . . Wait, how did you know about him?"

"I don't know who he is, but when I saw you both running and him sort of dragging you along, I was worried you might be in trouble, and I went after you. I followed you both but then I realized you wanted to be alone with him."

Mary was stunned.

"That's it, then? You're still involved with this guy?"

"No, no, no. Aw, you came after me? That's so sweet! You were worried about me, even back then, and you hardly knew me."

"So, am I competing with another guy or not?"

"Competing? That guy is a just a boy, a teenager."

"A teenager?"

Mary proceeded to tell Edward everything – about Joey, her parents, the fire, the envelope and notebook, and the meetings with Jude, Axel, and Raj.

As she talked, Edward quietly listened, hanging on her every word. She tried to interpret his expressions and wondered if he was having a hard time believing what she was saying. "Listen, this is who I am. I'm the girl with weird stuff going on. I can't blame you if you don't want to be part of my dangerous life. I wouldn't like it, but I'd understand."

"Give me a minute to let this sink in," he said, shaking his head.

"Take your time. You needed to know before you got off the list. Look, it's not too late. We can tell Doc to stop."

"That's not what I want, but I do wish you had trusted me. You shouldn't have waited until now to tell me all this. I mean, you really think the Program murdered your family?"

"I think so. I was worried the Outcasts might not let me continue to see Jude if they found out I told someone. I saw myself as a girl in trouble with the Program. Who wants to be with that person? I was afraid that I might scare you off."

"What did you think I'd do? Run? Run to the leadership committee? I'm crazy about you, Mary. I've been crazy about you since the day we met. You're all I ever think about."

"Ah, you mean the world to me, Edward, which is why if they did murder my family, getting more involved with me could be dangerous for you. You need to consider that."

"Don't you think it's too late to worry about that now? Hell, almost everyone knows I'm involved with you and, if you haven't noticed, I'm not going anywhere."

"You're not frightened?"

"Maybe, and I'm sure I'll have more questions – you're wonderful, you're dangerous, your life is a lot to take in – so can I trust you won't hide anything else from me?"

"Yes. I want us to be together."

"I want that, too. Tell me one last thing: how did your dress get dirty that night?"

"I didn't fall. That was a lie, although I could have fallen – I mean, I am clumsy, I didn't lie about that."

"Clumsy, I can believe. I've seen you run."

'Uh-huh, thanks. Way to charm a girl. Anyway, the tunnel I told you about was narrow, and we had to move fast. I probably brushed against the muddy walls as I climbed down the ladder into the tunnel, too. I was so elated to see Jude, I was on the ground playing with him in no time. I wasn't thinking about my dress. You noticed the stains before I did."

"An Outcast brother in the Care Place, clandestine meetings with children of Outcasts in abandoned buildings, trips through secret tunnels to the other side of the wall? I mean, holy shit, Mary, you're are a regular dissident."

"I don't think of myself as a dissident."

"Really?" he said, smiling, "Compared to my life? No, compared to everyone I know? You lead an incredibly dangerous life. Now I understand why Ena said you are the most exciting person she knows."

"She said that . . . about me?"

"She did, and she was right," he said, hugging her waist. "I don't know who is more likely to come after you, the Program or the Outcasts, but from now on I want to be a part of everything. And when I get off that list, we're going to celebrate."

"Oh yeah, with a big party – and we're inviting Outcasts!"

CHAPTER 33

PREPPING FOR THE FIELDS

Mary spent most of her workdays dreaming up discrete ways to meet Edward. On weeknights, during the busy dinner hour, he managed to slip past her nosy neighbors and spend long evenings at her apartment. He revealed how his dislike of the Program began as a sickly child. Mary retold stories of Joey's crazy talk and her regrets now that she knew the truth from her interactions with Outcasts. They consoled each other. After a bedtime review of the details for their next rendezvous, Edward would slip away before dawn.

Like all Program children, Edward had been taught that Outcasts were violent, dangerous leaches on the society. However, after hearing how Mary's brother became an Outcast, Edward questioned what he knew.

"It's so damn disturbing to think about how many people may have been tossed out to die like that. My parents told me that I could have been one of them if they had declared me a defective at puberty."

"What I can't understand is that intelligent people we know are fine with how the Program treats Outcasts. That includes Doc. I don't know why, but he doesn't like Outcasts. He even views the final injections as humane."

Edward was taken aback. "Really? It's not like I know him well, but that doesn't sound like the guy I met. He appears to be a caring, kind person, not at all callous."

"Hard to believe, huh? I've known him all my life, and I have no idea why he thinks that way. Maybe it's a generational issue."

"Maybe he had his own bad interaction."

"He's never mentioned any. Now I've got you thinking about all these things that are going on in my life, it's time you read this. Here, take it," Mary said as she handed Edward her great-grandfather's notebook. "Read it."

The next day, all Edward wanted to talk about was what he had read in the notebook. "These super-smart people from all over the world figured out a way to save humanity, survive the disaster, and then build a new society from scratch. Mary, that's a huge deal. Can you imagine what they went through, having to leave their families behind to die? And to think, we're their offspring."

"Yup, somewhere down the line we're probably related. Genetically we both came from that original group."

"But we're not any more related than anybody else in the community." Edward said, giving her a reassuring hug. "They had noble goals, trying to build a society where everybody shared everything – the work, the food, the medicine, the leadership."

"And, they accomplished it but, later on, things got screwed up."

"It was a great idea, and it still works almost a hundred years later. No fighting, no killing, no mass starvation. We're educated. We have jobs and a place to live. We get medicine, everything we need. The Program works."

Twisting her face with the disapproval he had teased out of her, she launched into the expected tirade. "Well, don't you speak like a true believer? You know things are messed up, that leaders don't come from the workers anymore, that one group holds power – and you know the horrible stuff they do."

"You're all warrior, and I love getting a rise out of you," he said coyly. "Their original goals for society were noble. Whatever that's morphed into now is something else entirely. Your great grandfather and the brilliant people he worked with had the right intentions, and they got most of it right."

"But not the society they wanted, ruled by a committee of its people. Clearly our ancestors didn't intend for this to happen.

And what about treating each person as a precious resource? That's certainly not happening anymore," she replied.

Edward had baited her, and it had worked too well. She was getting agitated. Understanding the folly he had unleashed, he didn't want their evening ruined. "Hey, I'm messing with you, so go easy, all right? I'm on your side. I don't know when or why things changed, but they changed."

Mary paused and closed her eyes. "Rub my shoulders?" Despite his teasing, she knew he agreed with her. She knew she had found a kindred spirit in Edward, and she wanted to spend the rest of her life with this man.

With her head on the table, her shoulders dropped, Edward thought it was a good time to change the subject. "You said something the other day that I don't understand, and I wanted to ask you about it."

"You're massaging my back. You're in a position to ask me anything."

"The final injection, the new one, the one they give to the Outcasts . . . "

"What of it?"

"Since Joey got it, why did he live for so many years afterward? You said the idea of the new shot was to make the Outcasts die quickly? If what Doc said was true about the final injection, he should have died much sooner."

Mary lifted her head. "Good point. I don't know. Why didn't I ever give that any thought? Ugh. I'll ask Doc." Revisiting Joey's misery and helplessness hijacked Mary's mood once again. She wiped her eyes. "All right," she said, sniffling. "My turn."

"Go ahead."

"Do you know anything about the fields where our food is grown?"

"Now that's a question out of the blue, isn't it? This means we're not talking about the notebook or the Program anymore? This means we're talking about what the Outcasts want from you, aren't we?"

"Yes, we are. I need to see the fields."

"Jorge's team handles shipments to and from the farms, so someone who works for him may be able to help us."

"I didn't even think about asking Jorge."

"I'll figure out how to ask him without raising too many questions."

CHAPTER 34

SICKNESS

"What a nice surprise. I didn't know you were coming by," Mary whispered as she held the door open late the next Monday night with one hand while clutching a blanket and a steamy mug of water under her nose in the other.

"I can only stay a minute." Edward quietly closed Mary's door behind him. "I talked to Jorge about arranging that trip to the fields."

"You did? I'm not feeling too well, so you might not want to get too close."

"That's why I didn't see you at work today. Sick, huh? I'm sorry. Guess that means I'm next." Edward took a step back. "So, he said his guy Vinesh makes regular pickups and deliveries to the farms. He's willing to take us along next time he goes."

"Did Jorge question why we want to do this?"

"Oh yeah – why did we care about the fields, that sort of stuff."

"And what'd you tell him?"

"I told him you wondered where our food came from, where it grew, how it was processed – the whole chain thing – and how it might be a fun date night. Not sure he totally bought it, but he didn't press me. He'll set it up with his guy. Now, humor me. What are we actually looking for?"

"Honestly, I have no idea. Axel said to go to the fields and that I'd understand. Guess we'll figure it out when we get there."

"Well, things are set for Wednesday night. We leave after work before sundown. Fewer eyes, less questions. Think you'll be well by then?"

"I'm sure I'll be fine. This is probably just a cold coming on. I need to rest."

"I love you."

Mary had been feeling odd all day, and now her stomach was queasy. A quick press of her palm to her forehead revealed a slight fever. As the last bit of the daylight pierced through her window, she crawled into bed early and fidgeted with her pillow until she found a comfortable position to read.

She cradled the partially missing cover and yellowed fragile pages one of her favorite books, *Animal Farm.* She read it once a year, at least. A few years back, she had traded Program food coupons for this prize on the black market, and it had been totally worth the hunger pangs. There was a certain sadness to reading about farm animals since, as far as she knew, most animals, except for the occasional sightings of birds and some insects, were now extinct. None of that impacted her enjoyment of reading about rebellious spirits standing up to the corruptly powerful. She pulled the covers and settled in for a long read. She got to page 4 before the book slowly slipped out of her hand and onto the floor.

She awoke from a deep sleep feeling sick to her stomach. She stumbled out of bed and ran for the toilet, one hand pressing firmly against her lips. Her head, covered in sweat, swooned back and forth in a rhythmic motion, her hands clamped to the cold perimeter of the bowl. Minutes later, she laid on the cool floor, which made her feel much better.

CHAPTER 35

THE FIELDS

"Let's get to the dock. Jorge said he'll meet us there. How are you feeling, still sick?"

"I feel better today. Yesterday I stayed home and rested. Look, here he comes."

Jorge met them but only stayed on the dock long enough to introduce Vinesh.

"So, I need to drop off a load near one of the fields," Vinesh told them, "but you two already knew that, right?" Edward didn't know about the drop off, but he nodded in agreement as Vinesh continued. "Jorge told me about the work you two do at the Distribution Center. That's great, now let me quickly finish something here, then we can go."

Vinesh checked his load a final time and watched Mary and Edward when they were facing away from him. Observing their body language, he could see they were standing too close to each other and touching each other's hands. Certainly, he thought, these two were more than just coworkers.

"Normally I do this type of run alone, but you two are welcome to share the experience," he said, chuckling. "Now if we get stopped along the way by the guards, let me do the talking. I'm doing a delivery. Lady, you're taking inventory, and guy, you're checking out distribution. Any questions? Hey, that's what you two do, inventory and distribution, correct?"

"Exactly," Edward said, without missing a beat, "You've got it. Mary tracks inventory, and I run distribution, scheduling. We want to see how the entire chain works, how all the pieces fit together."

Vinesh muttered to himself as he stepped up into the cab of his open bed truck. Once in the driver's seat, he signaled for them to enter. Mary stepped up first from the passenger side, sliding along the bench seat toward Vinesh as he brushed dirt off onto the floorboard. He then placed a tattered bible, which had been resting at his side, carefully onto the floor and under his seat. This made more room for Mary. Edward entered, making Mary into a snug sandwich between the two males. With everyone settled, Vinesh gave his passengers a onceover. "You're going to find this trip boring, but if you're ready, we can leave."

"We're ready and no, it won't be boring," Edward replied. "We've never seen the fields."

"Whatever," Vinesh said, unconvinced by their words. "So how long have you and the little lady been working here? I don't remember seeing either of you on the docks."

Fearing Mary might respond unfavorably to being called a little lady, Edward quickly replied, "About five years, I think. Not a bad place to work, but I never get to do things like this. We both sit behind desks all day. That's probably why we've never met."

To Edward's surprise, Mary seemed unfazed by the little lady comment. "Three years for me," Mary answered. "How about you?"

"You two are babies. Eighteen for me. Hard to believe, isn't it? Working at the same place, doing the same boring job. But I'd hate to sit inside all day. Hey, come on, it's just us, what's the real story with you two lovebirds?"

Edward now saw a clear expression of unhappiness on Mary's face, and this time she spoke. "Please don't. We're here to see the fields for work, that's all."

"No offense lady, but you two seem like lovebirds to me. But hey, I don't give a damn. Say whatever you want, nobody comes at night to check out the fields unless they don't want to be seen."

Edward looked at Mary, who was now visibly blushing in the fading light. "Listen, we were instructed to come at night. We couldn't come until when we got our regular work done. My partner already told you why we're here," she scolded.

"Like I said, lady, Jorge told me to take you two along. That's what I'm doing."

When they arrived, the three of them jumped down from the small cab of the truck.

"You two go on. I need to unload these sacks. Then we'll leave."

"Mary, maybe I'll stay behind and help him unload. You go ahead and check out the fields. I'll catch up when we're done."

"Fine," she replied somewhat disappointed that Edward was staying back. She looked at the bags they were about to unload and asked, "Hey, what is in these sacks, anyway?"

"Fertilizer, chemicals for the plants. Don't know how much it will help, farmers say the dirt's no good. They need new land."

"Chemicals for the plants?"

"Yeah, chemicals, fertilizer, you know, nitrogen, phosphorous, that sort of thing." He stopped and looked at his passengers, wondering how they could be interested in the fields but not know anything about fertilizer. "You two don't know a damn thing about plants, do you? You should get your butts out from under those desks more often."

"We told you, we don't get to see this kind of thing. Mary, go ahead. I'll be there shortly. Let me finish helping him."

"No, I'll wait."

The two men unloaded sacks from the truck. Edward struggled to lift then walk with the heavy bags. Vinesh shook his head in disbelief. Mary guessed he had expected his tall passenger to be stronger and more fit. Edward's face reddened in the moonlight.

For their benefit, and maybe to further embarrass Edward, Vinesh showed off by grabbing two bags at once. Holding the two bags he turned, "Look, guy, I got this. I do this all day long. I don't sit behind no desk. Thanks for the help, but you better go with pretty lady. Make sure she don't get into trouble."

"Sorry I wasn't much help. Hurt my back earlier this year. Guess it's still not recovered," he lied sheepishly.

Frustrated by Vinesh's attitude, Mary turned her back on the two men and slowly walked toward the field.

Edward placed his last bag and then stopped, "Hey before I catch up with her, what'd you mean when you said the farmers think the dirt's not any good?"

"Farmers have been complaining about that dirt for years. They won't say that to the bosses, but that's what they tell me. They need fresh dirt, new land. Evidently resources are running out, and they're having problems with the plants."

"Hmm, they need new dirt? That's sort of interesting, don't you think?"

"Not to me. Mister, I got to finish my job."

"Sure, thanks. Mary, wait up," he called out, "I'm coming."

"Go on, make sure little lady stays close, you know? We leave soon."

Mary was still close enough to hear what he had said. "Vinesh, I can still hear you so quit the little lady crap. I'm getting tired of it."

Happy he had riled her, he laughed, "You two are funny."

Edward caught up at edge of a large field where she was standing. The two scanned the field in the moonlight, neither sure what to look for.

"This is it. We're here. You see anything? Something that makes you understand whatever you were supposed to understand?"

"Nope," she sighed. "I don't have any idea what I should see. I do see a difference in the plants. They're not the same as the ones in the Outcast fields. Maybe that's it?"

"Different how?"

"This is a much bigger field than the one Axel showed me, but these plants are scrawny in comparison. Maybe they aren't finished growing?"

"Let's ask Vinesh when we get back to the truck. He'll know."

"I wonder what else I'm supposed to see. I hope I haven't missed it." Her voice revealed a trace of disappointment.

On the walk back, Edward took Mary's hand, squeezed it and dropped it.

"Lovebirds, are you finished? Can we go now?" Vinesh yelled out.

At that, the three of them jumped back into the cab of the truck, and they drove off leaving the fields and the fertilizer sacks behind.

Edward sensed Mary's irritation with not noticing anything outstanding about the fields and also with their driver's constant teasing, but he was glad that she was able to keep her focus.

"Vinesh, how much do you know about those plants?" she said, reflecting on the small size of the plants.

"I'm not a farmer, but I've been hanging around these fields for years. What do you want to know, lovebird?"

"Can you quit being a jerk, for starters? I want to know if the plants we saw will get any bigger?"

"She's a feisty one, isn't she?" Vinesh exclaimed, leaning forward to see Edward. As he did, the truck swerved, causing everyone to lurch.

"Hey, watch the road!" Mary yelled. "And I'm right here. Don't talk to him and act like I'm not here. Now answer my question."

"The plants don't get bigger." Then displaying an odd smile, he added, "Look at the fields. They are ripe for harvest."

"They're fully grown, then? That's normal?"

Vinesh was disappointed they missed his biblical reference. "Lady, there's nothing normal about those plants. They're grown from super-seeds. The farmers closely guard those seeds and those plants. Anything else that grows, they weed out. They make sure the seeds don't get contaminated."

These details caught her off guard. "What makes them so special?"

"The farmers tell me it took decades of genetic engineering to develop them, radiation-hardened plants. They bred the seeds and the plants to tolerate the UV rays. If those seeds get contaminated with stray seeds, the harvest next year could be a disaster. Then we'd all be in big trouble."

"No plants, no food. Guessing that would be bad," Edward mumbled.

"Alright, we're here. Hope you lovebirds saw whatever you were looking for – I mean, taking inventory, understanding distribution," he said sarcastically.

"Thanks for taking us along. We'll report back to our bosses."

Vinesh wasn't buying what Edward was selling. "Whatever."

After he drove off, Mary touched Edward's arm. "Remember how those plants were scrawny? They were much smaller than the ones Axel showed me."

"Right, you said that. So . . .?"

"It must mean there's something wrong with our seeds or the soil or both. I don't know, somehow the Outcasts must have better seeds."

"My guess is better seeds and better land. But seeing our fields makes me curious. I'd sure like to see the Outcast fields for myself. Do you think you could arrange that?"

"Lovebird, Axel contacts me, not the other way around."

"Well then, little lady, next time Axel contacts you, ask him if I can tag along."

"I . . . will," she snuck in between kisses, "but don't push it."

"Whatever you say, boss."

CHAPTER 36

TOO LATE

"There you are. I've been running around looking all over for you."

Mary smirked. "Hmm, what do you need?" she asked, perturbed by the implication in Ena's voice.

"Well, hello to you, too. You're never at your desk anymore. What's up with you?"

"Ena, you're beginning to sound like my mother. If you must know, all morning I've been in another one of my boss's worthless meetings. Now I'll probably be behind for the rest of the day, so can this wait until later?"

"No, it can't. Jorge just stopped by my desk. He was in a hurry, so I'm not sure what it's about, but I can tell something's up. He said for you to come find him on the dock after your shift ends. I'm just going to say this once, Mary, so take this warning for what it's worth. If my guy gets in any trouble because of that little excursion you and Edward took . . ."

Mary kept her eyes on the tall stack of invoices on her desk. "Stop jumping to conclusions," she said, slamming the pile. When she looked up, however, she registered a level of concern on her friends face she had not expected. "We didn't get him or anyone in any trouble."

"And, you aren't listening. Then again, no one knows better than you, right? Would it be so hard for you to think for one minute about somebody other than yourself?"

"I'll go after my shift ends and, if it makes you feel better, I'll come by and tell you what I know. Try not to worry your pretty paired head off. It's probably nothing."

"I hope you're right," Ena growled between her teeth.

Mary moved fast to catch up on her workload. How could that trip have caused trouble for Jorge? He had done them a favor, but the trip went smoothly, and nobody saw them. Still, Ena would never speak to her again if he were in trouble.

She finished her work 15 minutes early and headed to the loading dock. When she arrived, the place looked empty. She peered through the smudged office windows along the long wall. Two large doors swung doors open at the other end of the dock, and Jorge approached her. His greeting was formal. His smile, forced. Were they being watched? She looked around. She was certain his stiff body language was signaling bad news.

"Are you in trouble?"

Jorge shook his head.

She was relieved. "Then what's going on?"

"Go through those doors to my office. I'll meet you both in a minute."

"Both?" Mary pulled open the door to Jorge's office. Coffee stains and stacks of orders piled his desk. Two torn and yellowed maps were pinned to his wall. As she went to sit in his chair, she saw that it was ripped and in need of repair. She decided to focus on the bigger, more interesting of the two maps. The smaller one had few markings. She had never seen a map of the area before, so she was curious to decode the lines and symbols. Five long minutes passed before Edward walked in, looking solemn. He closed the door behind him.

"Edward? What are you doing here? Why are we here?" She turned to give him a hug, but as she did, he stiffened. The hair on her neck stood up.

"Yeah. Look, Jorge set this up, so we could talk somewhere safe, where we wouldn't be seen or heard. After today we can't be seen together inside or outside of work. At least until I figure things out." he said, clearly unable to look her in her eyes.

"What things? What's this about?" She said as she grabbed his hand and squeezed it, "Is this about us? Are we in trouble?"

"Yes, we are. I was afraid of something like this. Read."

Mary studied his facial expression then took the paper from his hand. "It says you've been paired. But what about Doc? What did he . . . ?"

"I haven't talked to him yet. My appointment isn't until Friday. Something must have happened that he couldn't fix." Once again Edward turned away, too embarrassed and upset to face her. "I got the letter today."

"Damn it, no!" Mary said to him, now realizing the significance of the piece of paper she was holding. Disgusted, she threw it onto the floor.

"I'm supposed to meet her soon. We're supposed to review the contract terms with someone from the Program. Mary, I don't think we have much time."

"We don't have any time! They've finished us. We're done."

"Don't. We have to figure a way out of this. I'm not going through with this."

"Workers lose in this system. It doesn't matter what you want or what I want. You've been paired. That's it. We don't get to choose."

"Why are you two yelling?" Jorge said, rushing in. "It's nobody's fault, so lower the volume or you'll get us all in trouble." Mary could see Jorge was upset and embarrassed to be in the room.

"There has to be a way out. Go speak to Doc. Find out what happened. I can't be seen with you until we fix this."

"Fix this? You keep implying there's a way to fix this. There isn't any. I hate this damn Program, I just hate them on that committee."

"Come on, that's not going to help anything." Edward went to hug her, but she pushed him away. "Hey, don't be mad at me. It's not my fault. Check with your friend. He's the one who didn't come through. This is not over."

Mary's lips tightened. "Don't blame Doc. We should have done something sooner!"

"Like what? Please, just go talk to him," he pleaded and left the room.

Mary stood in the middle of the dirty office, shocked. Jorge gave Mary a quick hug, letting her know he was sorry before she started the long walk back to her desk. The office had cleared out, thankfully. She grabbed her things and walked toward the exit. Ena was waiting for her. She could tell Ena already knew.

Without a word, Ena grabbed her friend and pulled her close as they walked away from the building. Neither spoke until they said goodbye and headed to their respective apartments.

CHAPTER 37

OUTSIDE HELP

"Your next patient is here. Do I bring him in?" Doc's nurse said in a particularly crabby tone of voice.

"Damn it, Delilah. If he's my next patient, why wouldn't you?" Doc replied, doing his best to match her curtness. Things were getting worse between them. He was convinced she had turned on him and couldn't be trusted. He felt certain she was leaking information about him to the Program. Later that day, he got word to Mary through Dr. Chivas that they needed to meet in the park. He had much to tell her about this and about Edward.

After work Mary sat on a weathered wooden bench at the secluded end of the park where they had agreed to meet. It was a cold but exquisite sunny day. She was upset with Edward's situation, which made her give in to the sunshine. It felt soothing. As a child, she had been taught to fear the sun. Today she didn't care. She had a few extra minutes to bask in its rays.

Time passed. Doc was later than usual, and Mary began to feel exposed, sitting in the open. As she stood to leave, she saw Doc a short distance away. He was huffing and puffing as he ran-walked. She had never seen him exert himself like that. Something was up.

He came to the bench, grasped her hand and, breathing heavily, plopped down, dragging her next to him. She wondered what was wearing him out more, dealing with a heart condition, the Program, or her. "I know I'm late, but there was something important I had to finish." He fumbled for a bit as he opened a crumpled handkerchief. His hands shook as he wiped his brow and cheeks.

Mary wanted to feel irritated at him for being late, but the irony was not lost on her. How many times had she been late for their appointments? Intentionally or not, the tables were turned, which seemed like fair play.

Still panting, Doc shielded his eyes as he squinted. "What sun. Wonderful day, isn't it?"

Mary nodded silently, her lips pursed.

Realizing she wasn't in the mood, he got straight to business. "Of course, I know why you're here. Edward must have received his notification. I'm his doctor now, so they sent me a copy." He paused waiting for a response. "You have to believe me. I tried, I did. He was already deep in the system. There was nothing I could do." Doc winced, expecting nothing short of wrath.

"Doc, I believe you. I'm going to lose him."

Her brevity made him feel guilty. "I went to his doctor. The guy's a friend, and I made up a reason why he should be my patient. That part worked, but I received his charts too late, no thanks to that bitch Delilah, and he was already paired."

"Yup," Mary said, "They're supposed to meet soon, then sign the contract."

Doc took her hand, "Look at me. We have one last long shot." He lowered his voice to a whisper. "I thought about this all night. I checked out things before I came, and I took a chance and got the ball rolling. That's the real reason I'm late."

Her face lifted.

"Don't get too excited, but what if I could buy a delay of a few additional weeks? Would that be worth something?" he asked, fidgeting with the damp hankie in his hands as he looked left and right.

"Of course, but how would you do that?"

"Turns out your guy was very sick as a child. In fact, it's hard to believe, given his medical records, how well he recovered. That gave me an idea, one that for anyone else would look suspicious but with his medical background would seem completely believable."

"How does his medical background help us?"

"What if, for some reason, he became ill again from a similar disease? I mean, seriously ill? Certainly, at the very least, that would delay things until he got better."

"He wouldn't really be sick, would he? We'd just tell everyone he was?"

"That's the problem. He'd get very, very sick, indeed. I'd have to make him sick because that's the only way his medical tests would show the abnormality. Otherwise other medical professionals might catch on. And, as his doctor, giving him these drugs wouldn't be risk-free for me, either. I would have to officially report his test results. That way, when the managers from his work or Program officials check his records, everything will be legit. Again, risky."

"You'd intentionally make him sick to buy us more time?"

"I can't hang around much longer. That's the other thing I need to tell you. My nurse is up to no good when I step away from the office, so let me make this quick. There's an outside chance that his illness could temporarily remove him from the list. In that case, they might go ahead and pair her with someone else. A reset for him puts him further down the list, which could buy you both additional time. It's a chance you can't count on."

"But it's something."

"This is important, so listen carefully. I can only keep him sick for two to three weeks. Any longer than that would be suspicious and dangerous for his health."

"I understand. I appreciate what you'd be doing for us, I do." Mary leaned over and kissed him on the cheek.

"OK, then. Done. You two make a quick decision about this."

"We'll let you know tomorrow. Soon enough?"

"Good. I started growing the cultures this morning, but I don't want Delilah snooping around while I'm gone. I'll prepare the shots for him myself."

CHAPTER 38

FATE WORSE THAN DEATH

That evening Mary sat with Edward holding his hand and explained things. "Doc said your records transferred, but he was too late to stop the pairing."

"Maybe he didn't like me or didn't want to help me . . . us."

"No, he's sorry it didn't work out."

"OK, but what do we do now?"

"He thought of something else, a crazy scheme. It's a delay tactic. I'm not sure we should consider something this . . . brutal."

"Brutal? How brutal? How long of a delay?"

Mary explained the details.

"Sounds awful. What kind of illness he would give me?"

"He didn't say."

"All right, I have to ask, you don't think he's trying to kill me, do you? A cover to make it look like he's helping, but he's not?"

"Don't be silly. Why would he try to kill you? I love you, so he loves you, or he will once he gets to know you better. He's like a father to me. Let's focus on the plan afterward. Any ideas?"

"Not me. I was counting on Doc getting me off that list permanently."

"So much for that. Listen, when I think about it, this plan has lots of risk without much benefit. Maybe keeping you on the list is a sign from the God of the Universe or something. Maybe it's time we go our separate ways before we really endanger our lives – and Doc's. One way or another, the Program wins."

"Why would God have anything to do with something as evil as this? And, no, I don't want us to go our separate ways. We're not giving up. The plan is . . . desperate, but we do it. What do you say?" Edward held up Mary's chin. "Will you come see me when I'm sick?"

"Stop. Maybe we should reconsider. I don't want to risk your life."

"Unless you have another plan, I say we do it. But we both better try thinking of a longer-term solution."

"And what if we can't come up with anything? Then what? You would have been as sick as you were as a child, maybe worse, for nothing. Promise me you'll sleep on it before you decide. I can't bear to lose you to her, but I'd never forgive myself if I lost you because of this."

Edward starred off into the distance. It was ironic, he thought, that for a chance to be with the woman he wanted so badly, he would have to battle the demons from his childhood. Had he grown stronger during the hiatus, or had they?

CHAPTER 39

TICK TOCK

"Mary, Jorge tells me Edward hasn't been at work lately. He's out sick?"

"Yeah, poor guy. Not sure what he's got, but Doc says he's not contagious."

"Hoping he'll mess up his pairing, huh?"

Ena's tone made Mary bristle. "That's a shitty thing to say, Ena. Can you stoop any lower?"

"Being sick isn't going to change anything, Mary. Let him go. You can't have him. He's not yours. The guy's been paired. Accept it."

"Whatever's going on with Edward's health is none of my business, so I can't imagine it's any of yours. You are way out of line." Mary marched back to her desk, both perturbed with Ena and irked that she was probably right. The Program would pair Edward once he was better. The clock was ticking, and she didn't know where to turn for a more permanent solution.

* * *

When Mary arrived at Edward's apartment, Doc was bending over Edward's bed, taking his vitals. Something seemed wrong. As she drew closer, Edward's eyes were closed, and his skin looked ghostly.

"We have a problem. He's had a toxic reaction to the medications. I need to transfer him to the Care Place, where I can run additional tests. This is serious."

"But he's going to be all right, isn't he?"

"Once he's there, I think I can pull him through. Unfortunately, that's going to raise eyebrows and bring up new issues."

Mary walked over to Edward's bed, placed her fingers in his hand and laid the side of her head on his chest. He was clammy and burning hot. Against her white blouse, his skin looked a little blue. Instantly she was frightened by what she saw.

Through the medication fog Edward was under, he managed a reply. "It's all right, lovebird. If Doc says I'll get better in the Care Place, let's do it." He started shivering.

"Now I wish you hadn't done this. This was so selfish of me. What a dumb idea."

"I'd be paired if we hadn't done it. What's our long-term plan?"

She looked away. "I'm working on it. You concentrate on getting better. Go to the facility. Do whatever Doc tells you."

"You'll come see me?"

"I will, and I'll be there when you get out." Mary wrapped an arm around Doc. "Doc will keep me posted on your progress every day, right?"

Doc cleaned Edward's arm before pulling out a needle from his medical bag. "As soon as I make the arrangements, I'll have my team move you to the facility. Now, young man, this will help you sleep."

Mary kissed Edward's hand until he stopped opening his eyes to look at her.

"Mary, before I leave, you need to know that I've got a problem."

"Is Edward going to be all right? He looks terrible. Worse than . . . I want to stay here with him."

"No, he's not the problem. He'll be fine once I get him to the facility. My problem is with the Program."

"What do you mean?"

"Years ago, I was accused of stealing medicines. Chivas managed to cast enough doubt, but the case remains open and on my record. Now I hear they are digging for other suspicious activity to pin on me and, as exhausted as I am with my own patient overload, I've been careless about covering my tracks about Edward's illness. It's an issue, a big one."

"What kind of issue?"

"First, medical records will show that I dug through Edward's files. From those, they'll be able to piece together that I pulled a favor to get him transferred as my patient. Those two moves would not be as big of a deal if I didn't need to admit him into the Care Place. Admitting him will look odd so soon after coming into my care. I never anticipated the severe reaction to this medication. Naturally, questions are going to come up. Other doctors will question why I stalled before getting him admitted. The combination will raise suspicion."

"Doc, this sounds bad."

"It is. Unfortunately, once I get him admitted, the clinic will have to run more tests, and those results will reveal the strange virus I gave him. I'm going to have a problem on my hands, take my word for it."

"But couldn't he have gotten as sick under his old doctor's care."

"Not likely, not with this disease. It's rare. I knew this virus would act quickly, but I was confident that he would recover quickly – maybe too confident there would never be a need for anyone to question me. His toxic reaction, these additional tests. . . when you pile things up, it'll mean an inquiry."

"Are you sure the virus could be traced back to you?"

"It can. Another unexpected problem is that while I was preparing the injections, the bitch came into the room. She saw me."

"How could Delilah have known what you were doing?"

"The syringes were in plain view. Her job is to prepare injections, not me. At the time she didn't say a word, but I have no doubt she reported me."

"You're being paranoid. You don't know that for sure."

Doc hurriedly packed his bag. "She came in on me. She saw what I was doing and gave me the oddest look. It was written all over her face. Edward, a new patient that I had specifically requested for transfer, so why I was preparing the injections instead of her?

I'm sure it all looked . . . odd. I tried to make up a cover story, but I'm not good at that sort of thing. She may have already gone to the authorities. It doesn't take a genius to see she isn't loyal, and my past will certainly make things worse."

"But Doc, if they're investigating, wouldn't they have informed you?"

"Maybe, maybe not. When Edward shows up in the Care Place, Delilah will have more questions. I know if I were in her shoes and had found out that Edward was this ill, I would have grave suspicions about his doctor."

"What can I do to help? There must be something . . .?"

"It's not yours to fix. I should have taken steps to make sure she didn't see anything. In a formal investigation, Delilah's not going to lie for me."

"I only thought about myself in all of this. How damn selfish of me."

"It was my idea. I didn't have to do this and either did Edward. Anyway, it's done. Now I need you to do something important for me."

"Anything."

Doc took a seat at the end of Edward's bed. "First, no matter what happens to me, remember I won't involve you in any way. Second, I'm certain Edward will never implicate you either. Third, and most importantly, I need you to distance yourself from him – and from me."

"Why? How will I know how he's doing?"

"You're not listening. This isn't optional."

"You just heard me promise Edward I would visit. I can't leave him there alone."

"I'll talk to him and figure out a way to get word to you. For now, you stay away or you'll be implicated. You absolutely cannot come to the Care Place. Everyone there knows you as Joey's sister. Your presence puts Edward and me in danger.

"But he's my coworker. Why can't I just be a coworker checking on him?"

"Don't be naïve, Mary. That flimsy cover won't fool anyone. You've been seen together. Rumors are probably already spreading. And, what can you honestly say? That you work with him every day? Once a week?"

"No, but . . ."

"Then don't come. I mean it. If you blow this, we're all in trouble. Very soon a lot of powerful people will be focusing on me and on him. I'll find a safe way to let you know what's going on. Now, get out of here, and please stay the hell away from us."

CHAPTER 40

DESPERATION FOCUSES THE MIND

Mary was handling a pile of invoices from her inbox when Jorge stopped by.

"Friend," Mary said brightly. "Nice to see you. Here to see Ena?"

"I saw her. Can we . . . talk for a moment?"

"I have questions about invoicing for you, so it's good you stopped by." She said, grabbing a stack of file folders and standing to see who was watching them.

Once safely out of earshot, Jorge wasted no time filling her in on his evening visit with Edward. "Doc says Edward has turned the corner. He's better than last week. He said he misses you. He's figured out, what did he say? Something about your plant problem, whatever that means."

She bent her head. "I'm relieved. Tell him that I'm waiting for him."

"He can't stop talking about you, that's how I know he's doing better."

Mary thanked Jorge profusely and turned back toward her desk.

"Can you do me a favor, Mary?"

Mary paused.

"Ena feels bad she said Edward was faking his sickness. She wants to apologize. If you'll let her."

"Of course. We'll set things straight," she promised. "Please keep me up on Edward's progress, all right?"

"You know I will. Oh, I almost forgot Doc wanted me to tell you that things have started. I'm guessing he means Edward's treatments?"

"Oh, OK." Mary shrugged, but her heart sunk. That coded message wasn't a good sign for Doc.

"I need to get back to the dock, but I want you to know that Ena and I care for you both. You and Edward belong together."

Mary didn't want Jorge to leave. When would she hear from him again? Time was running out, and she had more questions. "I can't tell you how much it means to me to hear you say that. Edward and I couldn't agree more. One more thing, Jorge? When you see Doc, tell him I said yes, that I will be able to meet him in the park at noon on Thursday. He'll know the spot. Can you pass that along for me?"

"Sure. Meet in the park at noon two days from now. Got it."

"Thanks. I'll stop by to see Ena before she leaves work today." Mary could see by the way Jorge walked away that she wasn't the only one feeling relief.

Mary knew she would have no problem patching things up with Ena. They fought like sisters, but the pit in her stomach kept nagging her. Edward had just gone through a lot for her, and Doc's paranoia about an investigation had been justified. She had to get them out of this mess before the Program took everyone down.

Desperate for possible solutions, she forced the fog in her brain to lift over the next two days. Once she settled on the best plan to save the three of them, all she had to do was convince Doc that a few far-fetched details would work.

CHAPTER 41

SETUP

"What a nice surprise!" Ena called out to Jorge as she opened the door. "Mary is here to see us."

Mary walked through the doorway and hugged her friend. "Sorry to stop by uninvited, but I need to ask Jorge something before work tomorrow. I forgot to ask him about it today."

"Of course. Come in. Let me take your coat. Jorge tells me Edward is beginning to feel better."

"That's what I hear."

Before either could continue, Jorge stepped in to hug her. "Mary, good to see you. Everything OK?"

"Yes, I dropped by to ask a favor. I should have asked at work, but I forgot."

"Sure, how can I help?"

"Well, I'd like to see Vinesh again. I want to thank him for taking us on that little trip, and I have a gift for him, a few books for him."

"Books for Vinesh? Really? He's the last guy I'd think would be interested in reading." When Mary didn't offer an explanation, he continued. "How about that? Well, let's see. Come by the dock before he leaves at 7:15 a.m., so you two can talk while I'm preparing his paperwork. He's scheduled to pick up things for me and then make a delivery. I'll give him a heads-up."

"Sounds perfect, and I wouldn't be so surprised to hear about Vinesh and books. He obviously reads because he had a ratty old bible on the seat next to him in the cab of his truck. I don't think he knew I saw it."

"Vinesh . . . religious? That's . . . I don't know . . . I'm shocked."

The three of them laughed.

"Good to know. Wonders never cease,"

Ena grabbed Jorge's arm and squeezed it.

"And, talking about surprises this is something I wanted to talk to you about. . . well, I'm guessing maybe you already know . . ." Jorge said, centering himself.

"About what?" Mary asked.

"Do you know Harman? He works on your floor."

"I know him," Ena answered. "He sits a few aisles from me. Mary, he's the older fellow who always wears that sleeveless bright green sweater?"

"Oh right. What about him?"

"He used to work on the dock. We're buddies. Anyway, his partner Delilah is Doc's nurse. I'm sure you know her."

"Oh wow. Delilah? Sure, I know her. She's sort of surly woman. She and Doc have worked together forever."

"Anyway, Harman told me that guards came to their apartment a few times to talk to Delilah about Doc. Harman thinks there's some sort of investigation? He shouldn't have told me about any of that, but I wanted to let you know. Have you heard about it?"

Ena's curiosity peaked. "Doc's not in trouble, is he? He's been a such good friend to you."

Mary was caught off-guard. "I'm betting it's a little dispute between him and Delilah. Those two argue all the time. I'm surprised they haven't killed each other yet, but who knows?" Mary made a feeble attempt to fluff it off. "OK, well, time for me to head home if I need to be at the dock before seven. That Vinesh is quite a character, isn't he?"

"A character all right. He told me how much he enjoyed teasing you and Edward. Believe me, as crusty as he is, he doesn't like many people. I'll let him know you're coming."

"Thanks, Jorge. Oh, almost forgot, a while back I had asked about Gus Weisman, did you ever get a chance to follow up on that fellow?"

"Yeah and, just as you thought, he's been reassigned to a processing factory. We get a lot of deliveries from there on the dock."

"Good, that's what I thought. I'll pass that on. Ena, see you tomorrow?"

"Jorge and I love seeing you," Ena attempted. "I'm glad Edward's getting better. Say hello to him for me when you see him."

A wave of sadness hit Mary as she walked away. She wanted to feel reconnected with her oldest friend, but Ena was clueless. She guessed that Ena would be questioning Jorge about Doc and maybe even about Weisman the moment she closed the door. She would worry about all that later. She had arrangements to make, and time was running out.

CHAPTER 42

TRANSPORT

"Didn't I make it clear we were not to meet until this thing is over? Investigators are watching me. Damn it, Mary, you're constantly putting me in a terrible position."

"Calm down, Doc. This is not your office. I got here early to scope out the park."

"Mary, help me for once. I'm already putting my life on the line. What else do you want?"

"I need to talk to you both together. I have a plan, but I can't come to the facility, and we can't meet in your office. When will Edward be well enough to go back to his apartment? If there is any way to get him out by tomorrow evening, do it. I have a way to fix this mess."

"Why do I have this feeling your attempt to fix things will only cause me more problems?" Doc rubbed his forehead.

"Is that a yes?"

"He's probably well enough to move him back, and getting him out of the Care Place might take some focus off me. I'll try, but that's all I can promise."

Mary kissed Doc on the cheek. "I'll be waiting for both of you at his apartment. I'll get us out of this mess."

"A plan, huh? It better be a good one."

CHAPTER 43

SITUATION WITH THE PROGRAM

Mary prepared herself for a long battle with Doc and Edward. She prepared answers to hard questions they might ask to challenge her game plan. Neither would be easily swayed.

To calm her nerves, she recalled what her father did when he needed strength. "While there are many religions, there is only one God, the one Creator of the Universe," she could hear him say. No one else she knew talked about God unless, like Doc, they were damning her. With the biggest task of her life in front of her, she bent down on both knees, as her father had, and asked the creator for strength and guidance. Somehow, she believed, her father's prayer must have worked.

The next night, she felt confident about the task at hand. The three of them met at Edward's apartment. He was thinner and still pale, but she was pleased to see he was more alert. Doc stood on one side of the bed, and she on the other.

"Guys, I need you to listen. I've got a plan for us. Please let me make my case before you interrupt or object."

Edward was happy to see Mary in control. She was the reason he had persevered during his illness. He had held out hope that she would find a long-range plan for them. "We're all ears," he said.

"First, and this shouldn't be a surprise, the UV levels aren't dangerous anymore. The ozone layer is working. I can prove it.

Edward and I have been out to our fields, we saw our scrubby wilting plants."

Doc glared at Mary.

"It's true, Doc," Edward added. "The plants we saw were pathetic, and Vinesh, who took us there, told us they were grown from special seeds, but they must not be very good."

With his support, Mary jumped back in. "Yes, genetically-engineered, radiation-hardened seeds. When radiation levels were high, it made sense to modify our seed stock. But over the years, the Program screwed something up because the current seeds are bad. With bad seeds and bad plants, is it any wonder the Program is cutting back on food?" She finally had Doc's attention. "No, it isn't, and the Program is hiding something else. Vinesh told us that the farmers are frustrated. They need new soil. Why do you think that is?"

Doc was listening but not following. "God damn it, Mary, what the hell are you talking about? I don't know a damn thing about plants, farming, or genetically-modified seeds, whatever. And forgive me if this insults you, but I doubt you or Edward know anything about that stuff, either. How do you know Program plants and seeds aren't any good?"

"You don't need to have studied botany or agriculture to understand that if the plants are scrawny and stunted, something is wrong with them," Mary shot back. "The seeds or the soil or both are sufficiently bad that farmers can't grow enough food. That might explain why the Program is dialing down the population – and maybe getting rid of people."

She gazed for a moment at Edward, hoping for continued support, instead he questioned her. "Makes you wonder why the Program would intentionally use bad seeds."

Mary stopped, not believing he didn't catch on to what she was implying. "It must be they don't have a choice. They over-engineered the modified seeds and can't go back. Now the soil they thought would yield more has been over-used."

"Maybe, but still . . ."

"For the sake of argument, suppose the farmers had access to non-genetically modified heirloom seeds, ones from before the climate change, and that these grew big healthy plants. Wouldn't that imply the UV radiation was no longer a problem? Would the program want that known? No more UV protection shots, no more addiction, no more clamps on our aggression?"

"Mary!" Doc snarled.

Undeterred by his outburst and unwilling to yield, Mary held her hand in front of his face. "Doc? Stop. The plants in the Outcast fields aren't like ours. They're big and plump. There's no comparison. And get this, the Outcasts even have trees growing everywhere. Trees!

"Because they didn't have the capability to develop genetically-engineered seeds back in the day," she raced on, "I think they must have found a supply of unmodified heirloom seeds. Those old seeds are growing healthy plants, which implies the UV levels must no longer be a problem."

She glanced at Doc. He still seemed unconvinced.

"Maybe years ago, all our heirloom seeds were accidentally or intentionally destroyed. Who knows? All that remains now are the Franken-seeds, and they're not reversible. They've lost the original genetic recipe." Mary paused. "I bet my dad figured this out. That's why they murdered my family, to keep that quiet." She looked across Edward's bed to Doc for conformation.

"I don't know, Mary. I'm not sure I buy all your conclusions," he said, but Mary detected something about his demeanor was weakening.

"Why don't we finish hearing her out?" Edward chimed in. "I want to get to the plan."

Edward's encouragement spurred Mary on. "OK, let's consider some other things, Doc: why did the Program change the final injection? Originally it was a booster for protection, then eventually Outcasts weren't getting sick and dying soon enough from the rays. Things changed. They no longer needed the protection drugs. That had to be bad news in the ranks of the Program. I mean, they couldn't let healthy Outcasts be seen on our side of the wall. Everyone would figure out the drugs were no longer needed if the UV wasn't deadly anymore.

"That forced the Program's hand. They changed the final injection to make it quickly kill the Outcasts. It became our insurance policy, a murder weapon disguised as a booster shot. Clever, huh? The Program administers a booster shot that looks compassionate!"

"Just more conjecture and speculation. Guess work."

"All right, Doc," Mary retorted. "Then let me share hard evidence: the offspring of Outcasts don't get sick. I've met them and so have you. I've seen healthy generations of children and adults with my own eyes. You can't fake being healthy. Axel, the boy from the funeral, very healthy. You saw him with your own eyes. The only logical explanation why Outcasts don't get sick is that the radiation level isn't a problem anymore. The ozone layer has repaired, the UV levels are safe again, no one needs injections, and you know it."

Doc looked away from them. When he broke the silence, he looked beaten by the past. "Congratulations. You've worn me down, and you're not wrong. Some of us surmised the UV levels were no longer a problem."

"Wait, you already knew the UV was no longer a problem?"

Edward struggled to sit up in bed. "I can't believe what I just heard you say, Doc. You agree with Mary?"

"Don't push it. You need to be very careful about exposing Program lies. Things like the UV are a hot button. Bad things happen to people who try to expose the truth. I've witnessed the Program take people away. Nobody ever sees them again. You are talking deeply dangerous information here. All these years, I've felt a duty to your father, my best friend, to shield and protect you, and that's what I've done.

"Protect me from what? The truth?"

"If knowing the truth could get you killed, then yes, that was my call."

Hearing Doc say that made Edward angry. "You knew this all along, and you never said anything to Mary?"

"Listen, Edward, don't you try to pin guilt on me. My first duty is to save Mary from the fate the rest of her family suffered. I'm not the only one who knows or suspects that a lot of things about the Program don't add up, but I am smart enough not to question them openly. You two are new to this game. Of course, people in the community are suspicious. They're also smart enough to know that it's better to keep quiet than ask for bad things to happen to them or their families.

"I know Mary. It's not possible for her to keep secrets. It's not in her nature. It's better for a person like her not to know some things. You two shouldn't take me for a fool."

Mary broke in. "I didn't realize you thought so little of my ability to keep secrets. Too bad you thought too little of my ability to figure all this out on my own. Maybe the one fatal flaw in your overprotective nature, but for the record, I never implied you were a fool. Maybe you were in denial about Program lies, like the ozone, and your stance on the Outcasts makes no sense."

"You thought I was in denial? I've withheld information from you, young lady, because, like your father and brother, your stubborn curiosity could get you killed."

"Maybe, but I know the difference between what is true and what is a lie."

"Your father used to speak to me that way. If that's all it took to get him and your family killed, then you can understand why I've been protective. You have no idea how I worried about what might happen to your father and me back then, especially when we were dealing with Joey after he became an Outcast."

"What do you mean? What does Joey have to do with this?"

"You demonize the Program. I get that but, at the same time, you shouldn't think the Outcasts are such great people. They're dangerous. I assure you they've done bad things."

"I've never seen the Outcasts do anything bad. Tell me one single thing."

"You two need to grow up and face reality. All people do bad things, some more than others." Doc took a moment to sit and catch his breath. He asked for a glass of water. His head throbbed as the cool water hit his throat. "When I was a young doctor, my partner and I had a baby. Thomas's birth was the greatest thing that ever happened in my life. Unfortunately, I didn't realize how troubled my partner was. She could be funny and vivacious one minute and irate the next. She refused to take her meds. That created problems."

Mary felt the sorrow in Doc's voice.

"My partner was a tortured soul with a demon dancing in her head, and that demon made our relationship . . . difficult. She blamed me for her problems and, truthfully, maybe I was responsible for some of them. I was busy becoming this great doctor and not paying attention to my family. She was constantly irritated, especially with me. Maybe she began to hate me. One particularly cold day, she left home with our son, without a coat for either of them, without a word. I was frantic. Everyone, including your father, helped me search for them. In that weather, it would have been impossible to survive. As you can imagine, I was upset but mostly afraid of what might happen to them. We formed a search party to look for them, and eventually we found Adaeze, lying dead in a field. Apparently, she had committed suicide. My son was gone."

"Dad never told me. Oh, Doc, how horrible."

Edward struggled to speak. "And, your son?"

"Searched for days, but we couldn't find him. I thought I would lose my mind. I considered suicide and might have done it, if not for your father. Anyway, days later I learned that a young couple working in the fields came forward to say they had seen a man running with a baby in his arms. They said he disappeared near the wall. We realized then that my boy must have been kidnapped by Outcasts. You can imagine my emotional state – my partner dead, my son kidnapped, my family gone. They took my Thomas." Doc's face dropped into his hands.

So the loss of Thomas was the sorrow Doc had been concealing, Mary realized. How did this involved Joey, who was born years later?

When Doc lifted his head, he looked bewildered. "Outcasts kidnapped my boy. I knew that even if Thomas managed to survive through infancy, he'd eventually die from a UV-related disease. Do you understand? Without medications, he was doomed. I learned to hate them for stealing my son."

"Listen," Mary added, "Kidnapping your boy is a terrible thing. But not all Outcasts are like that. What about my brother Joey? No one showed him more compassion than you. Doc, you can't believe all Outcasts are bad."

"Joey was the exception," Doc mumbled. "We'll agree to disagree, but there is more to this story, and it concerns your brother. As you are aware, your father secretly met with Joey while he was an Outcast. Many times. One day Joey told your dad that he had seen a man who resembled me. He thought the likeness was uncanny. He asked around the Outcast community and discovered that this man had nearly died in a field as a baby."

"My God, that means your son is alive? That must have been fantastic news."

"Sure, Edward. What parent doesn't dream of a safe return of his kidnapped child? At the time Mary's father promised that Joey would find out more. Then, her family died in that accident. End of story."

"Wait that's not the end of the story," Mary said, after thinking about the situation. "That's why you lobbied for Joey to be admitted into the Care Place. Now I get it, you needed access to my brother to learn more." Her sympathy mixed with distain.

"Yes, the rest of the story. Maybe I wasn't as altruistic as you might have believed. After the accident, I started pestering the Program to let Joey into the facility. I convinced them it would look good to the community if they admitted him since most of your family had died in the fire. I also reminded them that Joey's illness was quite advanced. If they wanted, they could parade him around in public, like they had done with other sick Outcasts, you know, to support the narrative, as you like to remind me. I assured them that with his advanced mental and physical state, he wasn't a threat to the Program or anyone else. Then I said something which they found much more important; that we should study Joey because, even though he had been given the final injection, he was living longer than any other Outcast. That got their attention and was probably why they agreed to let him in."

"That's why you put Joey in that God-forsaken clinic? To use him?"

"Mary, you of all people know how much I loved your brother but, yes, I admit some of what I did was for selfish reasons. Unfortunately, however, by the time the Program admitted him, he was too sick to tell me anything about my son. My whole life – a doctor who's always too late to save the ones he loves most."

"Any parent would have done the same thing," Edward said, rasping through a cough. "Mary always says the last years of Joey's life were better because you helped get him admitted into that place. That's not selfish."

"Thank you, Edward, but I am guilty of not being honest."

"Well, if the guy Joey saw was your son, and he lived to adulthood without injections, doesn't that mean the UV radiation isn't a problem? I'm not a scientist, but . . ."

"You're a smart man. So, now let me ask you, what can you do with that knowledge that won't get you killed? The information is worthless. We're dependent for everything, and we need to live within these walls for better or worse. They make the rules. When you get to be my age, you'll see that knowing they lie isn't an asset, it's a liability. Your precious revelation here tonight doesn't change anything for us."

"Maybe it doesn't yet change anything, but it certainly matters to my plan, which is why I urgently needed to talk to you guys."

Doc shook his head in disbelief, "All right, but before we get to your plan, let me finish my story. I have more to confess. Mary, the reason Joey lived longer than any Outcast was because your father and I smuggled drugs to him to boost his immune system. The meds we gave him were to mitigate what he had been given in the final injection. He certainly would have died years earlier without that medication. Stealing those drugs was risky, but I loved that boy, like he was my own son. No one was supposed to know about what we had done. That bitch Delilah was as suspicious then as she is now, but she's never had the evidence to take to the authorities. That's it, that's my story."

"Doc, why am I only now learning about what you did for my brother?"

"Smuggling drugs with your father?" Doc let out a shrill. "We weren't even sure they would work, so your dad decided we shouldn't tell you girls or your mother about it. Why get your hopes up? He felt the less people knew, the safer for everyone. I supported his decision."

"What you did for my brother was a courageous thing, but you have to now stop protecting me from the truth."

"Maybe I was wrong to hold things back, but I promised Simian that if anything happened to him, I would protect his family. It turned out only you and Joey survived him, but I think I honored his wishes."

"You did." Mary hadn't heard her father's name Simian, named after his grandfather, uttered in years. She wished he were here.

Everyone was now tired. Edward was clearly fading. Doc was also nearing exhaustion but, after a belabored breath, he started up again. "Let me add one final word about this secret knowledge you think you have. People in power do whatever they need to stay in power. That applies to the Program and the Outcasts. And remember, the people in power get to write the history."

"Then here is some history you can't deny: the Outcasts saved your son. He would have died out there alone in the cold."

"Well, that verdict is still out, but they should have returned him to me."

"Go find him," Edward said, his eyes closed now.

"Find him? And then what?" Doc said, slouching back in the nearest chair and putting his feet up on Edward's bed. "If my son is alive, he doesn't know me. Who knows what the Outcasts told him – that when he was a baby his father and mother abandoned him in a frozen field to die?"

Mary started to reply but stopped herself. It was getting late. She would have to wait to divulge her plan. Mary watched Doc stretch his neck over the back of the chair and rub his eyes with the palms of his hands. He was exhausted, and Edward clearly needed more rest. She was about to suggest they take a short break, but both men were already lightly snoring.

CHAPTER 44

ENERGY CONSERVATION

Edward and Doc slept while Mary's mind raced on. While she was pleased with how things were progressing, getting them to accept what she was about to tell them would be harder. Maybe, she thought, she should use this interlude to conserve her energy for the next round of talks. She needed to rest, but an occurrence earlier the day before kept gnawing at her.

Walking home from the park after her meeting with Doc, one of her coworkers, Malik, called out to her. She knew him both from the Distribution Center and from childhood. A few years older, Malik had bullied Mary and her siblings as children. Their fathers had been friends, but they hadn't, then or now. She dreaded seeing him. What could he want?

"Mary, wait a minute," he yelled, awkwardly buttoning his coat and running to catch her. "Mind if I walk with you?"

"Malik? Hi," she forced out. "I'm almost home and sort of in a hurry." She paused and waited for him to come alongside her.

"Hey," he said catching his breath. "Wasn't that Doc Brisko I just saw you talking to in the park?"

Damn, Mary thought. They had been spotted together. That wasn't good, and it was exactly what Doc had been worried about. "Oh, you know Doc? Yeah, funny, we were both passing through the park when I ran into him. Good thing, too, because he reminded me I had forgotten to sign some papers in his office. We set a time to take care of all that." She was getting better at make excuses.

"That's nice. Listen, just a few quick questions, and a few might sound a bit strange."

Mary paused and looked at him. The idea of talking to him here and now was also strange. At work they often passed each other in the hallways, on occasion they might have casually waved, but never spoke. What could he want? Was it a coincidence that he appeared after her secret meeting with Doc? Was he a snitch sent to spy on her? Maybe the Program using him to get to her since they knew their parents had been friends? Or did this have something to do with Jude or her trips to the other side of the wall? Her mind raced. She didn't trust him.

"You remember my dad and your dad were good friends, right?" he asked.

"Of course, I remember." Mary stayed composed but kept a distance. "And, Malik, I should have told you this before, but I'm very sorry about what happened to your dad." Almost before those words had left her mouth, she realized how insincere they must have sounded. Malik's father had been dead for years. He had committed suicide, and everyone had talked about it at the time. She hated knowing that her face must be reddening. Pull it together and focus, Mary admonished herself.

"Oh yeah, thanks," he paused, aware of the awkwardness. "I appreciate that," he said, his voice signaling his surprise. "Sure, and uh, very sorry about your family, also."

"Guess it's not a very good thing that we have in common, is it?"

"No, no, it isn't. But that does bring me to what I want to ask you. Did your dad ever mention to you someone named Emad? Or anything about his papers?"

Mary was leery about the direction the conversation was taking. "Emad? No, I don't think so. Why?"

"I'm not sure. This is probably me being silly, but I think this guy Emad is somehow related to my father's death." He looked around before speaking again. "Mary, I don't accept that my dad killed himself. He was always such an upbeat person. You remember him. Anyway, let me back up and explain. I once overheard our dads discussing a guy named Emad and something about his papers."

At this point, Malik had Mary's full attention. It had been years since anyone had asked her anything about her dad's work, and here was one story she had never heard.

"And what about him, this guy Emad?"

"I had never heard the name Emad before. Being a curious kid, I questioned my dad about him later that day. But when I started running around the apartment shouting stupid stuff like 'Emad, he mad,' my father became uncharacteristically upset with me. He grabbed me, covered my mouth, and scolded me, telling me never to mention Emad's name again, not to anyone. Of course, that scared me, but it also made me even more curious about the guy. Dad was so upset, I figured I'd ask him about it another time, you know, when he was calmer. Unfortunately, a few days later, two guards came and told me and my mom they found my dad in some old government medical facility. He had killed himself. I've been thinking about things for years, and the other day it occurred to me your father might have mentioned this Emad fellow to you. But I guess he didn't, huh?"

It dawned on Mary that she did remember hearing the name Emad. But it had been in a different context and from Joey, not her father. She decided it was best not to divulge that information to Malik. It was still possible he was a snitch sent by the Program.

"Sorry, no. My father never mentioned anyone named Emad."

"I was sure hoping you could help me figure this mystery out. Maybe it's time to let the secrets of the dead go, huh?"

Just as Mary was about to say a cordial goodbye, a booming voice yelled out to them.

"You two, stop right there!" In the distance they saw a tall guard running full tilt toward them. Mary and Malik froze. Moments later a second guard came charging up. He was obviously out of breath, but he ran up to the first guard. "Damn it, Henry, you didn't grab him? I was sure you got the bastard."

"No, I couldn't catch him. Son of a bitch got away. He was way too fast for me."

"And what's the story with these two? Did they help him escape?"

"Not sure yet. Did you two see the SOB I was chasing?" the first guard growled at Mary and Malik.

"No, sir, we didn't see anyone," Mary replied, her voice trembling.

"Lady, I saw you leaving the park. What the hell are you two doing here?"

She was nervous that this guard might have seen her with Doc, so she knew to be careful how she responded, "I was just walking through that park. That's all, it's a short cut. I wanted to meet my friend. We wanted to talk about work and stuff." Mary glanced over at Malik, hoping that he wasn't so freaked out by the interrogation that he might feel compelled to tell the guards she had been meeting with Doc. Instead he stood frozen, unable to speak.

"Lady, nobody should be going through that park unless they have to. You know that place is contaminated right?"

Mary was well acquainted with the rumor about the park, she had heard that all her life, but she didn't believe it. She figured the guards concocted that story so that workers wouldn't frequent the park or the Kabak. To be safe however, she feigned ignorance, "Contaminated? No, sir, I didn't know that."

"Well, it is. Anyway, you said you two were talking about work?"

By now Malik had thought of something to say. "Mary and I both work at the Distribution Center. If you like, you can check with our bosses. We just finished our shift. We were talking about the weekly department tally and, you know, other stuff."

Malik had lied, which made Mary feel better, most likely proving he was not a Program snitch.

"Stuff? What other stuff?" the first guard once again growled.

"What he means is," Mary said, showing Malik's sweaty hand in hers, "Boy-girl stuff. We just learned we've been paired, and he was walking me home. You know, to get to know each other."

The first guard turned to look at his friend. He contorted his face, conveying how surprised that this homely man had lucked out and was going to be paired with such a pretty girl.

"Paired, huh? I don't guess either of you saw which direction that Outcast ran?"

"He must not have come this way. Either that or we were too busy to notice. But sir, surely an Outcast couldn't get far, as sickly as those vultures are," Mary replied, hoping to appeal to his sensibilities.

"Well, this one was healthy. Son of a bitch was pretty fast, too, wasn't he, Paulie?"

"I couldn't catch him. I was just hoping to herd him toward you."

Mary looked at how tired and out of shape the two guards were. Neither one of them would ever have been able to catch Axel or Raj.

"Alright," the first guard said, "There's no point in holding you. Paul, you in agreement? We let them go?"

"Can't see how they're of any use to us now. Send them home."

"You heard the man. Get out of here before that SOB comes back. Outcasts are dangerous. And if you two know what's good for you, you'll stay out of that filthy park. Now move along."

"Yes, sir. Thank you. We will," she replied, pulling a shaken Malik along by his hand as they walked away. She had no idea what was going on with Emad or the Outcasts, but when she said goodbye to Malik, she noticed he looked nothing less than terrified.

CHAPTER 45

THE PLAN

She hated to wake them, they looked so innocent, but time was running out. They could all rest more later. She bent over Edward's bed.

"Was I dreaming that you kissed me?" he whispered, pulling her closer. "Your plan, we haven't heard it yet."

"I'm almost there, hon."

Doc stretched like a cat and pleaded, "Have mercy. You can't be serious. There's more? Your little test of endurance discussion on the truth wasn't enough? I want to go home. I need to sleep in my own lumpy bed. I can't talk anymore."

"Then don't. I have a plan, Doc, and it only works with your help. Bear with me for just a little longer." Mary noticed the look of exasperation.

"For God's sake," Doc whined, "make it fast."

"OK, then, answer this: is there is a way to break our addiction?"

"You can die. That will break it," he said, still not opening his eyes.

"Come on, it's late. Answer honestly. I need to know if there's a way to break the addiction . . . without dying."

Doc sat up and stared her down. "The Program has drugs they use with new guard recruits. Antipsychotics. They take them for a few weeks during training, so the Program can ween them off the regular injections."

Edward perked up, "They do? I thought they went through intense mental training regimen, like it said in the notebook. You know, so they can minimize their violent attacks."

"Maybe back then that was sufficient. Not anymore. Now they want the guards to be tough and aggressive toward Outcasts . . . and maybe toward troublemakers, like us."

"Then why don't the guards realize that they don't need injections?"

"I didn't say they don't get injections. They still get shots, but the formulation is different. It could just be a placebo, but something in their shots is addictive. The Program is not going to relinquish control over the guards."

"Are you saying that with these injections, they avoid the convulsions? How do you know about this?"

"Doctors talk. Might be safer if we kept our mouths shut, but we talk. The drugs they use to ween them are a combination of buprenorphine, clonidine, and loperamide. Don't let me mislead you, though. Even with those drugs, it's a tough withdrawal that can be deadly if handled incorrectly."

"So, you're saying tough withdrawal but possible," Mary asked, wondering how that would impact her plan. "And I assume you could you get your hands on these drugs?"

"Are you kidding? No. They monitor those drugs closely. What are you scheming, anyway? Why do you want to get off the injections?"

"We need to think big picture. I want the three of us to kick the habit."

"That's crazy talk. Do you realize how dangerous that would be? I know what you're thinking, but they'd kill us before they'd let us show the community we don't need those shots for protection from the UV."

Could that have been what happened to Malik's father? Mary wondered. "No, they couldn't kill us, not if we were somewhere else, somewhere safe."

Both men turned, perplexed by her comment.

"Doc, you're being investigated, and you said yourself that it's probably going to end badly. During the investigation, they'll figure out about you and Edward, and it's also likely they'll implicate me. We need to leave here."

"We may get into trouble after this investigation, but what choice do we have?" Edward asked.

"Hon, we do have a choice. What if the three of us get the hell out of here? What if we escape, go to the other side of the wall?"

"Live with the Outcasts? That's what you're suggesting? They hate us. They'd accuse us of being spies and hang us. Maybe torture us before that."

"No Doc, that's not true."

"And how do you propose we get to the other side? It's guarded night and day, they'll shoot us on sight. It's impossible."

"You know that my dad went numerous times, so don't pretend we can't get there. I know a way in without being detected. When I was with the Outcast community, they weren't hostile. I don't think they hate us, not all of them, anyway. A couple of guys there know me and, Doc, they know who you are, too, because they've asked about you several times. Think about it. When we're there, we could look for Thomas."

"Even if I wanted to go along, which I don't, I'm a sick man, I have heart issues. I can hardly walk. An escape attempt would kill me."

"I have a way to handle things. Edward and I know a guy who has a truck. He'll take us to the wall. I've . . . I've actually already arranged our passage."

"You're asking me to leave everything behind – patients who depend on me, colleagues, lifelong friends? I won't do it."

"Then tell me what is going to happen to you when this investigation is finished? What's the Program going to do to you? Chances are, make you work in the fields or give you the final injection, which would instantly give you a heart attack. You spent your life promising Dad you would protect me. Now you have the chance to get our protection."

Doc looked at them in disbelief.

"The three of us need to get the hell out of here. We're all implicated with this scheme that made Edward sick, so we're safer with the Outcasts than we are here." Mary paused to catch her breath. "And there is another reason for us to be afraid of the Program. . . ."Doc cut her off. "I'll stay behind and deflect them. If my final act is protecting you, so be it."

"Look how sick Edward is; I can't do this alone. He'll die on the trip without you. Once we take the withdrawal drugs, the three of us can support each other. If we stay, they'll murder us. We're done."

Doc shook his head, "I don't know. Maybe if I were younger. I'm not a risktaker."

"Are you kidding me? Look what you've done for us already. The way I see it, we've got nothing to lose. It's late. Think about a way to get the withdrawal drugs. I'll take care of transport."

Edward wasn't sure about the soundness of the plan, either. "Once again, why would the Outcasts let us in, and what exactly would we do there?"

"Love, believe me, they'll let us in. The three of us could teach reading and writing. They don't have doctors. Eventually Doc could teach them about medicine. We have a lot to offer."

"Mary . . . "

"Doc, please." Mary said, rising to the challenge. "why does the Program wait until people like me are older before they pair us? At work, so many unpaired men and women my age are waiting. Why are couples limited to one child? I bet I can tell you the answer."

"Why am I not surprised," Doc said flatly.

"Vinesh told us the farmers have no new soil, and we now know they don't have good seeds. The Program is limiting the population because they're dealing with failing crops, a food crisis."

Doc leaned back, nervously scratching his head. When it came to Mary, he was poised for lengthy arguments, but rarely agreements. Mary was making a connection that should have been obvious to him. "Well, actually, you could be right. Couples are being told to have fewer babies than your parents did, for example. Births are down, I know because I deliver them. Yes, could be the Program is running out of resources again." He began pacing the room.

"Again?" Edward questioned.

"When I was a boy, everyone in the community worked to tear down and then rebuild the walls farther out so we could claim new land. That's when the big troubles with the Outcasts began."

"Move the wall? Crap, if they're that desperate again, they're even more dangerous to us." Everyone took a moment to absorb the truth in what Mary had to say. "It's time for me to tell you the biggest news of all. Doc, you may want to sit back down for this."

CHAPTER 46

THE BIG REVEAL

Edward gasped as Mary placed his hand on her belly. "You're pregnant?"

Doc shook his head. "Unbelievable, simply unbelievable. How can you be so sure you're pregnant?"

"You can examine me later, but there is no doubt I'm pregnant."

"What the hell were you two thinking? You've made such a stupid mistake!"

Edward jumped in, still in shock, "How? We were so careful."

"I don't know, Edward. It happened. Life happens. Call it fate or God or just plain old-fashioned biology. I certainly didn't want to get pregnant, but I am, and now I'm happy about it. Truly happy."

Doc continued to shake his head in disbelief. "So, this is the real reason you tried to talk me to death tonight? Damn it, Mary, soon you won't be able to hide this – and anyway it'll be exposed in the next quarterly blood test. I'll be forced to perform the abortion. I warned you. This is bad!"

"Stop it, both of you. This is a good thing. No one is giving me an abortion. I'm having this baby, and you're going to deliver it. I would rather die escaping than stay and let the Program kill my baby."

"Is it hot in here? My ears were ringing again, Doc." Edward's head felt like it was going to explode. "Wow. One minute I'm close to death, the next a father? How crazy is that?"

"I'm scared, too, but now you guys understand why we must get out of here. All three, make that four, of us. We need to leave before the Program discovers and comes after Doc."

"Can you believe this, Grandpa? She didn't tell me, either," Edward rambled, his speech slurred. "Can you make the room stop swirling? We're having a baby."

"Lovebird, I didn't tell you because you were in a fight for your life. I thought you were dying. And I wasn't completely sure I was pregnant until recently. Isn't it wonderful news?"

Doc leaned over to check Edward's vitals and then Mary's. When he finished, he was indignant. "Hours ago. You could have shared this news hours ago," he growled, glaring at Mary, putting his stethoscope away. "While I appreciate the urgency, I need to be honest with you, taking withdrawal drugs while pregnant could impact the development of the baby. Listen, I have no idea what these withdrawal drugs do to a fetus."

"It doesn't matter, does it?" Edward said, struggling to get out of bed. "I'm with Mary. The three of us leave. If we don't, no baby. Withdrawal drug risks are better than forced abortion or a heart attack from their final injection. We escape, take our chances with the drugs."

"Lay back down. No one's dead yet," Doc whispered, as he lifted Edward's feet back in bed and covered his shaking body. "It's settled. Rest now. We leave soon."

"Peace at last." Edward curled onto his side, exhausted.

Mary followed Doc around to the other side of the bed and squeezed him. "After work, two evenings from now, you and Edward need to meet me at the loading dock. I'll handle the rest." Mary pulled two books off Edward's shelf and held them up to Doc. "Bring your books with you."

"So, we're giving books to the Outcasts?"

Hearing Doc's comment made Mary laugh. "The Outcasts couldn't care less about acquiring more books. They have half of what's left of a library full of books; they don't need ours."

Edward blinked through watery eye slits. "Huh?"

"What's so funny is that most of them can't read or write," Mary said. "The irony. They have a library full of books that would be the envy of anyone in the Program, but they can't read or write. Come on, don't you think that's funny."

"Not really," Doc said, unable to find the humor. "It's tragic. Why waste them if they don't need them?"

"The books are for Vinesh, the guy with the truck who will get us closer to the wall. He wants a load of books as payment for the trip. They're valuable on the black market. I've already sorted a bag of my own. Just bring books and withdrawal drugs, Doc. I'll see you both in two days. Edward are you listening?"

"Two days. Books. Meet at the dock."

Mary kissed Edward's forehead. "See? You're better already."

Once Edward's fever lowered, Doc sagged into the chair beside his bed, pondering the dangers of getting withdrawal drugs without getting caught and the dangers of delivering his first grandchild on the other side of the wall.

CHAPTER 47

ESCAPE ATTEMPT

To Mary, the long wait at work seemed interminable. With each passing minute, she grew more nervous until, finally, it was time to leave her desk. She smoothed her hair, grabbed her bag of books, and quickly headed to the dock. When she arrived, Jorge's office was vacant, just as she had hoped. He had already left for the day. Inside she anxiously she paced, peering out his window for Edward and Doc.

To stop the fear from engulfing her, she shook her arms rigorously. Where were the flaws in her plan? Was she about to get everybody killed? What if Doc or Edward were too weak to survive the escape or the withdrawal drugs? What if she couldn't remember the exact location of the entrance to the tunnel? And what if that tunnel had been sealed? Considering how easily the guards could discover their escape made her palms sweat. She felt nauseous.

She couldn't think of any improvements out of the mess they were in. The guys were committed to the plan and depending on her to succeed. That morning, her last day in the apartment, she knelt to repeat her father's prayer, asking for strength from his God of the Universe. Like previous times, she felt better afterward. She needed to get a hold of herself. She started humming to crush her doubts: she was pregnant, the man she loved was on his way, they would take care of Doc, Doc would take care of the baby, and they would live as a family. This plan would allow that dream to happen. She pictured it in her head. Now, everyone needed to show up.

When she heard a vehicle pull up, she peered out the window that faced the dock. Right on time, Vinesh was parking his truck. He glanced toward the window and waved from the cab. She noticed he was using a different vehicle. The truck had a back section completely covered with heavy canvas. Relieved to see him, she ran out of the office and onto the dock to greet him.

"Ready?" he called out.

"They aren't here yet, but they're on the way," she replied, trying her best to sound confident despite their tardiness. "Hey, Vinesh, fancy truck."

"Yeah, I thought this one should be a lot better for our trip. Listen, I'll be loading in the back, they need to get here soon. If I hang around, management will start asking questions about the timing of my deliveries."

"No, I understand, you won't have to." She marveled at what a good liar she was, but she had no idea where they were or how long they'd be. Had Edward's health taken a turn for the worst, or had the investigators detained Doc? Or worse, had her trust in Doc been misplaced? Surely, that was not possible.

"So, you brought stuff for me, like you promised?" Vinesh asked, still loading the truck.

"I have valuable books in this bag and better ones are coming with the guys."

"Good. So, exactly where do you want to be dropped off? A celebration venue?"

At that moment they both heard footsteps and saw Doc and Edward approaching. "Look. That's them now," she said excitedly. They were struggling and looked exhausted.

"Get them into the truck as quickly as possible. The less time here, the lower the chance someone sees us."

Mary's heart raced as she hugged Doc and Edward and hurried them toward the back of the truck. Vinesh stopped loading long enough to nod his head, signaling them to hide behind the bags and boxes he had already loaded. They understood and crouched in a huddle behind the large pile of bad-smelling fertilizer. The metal floor was filthy with rust and prickly coarse bits of debris from welded repairs. Nervously they waited for him to finish loading.

Vinesh made his way to the back of the truck and behind the stack of bags where they were hiding. "Payment?"

Doc took the four book bags he and Edward brought and dumped the contents out. He forgot that withdrawal medicines were in the bottom of one of his bags. As the pile of books fell out, so did a handful of brown bottles.

Horrified, Mary glared at Doc. He wasn't close enough to reach them. Luckily, Vinesh had been sufficiently distracted.

"What a stash," he exclaimed. "Better than I imagined. And so many of them. I'll get a lot for these in trade. I think I like doing business with you."

"We thought you'd think that," Edward replied.

Smiling at his booty, Vinesh turned his attention to Edward, "And how are you doing, lovebird?"

"Fine, fine. Thanks for doing this."

"My pleasure, but guy, I have to say, you don't look so good. Sick or something?"

For a moment, Edward's eyes inexplicably fixated on the bottles of drugs that had dropped from the bags. Catching himself, he looked away, hoping to divert Vinesh's attention. His recovery was too late. Vinesh had followed his glance down to the bottles.

Edward bent over and helped Doc put the bottles back into the bag. "Yeah, a little infection, but that's why Doc brought along meds," he said dryly.

Vinesh intuitively stepped back. "Hmm. Hope you get better soon," he said, watching as Doc and Edward collected the scattered bottles. "This is Doc? We haven't met yet."

"I'm his doctor. . . Breezeway. Glad to meet you. Vinesh, right?"

"That's me, Vinesh. Dr. Breezeway, the pleasure is mine. Those are great books you brought for me. Welcome aboard. Once I put the booty inside, we will get going. One last thing, if I get stopped and the guards want to do an inspection or anything else, stay back. Don't move. Stay hidden and keep quiet. Got it?" Vinesh didn't wait for questions. He jumped down and closed the back doors of the truck, causing a clatter of metal against metal.

The lock sealed and, a second later, they jostled from the weight of Vinesh jumping into the cab. They felt the engine vibrate and the gears crank beneath them. The old truck rattled as it built speed. There was no turning back.

It didn't take long for their cramped bodies to get hot and stuffy. The odor emanating from the bags was noxious. Mary willed herself not to vomit in such tight quarters. No one spoke, but Edward, now clammy, held onto her tightly. Clearly this trip was not going to be easy for any of them.

When the truck suddenly rocked to a sharp stop, it threw the three of them against the back wall. They froze in place, holding their breath, afraid to move or make a sound. Had the guards stopped the truck? They strained to listen, but all they could hear was the crunch of footsteps on gravel. The clanging of the truck's back door locks startled them. When the doors swung open, the moonlight that washed in with a cool breeze temporarily blinding them. Carefully they peered out from behind the fertilizer bags. It was Vinesh, but from their vantage point, there was no way to see if he was alone.

"Mary!"

She leaned out over the pile of bags, so he could see and hear her. "Yes?"

"Jump down, I need to talk to you. You two stay back."

Mary and Edwards's eyes met, and she could see the fright in them, "You shouldn't go alone," he whispered, instinctively grabbing her arm. "He can talk to you right here."

"I'll be fine, Edward," she said, gently easing his grip. She moved around the bags, jumped down, and followed Vinesh to the side of the truck.

Doc and Edward readjusted their bodies and sucked in the fresh air that rushed into the back of the truck. They strained to hear what was being said outside. A few minutes later a smiling Mary returned. They watched as she made her way back behind the bags.

Seeing she was well-hidden, Vinesh slammed the back doors once again shutting them in. Moments later the truck lurched forward, made a sharp turn, and barreled down another bumpy road.

"Damn it, Mary! What the hell happened out there?" Doc whispered.

"He got lost, so I had to help him figure out how to get back on track. We should be there soon. I think."

"My heart can't take this. I'm too old . . ."

Edward smiled, sighed a little breath of relief, and pulled Mary close, "That was scary, Mary."

"I know, we are all frightened, but I trust Vinesh. He's looking out for us. It's going to be all right. I promise."

"I want to believe that," Doc mumbled.

A short while later, the truck lurched to another stop. They waited for what seemed like an eternity before the back doors of the truck swung open.

"We've arrived," Vinesh said. "Sort of out in the middle of nowhere, don't you think, Mary? Should I come back for you in a while after I drop off this load?"

"No, we're good, thanks. This place is set up for celebrations, so it's perfect for us tonight. Thanks for taking us and for keeping this our little secret. Remember our deal. You never saw us, we were never here."

"As far as I'm concerned, I never met any of you. Anyway, I'd be in trouble if anyone found out I let you ride along with me. But I'm curious, what the hell are you guys going to do all the way out here at night?"

"If I said it had something to do with a religious ritual, would you believe me?"

"Ha, devil worshipping?" Vinesh joked. "No, you need to do better than that for me to believe you. You guys don't look like the type, nope, I don't believe that. Good one, lovebirds, ha!"

"You're always one step ahead of us, Vinesh."

"Fine, fine, never mind, don't tell me. Better if I don't know anyway. Doc, good to meet you, sir. Lovebirds, good luck. Whatever you're up to, stay clear of the devil. I'm out of here." Vinesh hoisted himself into the cab of his truck and sped into the darkness.

The silence was deafening. Mary hoped she remembered where the tunnel entrance was located as the three of them slowly trudged through the moonlit area. The walking grew harder for both guys, so she paused twice to let them rest as she tried to get her bearings in the dark.

Edward, watching her survey the area, spoke first. "Don't worry, Mary, you're going the right way. I followed you that night, remember?"

With that confirmation, Mary was more confident about their direction of travel and did her best to get them moving faster. The longer they were exposed, the more likely they would be discovered.

"Come on, guys. Please, we have to move a little faster. We're too exposed in this field. We're nearing the wall, and it'll be guarded. I promise it's only a little farther."

Only-a-little-farther took a full 15 minutes before she saw the small mound that covered the entrance to the tunnel. "OK, guys, we're here. Sit and rest while I figure out how to open this thing."

On hands and knees, Mary cleared away dirt and stones until she exposed the top of the lid to the tunnel. She knocked on it a few times to check if an Outcast member might be inside. As she banged she realized that making such a noise might be a bad idea. Edward and Doc looked terrified as the sound echoed off the nearby wall. She had to get the hatch open, but no matter how hard she pulled, the lid wouldn't budge. Fear sliced through her as she considered the possibility that the tunnel might be sealed.

"Guys," she whispered, "Come over and help me."

Edward and Doc lumbered over. Kneeling, the three each took a spot, grabbing a handle around the lid and in concert pulling as hard as they could. The lid squealed and released and, as they fell backward, the entrance to the tunnel opened.

Mary was surprised by its damp stuffy smell. Somehow, tonight, the tunnel was darker than she had remembered. Then she realized she forgot a flashlight. She had scolded Ena the night of their trip to the blue building. She now gave Ena the credit she deserved. Having a light would have been a handy tool to have.

The guys were oblivious to her mistake. Instead they exhibited a look of relief.

Edward beamed a smile easily seen in the dim moonlight. "Babe, you did it! You got us to the tunnel. I can't believe we made it."

Mary was pleased. "Edward, you sound surprised. You doubted me?"

"Never!" he replied, "Well, yeah, maybe. OK, for a little back there when the truck stopped, but I never doubted you'd come through for us." Edward's twisted about-face made them laugh. Obviously, they all had doubts about making it this far, including Mary.

"Well, guys, don't go thanking me yet," she said, taking Doc's hand and gently moving him closer to the entrance. "You first, Doc. Slide down in there. Hold onto the ladder. Edward will follow, and then I'll go after you two and close the lid behind us." Doc carefully stepped one foot at a time while gripping the ladder tightly with both hands. When he felt sufficiently stable he removed one hand and reached out touching the wet rock and dirt wall that surrounded him. It felt cool and slimy. He was not happy to be in this dark place. He then proceeded down the ladder and into the tunnel moving ahead just enough to make room for Edward and Mary.

They moved cautiously through the pitch-black tunnel, feeling their way along. Mary, pleased that she had found the tunnel, relaxed and thought of what they were going to say when they popped out the other end.

OUTCASTVILLE

Doc noticed a sliver of light surrounding the lid on the Outcast side of the tunnel. Dutifully he pushed himself against the lid and leaned in with his whole body. It didn't move. "Damn it, it won't budge."

Sensing Doc's panic, Mary squeezed around Edward. Together, she and Doc pushed on the lid to no avail. Suddenly her hands became moist, her breathing labored, and her face felt hot. She was getting claustrophobic. Axel had told about the test to see if she had told anyone about the tunnel. Was it sealed at this end? Had they come all this way for nothing? That thought made her feel worse.

No, they had come too far. Using the touch of her fingers along the dirt walls, she pressed along the wet walls searching for a rock she could dislodge. After a few unsuccessful attempts, she wiggled one that broke free. With a new-found might, she slammed the rock three times against the lid. Her fingers caught between the lid and the rock, and the pain they unleashed reverberated throughout the tunnel.

"The Outcasts had to have heard that," she said, squeezing her hands in tight fists trying to stop the pain. Her voice shook. No one moved, waiting to see if someone would come.

Above them they heard shuffling then the sound of male voices. Raising the rock a second time, she banged once more solidly against the lid. "It's Mary, Joey's sister. Open up." If people were outside, they wouldn't be able to ignore her now.

A moment later the lid popped open and the full moon blinded them as the scent of fresh cool air filled their nostrils.

Above them was the silhouette of two men. Mary couldn't tell if they were Outcasts or guards. One appeared to be holding a gun like the guards carried, but she was sure they had to be Outcasts.

Whoever's hands they were in no longer mattered as much as getting out of the tunnel. She was now at the top of the exit ladder and she wiggled her arm through the opening and waved. "Please help us out of here. There are three of us."

Two men reached down and grabbed Mary's arms and hoisted her up. Doc and Edward were next. For a moment, no one spoke. The five stared at each other in the dim moonlight. The man with the gun was the first to speak. "Who the hell are you, and how did you get in our tunnel?"

"I'm Mary, I've been here before. Axel brought me through this tunnel. Axel and Raj know me and were friends of my brother, Joey, and his son, Jude. These are my friends, Edward and Doctor Brisko."

"Holy shit, you're damn Program spies," he said, in a voice that conveyed he thought they were worthless. He pushed his gun into Edward's chest. "You three have made a terrible mistake. You can't be here, we don't like spies, not alive anyway!"

"Wait! You don't understand. We're not spies. We're running away from the Program. We're in big trouble. They'll kill us if they find us. Get Axel. He knows me. He'll tell you about me."

"Shut up! You'll be lucky if we don't kill you right now!"

Edward moved slightly toward him but, as he did, the man used the end of his gun to shove him to the ground. Edward braced himself as he fell backward into the hard dirt. His heart raced, and he realized he was in no position to challenge this huge man.

"You two, over here next to this guy. Get away from that tunnel. Sit down, shut up. Do it." The two Outcasts then backed away to converse. The man without the gun ran off into the darkness.

Mary made another attempt at reason. "Please, if you just get . . ."

"Shut up, lady! I told you to shut up! Not another word unless you want this gun down your throat."

As they sat in the dead zone with the light from the moon behind them, she could see in the distance three silhouettes running in their direction. The gunman yelled out, "We found them here, banging on the tunnel lid. This woman says she's been here before."

As the figures approached, Mary recognized Axel.

"I know her." Axel yelled to the man holding the gun. "Yeah, that's Joey's sister, and I know who this guy is, too. He's a doctor."

A third large stocky man spoke up. "Bravo, Dimitri. You and Ivan honor your people by capturing them. Axel and I will take over now. I recognize this lady, watched her play with Jude. We got this."

Dimitri, not yet satisfied with the situation, spoke. "And the other two, boss? Why the hell are they here?"

"No idea . . . Axel, what's going on?"

"I know those two, the doctor and the lady. Her name is Mary. That sick-looking one, I don't know who he is."

Mary rubbed her hands around her belly, hoping to indicate she was with child, but it was too dark for anyone to notice. "He's my partner, Edward, the father of my baby. He's with me."

"They look pitiful to me, harmless. All right, guys, Axel and I will deal with them. Dimitri, you and Ivan send somebody or go yourselves to make sure that tunnel is secured on the other end. Got that? Make sure it's hidden and secure."

"Yes, sir, got it," he replied, "But maybe I should stay and hold my gun to their jaws while you figure things out?"

"If I didn't need you elsewhere, that would be good."

Dimitri glanced at Edward and spit at him in disgust. "Boss, why don't we just kill them now? We could throw their heads over the wall. Now that would send a clear message to the Program. Pay 'em back for killing Israel."

"Do as you're told. And Dimitri? I've said this before, we don't know that anybody killed Israel or why he died, so don't go spreading those rumors."

"He came back from over there and then he died. They poisoned him."

"You don't know that. Now go. That's an order. In the morning, I meet with Mother. I'll announce what we're going to do then. And you know what will happen if I hear that either one of you has spread that Israel rumor."

Mary watched Dimitri and Ivan back off and wondered what kind of power this boss man held. Then she remembered the first time she visited Jude. She recognized him as the same guy who had signaled to Axel that playtime was over.

"Axel," the man commanded, "I want to talk to these people, especially her. You know her, so you may stay. If you hear her lie, you will tell me. Understood?"

Axel nodded to him and then to Mary. She took that to mean she was being given permission to speak.

"Lady, why are you three here?"

She seized the invitation. "My name is Mary. This is Edward and Doc. I'm pregnant with Edward's baby, but we're not a Program pair. They'd surely kill my baby if they found out. Edward's sick, and Doc is helping me care for him. He was my father's best friend and is like a father to me. You need to know it's not Axel's fault that we used the tunnel. He warned me not to tell anyone about it, but using it to come here was the only way I could get us out of danger."

"So, you think you're out of danger? Bad timing on your part," he went on, "People here aren't ever fond of your kind, and tempers are running high right now. Ivan and Dimitri aren't the only ones who might want to kill you. Everyone thinks the rumor about Israel is true, that the Program killed him. If they did poison him, it certainly wouldn't be the first time. The poor guy was just a teenager, and it was his first trip to gather intelligence."

"We don't know anything about Program killings or Israel. With our injections, we can't be aggressive toward anyone. But I'm sure you know that. Whatever happened to your friend, we had nothing to do with it."

"Hmm.

Mary glanced at Doc's pursed lips. She had better say something fast, or he was going to explode. "Sir, really, please, we need to stay.

We're in so much trouble. They'll kill us for sure. We know too much."

"Know too much? Is that right?" he said, wryly.

"Look at my partner. He's sick . . . I'm pregnant . . . and Doc, in the shape he's in, is trying to take care of both of us."

"Lady, none of that is my problem. Axel, grab that bag from the old doctor and empty it out."

Axel immediately dumped Doc's medical supplies on the ground.

"And what's all this?"

"I'm solely responsible for those medicines," Doc spoke up. "The bottle of green pills are for Edward's illness. The liquid is our withdrawal drug – to kick the habit, so we can get off the addiction to the injections."

"Addiction, maybe. Or, maybe Dimitri was right; that's the poison your kind used on Israel. Axel, gather those up and give them to me."

"Nonsense. I assure you, those are our withdrawal drugs," Doc defended.

"Prove it. Give some of those drugs to this guy," he said looking at Edward."

Doc shook his head in disbelief, but gave two pills and one of the bottles of withdrawal drugs to Edward. Facing their captors, Edward tilted his head back, stuck his tongue out as far as he could, and placed the pills at the back. Then he swallowed hard, chasing them down with a short swig from the bottle. Once he had swallowed them he again opened his mouth wide, scanning his head around for everyone to see.

"If that guy gets any sicker, you're all going to die and not in a painless way. Understand?"

"Yes, I do. It's medicine not poison. And it's for us, not you."

"Well until I see the results, I'm holding the rest of this stuff."

Doc spoke again, this time more forcefully. "Look, I'm a doctor. I've been one for more than 30 years. Those drugs are important. We could die from the withdrawal symptoms without them. You can clearly see how weak Edward is. You must give them back to me."

"Maybe later. Or, maybe I'll order my people to push all of you back through that tunnel. That would take care of my problem. Or, hey, better yet, maybe we do like Dimitri wants, and make an example of you. Chop off your heads, throw them over the wall, send our reply back to the Program about messing with us. That would satisfy more people than you can imagine. So many choices, and none of them are yours to make, old man. You think you can just show up here and tell me what to do?"

Doc stumbled backward. Instinctively Edward placed his arms around him.

"He's the best damn doctor you'll ever have," Mary blurted from somewhere deep inside. She stood up and approached the boss, wagging her finger in his face. "Now you listen to me. Joey was my brother, Jude is my nephew, and Axel and Raj pursued me and brought me here first. Outcasts show up on the Program side of the wall all the time. What's the difference?" she scolded.

Doc and Edward stared at their warrior, unsure if her confidence showed a lack of control that might get them killed or the courage of a leader they had not recognized before.

He chuckled at her brazenness, "Good point, now sit down. Our guys are trained spies. And, you three are . . . ? You're too pitiful to be spies. You should have seen your faces when I threatened to cut off your heads. And, if you were killers, like your Program guards, you would have moved aggressively toward me and been able to take my punishment."

"We haven't done anything to you, and we couldn't even if we wanted to," Edward told him.

"Fella, I already figured that part out. You three seem harmless. I'm not in the mood to kill . . . not yet, anyway. But you need to understand the bad position you've put me in."

"We understand," Doc said in a firm voice.

"Excellent. Now we appreciate each other's problems. So, here is what happens next. Lady comes with me, explains why the three of you are here and why I shouldn't send you back. If her story pans out, then no harm comes to you. Axel remains on guard. If I find out that you gave him any trouble, I'll hand you over."

". . . to the Program?" Mary asked her voice noticeably concerned. "To those men over there."

Mary looked over. A small crowd had gathered on a rise of land a short distance away. Their silhouettes reminded her of the crowd that watched the guards beat the boy who pushed her aside as he fled. But this crowd, she guessed, wasn't sympathetic. She shuttered at what seemed like another lifetime.

"And who knows what surprises they're capable of. Dimitri and his friends don't like your Program people, but they do what I tell them. For now, if you're honest with me, and don't give me any more problems, you'll be fine. You may call me King Solomon," he said, redirecting his attention to Axel. "Go tell Raj to bring Jude here first thing tomorrow morning, then get yourself back here and guard these two. I need to talk to Mother."

Mary watched Axel disappear into the darkness. A few minutes later, he came running back. "I took care of it. He'll bring Jude tomorrow," he said, hardly winded.

"Good, now guard them and make sure nobody hurts our uninvited guests. You two should rest, relax. You both look terrible," he said to Edward and Doc. "You, come with me," King Solomon said, pointing to Mary. "We need to talk."

Walking away, Mary glanced back at the guys. They looked exhausted but watched anxiously as she left with King Solomon. She shrugged it off, pretending she was not afraid.

The walk was longer than Mary anticipated, up one hill and down another. Solomon stopped at an old wooden building that looked like it could collapse at any moment. He pulled Mary inside by her arm and led her through the open entryway. Then he pointed downward, indicating she should watch her feet as they carefully stepped over jagged holes in the rotting floor.

Mary surveyed the little room. Hanging all along the top of the walls were large rusted metal hooks holding ancient-looking wooden tools. A narrow table lay rotted and slumped to one side. This place, she thought, must have been a work room or shed.

Solomon dragged a stump and placed it against the back wall and motioned for her to sit on it. He stood in front of her blocking the exit. His action made it was clear he meant business. Was this it, she wondered. This man was too big, and the side effect of the injections would never allow her to fight him off.

"Lady, you have put me in a bad position. You three came uninvited through the tunnels that I'm in charge of. I'm going to have some serious explaining to do to Mother. Now I want to know exactly what's going on here, and your story better be believable. Do we understand each other?"

From the sternness in his voice Mary knew that she should be completely honest about everything. "Absolutely," she replied, her voice noticeably trembling. She proceeded to tell him about Doc's investigation, Edward's willingness to become ill, her pregnancy, her family's murder – all the reasons they needed to escape from the Program.

He said nothing, but satisfied with her explanation, he pulled her up by her hand and they started walking back toward the others.

She was tired. Her feet and back throbbed with each step. A few hundred yards away at the top of a small hill she saw the flickering of a small fire and smelled wood burning in the cold night air. Both boosted her energy.

Arriving at the camp site, Solomon boomed, "Axel, I'll be back in the morning. Keep watch on the three of them."

"Yes, sir."

Solomon walked off, and a sleepy-eyed Axel nodded his head at Mary while he tended the fire.

She was glad he was not in the mood to talk. She was spent. Curled up near the fire, Doc and Edward slept on patches of wild grass. She snuggled next to Edward and went to sleep.

CHAPTER 49

MOTHER

Waking up sore, shivering, and feeling like she might need to vomit, Mary slowly bent herself upright. Only half awake, she waddled about fifteen feet from the guys and turned her back to them. Eventually the nausea passed. With them still sleeping and her dignity on hold, she took the opportunity to pull her pants down and pee.

She wondered if things would turn out all right. Nothing was settled. Would King Solomon and this Mother person, whoever she was, send them back? Would Axel, who was, after all, just a boy, be able to protect them from an angry crowd of Outcasts with revenge on their mind? Or, would they be allowed to stay and live in peace?

During her interrogation the previous night, she had been unable to read Solomon's poker face. No matter what their fate, she thought, at least this morning she would get to see her nephew one more time.

Freezing, she walked back to the campfire, rubbing the back of each arm with the opposite hand in a desperate attempt to stop herself from shivering. There curled up on the ground in front of her were the two most important men in her life, her lover and her surrogate father. They were sleeping comfortably on the ground, seemly unphased by the stresses of the previous day and the cold. It was good, she thought, to see them resting so peacefully.

She leaned back, yawning with her arms pointing skyward then inhaled a deep breath. The morning air felt good right down to her belly. She bent over and gently began rocking Edward back and forth until he woke.

"Mary," he said, squinting his eyes, "We made it. Burr, it's freezing out here. I guess I fell asleep last night before you got back. How did things go with what's his name? Did he say what they're going to do with us?"

"King Solomon. He didn't say, but I told him everything. He's a hard guy to read, and I think it peaked his interest when I said the Program might be planning to move the wall farther into their territory."

"Bottom line, do you think they'll let us stay?"

"Apparently he needs to talk to his mother before he decides. Hey, how old do you think the guy is? Five to ten years older than us?"

"Could be," Edward responded."

Doc, hearing their voices, sat up and looked around. For a moment, he seemed disoriented. Then he stretched out his arms and spoke. "You're back, good. I was worried about you. Ugh, I'm stiff. The ground is hard. I'm too old for this shit, and it's too damn cold. What happened to our fire?"

"It was raging when King Solomon brought me back last night, but it must have gone out. I'm cold, too, that's why I woke so early."

The three of them looked over at Axel.

Mary chuckled. "Heck, the guy who was supposed to guard us fell asleep."

"Yeah, some guard," Edward said. "Look at him. He's just a boy. Let's see if I can stoke the fire."

"Hey, you two, look at these little plants growing everywhere."

Mary laughed at Doc's comment. She had never mentioned the wild grass to him or Edward, and all night they had been sleeping on top of it.

"Curious about the plants?" Edward asked, "So Doc, why do you think these don't grow on our side of the wall?"

"Chemicals. The Program probably sprays the ground with poison to keep their ruse going. Maybe the same stuff that polluted the park near the Kabak."

Mary caught site of a group of people in the distance headed their way. Axel was asleep. Who would protect them from a crowd of angry Outcasts? Then suddenly, she jumped up waving. "Guys, guys, look! It's Jude, my nephew. Jude! Jude!"

Seeing the distant figures, Edward and Doc watched as Raj and Jude approach. Axel, now also awake, waved.

Jude waved back.

Doc gazed at the little boy in amazement. "I'll be God-damned! Even from here the kid looks exactly like your brother. Son of a bitch, would you look at that!"

"That's because he's his son. I'll introduce you when they get here," She said excitedly. "Doc, you've known me for how long? But you had to see before you would believe?"

Doc continued his gaze, pretending not to hear. He suddenly felt strong and proud and wasn't about to give her the satisfaction of being correct.

Raj walked with Jude tumbling behind. He nodded to the three adults, and, as on previous visits, the shy toddler hid behind him. Then he and Axel took Jude aside. After a short private discussion, Axel took Jude's hand, and Raj turned around and walked away.

"Jude," Axel said to the little boy, "You remember your Aunt Mary? These are her friends, Doc and Edward. Come say hello to everyone."

The little boy slowly approached his aunt. Mary reached out and hugged and squeezed him, and he giggled. The four adults played with Jude until Solomon returned with a basket full of brown and gray food, which smelled strong and different. They were famished.

"Axel, they need to eat before they meet with Mother. I think Jude has played long enough. Take him back now."

Jude took Axel's hand and waved goodbye.

"Thanks for letting us visit with you, Jude," Mary said, hoping to curry favor as her eyes followed her nephew out of site.

"Yeah, and thanks for food. After yesterday, we're famished," Edward added.

"I see a little sleep seems to have worked well for you, Edward. How impressive, you look so much better this morning."

"Maybe because of the medicine I gave him," Doc chimed in.

"Eat up, and then we'll go meet Mother."

The three of them held out the bowls Solomon had brought and eagerly received their allotment. Before eating, however, Mary and Edward looked at Doc, who brought the plate of food close to his face and smelled it. The others waited to see what he thought. He pressed his lips together and tilted his head. He didn't recognize the aroma. The texture and look of what he had in his hands was completely foreign.

Doc was the only one brave enough to speak up, "Thank you, King, but," he said, looking at what was in his bowl, "what is this?"

Solomon looked as surprised by the question as they were at what was in their bowls. "Bread and salted dried fish. You've never eaten this before? It's good," he said, taking a piece to his mouth and looking to see if the answer satisfied them.

"Bread, of course, but fish? Like in the old books, fish from the sea?" Mary asked.

"Fish from the lake," he said, pointing in the direction of a lake they could not see. "You mean to tell me, you've never eaten fish?"

"We've never eaten any animal, but we've read about animals. I thought all the fish died a long time ago," Edward replied.

"Well, shh--," Solomon laughed into their astonished faces. "Don't tell that to all the fish in the lake!"

Famished, they ate all they were given, despite misgivings about the food's pungent odor, salty taste, and dry, flaky texture.

"Watch out for bones," Solomon said, pinching a long, thin one out and holding it up an example.

"We have so much to learn," Doc whispered to his friends. Edward and Mary nodded as they continued to consume every bite.

After the meal, the four climbed a short hill to a small brick building that was in the opposite direction of the shed. Before entering, Solomon stopped. "Sit on the ground and wait for me. I'll come get you when Mother and I are ready."

As they waited, they were able to overhear the interior conversation.

"Mother, they're outside. Are you ready to receive them? Should I bring them in?"

"In a minute. We know a lot about Mary and about the doctor. Who's the other? What's his name and his story? Do you sense we can trust him?"

"Edward. We don't know much about him. He's been sick, and Mary says he's the father of her baby. He seems fairly safe to me, they all do but, of course, we're watching them."

"If you say they're safe, that's good enough for me. And the bag of bottles you took? What are they for? Anything we can use? Dimitri told me he heard they're trying to break their addiction?"

"That's what they said. I've got the bag. The doctor is anxious to have it back."

"Fine, bring them in. I'll decide what to do after we talk."

"Yes, Mother."

As soon as Solomon reappeared, the three of them followed as he led them into the building. "Mother, this is Mary, Edward, and Doc."

"Thank you, Solomon. Get Intu and come back quickly."

"Ha," he acknowledged, "I thought you might say that. I'll find him."

"You three, come closer. My hearing isn't that good anymore."

Obediently they moved closer to Mother, who sat in a roughly carved log chair with a high back at the top of a platform. Mary looked at her and guessed that Mother was a few years younger than Doc.

"Edward, I've been told you are sick?"

"Yes, ma'am, but I'm getting better. We rested, and King Solomon brought us food. That helped a lot."

"King Solomon? Oh my!" Mother bellowed. "Is that what he told you to call him? He's no king. I'm in charge here, so let's visit. Mary, we appreciated your honesty last night. Solomon said you confirmed a few things for us. We've suspected the Program was getting desperate. Their crops are failing. Not only have they over-farmed the land, their seed stock is bad. We guessed they've been plotting to get their hands on our seeds. Understand, that will never happen. Doctor Brisco, you were a good friend of Sim's, correct?"

"I was." Doc said, looking over at Mary, not sure where the conversation was headed.

"Of course. You come from good people, Mary. Your father Sim was a good man," Mother said, more as an aside.

"Sim was my best friend." Doc replied, sticking to the basic facts. "I was older, but we grew up together. I delivered all three of his children, knew them all their lives, and spent a lot of time with Mary and Joey."

"Obviously, you know Sim came here to visit Joey. What did he say about those visits?"

"Details weren't safe things to share on our side of the wall, but I am the one who pushed to get his Joey into the Care Place."

"We let that happen, let me remind you, but you did other special things for Joey, didn't you? You smuggled medicine to him through his father. Of course, we let that happen, too, didn't we?"

Doc wasn't about to acknowledge anything. He could sense that Mother had waited a long time to question a Program professional like him.

"And," Mother continued, "since he was helping Joey, we let Sim come and go as he pleased. But I feel certain the drugs you provided were responsible for Joey being able to father Jude. We thank you and Sim for taking that risk."

"I loved Joey, and his father was like a brother to me. I did what I could for them both."

"Yes, you did. Now Mary, what did your father tell you about things that happen here?"

"Unfortunately, he didn't tell me anything. I wish he had. My mom and I guessed he was meeting with Joey. I'd love to know what my father did here."

"I'm sure you would. Here's what I can tell you: the last time I saw him, he gave me something to hold for him. He never had the chance to come back for it. I'm certain he'd want you to have it, and I'll make sure you get it."

"You have something from my dad?" Mary couldn't believe what she had just heard.

"Patience, dear girl. Doc, I assume you wouldn't have any problem helping us with medical needs?"

"You can count on my help as a doctor. I can also give your best and brightest the medical training I received."

"I was hoping you'd want to do that. Now about these bottles Solomon took from you?"

"Yes, very important to us. One vial of that medicine is for Edward, since he's still sick, but the other is a withdrawal drug for the addiction, and we're going to need it soon or we're in trouble."

"Withdrawal drugs? No doubt from those destructive injections? I find those withdrawal drugs more interesting than you might imagine. I'll give those back to you."

"That's great to hear."

"One more thing. If we decide you can stay, each of you will have tasks in our community. Teaching, reading, writing, other things. I need to know that the three of you are willing to help in whatever way we ask. Are you? Willing?"

Mary spoke for the group. "We're completely on board. We want to help in any way we can. We want to be useful."

"Dear girl, that's the correct answer. All right then, here's your bag of medicine. For the time being, rest and get healthy. Then we'll get to work. I have several special projects in mind for each of you."

Doc took the bag from her. He had a feeling in his gut that something wasn't right, but he wasn't about to cause an issue. "Thanks. We appreciate the hospitality you've shown us. And, uh, I hope we can be safe here."

"Safe? Yes, good, good. I was certain we could count on all three of you. Mary, here, this is what your father left with me. Please take it.

Mother reached under her chair and handed Mary a large and rather ugly looking clay urn. Mary carefully took the urn from her. "Hey, you guys," she said with delight as she held it tightly, "look what's engraved in the base, my father's initials, SDD." Her cheeks flushed showing how happy she was to receive something that was her father's. The urn however looked to Mary like it must have been made in a hurry or by someone that wasn't very skilled at making pottery, but that didn't matter. Smiling at her new-found object, she held it in the air for others to see. As she did she heard a slight rattle noise coming from its base. She decided not to mention the rattle in front of Mother.

"Thank you, ma'am. I'm thrilled to have something that my father made."

"You're welcome. Motherhood is a gift, so off you go. Rest, all of you. Shoo, shoo. We will talk again of special things I have for you to contribute."

"Whatever you like. I want to help any way that I can."

"Good, good. I like knowing we're all going to get along. And Edward dear, your baby. I hope it's a girl."

Before they could exit, Solomon leaned his head into the building, "Should we come in now? Are you ready for us?"

"Ah yes! You three wait. I'm forgetting the best part. Come, King Solomon," Mother joked. "Set them up with a place to stay. See that they're safe and comfortable while they recover. Get them each a blanket and more to eat. Make sure all others know my wishes. So Solomon, is Intu here?"

"Yes Mother, he's waiting outside."

"Does he know why I wanted you to bring him," Mother said, now grinning from ear to ear.

"No, he hasn't a clue."

"Oh good, that should make this more fun. Bring him here so our special guests can meet him. Then escort them all outside, where they will surely want to visit for a few minutes."

Intu walked into the crowded room. He gazed at the three guests while they stared back at him in amazement. For a moment no one spoke.

"I . . . I can't believe it," Mary shouted.

"Damn, that's twice in the same day!" Edward added.

"Mary, dear, after the four of you visit, return to me. Alone. We have important matters to discuss."

Then everyone in the room turned and looked at Doc, who slowly sunk to his knees, sobbing.

CHAPTER 50

THE TASK AT HAND

Solomon escorted Mary back into the room with Mother. "Dear, what did you think of Intu?" Mother asked her.

"Wow, that meeting was such a shock. The look on both of their faces when they saw each other, both speechless. Now that was special."

"It was great to see their reunion and embrace, wasn't it? I hope they will get to know each other and find a way to connect. Now about your father's urn? What do you think of it?"

"The urn? It's great, I love holding something in my hands that was my father's. I don't want to ever put it down, but I guess that sounds silly, doesn't it?"

"No, I understand completely. He was your father; he was a good man, and you miss him. And we miss him, too. Now, tell me honestly. What's your opinion of the Program?"

"I hate it, I really I do. That's why I'm here, I hate everything about it. They control everything, manipulate the truth, and lie to innocent people. If I stayed, they'd surely force an abortion. And, I think they killed my family. You wouldn't know anything about that, would you?"

"No, but that wouldn't surprise me. And Mary, do Doc and Edward feel as you do?"

"Edward certainly does, but Doc, well, it's complicated for him. There's the whole situation with how his son, Thomas, I mean Intu, was taken away from him. He struggles with that, but he's in an impossible situation in the Program. He can never safely go back now that he's under investigation. I worry he will miss his friends and patients, his life. On the one hand, he loved my brother, the only Outcast he had ever known. At the same time, he believes Outcasts kidnapped his son."

"Say no more. I understand. I'm a parent, too. I know Doc did all he could to help Joey. I think he will eventually understand he should thank us for saving Intu. I assume he's told you the story about all that?"

"A little."

"That baby would have died in the elements if we hadn't saved him."

"Part of him realizes that, but he also believes his son should have been returned."

"It would have been impossible for us to safely return him. We would have been blamed for what happened to his mother. They would have made an example of us. No, we did what was best for that baby boy. Doc will come to accept that. Intu is alive today because of what we did."

"I'm sure in time he'll come around."

"I agree." Mother paused, taking a long and piercing stare.

Mary wondered if she had shared too much too soon, leaving Doc vulnerable.

"Tell me what you've observed about our community. What stands out?"

"Well, I haven't seen many of you, but you all seem to be healthy. No one appears to be sick from the radiation."

"That's true, we're a small community, and we are healthy. The UV clearly isn't a problem. What else?"

"Let's see, uh, most of the people I've met are young, except maybe for you and Solomon? Intu appears to be not that much older than me, which makes sense because, obviously, he's Doc's son."

"Yes, you're right about all of that. Anything else?"

"Uh, I haven't met any women other than you." Mary began to feel tired and nauseous.

"What would you think if I told you that I had thirteen children?"

"Thirteen? I'd say that's a lot of babies. The Program would never allow anyone have that many children. That's hard to believe you were able to do that way out here."

"Oh, not all survived. Medical care here is primitive at best. The interesting thing about my children is that between all those babies, only two were girls. I birthed eleven baby boys. Do you think you've met any of my children or their fathers?"

"I don't . . . well, maybe Solomon? Is he one of the fathers?"

"Excellent. Solomon is one of them, and there are others. Did you realize that Axel is one of his sons? Which, of course, makes him my son."

"He's a very smart young man. You raised him well, I'd say."

"And Solomon? What do you think of him?"

"Now that you mention it, I do see the resemblance between father and son. To be honest, Solomon was gruff at first. He can be scary, but he seems all right."

"Good. Intu is also one of the fathers. What do you think about that?"

Mary stopped to consider what she had just heard. Both Solomon and Intu were much younger than Mother. "Are you saying only two women live here other than you?"

"No, I said I had two daughters. We have a few other women here and, in time, you'll meet them. And now that you're here, we have one more woman in the community. Women should stick together don't you think?"

"I guess . . ."

"You're pregnant, so you're obviously fertile? Which also means Edward is virile."

"Of course, but . . ."

"If our little community is going to grow, we have to build our numbers to defend ourselves. Mary dear, look at me. I'm getting old.

We need new mothers to mate with our men. And unfortunately, not all the men here are virile. Do you understand what I'm saying?"

"Are you asking if I will mate with men other than Edward and if he will mate with other women?" Mary's mind raced, her stomach unsettled. "Edward and I . . . with other people? Is that what you're saying?" Had she misinterpreted Mother's implication?

"That's exactly what I'm saying. But having only you and a few others to produce a larger adult community would require too many years, too much risk. What if we could bring other women here, girls old enough to conceive? And what about bringing other adults here? Now that we know about withdrawal drugs, the addiction won't need to be a problem anymore, right?

"I'm struggling to keep up with what you're saying. First, what makes you think there are other people in the Program, young or old, who would want to come here?"

"Mary, surely there must be others like you. Women who want families. People are better off here once they get to know how pure life is on this side, no question."

"There might be willing participants, but I don't know any." Mary thought of how desperate Ena was to have children and wondered if other unpaired women in her office felt the same way.

"I bet you do. Take a little time to think about it."

"Thanks, I am getting nauseous again. May I sit?" She sat without waiting for a reply. "So, you are asking me, asking us, to recruit other from the Program? To get other women to come here permanently?"

"And if I was? You just told me how much you hate the Program, how bad it is, that they lie and kill people. Others must feel the same way. We have clean land, clean food. Isn't the way we live here better?"

"But, I . . . "

"And Mary, just think, what if we were to welcome boys and girls before they became addicted, before they started those horrible injections? Wouldn't they be better off living here with us? Wouldn't the lives of those children be safer if they grew up drug-free? Look how healthy Intu is, born in the Program but raised here. Stronger because he didn't get drugged."

"Are you suggesting kidnapping children from the Program? Stealing them from their parents? Is that what you're saying?"

"Kidnapping? Saving young families! Don't you agree the quickest way to grow the community is by bringing in people from the Program? Is rescuing humanity bad if, in the long run of their lives, individuals are healthier and better off? Doesn't every community want the best for its people, every mother want the best for her child?

"Here those children would have a whole world to roam around instead of being cramped behind a walled prison. Here they can eat healthy food, play in the sunshine, and learn how to be strong, protect themselves and their people. We don't medicate to keep people in line. No calming drugs for children here. Is that an option there?"

"No, but kidnaping children from their parents?"

"Mary, if their parents don't want to come with them, we rescue and give their children a freedom they could never have in the Program. That's a good thing. Isn't that why the three of you came here, to free yourselves of that repressive regime?"

Mary stopped for a moment to carefully think before she replied, "Yes, that's why we're here, but does that freedom apply to me and Doc and Edward?"

"That's up to the three of you. But you should remember that you came to us -- uninvited. We didn't kidnap you, did we? No, you came on your own, and you said you wanted to join our community. You told me you wanted to do anything you could to help, or was that idle talk? I've now told you how the three of you can help, especially how you can help. Everyone has a job to do. Do you want to be a contributing member of our community or not?"

Suddenly Mary felt cold and alone. For a moment she was speechless. How should she answer without jeopardizing their safety? This was not the discussion she had expected to have, and there was a lot to think about. She had an urge to run, but she had no idea where Solomon had taken Doc and Edward. "Yes, that's why we came, and we want to help, but I need to think about what you're asking and talk to the guys."

"I have given you a lot to think about, I understand. Because the Program has conditioned you, you are not used to our cultural honesty, openness, or transparency. That is our happy way. After you discuss things with your friends, you need to let me know your answer. Consider your alternatives and . . . don't lie. We certainly don't want to believe you have come here only to disappoint us."

A chill ran up Mary's back and arms. How naïve she had been? Obviously, it was meant as a sort of threat.

"Before you leave, consider this: in our community, the women are like queen bees, and the men are like worker wasps. We have the babies, but men take care of them along with all our other needs. As queens, we run things and have whatever men we want, young or old, whenever we want them. There is room here for multiple hives, multiple queens. Think about that. You, Mary, a powerful leader, a queen."

CHAPTER 51

THE URN

Mary staggered out the meeting, dismayed and frightened. The guys would be very upset once they heard what Mother expected. She decided to wait until they were alone to talk to them about their options.

Solomon led the three of them back to the same area where they had been in the morning. "Mother wants me to set up a place for the three of you. I will, but you'll stay here until then. Axel will be back to guard you when he finishes a task I gave him. For now, the three of you are to remain in this area. Do you understand?"

"Yes," Doc answered.

"If you wander, I can't be responsible for what happens. Axel should be here soon, and I'll be back later to check on you." Solomon walked off.

Mary waited until Solomon was far enough away. "We've got a lot to talk about. Doc, how incredible! You and Intu, you must be in shock. He looks exactly like you, only younger and taller."

"I'd be lying if I said I had any words to describe what I'm feeling right now, what's going through my mind. Obviously, he's my son, and it's overwhelming. All these years not knowing, just hoping, and here he is." He wiped his face with his crumpled handkerchief, and Mary wrapped her arms around him, hugging tightly.

"It's wonderful," Doc continued, "that he's alive, that I've met him at long last, but this is also hard. So much stuff going through my head. So many emotions all at once. And it may be worse for him; neither one of us was prepared for this."

"Doc, we're in this with you." Edward said, half dozing. He struggled to keep his eyes open.

"Thank for the support, I appreciate that. I'll lean on you and Mary. No, this is a good thing; in fact, it's amazing. I mean I'm a father and a grandfather. I need time to process all this."

Meeting a parent as an adult must be as hard as losing a parent as a child, Mary thought.

"Mary, tell us what you and Mother talked about," Edward struggled to wake up.

"Oh sure," she said, realizing Edward was trying to change the subject. "I will, and you guys won't believe the crazy things she expects us to do, but first I need your help. How can I crack this urn open before Axel or Solomon get back?"

Both men were confused by her request. "Now why would you want to do that? That was your dad's. Why destroy it?" Doc asked her.

"Guys, look at this ugly thing. The neck is long, but if you peek inside it's closed off just four or five inches from the top, it can hardly hold anything. Why? Don't you think that's odd? A tall urn that can't hold very much? And look how much bigger the bottom is than the top, it's sort of useless as an urn. He hid something in the base. I know my dad, and he didn't care about pottery. Something's definitely in there. Listen." Mary held the urn in front of them and shook it vigorously. "Did you hear that rattling?"

Edward's eyes were closed, but he took the urn, placed it by his ear, and shook it. "Yeah, I hear something. But it could just be a piece of clay. Sure you want to ruin it?"

"I am, absolutely."

"Hand it to me," Doc said, grabbing the urn and shaking it for himself. "Nope, don't hear a damn thing. Don't know what you two are talking about."

"That's because you're old and deaf, like our new mother," Mary said, giggling. "Come on, I can't wait any longer. Crack it open. Let's see what's in there."

Doc slammed the urn a few times against a rock until a large crack grew in the base and up the neck. "You're right. Let me give it one more good whack." When he did, a bundle of rolled, tattered papers fell out. He picked them up and handed them to Mary. Gleefully she took the papers from him and carefully unrolled them. "I knew it!"

"Is it a treasure map? Show it to us," Edward said, his eyes still closed.

"I will, Edward. Give me a minute. I don't want to tear the paper. They're notes, scribbled in my father's handwriting, maybe written in a hurry. It's so tiny, it's barely legible. There's a lot crammed on here. I'll read it out loud real quick."

* * *

Today Joey introduced me to Emad, an Outcast man. He was very sick and seemed close to dying. He said he was 75 years old. He had worked as a scientist with my mother in the old CAIHR site. Somehow, he had gotten himself crosswise with the Program and, even as an old man, they made him an Outcast.

Whatever injection they gave him, it was killing him. Joey had mentioned to him about my trips back and forth through the tunnels. Learning that he urgently wanted to talk to me, we met. Emad told me that my mother Phoebe had been a good friend, so he knew he could trust me. He had information he wanted to give me before he died.

He said that when he was a young researcher, two older scientists had passed on interesting things to him that had forever changed his life. The old scientists evidently had been curious about the cause of the climate change. They had secretly spent years conducting their own covert investigation looking for clues in old documents. They concluded that the change had been accelerated by the eruption of a super-volcano in Yellowstone. That eruption had been ground zero for most of the devastation that occurred afterward. They were convinced that the eruption had been the final straw in the climate disaster.

More importantly, they believed it had been intentionally detonated. The old guys, however, never figured out why that had been done or how that was accomplished. They didn't want their work to stop, so they asked Emad to carry on their investigation. They believed the answers might be contained in documents still hidden throughout the CAIHR facility. Emad agreed to take on their challenge.

He spent years secretly searching and collecting documents and found two that he thought were particularly interesting. One was a military manual labeled, **Nuclear Fallout Emergency Operations Center, N.F.E.O.C.** *and a second very similar manual published at a later date,* **The Center for the Advancement of an Intelligent Human Race, C.A.I.H.R.** *The emergency manual described a plan for a totally self-sufficient facility for use by U.S. government officials and select military personnel as a command and control operations center in the event of nuclear war. He found other documents tucked inside the pages that indicated the government had started the construction but then stopped work on the project. He assumed funding for the site was probably cut off.*

The intelligence manual, which was similar to the emergency guide, showed the site objective had changed. Now it was a plan to preserve the human gene pool and ensure the breeding of highly intelligent humans for future generations. There was no mention of why this plan was implemented.

Other documents indicated that numerous wealthy and connected international families became aware of the partially completed site. Emad uncovered records of negotiations between the government and these families for purchase of the unfinished facility. They showed that eventually the private parties had secured joint ownership of the facility along with the government. The families had agreed to supply the massive funds required to finish the build out without further government investment.

Emad wanted to know why these families felt the need to do this. Evidently both the families and the US government were gravely concerned about global warming. They were also concerned about the exponential growth of the world's population, the associated unquenchable thirst for more resources and other impacts on the climate. One document listed the depletion of the world's rain forests, the explosion of factory farming, too many animals producing methane gas, and the endless use of atmospheric polluting fossil fuels as issues. This struck Emad because these same families of wealth and power had most likely been the ones to directly benefit from the sale and ownership of the world's resources.

These connected families had firsthand knowledge of the climate impact, the drought, wild fires, and flooding that were affecting the world's food production. They also had a window into how this was impacting the stability of governments around the world. He guessed they realized their wealth, power, and ultimately safety was about to be threatened. They assumed that in the near future, in desperation, the poor would rise up against them and their governments and try to reclaim whatever scarce resources remained. They needed to complete the CAIHR site for the safety of their own families.

Emad eventually found the actual agreement between the government and these oligarchs. The document detailed names and the financial contributions including what was promised in exchange for the funding. Each family was assured a place for themselves in the CAIHR site. They would have to wait out the climate disaster but could do so in the safely offered by the site. By entering into this agreement, they were ensured their lineage would continue. Their legacy, wealth, and power would be passed on through populating the new site with family members in the roles of generals, guards, and managers. In a similar manner, the government's position in the future world would be secured by supplying members of certain U.S. diplomatic families along with a few military members and some of the brightest scientific minds in the world.

The site was immediately occupied by family members of the oligarchs after construction was completed. These families and the government became impatient, however. He guessed they were worried that the climate change was too slow and that their resources might be depleted before it ran its course.

Soon after their occupancy, they somehow forced the eruption of the Yellowstone super- volcano to accelerate things. This would have been an extremely difficult and expensive endeavor. The forced eruption of the volcano happened under the assistance of the U.S. government.

Emad realized possession of this collection of documents potentially put him in peril, so he hid the collection in the waste water processing module of the CAIHR site, an area no longer used. His plan had been to retrieve the collection when he could find a way to do that safely. His goal was to give this information to the community and expose the current Program leadership, which he felt was corrupt. Now, however, he was close to death and, as an Outcast, he no longer had access to the site. He wants me to retrieve those documents and expose the Program. I will take on this responsibility.

* * *

She waved the notes in the air. "Guys, it's all here. Now we know why my family—"

"Damn those selfish bastards. This proves the climate change was manmade. It was intentional. They caused the whole damn mess."

"No, I don't think so, Doc," said Edward. "That's not what those notes imply, at least not entirely. The climate change was happening due to overpopulation. The world's resources were being overused. These families no doubt accelerated things for their own benefit, but overuse and overpopulation would have made the disaster inevitable no matter what."

"Edward, you can't be serious? When they detonated that volcano, they pushed things over the edge. Those bastards were the ones who forced the devastation on a global scale. What they did killed everyone else while they or their families were protected in that facility."

"I agree with Doc," said Mary. "Those families were directly responsible for what happened. When that super volcano erupted, it was all over for everybody except those in the CAIHR site. If Yellowstone hadn't been detonated, then maybe the climate change wouldn't have been as severe. Maybe it would have stalled or reversed course or something. Maybe millions of more people would have survived. But, once they blew up the volcano, that chance was lost forever. No, they callously made things worse for everyone else to protect themselves."

"OK, you two can speculate about what might have happened if they hadn't set off that volcano, and who is at fault. All I'm saying is that overpopulation was the original cause of climate change. And, at this point, who really cares? It doesn't matter anymore."

"We can't go back and change history, but I care, Edward," said Doc. "All that devastation was caused intentionally by those families. I care."

"Fine, but if those families were responsible for detonating that volcano, wouldn't the descendants of those oligarchs want to cover themselves? Why leave documents around with names all over them? That risks possible exposure. Why not either destroy the documents or at the very least, change your family name so that nothing could be traced to your future relatives?"

"I can answer that," Doc replied. "Arrogance. These families were among the richest, most powerful people in the world. They were used to being totally in charge, in control of everything and everyone. Back then they had no reason to believe that any of these documents or what they did would ever see the light of day. Second, I've read about wealthy families like that and their names are very important; it's their brand. Their names are an integral part of their proud legacy. No way were those families or their descendants going to change their names and lose that standing."

"OK, I know nothing about people like that," said Edward, "but if you say they would care that much about their names, I believe you. The question is, where do you two think that collection is today? It stands to reason this Emad must have told Mary's dad exactly where it was hidden. And I'm guessing he would have retrieved it."

"Possibly, love," said Mary, "but I doubt my father ever had the opportunity to do that. And if Dad did have that collection on him during the accident, then they're gone forever. They would have burned along with my family. But I'll bet he never got his hands on them. They're probably still there, hidden somewhere in the waste water treatment area of the CAIHR site."

"What are you basing that on?" said Doc.

"Logic, Doc. How would a guy like Dad have gained access to the site? You said Dad acted nervous when he gave you the envelope prior to the accident right?"

"That's right, he was very nervous when he gave it to me. In fact, he scared the hell out of me."

"But we know those Emad documents and these notes weren't in there. Doesn't it seem likely that if he had them at that time he would have given them to you to hide? They would have been in that envelope, and they weren't. He probably never had a chance to find the collection. And I think these notes could have been for the missing second letter that he never had a chance to write. No, I think that collection is still out there."

"Damn," said Edward. "Either way, if he did retrieve the collection and it burned in the accident, or even if they are still hidden, they're lost to us. It's a shame because both he and Emad are dead, and no one knows where those documents are. Emad and those old scientists spent a lifetime trying to uncover this stuff, but it was for nothing. The Program committee better hope nobody ever finds them."

"Maybe that's why the Program used arsonists to kill my father," said Mary. Before she could continue that line of thought, however, she saw Axel walking toward them. "We'll talk more later. He's coming. Cover me while I hide the notes under this rock. Quick."

Doc and Edward stood in front of the rock hoping to distract Axel's gaze while Mary hid the papers. When he arrived, his eyes were drawn to the shards of broken urn scattered on the ground. "Isn't that's your father's urn? You broke it? You know I think I remember when your dad and Joey were making that."

"Clumsy of me. I was so tired, it slipped out of my hands, shattered into a million pieces," Mary said, shaking her head in disgust.

CHAPTER 52

ISSUES

Mary, Doc and Edward were grateful for the small building that Solomon arranged for them to use. The walls of this crude stone structure held together with dried mud and moss growing on the outside. The shelter had no roof, offering a direct view of the sky above. After seeing dark marks on the top edges of the walls, Edward suggested that the structure probably had some sort of roof many years ago.

Walking inside for the first time they saw a dirt floor that had been partially covered in thick piles of dead grasses. Edward and Doc bent down and scooped up the piles, pushing them into the corners to make seats. In the middle of the room sat an old rock fire pit still containing the remains of charred pieces of wood. From the lingering smell it emitted, they surmised the pit had been used recently. Though the room left them vulnerable in the event of rain, they were happy to be in the shelter, since it afforded some level of privacy.

After two days, Doc and Mary could see that Edward looked better. He had come a long way from the beginning of the trip. Fresh food and the open-air rest agreed with him, and he was recovering faster than Doc had anticipated.

Mary was especially pleased with his progress, but she also knew that time was running out. They would need to figure out what they could do, what they would do next. She was grateful for the food and shelter, but no way was she was going to be part of Mother's population growth plans, and neither was Edward. The guys were shocked and upset when she told them Mother's grand plan, and they had been stewing about it ever since. Doc appeared especially distraught.

Before breakfast, she watched Doc sit quietly in the corner with his head in his hands. She guessed Mother's plans to involve them in kidnapping children must have been particularly painful for him. What could she say to make him feel better? Probably nothing.

Feeling antsy, she decided to take a short walk outside. She knew to always stay in sight of the shelter. As she walked about thinking, she noticed a few patches of tiny yellow flowers growing on the ground. She bent over and carefully picked a dozen or so, delighting in them and making a small bouquet. These flowers, she thought, might give Doc a reason to be happy again. Smiling to herself she trotted back to the hut and handed the bouquet to Doc.

"Listen, I promise we'll think of something to get us out of all this. No way any of us will get involved in kidnapping or any of that other stuff. Maybe we're still not done escaping. Maybe we need to figure out how to go somewhere else."

"Young lady," he replied, rubbing each bloodshot eye one at a time with one hand while holding the little bouquet in the other, "we better figure something out, but right now that is not our most pressing concern." Doc took the bouquet and meticulously removed a petal at a time from the tiny flowers and blew them softly into the air.

Edward, who had been in his own sort of funk, perked up. "Really Doc? What in the hell could possibly be more pressing?"

"Our withdrawal drug situation, that's what. You two were counting on me, and I must have messed up. I've checked this out ten times if I've checked once, but we don't have enough withdrawal drugs. Not even close."

"How can that be possible? I watched you put a bunch of those little bottles into that book bag at my apartment."

"It's not that I didn't bring enough, Edward. Remember when all those meds fell out in Vinesh's truck? All I can think of is that in our rush to grab them, we must have missed some. The light was dim. They could have rolled under the fertilizer bags. Of course, it's also possible that Mother or Solomon kept a few back, though I'm not sure why they would do that. Anyway, this is on me. My responsibility was to care for those meds, and now we don't have enough."

"Can't we just ration what's left?"

"Edward's right, Doc. We'll ration them."

Doc held up his hand to stop them from speaking. "There's not enough for three of us, but I still might have enough for you two, maybe."

"And what about you?" asked Mary.

Doc could see red flushing Mary's cheeks. "Let's just say I'm an old man with a heart condition and, now that I've seen my son again, I've lived a full life."

"Oh no, that's not going to happen. You can forget about it. With your heart, withdrawal without those drugs would likely kill you. We're a team, and that isn't in the plan. We support each other. There has to be another way."

"You two don't get it. There's no contingency plan for lost drugs. Be pragmatic. Without the withdrawal drugs, you might abort, and Edward is still recuperating. You two have your entire lives ahead of you. I'll administer the remaining drugs to you two."

Mary grabbed him as if to shake him but instead just held him tight. "Doc, I love you, and we appreciate the thought, but we're not going to allow you to do this."

"You're not listening; there's no other way."

"And every time you say that, we find there is." Edward finally had the floor – and Doc and Mary's attention. "Here's an idea. How about I go back and get more drugs? With the investigation on, you certainly can't go, and we're not going to risk Mary's pregnancy. The only option that makes sense is for me to go. Tell me where to get the meds, and I'll bring them back."

"He's right, Doc. He's the only one who can go back. Nobody probably knows he's gone. He's sick at home and recovering, which means his bosses aren't looking for him yet."

"It's true, I'm the only one who would be safe. It has to be me."

"Let me think, let me think . . ."

Seeing Doc pace again, Mary felt hopeful. "Now we're talking," she said, leaning in to give Edward a kiss.

"Edward, that's a thought," said Doc. "I could give you a much bigger dose than normal to buy you extra time. Maybe that would work."

"And if I can't get back in time, what happens then?"

"We're screwed."

"Then give me the normal dose. Let's talk about how I get those drugs."

"Well, there isn't any more where I got those; I cleaned out the supply. And when it comes to the black market, the only thing to do is go to the guy at the top."

"And you know who that is?"

"Don't act so surprised. Go to my man, Chivas. You can meet him in fairly safely at the Kabak any day around the same time. I'll draft a note that you can give him. If I ask, he'll come through for us."

"Good. Now, will our queen and king let me go . . . and then let me back in with the drugs?"

"Why would they do either?" said Mary. "Especially now that they've revealed their plans."

"Guess they'd think I was a spy for the Program?"

"Wouldn't you?"

"So, how do we get them to let me go?"

"Damn it, you two, there is no way," said Doc. "But apparently neither of you are sane enough anymore to listen to a physician — or to reason."

"I'm not sure how we get them to let you go, Edward," Mary interrupted, squelching Doc's rant, "but every time he says there's no way . . ."

". . . we find a way," they said in unison.

"I give up," Doc said and stormed out of the building.

CHAPTER 53

INSANITY

The three sat huddled together around the fire pit in the middle of the hut that evening. Usually Axel watched them, but tonight he attended prayers with his community to the Lokapalas, so this gave them another opportunity to talk. Though Axel had become quite friendly with them in recent days, he was still Solomon's son. They did not dare discuss certain topics in front of him.

"Doc, what do you think we can offer the Outcasts so they'll let Edward make the trip?"

"The obvious stuff is covered. They already believe we owe it to them to teach them to read and write and help with medical needs. I don't know, maybe we're thinking about this all wrong. How, for example, can we help to ensure that bad things don't happen?"

Edward contorted his face, clearly confused. "What bad things?"

"What happens if the Program invades, pushing the walls out again? Outcasts don't want the Program to steal their land, their seeds, their food, their supplies, or kill their people in the process."

"OK, but how can we help stop that? Oh wait . . . I get it. You're suggesting that we'd broker a deal for them with the Program? Doc, that's damn brilliant! We'd be the ones to negotiate with the Program and stop the invasion. The Outcasts would trade food, heirloom seeds, fish, whatever, to stop the wall from being moved into their territory."

"Nah, Edward, nice idea, but that's not what I'm saying. The Program is never going to negotiate with us or them. They need the Outcasts to remain the enemy, their biggest threat. They want the community to hate and be frightened of Outcasts. We would never be able to broker a deal."

"Then I'm lost. Where does that leave us?"

"Stick with what the Outcasts don't want to see happen. What other ways can we help them stop an invasion? Maybe we consider their defensive capabilities. Is there any way to help them there?"

"Do they even have defensive capability? We know they have guns, given that Dimitri kept sticking that thing in my chest. Even if they have a stash of weapons, they don't have a trained militia that could hold off the Program guards. In a fight, they'd be terribly outnumbered, slaughtered. I don't see what we have to offer that can fix that."

Mary decided she should try to redirect the discussion, "You guys are thinking too militaristically. What if we could convince Mother and Solomon that we have a way to stop the Program by turning the guards against the leadership committee? Then the Outcasts wouldn't need to fight them. I mean you already said fighting them would be a disaster. Why go down that path? Instead, as I see it, we have two goals, convince the guards not to fight and convince Mother and Solomon that by sending Edward back we have a way to accomplish that."

"First of all," said Doc, "in what fantasy world do the guards turn on the committee?"

"Doc, that happens in a world where we've influenced them to behave that way. We give them a reason to have a crisis in confidence. We show them — no, prove to them — how their bosses on the leadership committee lead fantastic lives while they and the rest of us ordinary workers are treated horribly."

"Sure," said Doc. "And how the hell do we make that happen?"

"I don't think that's so hard to do. You guys are forgetting that the guards live just like we do. They live in the same crappy rundown apartments, lead the same bland and ever more restricted lives. Those poor guys don't make the rules, they're just expected to enforce them. So, with a little help from us and a few proof documents, we make them more aware of things. We get them frustrated with their situation, give them a reason to doubt their committee bosses. Think about it, frustrated armed guards? Now that's a combination that works for the Outcasts as well as us."

"Even if we could do that," said Edward, "and you still haven't said exactly how we make that happen, they're not going to stick their necks out and disobey. That could get them killed."

"They will if most of the other guards are on board. Listen, honey, I know exactly how we can prove to them that they're being screwed over. We start by showing them the plans for that new luxury place."

"And we get those plans how?"

"I'll explain. But first we also need to prove to the guards that the UV rays are no longer a problem. Show them they've been duped by injections that trap them into addiction but do nothing. We tell them we know how to break that addiction. We let them reflect on how they spend their miserable lives protecting committee members who live like royalty. And one more thing, we show them documents that prove the leadership committee is now only composed of descendants of the original wealthy families, the same families that pushed the climate change over the edge and nearly killed everybody."

"But why should the Outcasts care about any of that?"

"If the Outcasts believe we can convince the guards not to fight because we obtained proof documents from the other side, they would definitely see value in that. If they believe, as I do, that getting those documents is the key to flipping the guards, then we won't need to convince them. They'll force you to go. Do you boys really not see where I'm going with this?"

"You know what, Mary?" said Doc.

"What?" she fired back, expecting him to spout ridicule in her direction.

"Your outlandish plan to flip the guards doesn't actually have to work. All we really need is to make it sound convincing enough for Mother and Solomon to buy it. And, my friends, I might have a way to make them open to it. We start with fear."

"I'm listening," Edward replied.

"We instill in the Outcasts the idea that we know they are in imminent danger of being invaded, attacked. Raise their anxiety and danger level. Reinforce the idea that it isn't safe to sit back any longer. They need to prepare to take action now to stop things.

"They're not stupid. They know they can't win in a fight. But the fear of losing everything will open their minds to our suggestions, no matter how crazy. The history books tell us you can never go wrong playing to a community's fears. We convince them that with our help — which, of course, requires Edward's trip back to retrieve the documents — our scheme has a chance."

"And how am I supposed to get these proof documents?"

"Easy. Reyanne," said Mary.

"Reyanne?" said Edward. "That woman is such a gossip!"

"No doubt, and you also know her partner, Ajay?"

"Yup, met him a number of times. Seems like a good guy. Not sure how he puts up with her incessant whining. But what do they have to do with this?"

"Well, Ajay is one those engineers, architects on that leadership committee complex. Reyanne and Ajay hate what's going on in the Program, so I'm sure they'll be willing to help us. Ajay should be able to get you a copy of the plans for the leadership complex along with all the details of the furnishings, food supplies, you name it. That is the convincing proof we need. Ajay also has access to the layout of the old CAIHR site."

"And why would we need that site layout?"

"Because with the CAIHR layout, you could find the wastewater treatment area and bring back Emad's document collection."

"What?"

"Damn it, you two, enough!" said Doc. "Don't go making this complicated. Remember, all we really need to do is sell the concept to Solomon and Mother. If they believe it can work, then they'll let Edward go. If the time ever comes for flipping the guards, I'll bet Chivas can help us. I'm pretty sure he and the guards have been doing business together for years. But let's not worry about that for now. Just keep things simple with Mother and Solomon. Don't say more than you need to."

CHAPTER 54

REENTRY

Solomon had his men unseal the tunnel that was closest to Mary's apartment. Axel and Edward traversed it, and that evening the two of them slept on the floor in the blue building. Fear was an easier motivator than Edward could have imagined. The Outcasts bought their story completely.

In the pre-dawn morning, Axel returned while Edward headed for the distribution center. He was confident that as long as he stayed hidden, he could intercept Reyanne on her way to work. As he walked in the dim light, he wondered how much he should divulge to her. She was curious by nature and would demand to know more.

Nearing the distribution center, he saw his chance. Reyanne was walking alone. His heart raced as he approached her, not wanting to be seen but also not wanting to scare her. "Reyanne," he whispered barely loud enough for her to hear, "Quick. I need to talk to you."

Reyanne jerked her head around, searching. Edward immediately put his index finger to his lips, warning her to be quiet.

"Edward, you frightened me. What are you doing? I heard you were really sick."

"I was. I'm much better now. Can we talk?" Edward scanned the area and eyed the edge of a nearby building. "Over here," he encouraged, gently taking her arm and guiding her to where they would be more concealed from prying eyes. "Mary and I need a big favor. I guess you know about us, I mean being a couple?"

"Of course I do, silly," she replied, giggling. "I know all the gossip all the time. Anyway, where is she? She hasn't been at work in days. Everyone is —"

"Listen, we're in trouble. Can you get Ajay to meet me tonight after work at my apartment?"

"Yeah . . . I can make that happen . . . what's up?"

Just then a group of workers walked by the building. He covered Reyanne's mouth and pulled her further back. "There isn't time to explain, and I can't risk being seen. Ajay can tell you everything after we meet."

"Got it. You're incognito, right? I love it. Don't worry; he'll meet you tonight."

"And don't tell anyone else — and I mean no one — you've seen me, got it? This is important."

"Your secret is safe with me," she whispered, peeking around the corner. "Tell Mary . . . Edward?"

He was already on the move. All morning, he had been nervous about being seen, but as he approached the Kabak, he decided it was better to look as normal and relaxed as possible. This place was strictly for workers. Managers knew they were not welcome. The Kabak was a snitch-free zone, but it was important not to seem desperate or raise questions.

He walked through the sole entrance and scanned the crowd. He hoped he could remember what Dr. Chivas looked like. The last time he had seen him was more than two years before. Just as Doc had said, he saw the man's familiar face, sitting alone at a table toward the back of the room.

"Dr. Chivas," he said, holding his hand out to the aging man, "don't know if you'll remember me. I'm Edward Verlander. Doc B. said I'd find you here. May I?"

"Certainly, I do remember you. Have a seat. I believe I treated you a while back."

"Yes, sir."

"A kavas for you, Edward?"

"No thanks, I only have time for a quick message."

"How is our mutual friend B doing? We've been worried about him. The rumor is he's stumbled upon a bit of trouble."

Edward wondered what it might be like to know who the doctor's 'we' are. They must be pretty powerful. "Yes, sir. That's why I'm here." Edward took a moment to look around the room, then leaned in and whispered, "Doc wanted me to give you this."

The doctor held a kavas in one hand and the other on his lap. Edward tried to discretely slip the note into his free hand. To his chagrin, the old doctor instantly pulled the note close to his face to read.

Edward waited, fidgeting with an empty glass on the table. He was silent until he felt he had to speak. "That letter, it should explain our situation. I hope you can help."

The doctor placed his glass on the table, crushed the note, and stuffed it into his pocket. "Let's leave so we can talk," he said, taking his turn to scan the room. Once outside he pulled no punches. "Son, you and Mary are in trouble."

"Yes sir, I'm afraid we are."

"I know Doc feels like a father to her. But your turn of events is very surprising to me. Thinking about it all, I'm not sure what to say. The three of you on the other side of the wall, living and working with the Outcasts. The Outcasts, imagine that? And exactly what are you're doing with them? I mean, it's nothing short of brilliant. We want in. That's going to be our next biggest untapped market."

"Well, sir, I guess it could be, but right now we're trying to help them stop the Program from moving the wall, invading, and taking their land. That's why they let me come back here."

"Yes, I've heard rumblings of the Program plan to move the wall. Didn't think it would be so soon. That could be very disruptive for me and my friends, you see. Anyway, interesting, very interesting. I'll certainly follow up on that.

"But back to your immediate needs, tell you what, son. You come back here tomorrow, same time. I'll get you what you need. Now is there any chance you could take me back with you to see my buddy?"

"No sir, I don't think so, not without messing things up. Listen, Dr. Chivas, I appreciate your help and all, but I'm feeling a little exposed right now. If the wrong person sees me, they might talk to my bosses. Maybe we could talk more tomorrow at the Kabak when I come back, same time?"

"Certainly, no problem, son. I'm glad that I might be of service to an old friend."

"Thank you, Doctor, from all of us."

* * *

Having successfully made the first two contacts, all that remained was to wait for his meeting with Ajay tonight. At his apartment, Edward noticed a note pinned to the door: *Came by to see you today. Must mean you're feeling better, Jorge.* While he was happy to know his best friend had been checking on him, he also felt a wave of guilt. Someday, maybe soon, he hoped to explain all the craziness that was happening.

He took off his coat, tossed it on his bed, and sat in his chair. Sitting in his own apartment felt almost normal, safe. He closed his eyes and thought about what he would say to Ajay.

He wasn't sure how long the loud rapping on the door had gone on when he jumped up from his nap. Trying not to look half asleep, he rubbed his hands across his face and through his hair before opening the door. "Ajay, come in. Thank you for meeting me."

Edward took time describing their escape to the other side of the wall and their predicament. Ajay seemed totally enthralled. Then Edward hit him with the request for the layout of the CAIHR facility.

"Listen, guy, I can probably get that for you, but why the hell would you want it?"

"I want it because I need to locate the wastewater treatment processing area. Oh, and I also need help actually getting in there." As Ajay's expression changed, Edward stopped talking for a moment and tried to read it. "But maybe I'm getting ahead of myself. Look,

I brought something for you and Reyanne. A sort of thanks for helping us." He reached and slid a large bag across the floor to him.

Ajay pulled it over and looked inside, "What's all this? Are you kidding me? Books?"

"Yeah, they're from the Outcasts. There must be thousands of them on the other side of the wall. Many are still in good shape and readable. Mary thought you might like these, or you could trade them on the black market for something else."

"Trade? I'd never trade these. Very nice. Tell Mary thanks. Now explain why you want that CAIHR layout."

From the tone of his voice, Edward could tell he had piqued Ajay's interest but had not yet convinced him to help. This was a bad sign, because he still had to request something that would be much more dangerous for Ajay to pass on to him, a copy of the leadership complex plans.

Just tell him, Edward thought. "Well, the truth is that years ago a friend of Mary's father hid documents in that site. Mary wants me to retrieve them."

"Wow," Ajay replied, "What is hiding behind that story, huh? Can't believe you want to go in there. You do know no one is allowed in that old site except for maybe the guards, and I'm not so sure about them. They'll kill you if you get caught."

"Yeah." Edward cringed a little at the honesty of what Ajay just said. "So, about that. I also need a copy of the plans for that new leadership complex you're working on. And documentation for all the furnishing, fixtures, everything."

Ajay immediately stood up. "I don't think you realize what you're asking," he said in a now very serious tone of voice. "That stuff is extremely sensitive. How do you know about that place?"

Edward cocked his head, and in an instant, Ajay had the answer. "Damn that woman, she is going to get me killed, isn't she?"

Edward figured he had said enough. He was better off letting Ajay speak.

"A copy of those plans would be so dangerous in the wrong hands. No one outside of the committee itself or anyone directly involved is supposed to know about the place."

"Ajay, that's ridiculous, isn't it? There's only so much land; don't they think farmers and everyone else are going to notice the construction? You can't hide something like that. Surely they're aware that we all know about the perks they get?"

"Maybe, but who is going to be brave enough to confront them?"

"Look, I know this ask is a big risk, but I promise no way will it ever get out that you got this stuff for me. I wouldn't ask if I didn't think it wasn't a matter of life or death. We need your help."

This caught Ajay off guard. Edward seized on the moment. "Listen to me. Mary, Doc, and I are in a lot of trouble. We made promises, so the Outcasts would let me come back and get the drugs we desperately need. If I go back without proof of what the Program is doing, it could be really bad news for the three of us."

Ajay looked unconvinced. A knock at the door made both men jump. Edward signaled Ajay to get under the bed. He quickly complied, taking the bag of books with him. Edward draped the bedsheet down to the floor, ensuring Ajay was covered from sight. A second, more insistent knock, quickly followed. He gathered his nerve and opened the door. It was Reyanne.

"Damn, you scared the hell out of me. Come in."

"Yeah, I tend to do that to people." Reyanne pushed Edward aside and moved into the room surveilling it as she entered. "I can see you, Ajay," she giggled. "You can come out now."

Rumbling came from under the bed. "Honey, what are you doing here? Help me get out from under here, will you?"

"I wanted to talk to our friend about Mary. And I'm not leaving until I understand exactly what is going on."

Edward smiled. "I do get it." Clearly, he was going to have to tell them both everything after they got Ajay unstuck.

After an hour of questions, Reyanne stood and proclaimed, "I've heard enough. At last someone is trying to do something to stop that damn committee. I love it. I don't know about your plan, but we're going to help, aren't we, Ajay?"

At that point, Edward and Ajay both realized Reyanne was making a statement and not really asking a question.

"Honey, Mary came through for me," she told Ajay. "You make sure Edward gets whatever he needs. Bye, boys."

Then, as abruptly as she arrived, she walked out and slammed the door behind her.

"That's one tough, crazy woman, huh? Don't you just love her fire? I guess if the boss says to get what you need, I get you what you need. Back here tomorrow night?"

Edward nodded, still processing Reyanne's arrival and departure.

"And we'll figure out a way to get you into that site. Good enough?"

"More than good. Fantastic!"

"Books, man. This is great." Ajay hugged the bag and, as if without a care, headed out the door.

Edward wasn't sure what to make of either of them, but he liked their style.

The next afternoon, Edward met Dr. Chivas at the Kabak. Something about this man, maybe his confidence conveyed he had connections you needed but didn't want to know personally, like mobsters in old stories. Of course, Doc had indirectly implied that might be the case.

As promised, Chivas slid a small padded black purse under the table. The bag was small enough that Edward could stuff it in the oversized pocket of his heavy coat.

"This is what I could get on short notice; could be more later if you still need some. Called in a favor with, well, never mind. B will know. You tell him to be careful with this stuff, OK? And Edward, a bunch of us here are ready to help you guys with whatever you need. He'll know who we are and all the ways we can get involved with anything you're planning. Helping the Outcasts sounds very interesting. And, son . . . you can also tell him we expect to see him again. Soon. Good luck. Glad we could help."

After they shook hands, a chill ran down Edward's spine. He watched as Chivas slowly headed toward the clinic. How could this guy act like he was untouchable?

CHAPTER 55

PLANS

Just when he was convinced Ajay might be a no-show, he heard the knock at the door. Standing outside, to his great surprise, was a smiling Jorge.

"Damn guy, I've been around a bunch of times looking for you. Why are you keeping things from me?"

Edward found it hard to conceal how glad he was to see his best friend, but he had mixed emotions. On the one hand, he had so much he wanted to share and, on the other, the last thing he wanted to do was to get Jorge mixed up in things.

Unable to resist, Edward pulled him inside and hugged him tightly. "Buddy, it's great to see you, but you seriously can't be here. I'm sorry that I've had to keep you in the dark and maybe another time I'll be able to explain things, but you need to leave. Now."

"Eddie, my friend, that's not happening," Jorge said, pushing him out of the way and plopping down in a chair. "I know what you're up to. Reyanne told me. So, you can forget about feeding me shit. I'm here, I'm staying, and I want to help."

"Damn, I can't believe that woman," Edward said. "I wonder who else she told?"

"No idea, and don't start in on Ena either, because, I'm telling you, man, she already knows. She's worried sick about you guys and said I should help. So, hurry it up, Eddie boy. Fill me in."

From Jorge's tone, Edward knew his best friend was not leaving. Ajay would be there soon, so he decided he might as well bring him up to speed.

After a short while, there was another knock at the door. As expected, it was Ajay.

"Come in. You know Jorge?"

"Sure, hey." Ajay looked at Edward, waiting for a sign that it was safe to talk about things. When he didn't get an indication either way he went ahead and spoke. "Then he knows why I'm here?"

"Yup, and hell, Ajay," Edward said with a smirk, "you can guess how he found out."

"Nothing surprises me about that woman anymore," he replied, unfazed. "OK, you're sort of in luck. These buddies of mine from the maintenance group scrounged up a few things. They gave me these goodies, and they didn't ask too many questions." At that, he reached into his dirty cloth bag and dragged out a large rectangular piece of paper, unfolded it, and placed it on Edward's kitchen table. The three men cleared chairs and huddled around it studying the layout of the CAIHR facility. "You guys need to appreciate that the old site was shuttered, mostly shut down years ago. That might work in your favor."

"That definitely could be helpful."

"Now, look over here," he said pointing to a spot on the layout above the site entrance doors. "See that scribble?"

"Yeah, looks like numbers: 0, 4, 2, 0, 3, 8, correct?"

"Exactly, Jorge, exactly. You want to commit those six to memory. They could be your salvation. When that site was being decommissioned, they added key pads at a few of the entrances for the workers. I'm guessing those numbers are an entrance code that someone scribbled on this layout. Might be different now but, in the past, that was probably the code."

"Fantastic. Keypad codes," said Edward. "Does that imply that the entrance is no longer guarded?"

"I'll get to that. Look at this layout. The site is basically built in concentric circles. The most secure areas are in the center and farther underground. More fortified. The outermost ring is at ground level.

It's a giant hallway connecting interior bays. Now look at this. The waste water treatment area, 5A, is here down the hallway to the left, counter-clockwise from the 1A entrance doors."

"Close to the 1A entrance, that's encouraging," Edward said. "And what's this room?" he asked, pointing to a place on the layout directly across from the entrance doors.

"That's the main security monitoring bay, 1AB, an intra-site guard station. It has all the monitors and controls for the cameras and door locks for the entire facility. Back in the day, that area would have been crawling with armed guards. I have good news and bad news concerning that. Since the site is officially shut down, there is no reason for that room or any of the entrances to be guarded."

"And the bad news?"

"My guys told me that sometimes the guards still use that place. Evidently, they beg off from their duties and go in there to drink and play cards. They use one of the large meeting rooms, 17A, which is here," he said, pointing to a spot along the hallway in the clockwise direction from the waste water treatment bay.

Jorge, whose nose and brow was furled, turned to Edward, "Card games? Well, that's terrible news for us."

"What do you mean, 'us'?" Ajay asked. "You mean you're going in there with this lunatic?"

"I do," Jorge replied, smiling and slapping Edward on his back hard enough to make him stumble forward. "I've been protecting this guy since he was a scrawny kid. No reason to stop now. Anyway, with two of us looking, we have a better chance of finding those papers."

"Then you're both officially crazier than Reyanne," Ajay whispered, making sure she wasn't around.

Jorge looked at Edward and winked. "We might be."

Ajay gave them two thumbs up. "OK, then! You're gonna love the handy extras I brought in this goodie bag." Once again, he shuffled through his bag. "Here are a handful of old maintenance shirts and, in this ratty little box," he explained, carefully opening the distressed container, "are a bunch of crew IDs. They must be ancient. Maybe you carry one on you to look official, in case someone sees you."

Edward took the box. "Thanks, but I doubt those IDs would do much for us if we got caught. We'll definitely check them out, though."

"Get caught? In my opinion, that's probable, so why go in there in the first place?"

"I don't think we're going to get caught, but no matter what happens, nothing is on you. We're just thankful for your help."

"Hey, your gig, your funeral. Moving right along." He paused, milking the moment as the guys watched him take a thick manual of the leadership complex plans from the bag. "One of you will have to eat this if you get caught," he said, handing it to Edward. "Seriously, they've been trying to hide all of this from the community. If anybody from Program leadership finds out you have this, they're going to kill the two of you and then come after me and Reyanne."

"I told you, we're not going to get caught. If we do, I promise I'll get rid of it."

"You better and, I still say, entering that old site is a bad idea. Gotta go, boys. Make this revolution happen." He made his way to the door.

After saying goodbye, Edward perused the box of old IDs. He went through them until his fingers stopped on one he found particularly interesting. "Would you look at this? Surely this is a good sign."

Jorge took the badge from him and struggled to pronounce the name that was on it, "Emad El-Ghazzway? Ah, I get it, you think this is your Emad, the document guy."

"Don't you? It's the only Emad in the box. I think it's good luck." With that, Edward carefully put everything, including the layout, in his backpack. Then he clipped Emad's badge onto his shirt and stood up. Jorge followed, and the two men headed toward the door. Before Jorge left, the men agreed to meet the next evening at sundown for the real test of character.

CHAPTER 56

THE CAIHR SITE

At the first signs of darkness, the two men headed toward the site. "I thought with the power being off, we could use these," Jorge said, revealing several flashlights. I signed them out from the dock utility closet; they're really bright. They're great during night loads."

Edward placed one flashlight in each hand and moved them up and down, weighing them. "This one is too big. I'll take the little one. Thanks."

They walked through the moonlight until they got within range of the site, then they stopped to assess the situation. Out of nowhere, a guard twenty yards from them whisked by in the dark. They quickly hit the ground and held their breath. Luckily, they had not been discovered. They watched as the guard ran to the keypad. His quickly fingers punched in numbers and then a small light on the bottom of the pad changed from red to green. With that he pulled open one of the entrance doors and disappeared inside.

"Holy Crap! That was too damn close!"

"That must kill the plan for tonight, right?" Jorge said.

"It doesn't change anything. I still have to go for it."

"Hell guy, you just witnessed there's at least one guard in there already. You're fine with that? What if he's waiting for his friends behind those doors?"

"No way, that guy was in a big hurry to get to his card game. If there are other guards in there, they're probably in the same place. Anyway, their game room is far away from where we want to be. Look, tonight is it for me; either I do this thing now or never. I understand if you need to wait out here."

"No, Eddie. I can't believe I'm saying this, but if you're going in, then so am I. But maybe we should check the layout one last time? Make sure we know where we're headed, once in."

"I'm good with that." Edward pulled the layout out of his back pack and laid it on the ground. Lit only by the dim moonlight, they struggled to review it. The couldn't risk turning on a flashlight. "We go through entrance doors 1A, move down the hallway to the left, away from any guards playing cards in 17A."

"Yup."

"OK, I'll go first. Here, you keep the layout in case I get caught." Edward's voice choked, revealing his nervousness. Jorge folded the layout and put it into his pants pocket. Edward continued, "if it's clear when I get in, I'll signal with a quick hand wave out the door. I won't hold it the open for you, in case there's a door jam timer with an alarm. You run up, enter the code yourself, and meet me down the hallway. If you don't see a signal from me a few moments after I'm in, assume the worst, and get the hell out of here. Understand?"

"Got it."

Jorge watched as his friend dashed to the keypad. He could see his fingers move slowly and deliberately entering the code. The little light, however, failed to change from red to green. Something was wrong. Maybe he was nervous and had entered the code incorrectly or, worse, the code had been changed. He moved much closer, anxious for his turn. At this distance, he could make out what appeared to be a frustrated look on Edwards face. He hated seeing his friend struggle in the open. Another guard could come by any minute. Clearly, Edward needed assistance. A rush of adrenaline over took him over, and he dashed toward the keypad.

"Damn it, Jorge," Edward whispered, "what the hell are you doing here?"

"Get out of my way," Jorge firmly whispered, pushing him aside. 0-4-2-0-3-8.

"I'm not stupid. I already tried that code twice. It doesn't work." Jorge entered another code: 1-4-2-0-3-8. Again, no green light. Cursing, he entered another code: 0-4-2-0-3-9 and, to both their surprise, the little light cooperated by turning green. Edward yanked the door open, and they both rushed into the site.

Unfortunately, the lighting near the entrance was unexpectedly bright. Realizing how precarious it was to be so exposed, they dashed down the hallway to the left, away from the doors.

With each step, the hall grew darker, which made them feel more secure. Edward, no longer able to contain his curiosity, yanked on Jorge's shoulder, "How the hell did you know that entrance code?"

"I didn't," he smiled, "I tried adding one to the first digit and, when that didn't work, I added one to the last digit. Wham, baby!"

Edward looked at him incredulously. "Well, I would have eventually tried that, if you had given me an extra second."

"Uh-huh." Jorge replied. "Keep moving, Eddie, keep moving."

The only remaining light reflected off the walls from the entrance way.

"Seems like we should already be at the waste water treatment bay, don't you think? Maybe it's around the corner?"

After another few feet, Edward became irritable. "Where the hell is it?"

"Wait, look, I think we're here."

"Yeah, I think so, too. Let's get in. This hallway is creeping me out. I keep expecting someone to come out from around the corner. Jorge, it has another keypad. Try your new code."

Hopeful that his magic would once again work, Jorge moved to the pad and entered the code. "Nope, nothing. Crap, this code could be anything," he said, out of tricks, "Do we try to break in?"

"I don't think we have to," Edward replied, reaching out and pulling the bay door open.

"It wasn't locked? How in the hell did you know that?"

"No hallway light, right? Meaning no power in this area. No little red light was glowing on that keypad, either."

Jorge looked. Sure enough, the red light was off.

"No electricity, no electric lock. Nobody is expected to be here."

"Eddie boy, you're in the lead," Jorge teased.

"Come on, let's search. You take the drawers, cabinets, and closets on the left. I'll take the ones on the right. Cover everything, those documents could be hidden — anywhere. Maybe it's stuck up inside or under a drawer. Pull them all the way out, feel around underneath."

Flashlights blazing, they searched everywhere.

"I got nothing," Jorge told him.

"Yeah, me either. Maybe this isn't the right place. Pull out that layout one more time? What should we be looking for?"

Jorge spread the layout on the floor between them. "I don't know, something we missed. Ah, over here. Whoa, how brave are you feeling tonight, tall skinny guy?"

"What am I missing? And why are you smiling like that?"

"Look on the layout, buddy. Do you know what that symbol means?"

"No idea."

"That usually means a hatch door. Now look back there toward the bottom of that offset wall, just below the shelf," Jorge said while pointing with his flashlight.

Edward grabbed the layout and hastily threw it in his backpack as both men ran over to check things out. "A wheeled hatchway? How'd we miss it?"

"Got me. It's on your side, Eddie; you're the one who missed it. Now read that sign."

"*Danger, Methane Gas*. Is it OK to open?"

"Oh sure, we're going to open it. The thing, though, about a buildup of methane gas is it's odorless, explosive, and poisonous. But methane, that makes sense, because this is probably a sewer system, a clean out. Shit, literally. We're in a waste water treatment bay."

"Great, so we're facing nasty waste water and poison gas once we open the hatch? You really think someone would hide stuff in there?"

"Got me. Guessing that Emad fella was a smart one, and this is the only place we haven't checked. If I was going to hide something dangerous in a waste water treatment bay, that's where I'd stick it — someplace disgusting."

"Hard to argue with that logic."

"Maybe we open this hatch slowly, though. We listen for the hiss of high pressure gas. If we hear it, we do our best to close it quickly before we're overcome. We'd better turn off the flashlights first. We don't need any sparks."

Now, completely in the dark, together they turned the crank wheel of the hatch door, waiting.

No hissing.

"No gas, right? Then we're safe? I can turn on my flashlight?"

"Might go boom, but go ahead. Just kidding. I don't smell anything."

"Would you quit that! I'm nervous enough as it is. Is it safe or not? You said methane was odorless?"

"I did, but I also don't smell any sewer gas, so go ahead."

Edward shone his light down into the dark narrow shaft. Below him he saw a rusty metal ladder leading down into a tunnel. "And I have to go down there because I'm the skinny one?"

"Listen, I think it'll be fine, but there still could be pockets of residual gas so don't stay down there too long."

"You don't have to tell me that twice," he replied, throwing his backpack on the shelf before squeezing himself through the tight opening. He placed each foot one at a time onto the rungs of the squeaky metal ladder and began descending into the shaft. "Hey," he yelled after a few minutes, "I think I may have found something. There's a black metal tube with a cap on one end lodged between one rung of the ladder and the wall. It's big enough to hold rolled up documents."

"Good, grab the damn thing and get yourself back up here. We've already been here too long."

"Will do, will do. Patience. I'll come up when I can work it loose from the . . . ."

Jorge didn't hear the last part. He was distracted by footsteps approaching from the hallway. "Edward," he whispered, bending over and sticking his head into the tunnel, "We have a problem! Someone is coming!"

"There isn't time for me to get this and climb up and out. Just close the hatch and hide."

Jorge quietly closed the hatch door, shutting Edward in. He squeezed himself into a nearby closet and pulled the door almost shut. In that moment he looked in horror at the backpack sitting on the shelf above the hatch. But it was too late to retrieve it. The footsteps were louder. He shortened his breathing, desperate to be still.

He knew he shouldn't, but he felt compelled to look. Peering through the cracked closet door, a large presence waddled into the room, a man, a guard, shining a flashlight. As the big man weaved and swayed, the beam from his flashlight danced against the floor and walls, passing over the closet. The man hummed loudly, banging into everything as he sauntered a few feet from the backpack and the hatch. Oblivious, the guard placed his flashlight on a table, pulled down his pants around his knees, and relieved himself, gleefully humming and spraying the walls everywhere.

It was possible, Jorge thought, they would dodge a bullet, literal and otherwise. Soon the guard would be done and leave without noticing them. Then a loud clang came from the direction of the hatch. The guard quickly pulled his pants up, grabbed his light, and moved toward it.

Jorge panicked. If that guard discovered the backpack and Edward in the shaft, they would both be screwed. Moving as stealthily as possible, Jorge emerged from the closet and crept up behind the guard.

Edward, still in the shaft, heard a loud banging noise come from the walls above him and then a dull thud. Was Jorge in trouble? As quickly as he could he scurried up the ladder and slammed his hands against the hatch, hoping Jorge had not turned the crank and sealed him in. The metal hatch squealed loudly as it opened and there in front of him, on the floor, was a large man, lying in a pool of blood.

Also, nearby, and obviously doubled over in pain, was another man, breathing loudly, clutching his chest and slowly writhing back and forth.

"What the hell happened here?" Edward mumbled to himself nervously.

"Edward . . . ."

"Damn, guy . . . what happened?" Edward smelled a foul musty odor. It was urine. "We're getting out of here — now." Edward grabbed Jorge's bloody flashlight from the floor and threw it and the metal tube he had dislodged from the shaft into his backpack. Then he placed his arms tightly around his friend's waist and moved slowly backward, dragging Jorge out of the bay.

Edward felt exhausted about thirty feet down the hallway. He stopped and leaned Jorge, who was now breathing better, against the wall.

"Is the attack dying down?"

Jorge didn't respond.

"You're going to have to help me now, buddy. We've got to get out of here before that guard comes to or one of his friends comes looking for him."

Jorge nodded his head slightly in agreement.

Edward helped him to a standing position. He wrapped Jorge's arm around his back and shoulder, and the two slowly advanced down the dark corridor. As they plodded along a dim light reflected off the shiny yellow tiles that lined the walls. Eventually, they came closer to the exit doors. Seeing no guards, they stumbled out, Edward led them into a shadowy alcove just beyond the entrance.

Jorge released his grip on Edward, indicating that he could walk on his own. With the ability to progress a little faster, they continued moving farther away from the site. They were grateful for the darkness.

When Edward was sure they were sufficiently away, they stopped. "We can rest here for a few minutes. Take your time. Catch your breath." No sooner had he spoken than they noticed to their right the outline of two guards headed toward the site. They flattened themselves to the ground.

One of the guards, walking slightly behind the other, grabbed the guard in front of him by the shoulder.

"Hey," the guard whispered, "did you hear that? Over there."

"Hear what?"

Now standing still, the two men surveyed the area, slowly scanning with their flashlights. The beams came perilously close to Jorge and Edward but passed them by.

"You're hearing things. Come on, we're late for the game."

Satisfied, the guards again headed toward the site.

Shaken, Edward slowly lifted himself from the ground then helped his accomplice do the same. Once standing, Jorge teetered as he struggled to compose himself. He paused to catch more breath, then spoke in a low, raspy voice. "That pissing drunk was headed toward the hatch. He would have found that backpack on the shelf and then you, so I hit him as hard as I could with the back of my flashlight. Wham, that big dude hit the walls and then the floor. I swear I didn't want to hurt the guy, but I couldn't see any other way. After I hit him, my body unleashed excruciating pain everywhere. I couldn't breathe."

"Dude, I am so sorry. I dropped my flashlight. The damn thing bounced all the way down. Hanging onto that ladder, I was so nervous, and sweating and then everything started slipping away from me."

Edward stopped talking for a moment to dig around in his backpack. "But I did manage to hold onto this." His hand emerged from his pack with his fingers wrapped around a 10 inch black tube that was still caked in a sticky crud.

"That's it? The documents are in there?"

"After all this, I sure as hell hope so."

"Well open the damn thing."

"Not here; when we get you back to Ena. Right now I need to ask you . . ."

"What?"

"Did that guard see you? You know, before you hit him?"

"Nah, I came at him from behind. He never knew what hit him. But he's going to have a hell of a headache when he wakes up."

For the next few minutes, they rested in silence, each revisiting in their minds what had occurred. No doubt they had been very lucky to not to have been discovered.

"Why do you think that guard was doing there in that bay? Was he looking for us?"

"Not until he heard the noise of your flashlight falling. That drunk was happily taking a leak all over the walls, the floor, everything. Maybe his way of sticking it to his boss? He had no idea we were there until then."

"When you heard him hit the walls and then the floor, what did you think?"

"I was so scared I almost crapped my pants. I didn't know what the hell that noise was. I scrambled up that ladder and popped through the hatch as fast as I could. I saw you writhing and that guard lying face down on the floor. But when I saw your bloody flashlight next to him, I guessed what happened."

"Well it's a damn good thing you did because I was in bad shape. I could hardly breathe. I thought I was going to die. Thanks for dragging me out of there."

"No way I would have left without you."

"I knew you wouldn't. So, and I hate to ask this, but is there any chance you closed that hatch behind you before you got us out?"

"Shit, Jorge! I'm an idiot! I didn't think about that."

"Don't worry, probably nothing. One last thing, your flashlight, did you retrieve it?"

Edward starred at his friend, his eyes growing larger and gleaming in the moonlight. "No I didn't have a chance, and I don't even know if I turned it off." He said questioning his own recollection of what happened. "Damn I should have closed that hatch."

"Hey, don't get too worked up. When that drunk wakes up, he isn't likely to remember much. Anyway he isn't going to be too eager to say anything to anyone or he'd have to explain why he was in that shuttered site. Nobody should have been in there, especially guards drinking and playing cards when they were supposed to be on duty."

"Well, we shouldn't have been in there, either. I'm sorry I involved you in this."

"Buddy, I didn't give you a choice. We got what we were after, and I learned something important tonight; I can survive one of those violent attacks — not that I recommend it."

"Hey, how about let's get out of here, get you back to Ena?"

"Best idea I've heard all night."

Edward couldn't shake the thought that his mistake could have killed his best friend — and still could.

CHAPTER 57

REPERCUSSIONS

"Mother wants to see you. Let's go."

Edward glanced at Mary, and it was clear from his face that he was caught off-guard by Axel's abrupt request.

"Shouldn't she come with us?"

"No, just you. Now."

"It's OK, go. You can tell me when you get back," Mary told him, acting calmly. She knew the trip had been successfully completed days earlier. The documents had all been reviewed, so she wondered what Mother could want with Edward? Whatever it was, this private meeting probably meant nothing good.

* * *

"I'm dying to know. Tell me what Mother said."

"Things are bad, honey. I need to go back over, and I leave tonight."

"Why? Doc said we've got more than enough of the withdrawal drugs, and we've got all the documentation we could possibly need. Mother and Solomon seemed so happy with everything you brought back."

"Yeah, but this has nothing to with all of that, not directly anyway." Edward replied, hanging his head and looking away. "And it's all my fault."

"Why go back?"

"Axel took me to meet Mother at that same little building where we've met before. She was sitting on her throne or whatever that chair is with Solomon standing beside her. As soon as we got in there, Solomon growled at Axel to leave but not go far. From the tone of his voice, I knew that whatever this meeting was about wasn't good.

"Then Solomon got inches in front of my face. It really frightened me. He wanted to know what I knew about the murder of a Program guard that happened the same night that I got back."

"My God, a murdered Program guard? Shouldn't he be talking to Dimitri or Ivan or one of his other Outcasts? They must have done that. Why question you?"

"I didn't have any idea, but it was clear that Mother and Solomon knew something I didn't. So I carefully retold them everything that happened that night. I told them about being inside that maintenance bay to retrieve those documents and Jorge having to hit that drunk guard with his flashlight. As I told that story again, I shivered, hoping to myself this had nothing to do with that guard Jorge hit."

"They listened and believed you?"

"Pretty sure they did. Then I told them that when we got out of there, I realized the guard was hurt badly but not dead because I heard him moaning."

"So was a different guard killed that night?"

"No hon, the guard who died was the same one Jorge hit."

"Shit, he died? That's terrible. I'm sure Jorge never meant to hit that guard hard enough to kill him. You told them that?"

"He didn't do it intentionally, but it was a panic situation. I wasn't actually there when it happened. I was still down in that shaft, not that any of that matters now. The fact is the guard died. The blow must have eventually killed him. And the mess gets bigger."

"Bigger?"

"Mother's spies told her that the guards found the guy lying dead on the ground near the CAIHR site. They're blaming the Outcasts. Now the entire Program community are on the lookout for Outcasts."

"And Solomon and Mother want to give you and Jorge up to appease them?"

"No, surprisingly no, not that I would blame them, but no, that's not it."

"Then I'm confused."

"I explained to Mother and Solomon what had been told to the Program by the guards was probably just a cover story. They made it up to protect themselves from the committee. The guards couldn't risk letting the committee know they were not on duty that night and not at their posts. Instead they were down inside that shuttered CAIHR site playing cards. They blamed the murder on the Outcasts, everyone would suspect them anyway. Not a bad plan on their part."

"But if that guard was so mortally wounded, how could he have gotten himself out of the site?"

"I don't think he could have, not without help anyway. I'm guessing his guard buddies dragged him out of there and placed him on the ground to support their story. That way he wouldn't be found inside. And now that I think about it, they could have even finished him off to protect themselves. They certainly wouldn't have risked having him interrogated while he was recovering in the Care Place. That might screw up their story. They'd all be in jeopardy."

"Is this the end of it? An Outcast is blamed, nothing new. What else do Mother and Solomon want from you?

"I'm certain that before they talked to me, their spies had informed them that an Outcast had not murdered the guard. I think they were testing me to see if I'd tell the truth. And they asked more questions, they wanted to know about my exposure to the murder."

"Nothing, right? That guard never saw either you or Jorge."

"That's true, he didn't, but we still have exposure, especially Jorge. I told Mother and Solomon that if before that guard died, he mentioned that he heard a noise coming from the shaft, then there could be an exposure problem. If guards found that shaft door open and they went down inside and found the flashlight I dropped it'll be linked back to the dock. I explained that the Program inventories everything and, since Jorge is the dock manager, it would eventually be linked to him. If that happens, those guards will surely kill him.

They wouldn't just do it for revenge for their buddy but also to make sure Jorge couldn't blow their cover story during any Program interrogation. They'd never risk that."

"I imagine Mother and Solomon must be so angry with you for this mess. Outcasts falsely accused of murdering a guard, damn."

"You would have thought so, but surprisingly they weren't. In fact, quite the opposite, they looked pleased. In fact, Solomon reached over and slapped me on my back. I think they were comforted that I didn't lie to them, I manned up and told the truth. I guess it didn't really bother them that much that a Program guard had been killed.

"Solomon said I surprised him, that he had been wrong about me. That he couldn't believe I had enough moxey to murder a Program guard getting in the way of retrieving documents for them. He even said I was now one of his soldiers."

"One of his soldiers? He said that?"

"He did."

"But what about Jorge? The guards could find out about him."

"That's why I have to go back and get him, bring him here. I'm the one who I got him into this mess, and I need to get him out of there as soon as possible."

"And Mother and Solomon will they let you do that?"

"They will. I explained that I wanted to go back and get Jorge and his partner Ena. That Jorge was the guy who helped me get the documents. They understood why I wanted to do that, and they even agreed to have Axel help me."

"Edward, this is crazy. Think about it, Jorge and Ena on this side, living with us, living with Outcasts?"

"Yeah, I know, pretty strange, but it has to happen. Of course, I'll still have to convince them that they're in danger. I'm sure Ena will balk at coming here."

"Oh, convincing them is not going to be easy. They've have never been around Outcasts. They don't know anything about them, and what they think they know isn't good. They're going to be terrified, especially Ena. Maybe I should go with you to talk to her."

"No way. The baby. No, I'm going tonight. Jorge is a smart guy and, when I explain the situation, he'll convince Ena that they have to leave."

"Does Jorge know the guard has died?"

"I doubt it, not yet anyway. He'll understand the risk, though, of waiting things out. It's only a matter of time before they find my flashlight."

"Damn, it's hard to believe you guys murdered a Program guard, and now you're going get our best friends and bring them here. It's almost unbelievable. Listen, I know you have to do this, but I still hate that you're going back there. I'll be worried every moment you're gone." Mary placed her arms around Edward and squeezed, burying her face in his chest.

"Honey, really, you don't need to worry about me. I've got this, I do. Cause you know what?"

"What?"

"I found out I'm pretty damn good at this spy shit."

Mary pulled her head back slightly from his chest and looked into his eyes. "Yeah, you are. You're my brave soldier." Wiping her sniffling nose and trying to look brave, she added, "Listen, you tell Ena I'm going to have a baby, so she's going to be an auntie, and that I need her here with me. And, hon, when you get back, after we do whatever we need to do to help out with this coup, we have to figure out where we can go. Because we can't stay here. I don't want to be a queen wasp. Ena won't want to be one, either."

"Leave the Outcast's encampment? Go back to the other side, to the Program?"

"No, never back there, too many bad memories, but we'll leave."

"And go where?"

"There." Her index finger pointed southward.

"Hmm, yeah, I think that's a fantastic idea."

"Good. Now go get our friends . . . and hurry back to me."

CHAPTER 58

THIRD-PARTY INTERESTS

"Why are you snickering?" Doc said, his brown eyes looking sternly into Mary's.

"It's just I find your total conversion about everything so funny."

"My conversion?"

"Yeah, your conversion. Your change in attitude toward the Outcasts. Look at you. You're busy working with Chivas, Intu, and the Outcasts on all this coup-planning stuff."

"Oh, so now you don't want me to be involved in the things you once begged me to believe?"

"No, no, of course I do. I think it's great. But a few months ago, weren't you the one that acted like my idea of convincing the guards to stand down was so dumb? I distinctly remember you telling Edward and me, in your typical condescending fashi͏ ͏ ͏ ͏ ͏ ͏ oesn't need to work, only needs to convince Mother and ͏ ͏ ͏ ͏ ͏ ͏ ͏ ͏ ͏ ͏ ͏ ͏ ͏ ͏ ͏ ͏ do remember saying that, don't you?"

"Yes, I remember and, at the time, ͏ ͏ ͏ ͏ ͏ ͏ ͏ ͏ nothing condescending about it, it was tru͏ ͏ ͏ ͏ ͏ ͏ ͏ totally different."

"Oh yeah? Other than a few months, wha͏ ͏ ͏ ͏ ͏ ͏ conversion?"

"For one, and you're aware of this, now we're ͏ ͏ ͏ ͏ ͏ ͏ position to expose those bastards, and two, mc

Chivas is onboard. The guy is connected, Mary. He's in bed with the head guards. That's a tremendous asset. He's even been working with some of them to stockpile weapons for this thing."

"Stockpiling weapons? If the guards are standing down, why the need for weapons?"

"Come on, be realistic, they're for the Outcasts and the workers."

"So everyone will be armed, and you think this will be a good thing?"

"Actually, yes. I think our side having guns is a good thing."

"Then you're OK with people getting hurt, killed."

"If that's what's required, yeah, I am."

"Well, good to know your position, I guess. But tell me, why is your buddy Chivas so involved with all this? What's in it for him?"

"He's a close friend of mine, so obviously he wants to help. But he has other reasons."

"Ah, you have that look. What reasons?"

"I guess he wouldn't mind me telling you. Surely it's not a secret. Chivas is Intu's uncle."

"What?"

"You heard me, his younger sister was my partner, Intu's mom."

"Doc, you son of a bitch!"

"Ouch! Mary that really hurt my arm. You just punched a sick old man."

"And I should have hit you harder. His sister was your partner? The mother of your son? Intu's mom? And you never told me?"

"Well, think about it, until recently, there wasn't a reason to discuss it, was there? You didn't know anything about her or my son. Anyway, yes, Chivas and I now have our boy Intu, but he's not really a boy anymore, is he? Hence the change of heart toward Outcasts."

"And are there other reasons for Chivas to be involved? Come on, spill it. What are they?"

"You already know. Think about it, the guy controls the black market. He's been doing that for as long as I've known him.

He's not a hard man to read, he sees this coup the same way he sees everything, a business opportunity. An opportunity that, for some reason, he can't take advantage with the current leadership committee; they're in the way. Guys like Chivas and his friends won't stand very long for that. He'll punish them."

"You think he'll have them killed?"

"I don't know, but with Chivas involved, you can bet that once this ball gets rolling downhill, there's no stopping it. There's no halfway in for anyone and, along the way, some people are going to get hurt, even killed. Anyway Mary, remember, you're the one who always said how you much you hate that committee, how you want revenge. Well, now your wish is about to come true."

"Yeah, but I never said I wanted them killed, just removed. I didn't think we'd be stooping to their level to make that happen."

"Oh, did you think those selfish bastards were just going to walk away peacefully?"

"I don't know. I guess I didn't think that part through, but I never considered we'd have to kill."

"Well, then, you better listen up because no matter how much evidence we show the guards, detailing how corrupt that committee is, some will still remain loyal. Those loyal guards are not going to stand down or look the other way. They'll fight to the death. Killing them along with some of the committee members may be the only way this gets done."

"No, I understand. It's unrealistic to think we could convert all the guards."

"That's right, so you need to keep reminding yourself that removing that committee is the goal . . . whatever the cost. It's what you've always wanted, right?"

"Yes, but . . ."

"No but's, Mary. That time has passed. This is in motion. People are committed. Think of all the good that will happen once the bastards are gone. Maybe the Program can even return to the old way of governing."

"Wow, wouldn't that be something? One can only hope. Doc, ever since I finished reading that notebook, I've wondered what it would be like to live in a society that operated the way my great grandfather and his fellow scientists envisioned. You know, one where everyone has value, everyone has a chance to govern."

"Not sure that will ever happen in this community, but who knows? Maybe you can make that vison happen back there. Of course, it's all predicated on Chivas eliminating the current committee. But with them out of the way, he'd be free to make a trade deal, get his business opportunity, and we'd get a virtual tearing down of the wall. In the end, everyone except those committee assholes would win. We'd all be safer."

"Yeah, I guess . . . So, Doc?"

"Uh-huh?"

"I was just thinking, your friend Chivas, with his connections? If you had stayed behind, and that investigation had gone as badly like you thought, could he have saved you?"

"I have no reason to think otherwise."

"Then why did you let me spend all that time and energy convincing you to come with Edward and me? Why didn't you just say no and stay behind?"

"I thought someone needed to be the adult on the trip."

Mary roared. "I can't believe you! You came because you felt you still needed to protect me, didn't you? Because of that promise to my dad."

"Mary, you told me you were pregnant, and you know I do love you as if you were my own daughter. So sure, maybe I thought it would be best if I accompanied you two. Since your parents died, I think I've done my best to protect you. And you can be assured that will continue for you, Edward, Jude and that little angel, whenever he or she arrives."

"That's good to know Doc, 'cause," she said, rubbing her belly, "my little angel will be counting on you."

Leonard J. DiSanza is a retired registered professional engineer and holds graduate and undergraduate degrees in electrical engineering. The holder of several patents, DiSanza was an analog circuit designer and technical manager and has been involved in numerous startup companies. When not walking, biking, or philosophizing on science, politics, and religion, he enjoys writing poetry, short stories, and plays. His author page is www.LeonardJDiSanza.com and his rants on various subjects can be found at www.LennyDoesRants.com.

Made in the USA
Coppell, TX
09 January 2020

14281572R00182